City of Darkness and Light
Agatha Award Winner

"A beautifully rendered portrait of the city and the period, seen from Molly's eyes as she deals with one of her most challenging cases yet."

—Deborah Crombie

The Family Way

"Feisty Molly unravels another knotty case while providing insight into life just after the turn of that other century."

—*Kirkus Reviews*

"Highly entertaining." —*RT Book Reviews* (4½ stars)

Hush Now, Don't You Cry

"For pure entertainment value, Rhys Bowen simply cannot be beat. . . . Her skill as a storyteller is almost unmatched." —Aunt Agatha's

"A charming combination of history, mystery, and romance."

—*Kirkus Reviews*

Also by Rhys Bowen

The Molly Murphy Mysteries

The Ghost of Christmas Past
Time of Fog and Fire
Away in a Manger
The Edge of Dreams
City of Darkness and Light
The Family Way
Hush Now, Don't You Cry
Bless the Bride
The Last Illusion
In a Gilded Cage
Tell Me, Pretty Maiden
In Dublin's Fair City
Oh Danny Boy
In Like Flynn
For the Love of Mike
Death of Riley
Murphy's Law

The Constable Evans Mysteries

Evanly Bodies
Evan Blessed
Evan's Gate
Evan Only Knows
Evans to Betsy
Evan Can Wait
Evan and Elle
Evanly Choirs
Evan Help Us
Evans Above

Wild Irish Rose

Rhys Bowen
&
Clare Broyles

MINOTAUR BOOKS
NEW YORK

This is a work of fiction. All of the characters, organizations, and events portrayed in this novel are either products of the authors' imaginations or are used fictitiously.

Published in the United States by Minotaur Books, an imprint of St. Martin's Publishing Group

www.minotaurbooks.com

The Library of Congress has cataloged the hardcover edition as follows:

Names: Bowen, Rhys, author. | Broyles, Clare, author.
Title: Wild Irish rose / Rhys Bowen & Clare Broyles.
Description: First edition. | New York : Minotaur Books, 2022. | Series: Molly Murphy mysteries ; 18 |
Identifiers: LCCN 2021043909 | ISBN 9781250808059 (hardcover) | ISBN 9781250808066 (ebook)
Subjects: LCGFT: Detective and mystery fiction.
Classification: LCC PR6052.O848 W55 2022 | DDC 823/.914—dc23
LC record available at https://lccn.loc.gov/2021043909

ISBN 978-1-250-80807-3 (trade paperback)

Our books may be purchased in bulk for promotional, educational, or business use. Please contact your local bookseller or the Macmillan Corporate and Premium Sales Department at 1-800-221-7945, extension 5442, or by email at MacmillanSpecialMarkets@macmillan.com.

First Minotaur Books Trade Paperback Edition: 2023

10 9 8 7 6 5 4 3 2 1

This book is dedicated to our family. Thank you for the words of encouragement, the frequent check-ins and Zoom calls that made us feel that we were not alone during a scary and unpredictable year. Though we span in ages from seventeen to eighty-seven we find many things to connect us, especially our loud and constant jokes! So here is to our clan: John, Rhys, Clare, Tim, Anne, Jane, Tom, Dominic, Meredith, Sam, Elizabeth, Meghan, TJ, Mary Clare, and Little Dom. We love you all.

And to the many Rhys Bowen fans who spent time with their favorite characters while they were staying home this year: you are a part of our family too. This new chapter of Molly's life is for you.

One

New York, February 1907

One thing about New York that is never predictable is the weather. The other thing that has not always been so predictable is my life. I suppose I was destined for trouble in many ways. Never the good child who didn't question authority. Always with big dreams. My mother used to chant with monotonous regularity that I'd come to a bad end, rolling her eyes as she said it and probably invoking a saint or two as well. Well, the bad end hadn't happened yet, but I'd certainly come close a few times.

Now that I was no longer working as a private investigator (at least not officially), things were different. I was a New York housewife like any other, looking forward to a time of settled tranquility with my family and friends around me. Hoping for another baby, actually. The doctor had said there was nothing wrong with me so I should get on with my life and not worry. So that's just what I was doing—taking care of my husband, my son, Liam, and Bridie, the young Irish girl we had saved from a life of servitude and had now made our ward. All was going remarkably smoothly until a snowman appeared outside my door one February afternoon.

After a mild January, just when the first snowdrops were blooming, there came a vicious arctic blast that froze any spring flower that had had the nerve to appear. It was bitterly cold and snowed for two days without stopping, making leaving the house almost impossible. Daniel had joined the other men from our little street and dug a narrow pathway to Greenwich Avenue so that he could go to work and Bridie to school. I had been forced to stay home, making do with the supplies on hand. Although I hoped our supply of coal would last, it was rapidly dwindling and everybody was rushing to buy more. We shut off the front parlor and instead huddled in the back room that was normally Daniel's realm, or sat around the kitchen table, enjoying the warmth from the stove.

Usually my days involved a visit to my neighbors Sid and Gus. (And in case you are not familiar with my friends and think I am befriending a couple of Irish laborers, let me tell you that they are both young ladies of good family whose given names are Elena and Augusta.) But I had not seen them recently. I suspected they had been busy with their latest project. There was always something new that attracted their attention. They were true Renaissance women, dabbling in art and music and foreign cooking as well as social causes like the suffrage movement. But this wasn't the time of year for suffrage parades. So I had been wondering if it was just the harsh weather that had kept them away when there was a knock at my front door, late one afternoon.

"Aunt Sid, Aunt Gus!" Liam shouted excitedly, pushing to the front door ahead of me. Actually it sounded more like "Aaa-Si? Aaa-Gu?" but I knew what he meant.

"Hey, young man, you stay inside." I grabbed him by his sweater at the last minute. "It's cold and snowy out there. And we don't know if it is Aunt Sid and Aunt Gus."

I swept Liam up onto my arms so that he didn't run out into the snow, then opened the door cautiously, letting in a frigid blast. Liam had been right. It was Sid standing there, her face only just visible under a big shawl.

"My, but it's bitter," she said. "How are you faring, Molly?"

"We're huddled in the kitchen. Come inside."

"I won't stay," she said, "but I've brought you some of the Indian vegetable curry we made. We're devoting ourselves to Indian food at the moment, having decided it's wrong to kill and eat animals. It's so good and it will keep you warm. I made far too much for the two of us and there was no way of halving the recipe."

"It's very kind of you," I said, reaching to put the casserole down on the hall stand. "Are you sure you won't have a cup of tea?"

She shook her head. "No, thank you. I must get back. We've work to do. We have a great pile of clothing to sort."

"Clothing? Are you going through your wardrobes?" It did cross my mind that a few good cast-offs might be coming my way. They had before.

"Not ours. The Vassar Benevolent Society, of which Gus is currently president, is having a warm clothing drive. So many poor wretches freezing to death in the city. We've been collecting items and now our front parlor is full."

"I could come over and help you, if you like," I said.

"Oh, that's kind of you, but I think we can handle it," she said. "Besides, there isn't space for more than two people in that room at the moment. Sometimes I can't find Gus under all those clothes." She smiled. "I'd better not let any more cold air into your house . . ." She turned to go, then paused, mouth open, and said, "What in heaven's name?"

I followed her gaze down the alleyway and there coming toward us was a walking snowman. As it approached it revealed itself to be a person, wrapped in a big white shawl but now covered in snow. I recognized that shawl at the same time that Sid called out, "Bridie? Is that you?"

"Jesus, Mary, and Joseph!" I started toward her. "What on earth were you doing? Rolling in the snow?"

Bridie staggered toward us, snow falling from her as she came.

"Oh, Molly," she said, and I could tell she was near to tears. "The boys set on me when I was crossing Washington Square. They were having a snowball fight, then they saw me coming and they all turned on me. They pelted me with snowballs. They wouldn't stop and I couldn't run through that snow."

"Which boys?" I demanded. "Let me get my cape on and I'll give them a piece of my mind. I'll teach them to attack young girls."

"I'll come with you," Sid said. "We'll teach 'em, won't we, Molly?"

Bridie put up a hand to stop me. "It's no use. The constable on the corner saw them and came after them. They ran off, laughing. Besides, you'll only make them hate me more."

"And why would they hate you?" Sid asked.

"Because I'm Irish," she said flatly.

"Because you're Irish?"

She chewed on her lip, which made her look much younger than her thirteen years. "They are mostly Italian in my class. They get into fights with the Irish boys. They call us names."

"Don't they know they're in America now and everyone is welcome?" Sid demanded. "You need to talk to that principal, Molly."

"I most certainly will," I said.

I put an arm around her shoulder. "Come inside, my darling. Let's get you out of those wet things and have a nice hot cup of tea by the fire." I turned back to Sid. "Thank you for the curry. I must take care of her."

I put down Liam and he went up to Bridie, who was now shaking snow off the shawl into the alleyway. "Bwidie all wet," he said.

As I was about to close the door Sid grabbed my arm. "Now do you agree with what we've been saying? About Bridie, I mean. We can't leave her at that place any longer."

"Let's not discuss it now." I shot a warning look at Bridie.

We went inside and I closed the door. I was tempted to go straight down to that school, or find the boys for myself, but Bridie was shivering and still one step away from tears. "You should get out of those clothes right away. Would you like me to run you a hot bath?" I asked her.

"No, I'd rather have a cup of tea by the fire," she said. "It's awful cold in the bathroom."

"It is," I agreed. "Well, you go up and get changed. We won't even mind if you put on your nightgown and slippers."

She gave me a grateful smile and went up the stairs, snow still falling from her hair.

"Bwidie cold," Liam commented as we went through into the kitchen. "Bwidie make snowman?"

"I think Bridie was a snowman," I said, having to smile. Out of all of us Liam was the only one who didn't seem to feel the cold. Still, he had the energy of a naughty two-year-old and was always running, jumping, climbing, and getting into things he shouldn't.

My mother-in-law stood up as we came into the kitchen. "What on earth was all that about?" she said. "You kept the front door open for ages, Molly. What were you thinking letting all that cold air in? We'll never manage to heat up the place again."

My mother-in-law felt the cold most cruelly. We had brought her down to stay with us after she'd suffered a bad bout of influenza. She had lost her maid, Ivy, who had gone on to better things, and her one aging servant, Martha, was finding the big house too hard to take care of alone. So until we could find a new maid and possibly a cook for Mrs. Sullivan, Daniel was insisting she stay with us.

Of course I couldn't say no, but it was certainly a challenge having so many people crammed into one little house. The real challenge was Daniel's mother watching me every moment, ready to comment on things she did differently. "Oh, so that's the way Daniel likes his pork done these days? He always used to tell me that pork chops should be grilled." I couldn't quite tell whether she meant it to rankle, but it certainly did. I was all too aware that she had been disappointed when Daniel chose me over a society beauty called Arabella Norton. To be frank, I was a little surprised myself. After all, I had nothing—having escaped from the wild west coast of Ireland, where I had grown up in a peasant's cottage.

"It was Bridie," I said. "A gang of boys set upon her in the square. Absolutely pelted her with snowballs, poor little thing. I've sent her up to change out of those clothes and I'll pour her a cup of tea. Can I pour you one at the same time?"

"I wouldn't say no," she said. That was another thing that annoyed me about her. She rarely said either please or thank you. "But that's not a nice thing to happen to a young girl. It's quite different if she was part of the snowball fight. I remember Daniel always enjoyed a good snowball fight when he was a boy." And she smiled at the memory.

I'd just put a generous helping of sugar in the tea when Bridie came down, wearing her robe and bedroom slippers.

"Saints preserve us!" Mrs. Sullivan exclaimed. "Is bedtime now at four o'clock?"

"I told her she could," I replied. "She needs to warm up. Come and sit by the fire, my love."

Bridie shot a glance at my mother-in-law as she accepted the seat by the fire. She cradled the cup in her hands, took a sip, then gave a sigh of contentment. I watched her fondly, feeling a great surge of maternal love for her. She'd been mine on and off since I brought her across from Liverpool all those years ago—a terrified little mite who had just been taken from her own mother. Now she'd blossomed into a bright and confident young girl—at least until her schoolmates started giving her a hard time.

She looked up from her cup of tea. "What were you talking about just now?"

"When you came down? I can't even remember."

"No, to Aunty Sid. She said something about you agreeing with her."

"Oh," I said. "Sid and Gus feel that I shouldn't keep you at that school any longer."

"But I don't want to leave school," she said. "I love learning. I know I'll have to leave in the summer, but . . ."

"That's just it," I said. "Clearly we're not going to let you finish your education there. We'll find a private academy for you. It's just that—well, you know how passionate Sid and Gus are about educating you and sending you to Vassar one day? Well, Gus has suggested that she would pay to send you to her former ladies seminary."

"And where would that be?" she asked. "I thought Aunty Gus came from Boston."

"She did," I replied. "It's a boarding establishment out in Massachusetts."

"Boarding? You mean I'd live there?"

"Yes," I said. "And I think it's a horrible idea. I nearly lost you before and I don't want to let go of you."

"I don't want to go away either," she said.

"Then you won't. There must be schools in New York we can afford, or maybe Sid and Gus will insist on helping to pay since they are so keen on your education." I realized, of course, that Daniel's policeman's salary was not going to stretch to a good private school, and Sid and Gus were so fond of Bridie and dying to help, but my pride was going to make it hard to accept. I took the cup from her and refilled it. "When they are done with their latest project we'll put them into finding the best place for you."

"That would be grand." Her whole little face lit up. "I'd love to go to a school where wanting to learn wasn't a sin."

"If that's the worst sin you've committed, I don't think you need to worry, child," Mrs. Sullivan exclaimed. "And if you want my opinion, the girl could benefit from going to a select ladies academy and mixing with a better class of person."

I tried to keep my calm demeanor—not always the easiest thing for me. "But Mother Sullivan, think about it. Daniel is a policeman. We live in this little house. How could Bridie possibly feel at home among the daughters of the rich and powerful?"

"Daniel might not always be a policeman," she replied with a knowing nod. "We have discussed his going into politics, haven't we, and any connections that the family could make . . ."

"Daniel will go into politics over my dead body!" There. The calm demeanor hadn't lasted long. "And I am going to be selfish and say that I want Bridie at home with me."

"Then you could always think about the nuns," she said. "There must be good convent schools in the city. Daniel might know. Those neighbors of yours won't, not being of the true faith."

"Absolutely no nuns," I replied. "I remember my own experience with nuns all too vividly. Sadistic, that's what they were. If I dropped my slate pencil, out came the cane. If I spelled a word wrong, it was hold out your hand for the cane. One of them used to hit us over the head with a Bible. So no nuns for Bridie."

Bridie looked up and gave me a grateful grin.

I drained my own teacup. "There, now I better think about supper."

"What had you planned for your man's meal tonight?" Daniel's mother asked. "I noticed we were out of meat and I didn't see you going to the shops today." She paused, then added, "Understandable in that blizzard, of course."

"I have our supper. I left it on the hall table when Bridie appeared," I said. "My neighbors kindly made us an Indian curry."

"Curry?" Her nose wrinkled. "So Daniel actually likes heathen food now, does he?"

"He'll have to like it or go hungry," I replied smoothly as I went down the hall to retrieve the dish. I suppose it was a result of being cooped up together in a too-small house, but my patience was wearing very thin with my mother-in-law and I noticed she had become more barbed in her comments recently. Something would have to change.

That night in bed I recounted Bridie's ordeal to Daniel. I could see I took it a lot more seriously than he did.

"Does she know the boys?" he asked.

"Yes, they're from her school."

"Well, it was only snowballs. I used to have a bit of fun throwing snowballs myself."

"Yes, your mother told me. But this is different. They weren't including her in the fun. They were attacking her. I'll have a word with her principal in the morning." I tried to control my anger. "Picking on a young girl. That's what cowards do."

"Don't bother," Daniel said. "It won't do any good. He'll say it was only snowballs—a bit of boyish fun. You have to choose your battles."

"This *is* my battle, Daniel." I flared up. "She came home in tears saying that they hate her."

"Why would they hate her?"

"Because she's Irish and she's the teacher's pet," I said. "She likes to read and learn things. Those louts know they're done with school in the summer and they just want to get out."

I told Daniel what Sid and Gus had proposed for Bridie. "Your mother thinks it would be a good idea to help you get into politics."

Daniel chuckled. "My mother always did have big ideas," he said. "If you hear her speak you'd never believe she was raised by parents who'd escaped from the famine. But if Sid and Gus want to educate Bridie, I wouldn't say no. They can look into finding a private school for her in the city. And you leave well enough alone." He looked at me sternly and I gave him what I hoped was a meek smile as I snuggled close to him, deciding that whatever he said I would let that principal have a bit of my mind. I had never gotten anywhere by letting people walk all over me and I wasn't going to let them walk all over my ward, either! I was surprised at how much of my life was now wrapped up in being a mother and taking care of my home, a far cry from the exciting days of running my own detective agency. Sometimes life felt rather dull after dealing with gangsters and murderers. I was sure I could handle a school principal.

I was glad to hear that, whatever Daniel's mother said about politics, his own views hadn't changed. His career was once again back on track now that there was a new chief of police who was not in the pocket of Tammany Hall. I was so relieved he was happy in his work again. Last year there had been talk of him accepting the position of chief of police up in White Plains, near his mother's house, and of us living with her. Mercy me! I went hot and cold at the thought. Also President Roosevelt had offered him a job, and that would have meant moving to Washington. But now we could go on living where we were, in our little house on Patchin Place, opposite my dear friends Sid and Gus.

At least I had assumed we could go on living here until, just as we were falling asleep, Daniel mentioned that he thought his mother might now make her home with us and we'd obviously need a bigger house. With his recent promotion, in charge of the new homicide and major crimes division, we'd have more money and should consider where we'd want to live. Now was not the time to make my objections. With any luck the weather would improve and Mrs. Sullivan would want to go home.

Two

Next morning the weather had improved. We awoke to a landscape of sparkling crystal. Normal mundane objects like garbage cans and garden sheds now were disguised under mounds of snow. "Liam can build a snowman today," Daniel said as he looked out of the window. "He'll like that. Too bad I'm working or I could take him up to Central Park and go sledding."

"I can take him to the square and let him play," I said. "Unless those mean boys are there again." I paused. "I think I should keep Bridie home from school, don't you?"

"Is it the right thing to let her aggressors know they have won?" he asked. "Shouldn't she go and face them?"

"I'll leave it up to her," I replied.

"You do that, Molly." He wagged a finger at me. "The girl has to learn how to stand up for herself. It won't help if you wrap her in cotton."

"No, dear," I replied, turning away so he couldn't read my expression.

When Bridie came down to breakfast, I read from her face instantly that she was not looking forward to going to school.

"It's all right, my darling, you can stay home if you've a mind to. I'll write a letter to that teacher of yours telling her why."

"No, don't do that." She chewed anxiously on her lip. "It's only half a year. I can get through it."

Daniel had gone off to work and I was just clearing away the breakfast things when there was a tap at the front door. Sid and Gus stood there. "We've been thinking," Sid said, and there was a defiant jut to her chin. "Bridie shouldn't go to that school a moment longer. So we've decided to put aside our other activities for now, as soon as this clothing drive is over, and take over her education until we can find the proper school for her."

They came through into the kitchen. Bridie had overheard—Sid had a commanding tone of voice. I saw bright expectation on her face. "You'd teach me? That would be wonderful. When can I start?"

"Not today," Gus said. "In fact we came over to recruit Molly to work with us. And you too, if you're not going to school."

"What do you need?" I asked.

"We've sorted the warm clothing and we've been assigned to distribute it to the new immigrants on Ellis Island. There are an awful lot of clothes, so we hoped you'd come with us."

"Ellis Island?" I said. Conflicting emotions flooded over me. I had not returned to Ellis Island since my first month in America. The first time I had been there I was fleeing from a murder charge in Ireland and the second time I was trying to clear my name and prove I was not a murderer. I remembered the feelings of utter panic and helplessness. I was in a strange country, fleeing for my life at that time, and I had nobody I could turn to. Then my heart went out to the people who might be going through similar situations right now. Here I was, safe and warm with a loving husband, children, and friends. I would be a heartless person not to help when I could.

"I'll be glad to help," I said. "Those poor wretches must be freezing to death. I don't remember it being well warmed or very comfortable."

"Of course!" Sid looked animated. "You came through Ellis Island. I forgot. You will be our tour guide to the island. Our own immigrant: Give me your tired, your poor, your huddled, coatless masses," she recited, loudly and incorrectly. "What is it like?"

"It mostly feels like waiting in an endless line," I said, omitting the part about fleeing a murder charge, "and being terrified that you'll be turned away at the end. A horrible medical inspection in which they turn back your eyelids and ask embarrassing questions. But that wasn't the worst part for me." I paused. I realized that, as well as I knew Sid and Gus, I had never told them about my ordeal. Now was not the time to bring it up. "At least I am from an English-speaking county and was educated," I continued. "Some of the people with me didn't speak a word of English and couldn't even spell their names for the officials. Bridie was there too with me. Do you remember much about it, Bridie?" I turned to her. Strangely, this was not a subject we had discussed before. I had brought Bridie and her brother across to their father at the request of their dying mother—and in case that makes me sound like a saint, I have to confess that it helped me to escape the law in Ireland. At first we were just busy trying to survive, and then since Bridie's mother, Kathleen, had died I didn't like to bring up those early days and see the sadness in her eyes.

"I remember I had to pretend that you were my mother," she said. "I was scared I would lose you and get lost in the crowd. I told myself just to follow your red hair."

I laughed. "It is a good thing I stand out in a crowd, then. But you are sure you won't feel too sad to go back there?"

"I would be very selfish not to want to help those who have nothing when I have everything now," Bridie said softly.

"Quite right!" Gus chimed in forcefully. "You see, Molly, she is wasted on the local school. She is made for better things!"

"What time are you thinking of going?" I asked.

"We're meeting the other ladies to go across to the island at one," Gus said.

"Fine. I promised Liam to let him play in the snow this morning, but let me see if Mrs. Sullivan will watch him for the afternoon and

I'll be happy to help. But how on earth are we going to get there? If you have enough clothes to fill a room, I don't see how the four of us can carry them all and fit in a cab, even if it would attempt to come down this street in the snow." Patchin Place was such a narrow cobbled lane that cabbies often refused to come down it since it was almost impossible to back up the horses.

"Not a problem." Gus waved this thought away. "Mrs. Sage is sending her automobile for us. We can put about half the clothes in there. The chauffeur can help us carry the other half to the end of the street and put them in a cab."

"Mrs. Sage?" The name was not familiar to me.

"One of the doyens of New York society, my dear. And very involved in philanthropy."

"And a Vassar graduate to boot," Sid added smugly.

"Can I ride in the automobile?" Bridie's face lit up with excitement.

"Yes, all right, then," Sid said, linking her arm through Bridie's. "You and Molly can take the auto while Gus and I follow in a cab. But you'll have to come over now and help me bundle up the clothes. Can you spare her, Molly?"

"Of course, go along with you, then." I put a hand on Bridie's shoulder. "I'll get Liam ready to go out."

"Going out? In this freezing weather?" Daniel's mother appeared behind me, giving me a disapproving glare. "You're not taking the young boy, surely?"

I was about to remind her that she had chided me for not going to the shops the day before, even though the weather had been decidedly worse. "I promised Daniel that Liam could play in the snow this morning and this afternoon I wondered if you could watch him for me." I struggled to keep my tone pleasant. "I have an errand with Miss Walcott and Miss Goldfarb."

"What will you be doing, then?" Her expression made it quite obvious that she didn't think that I would be up to much good with Sid and Gus.

"Actually, Mrs. Sage—you know, one of the wives of the Four Hundred who appears in the society columns—will be sending a chauffeur for us." I was always trying to be a better person, but I have to admit I enjoyed the look on her face.

Especially when Gus added, "I expect the police commissioner's wife will be there as well, Molly. She is a member of our Vassar Benevolent Society." She winked at me. Sid and Gus had heard about my struggles to keep my temper with Daniel's mother over many cups of too-strong coffee as I frequently fled the house to get away from her critical looks and comments. She knew that Mrs. Sullivan had big plans for Daniel and that I was not too happy about them. "It's important that Molly mix with the right people, Mrs. Sullivan," she said, turning an earnest gaze on my mother-in-law. "For Daniel, I mean. We all consider Daniel's career of the utmost importance."

I bit my lip to keep a straight face. "Perhaps I shouldn't leave Liam after all." I winked back at Gus. "It is a lot of work for you, Mother Sullivan."

"Not at all, no work at all to watch the little darling. Mrs. Sage, no less. Fancy that. Where is this event? Will you be going to Mrs. Sage's house? Isn't she up on Fifth Avenue?"

"Nothing that nice, I'm afraid. We'll be going to Ellis Island to give out warm clothes. Part of the society's charity work. But we shall be freezing beside New York's finest. I understand several daughters of the Four Hundred will be there." Sid steered Bridie out the door.

Mrs. Sullivan was quite pleasant to me as I bundled Liam into his leggings and overcoat, then wrapped him in rugs in his pram. "I'll bring back some meat for Daniel's supper," I said. Daniel hadn't actually complained about the vegetable curry the night before but had described it as "interesting." His mother hadn't been quite so polite. "Well, I suppose it's good enough for people in heathen countries who can't get any better food" was her comment. I actually had found it rather tasty.

We set off, Liam's buggy bouncing over the snow and ice. It was hard going and I rather wished I'd left him behind, because, you see, my mission wasn't actually to let him play in the square. I was going to give that school principal a piece of my mind. I know Daniel had told me to leave well enough alone, but I've never been good at doing what I was told.

I kept an eye out for the boys as we crossed the square. There was no sign of them, which meant they must be in school already. As I continued past the square and down McDougal Street my gaze went to the post office. I remembered how my senses would quicken when I went up the steps to see if there were any letters for me—or actually for the detective agency I had inherited. A new case to sink my teeth into! How long ago it all seemed. Almost in a different lifetime. Now I was Molly Sullivan, mother and wife, and I had to learn to be content with that.

But memories of past triumphs had riled my fighting spirit. I hauled Liam from his pram and marched into the principal's office.

"I'm Mrs. Sullivan. I'm here about my ward, Bridie O'Connor," I said. "She was set upon yesterday by a gang of boys from your school and is naturally upset. I hope you will be taking positive action against this sort of unacceptable behavior."

"Set on her?" the man looked worried. "Attacked her, you mean?'

"Pelted her with snowballs," I said.

He burst out laughing. "You're here because some children had a snowball fight? My dear woman . . ."

"I am not your dear woman." I gave him a cold stare. "A snowball fight implies both sides are willing. A gang of boys pelting a lone little girl is bullying. And Bridie says they attacked her because she is Irish and she is smart."

His smile was patronizing. "I know the girl you're talking of. If she spent less of her time with her head in a book then maybe she'd learn to get along with her schoolmates."

"Well, we won't need to worry about that anymore, because I'm withdrawing her from school as of today," I said.

He came around his desk toward me, in what seemed to be a threatening pose because he could tower over me. "Now, let's not get hasty, little lady. I can see you're upset, but surely you want the child to finish her education. She seems so keen on it. Why don't you talk it over with Mr. Sullivan first? Get a man's perspective. Less emotion and more reason, huh?"

It was lucky I was holding Liam or I would have punched him in the nose. "For one thing, it's Captain Sullivan of the New York police, and if you can't instill discipline and compassion into your boys, then my husband will be instructing his men to keep a good eye out for those boys. Good day to you, sir." And I stormed out. Liam took one look at my face and started to cry, which made me feel bad.

"No, you haven't done anything wrong, sweetheart," I said. "Let's go and play, shall we?"

After half an hour of building a snowman, throwing snowballs, and even making snow angels we headed home, stopping by the butcher for pork chops on the way. Then I fed Liam some soup and put him down for his nap before I put on my best cape and fur muff to meet my friends.

"Don't worry about a thing," Daniel's mother said. She even offered to make some dinner for Liam and Daniel if I was kept late. I think the idea of an automobile calling for me with a chauffeur had a marked change in her attitude. People would see me getting into Mrs. Sage's automobile. Finally I was behaving like a proper daughter-in-law!

"I wish those boys could see me now," Bridie said as we backed out of Patchin Place and then drove around Washington Square in the back of a swank automobile. The streets were icy but we were very warm, as every inch of the car was full of cloaks, coats, and shawls. Bridie draped a particularly fine purple shawl around her head. "Sorry to see you out in the snow," she said, waving to imaginary boys outside the window and making her voice sound like Gus's at her most posh, "I am being driven by my chauffeur."

She turned back to me with a wicked grin. I gazed at her with surprise and realization that she was growing up fast. I think that moment when she refused to go back to Ireland with her father and his new wife had somehow changed her. For the first time in her life she had fought for something precious to her and won. She realized she had power. I returned her grin.

The auto negotiated piles of ice and snow along Christopher Street, the tires slithering on ice, until we came out to the Hudson waterfront and turned north onto West Street, past all the docks. Here we got the full force of the icy wind and I realized I wasn't looking forward to that crossing to Ellis Island—in more ways than one. To tell the truth, I wasn't at all sure I wanted to go back there at all—my memories of it being so dark. But I could hardly back out now.

At last the automobile pulled up beside an enormous steamship. It had clearly just arrived because people were coming ashore. One lot of people, well dressed in furs, were emerging from the cabins and proceeding to waiting cabs or autos when at the other end of the ship a more tattered mob was streaming down the steerage gangplank and being herded into a ferry that looked tiny beside the liner.

I leaned forward to speak to the chauffeur. "Do you know where we are meeting Miss Goldfarb and Miss Walcott?" I asked.

"No, ma'am," he replied. "I was just told to go to the ferry pier for Ellis Island and this is it."

I was wondering what on earth I was going to do with an automobile full of clothes and whether we were to travel with the steerage passengers onto that crowded ferry. But at that moment Sid and

Gus pulled up, waving wildly out of the cab. "One pier down," Sid yelled. "They've sent a private boat for us. Follow us."

Our chauffeur obliged, weaving between piles of luggage, cargo, and people on the dock until we came to a pleasure craft moored at a smaller pier. There were several automobiles beside it and chauffeurs or footmen were staggering under loads of clothing, while fashionable young ladies walked beside them, waving to newly arrived friends. Gus and Sid were greeted and footmen were recruited to haul the loads we had brought.

"Mercy me," Gus said as we approached the gangplank to the ship, "we'll be lucky if there is room for us on board. You might have to swim, Bridie."

Bridie laughed as she took Gus's hand.

"Well, if it isn't Augusta Walcott," said a voice, and a young woman, dressed in a white fox fur coat with matching hat, came up to us. "Put the bundle down there, Jackson, and then you can go," she said. "But make sure Tompkins sticks around with the automobile. I don't know how long I shall be."

She turned back to us. The smile she had used for Sid and Gus faded as she focused on Bridie and me. "And you've brought your own little helpers with you. How clever."

"These are our neighbors and good friends, Mrs. Molly Sullivan and her ward, Bridie," Gus said. "Molly, this is our college classmate Cordelia Ransom."

"Maybe not Cordelia Ransom for much longer," the woman replied, giving a coquettish smile. "I have just returned from a long trip to Europe and if all goes well, I might just have snagged me an English aristocrat. A viscount no less. We met in London last month. He is coming to America to join me and meet my family any time now. So I'll be a lady and you'll have to curtsey to me. Won't that be a lark?"

"Congratulations," Sid said in a tone that made me want to grin.

The woman's gaze narrowed as she focused on Sid. "Not married yet, Elena?"

"Not exactly," Sid replied. "But quite happy, thank you."

"If you were in London, did you happen to go to the theater?" Gus asked, steering this conversation rapidly to safer ground.

"Why, yes. Of course. One always goes to the theater," Cordelia said.

"Did you happen to catch our friend Ryan O'Hare's latest play?" Gus went on. "One hears it was the rage of the town. *Queen of Diamonds.* Very witty and a little naughty, so we understand."

"Oh yes, I did read something about it," Cordelia said, waving a dismissive hand. "The critics seemed to love it, but the people at the hotel said it wasn't at all suitable for a young unmarried woman like myself."

Sid stifled a chuckle at this description of Cordelia. "Well, if you change your mind he's on his way home now, bringing the play to New York. I can't wait to see him again, can you, Molly?"

"Absolutely dying to see him. And his play." I gave Cordelia a knowing little grin.

Where this little polite confrontation might have led was interrupted by another voice calling, "Let's all pick up a bundle and get going. The boat is waiting for us."

We obeyed, following the fashionable Miss Ransom onto the boat. Ice floes had piled up against the piers and the boat creaked and crackled as it steered through them, out into the waters of the Hudson. Then we were free of the ice and out into the stream. The black water swirled by, looking dark and menacing. The air coming off the Atlantic Ocean was frigid. I leaned on the rail and watched the island as the big brick buildings came closer. "It looks like a fairy castle." Bridie came up and stood close. I saw what she meant. The domes and spires were covered with snow and ice and glittered in the clear winter sun. "I don't remember it being pretty."

"Well, you were so little." I tried to smile at her, but my cheeks were too frozen to move. "I doubt you could see anything but boots."

Workers rushed out to tie up the boat as we came in to dock and a uniformed official put a gangplank into place, saluting us.

"Everyone take a bundle," Gus said forcefully, and young women leapt to obey.

"Welcome, ladies," the official called. "Commissioner Watchcorn asked me to make sure you have everything you need. So follow me, please. Another ferry has just come in and we will want to make sure that you get safely to the tables we have set up for you before you are overwhelmed."

The ferry must have just come from the ocean liner we had seen. It was tied up right beside us, and I watched a line of men, women, and children stream off it. As the group on my boat leapt efficiently into action I felt frozen. The people getting off the ferry looked like they could have been from Ballykillin. When you are far from home and see people from your country, every face looks like a family member's. These faces, the clothes, some worn and ragged and some the Sunday best, and even the baskets and cloth of the bundles—it all took me back to my childhood. And my childhood as an Irish peasant, looking with envy at the English who ruled us, was not a happy one. My heart began to pound. I half expected someone to look up from the line and say, "Look at that Molly Murphy putting on airs and graces and thinking herself better than us. Get back into this line where you belong!"

"I'm Molly Sullivan now," I reminded myself. "I'm not a girl from Ballykillin with nothing, but the wife of a respected policeman." Still, as we walked away from the boat, arms full of coats and shawls, I kept close to Gus and Sid. Even though I knew it was ridiculous, I couldn't help feeling that if I got mixed into that line of immigrants heading toward the building, I would never be allowed to come out again. Or, more ridiculously still, I would be sent back to Ireland, where there could well be a price on my head for a couple of crimes I had committed. As we neared the main entrance, our group had to cross the line of people waiting to get into the baggage room on the ground floor. The men stepped back politely and touched their caps to us.

"We set up a couple of tables for you on the far side near the money changers," the official who was guiding us said. "That's where the women can find themselves some warm clothing while the men wait in line to change their money. And there are also more tables out by the kissing post."

"The what?" one of our group asked in astonishment.

The man grinned. "That's what we call the dock area where the immigrants catch their ferries to Manhattan or to the train station on the Jersey shore," he said. "It's where their long-lost relatives can wait for them. There is always a lot of kissing and hugging and crying going on."

Miss Ransom turned back to Bridie and me. "Why don't you ladies take the table out on the ferry dock," she said. "I don't think I'm well enough equipped for the cold. If I'd known I'd have worn my ski outfit I acquired in Switzerland." And she gave us the sweetest smile.

If she had actually said, "because you look more like the arriving peasants," she couldn't have made it clearer.

"We'll be happy to man the dock area," Gus said. "We're made of sterner stuff, aren't we, Bridie?" And she swept ahead with her bundle of clothing.

We skirted the building and came to some tables set up for us. More immigrants were coming out, ready to board the ferries for New York or New Jersey. Most of them, especially those from southern Europe, were shockingly under-equipped for the weather. Some women had on cotton dresses, and the men's light jackets or vests must have done nothing to ward off the cold.

I didn't want to let a single one go further without a warmer item of clothing, and it seemed that the other women in the group felt the same. We started handing out the coats and cloaks before we even got to the table, which resulted in people swarming around us, much to Gus's annoyance.

"Ladies, please put your clothes down here. And everyone form a line if you want warm clothing." Gus's voice rang out in the frigid air. She had us set down the clothes in piles on the tables, and a line formed of people who were exiting the main building. Many of them dragged baskets or suitcases, the women held tightly to children's hands, but some of the young men seemed to have nothing but the clothes on their backs. Now that they were out of the building, everyone was smiling, slapping each other on the back or hugging.

I undid my bundle and started handing out coats, shawls, scarves, all eagerly snatched from my hands. I didn't have a second to breathe, but the first time I glanced up I spotted a young woman rushing into the arms of a man on the dock. It was so touching it brought tears to my eyes.

"Do you remember how surprised your da was to see me? I was dreadful afraid that he was going to give me away and blurt out that I wasn't his wife." I turned to Bridie, but she wasn't there. I looked around the dock area, down the line of tables quickly, but couldn't see her among the crush of people. "Sid, have you seen Bridie?"

"No." Sid called down the tables to Gus, "Have you seen Bridie anywhere?" Gus looked up and shook her head. "When was the last time you saw her?" A feeling of panic started to build in me as I scanned the crowd streaming out of the building. She must be here. I spotted an iron staircase going up the side of the building and climbed up to get a better look. But looking down over a sea of people, I couldn't see Bridie anywhere!

Three

I retraced my steps around the building, trying to remember when I had seen her last. She had been beside me when the Ransom woman had made her cutting remark, of that I was sure. The ferry had filled again with immigrants heading back to Manhattan. I watched it pull away from the dock. Surely Bridie couldn't have boarded by mistake or been swept on board in the crowd of immigrants. Our smaller boat was still moored, but the deck was empty. She had been right beside me as we got off and when we were escorted around the building. I had been following Gus and she had been following me. But then we had been besieged as we started handing out clothes and I hadn't had time to see what happened to her.

Panic rose inside me and I told myself to be calm. She wasn't a little girl anymore that I couldn't let out of my sight. Just as I was determined to go into to the baggage entrance and ask if anyone had seen her, she appeared from the darkness inside, forcing her way past the waiting line of people, and ran toward me, still carrying her large bundle of cloaks. "Oh, Molly," she said. "There you are!"

Relief spilled out as anger. "What were you doing in there? I was worried sick. I thought you were following me and then I looked and you weren't anywhere." My panic made my voice sound harsh and a bit shaky.

"I was following you!" she protested. "At least I thought I was. I saw your bright red hair disappear into the building and I went after you into it. I suppose I couldn't see much more over the cloaks I was carrying. I followed the woman through the baggage room and then up a big staircase and there were doctors waiting and checking out everyone, and I thought that wasn't right, then she turned around and it wasn't you! She looked so much like you, though. Bright red hair, pale skin, and freckles. And just the same height, too. I tried to run back down the stairs and out of the door, but the man at the door said I couldn't. He said I had to wait my turn and go through registration in the building. And I realized that he thought I came on the ferry with the immigrants."

She stopped talking as we made our way back around the outside of the building, and the full force of the icy wind met us. At last we came to the outside tables where we had been working. Sid came up to us. "Well, those went quickly," she said, pointing to the dwindling pile of clothes. "Those poor people with nothing but the clothes they traveled in. Bridie, where did you disappear to? I think Molly was worried."

She turned to me, "I'm glad you found her, Molly, although I don't think any harm could come to her on an island. There is nowhere to go."

"I'll have you know I was almost kidnapped!" Bridie said dramatically.

"Kidnapped?" Sid shot me an alarmed look.

"She got into the Registry Room by mistake, following a woman she thought was me," I explained. "And they thought she was one of the new immigrants and wouldn't let her out again." I took Bridie's bundle from her. "But how did you finally manage to make them let you out?" I realized that the very nightmare I had worried about for myself had almost come true for Bridie.

"I told them I was not a newly arrived immigrant but the goddaughter of the head of the Vassar Women's Benevolent Society and if he didn't let me go back to the ladies right away I would scream and then tell Commissioner Watchcorn."

"That's my Vassar girl!" Sid put her arms around Bridie. I could tell that she was enjoying being the center of Sid's attention now that she was safely back with us. And if I thought about it, I was glad that Bridie could speak up for herself. No harm had come to her and she had shown herself capable of taking care of herself. Perhaps my spirit was rubbing off on her. It would have been just like me to get myself into trouble and have to find a way out of it!

By the time she retold the story to Gus on the boat ride home she had added some touches to make it more exciting. The woman she had followed in line had looked like my identical twin and the uniformed officer had been seven feet tall and told her he would lock her up if she did not get back in line.

"You are full of blarney, my love." I laughed, and Sid joined in. "Is this the shy little girl who wouldn't say a word to speak up for herself?"

"It is our good influence, I imagine. We have been giving her adventure novels to read lately," Gus added.

"So that's it, is it?" I chuckled as I said it. "Too full of imagination to watch where she is going. Did that woman really look like me or were you making that up too?"

"Oh, she did, Molly, her hair looked just like yours from behind." Bridie nodded earnestly. "And her face too when she turned around."

"Well, we'll have to tell Daniel, then. History is repeating itself at Ellis Island."

"I suppose it's not unexpected to find a woman with red hair arriving from Ireland, is it?" Gus said.

I looked around. "What happened to the one who was giving herself such airs and graces? Ransom, wasn't it?"

"Oh, her!" Sid gave Gus a knowing look. "Always was a pain, even in college. The number of times we had to hear how much money her father made and how many rooms they had in their cottage in Newport, Rhode Island."

"She wasn't very nice," Bridie chimed in. "The way she looked at me and Molly as if we had no right to be part of her group."

"Clearly insecure," Gus said. "I'm glad I studied with Professor Freud. Now I know all about complexes, and she definitely has some."

I was glad that we could laugh together about this and that they found her as tiresome as I had done. "So where did she go?" I asked.

"Left early. Said she had strained her back lifting her heavy bundle and needed to rest," Gus said. "I expect she actually had a dinner engagement for which she had to get ready."

The boat crunched its way through the ice floes toward the pier. Our faithful chauffeur was waiting and we all piled in this time, having no extra baggage taking up room.

"So how did it go?" Mrs. Sullivan asked as we arrived home. "Was Mrs. Sage there herself? And the police commissioner's wife? Did you manage to have a good conversation with them and mention Daniel?"

"Mrs. Sage didn't come herself," I said, going over to the stove to pour myself a cup of tea. "She kindly sent her automobile, and her poor chauffeur had to wait all those hours for us to return."

"That's what chauffeurs are supposed to do," Mrs. Sullivan commented. "Here, sit down, both of you. I've baked scones. The little one was good as gold. After he woke from his nap he wanted to go out and play in the snow again, so I took him into the backyard for a few minutes and we built a snowman. Not a very satisfactory one, but good enough for Liam."

"That's very kind of you, Mother Sullivan," I said, helping myself to a scone. "I know you don't like the cold."

"And did you have a good time, young woman?" she asked Bridie, who had now come to sit beside me.

"She got herself lost and mistaken for a new immigrant." I glanced across at Bridie with a knowing smile.

"In the crush of people I followed someone who looked like Molly and then they didn't want to let me out of the big room again," Bridie said shyly.

"But this young lady was smart enough to tell them she was with the Vassar ladies and she'd call for the commissioner's wife if they didn't let her out." I gave her a fond look.

"Did she now? So your mission was appreciated, I take it?"

"Oh, Mother Sullivan, you've no idea. So many of those immigrants were from Italy and other warm places. Their clothes were so thin. They were so grateful. It was a good day, wasn't it, Bridie?"

She nodded. "Yes. It's nice to be able to help people. I think I'd like to do that when I'm finally out of school. Maybe be a teacher, or even a doctor?"

"Big dreams," Daniel's mother said.

"And you hang on to them," I couldn't resist saying.

After we'd revived ourselves with tea and Mother Sullivan's scones, I got started on the evening meal, cooking the pork chops, along with cabbage and potatoes, then a sponge pudding with jam sauce to follow. By six thirty it was all ready to be served. At seven thirty I was getting a trifle annoyed and declared that we should go ahead and eat, putting Daniel's chop, the biggest of the four, into the oven. We finished eating, I put Liam to bed, then sat by the fire in the back parlor while Bridie read a book and my mother-in-law knitted, but still no Daniel. By nine o'clock I was getting worried. I reminded myself that a policeman's job was never without danger. He had been shot at before, and nearly lost his life on a couple of occasions. Now that he was the head of a homicide division he shouldn't, in theory, be out confronting criminals on the streets, but merely doing the investigation after the crime had happened. So where was he?

I sent Bridie up to bed. Mrs. Sullivan declared she was tired and would go up as well. I filled their hot water bottles and then settled myself again by the fire. It was now down to embers and it didn't seem right to add more coal at this time of night, so I moved my chair closer and wrapped my shawl around me. Where was the dratted man? Why did I not think it was a good idea for him to go into politics where nobody would be shooting at him? Then I remembered that several presidents had been shot. So not such a safe profession after all!

At ten thirty I was dozing off when I heard the front door open. I was up, out of my chair, and rushed into the hall. "There you are at last," I said as he closed the door behind him. "I was worried sick about you. Why didn't you let me know you were going to be late? You could have sent a man to tell me."

He unwound his scarf and hung his overcoat on the peg in the hall. "I'm sorry, Molly. I realized you'd be worried, but there wasn't anything I could do about it. You see, I was stuck out on Ellis Island with no access to a telephone."

"Ellis Island?" I almost shrieked out the words. "And what in God's name were you doing there?"

A wry smile came over his face. "You'll never believe this in a million years, Molly, but there was a man found murdered on the island today. And the woman who is the prime suspect looks exactly like you!"

Four

I stood like a statue in the hallway, staring at Daniel in disbelief. "A murder, you say? Are you sure? It wasn't just an accidental death?"

He gave a grim smile. "People don't usually stab themselves neatly in the chest."

He started to walk toward the kitchen. "Is there any dinner left? I haven't eaten since midday. And I'm frozen to the marrow, crossing on that open boat."

"I've saved your pork chop," I said, "and I can easily heat up some tea for you. Or cocoa if you'd prefer."

"Whiskey is what I'd prefer," he said, looking back with that wicked grin. He ducked into the back parlor and poured himself a glass from the decanter on the sideboard. I waited, fighting to be patient. I told myself he'd had a trying day and needed to unwind, but my curiosity was about to explode. I went through to the kitchen, removed the now rather dry pork chop from the warming drawer on the stove, then put on the kettle as Daniel came through, taking a gulp of whiskey as he walked.

"Ah, that feels better already," he said. "I can feel the life coming back to my hands and feet. My, but it was bleak out there."

"So tell me all about it," I said. "A woman who looked like me, you said."

"She did. Remarkably like you. Irish. Long red hair over her shoulders. Neat little nose like yours, pale skin. Strong brogue, too."

"She wasn't called Molly, was she?" The coincidence had shaken me.

He chuckled. "Rose," he said. "Rose McSweeney, but she came from your part of the country. Galway. The far west. Not too far from you?"

"Not too far," I agreed. "But the funny thing is that we met her today too."

"What?" He put down the whiskey glass with a thump. "Where did you meet her?"

"On Ellis Island. We lost Bridie and it turned out she got separated from us in the crowd and followed a woman she thought was me—only it wasn't. Poor Bridie had a scare, actually. She followed the woman into the baggage hall and up to the registry, and they wouldn't let her out again. They thought she was one of the newly arrived immigrants trying to bypass the line."

Daniel was frowning now. "What in God's name were you doing on Ellis Island?"

"Helping Sid and Gus with their warm clothing drive. We handed out capes and scarves and things to the new immigrants, and Holy Mother of God did they need them! Some of those children were in cotton dresses with just a shawl."

Daniel shook his head. "This really is too strange for words, Molly. You go to Ellis Island on the actual day that this woman arrives and is arrested for murder. And do you know what else is strange? I could have sent any one of my detectives out on that case, but when I heard it was on Ellis Island I remember thinking about how I met you and I decided I really had to go myself."

"It was fate, Daniel," I said. "Fate sent you there so that this poor woman was not unjustly accused."

"Why do you not think she was guilty?"

I gave him a knowing look. "Well, you accused me of murder, didn't you? And yet I was innocent."

He pulled out a chair, sat at the table, and picked up his knife and fork. "That doesn't mean that this woman is innocent."

"But don't you think it's a sign? That I was there today and you felt obliged to go yourself? If it had been one of your men instead he would have jumped to conclusions. Why was she the prime suspect? What made you think she was guilty? Don't tell me she was found with the knife, dripping blood, in her hand?"

Daniel had managed to eat a couple of mouthfuls before he answered. "She was spotted coming out of a disused storeroom, well away from the parts of the island that the immigrants would use."

"And?"

"When that storeroom was checked a man's body was found on the floor. He'd been stabbed."

"And the murder weapon?"

"No sign of the murder weapon."

"So the young woman who was spotted coming out of the storeroom was not carrying a knife in her hand at the time?" I waved a triumphant finger at him. "And what happened to the weapon if she didn't have it on her?"

"She was wearing a big cape," Daniel said. "She could easily have hidden a knife under that cape."

"And did any of her clothing have bloodstains on it?" I asked sweetly. "If you're carrying a bloodstained knife under your cape, it's bound to touch your skirt somewhere. At least there would be the tiniest bit of blood spatter on her."

He looked up at me and smiled. "You're too good at this, you know. It's a shame you're not a man and I can't use you on the force."

"You're damnty right I'm good at it," I said. "I've had plenty of practice. Solved plenty of murders, haven't I?"

"Not all of them went so well for you, remember," he said. "There were a couple of times I could think of when you had a lucky escape."

"Maybe a couple," I agreed. "And you do have female detectives on the force now, don't you? What about Mrs. Goodwin? She's as good as any man."

"She is, in her way," he admitted grudgingly. "But that doesn't mean that Mrs. Molly Sullivan is going to apply for a job anytime soon."

"You could use me, Daniel," I said. "Behind the scenes, share your cases with me more often and hear the woman's point of view. Let me keep my hand in." I was struck with a brilliant idea and tried to be nonchalant as I tossed it out. "You know, I could come out to the island with you tomorrow and talk to this woman for you. Interview her for you. She may relax her guard and reveal things to me she'd never say to a strange American policeman. You know, Irishwoman to Irishwoman. You know how we like to gossip."

"Absolutely not, Molly. I cannot have you getting involved in any way in my cases. And especially not in a murder investigation."

"I could be helpful, Daniel. I'm only trying to help."

"I'm sure you are," he replied, shaking his head as he spoke. "But it can never happen, Molly. I know you were a good enough detective in your own way, and that was fine. It was also not a job for a married woman with family commitments." He paused. "Besides, I'd be the laughing stock of the NYPD if it was found out. Look at poor old Sullivan, having his wife solve his cases for him."

"Who would find out if you didn't tell them?" I asked, then decided this was not a battle worth pursuing at the moment when I had more important things. "But you didn't answer my question. Were there any bloodstains on her clothes?"

"No, at least not that I could see. But we don't know how much time passed between Rose McSweeney being observed and the body being found. She probably had enough time to sneak back into the room, recover the knife, and toss it into the harbor. Maybe enough time to sponge any blood off her hands or clothing."

"If some time elapsed," I said, weighing the words as I spoke, "who is to say that other people didn't pass that way unobserved? If it was a part of the island not normally used, as you say. Was a guard on duty at the end of the hallway who can attest that she was the only person seen during that time?"

"There was a man on duty at one end of that corridor," he said, "but his job was to observe the Registry Room and the incoming immigrants, so he would have had his back to the hallway leading to that room. And it was pretty dark there. No electric light in that corridor."

"So anyone would have had to pass this guard to go down the hallway and get into that room?"

"Not necessarily," he said as he cut off another large bit of pork chop. "Let me eat first, will you? Then I can concentrate more on my answers."

"All right," I agreed. "I'll make us both a cup of tea, shall I?"

"Good idea. Give you something to do, because I can see you're itching to ask more questions."

I went over to the stove and made a fresh pot of tea. Daniel had cleared his plate remarkably quickly, so I replaced it with the steamed pudding. I poured the tea, put two cups on the table, and sat facing him as he finally put down his spoon. "Very tasty," he said. "Thank you. Now you can fire away."

"So let's recap," I said. "This Rose McSweeney was spotted coming out of a disused room where a man's body was found later. Who spotted her? One of the guards?"

"No, one of the incoming immigrants, actually," he said.

"A fellow Irishman?"

"No, an English fellow. Name of Edwin Cromer. Quite well spoken."

"What was he doing on Ellis Island, then, I wonder. Why did he not travel at least second class if he was well spoken? And how did he come to be in a part of the facility not normally used by immigrants?"

"A good question. I wondered myself why he hadn't the means to travel in more comfortable conditions. He claims he was banished by his family for running up gambling debts, given a small amount of cash, and told to go abroad and make something of himself. He decided to travel by the cheapest means possible."

"I see." That did have a ring of truth to it. I had heard of younger sons being sent abroad to make their own way. "And what was his explanation for being in a part of the building not normally used?"

"He claimed he was trying to find the dining hall. He was near the back of the line and hadn't eaten since breakfast. He heard there was food available in the dining hall and decided he'd rather eat than wait his turn, since it was possible he wouldn't be processed that day and he'd have to spend the night."

"Did that corridor lead to the dining hall?"

"Where the man was stabbed, you mean? No. It was just a small side hallway leading off the main corridor, but as he went past on his way to the dining room he happened to see a flash of color in the darkness down there. He glanced down it and saw the woman coming out of a room and carefully closing the door behind her."

"Definitely Rose McSweeney?"

"Yes. He'd met her on the ship, apparently. That was why it remained in his mind. He was curious as to what she was doing poking around in a dark little area like that."

"And what did she have to say about it? Why did she claim she was there?"

Daniel grinned. "She claimed she was looking for the nearest WC. She said she'd been standing in line for hours and felt rather desperate. She couldn't find anyone to ask, so she set off in search of one."

"Also a reasonable explanation. The place is certainly confusing,

Daniel. I remember getting lost myself while I was there." I took a big swig of tea, then another thought struck me. "What time was this?"

"The doctor reckons the man was murdered between four and five."

"And what time was the body found?"

"A little after six."

I frowned. "And Rose and the Englishman were still on the island? We saw her in line ages before that. They should have been processed and long gone."

"They had a holdup, apparently."

"A holdup? With a gun, you mean?"

"No." He laughed. "I meant a glitch in processing. The ferry going into Manhattan from the island struck a big chunk of ice and they had to determine if it had done any serious damage to the hull before it could be put back into service. There was no ferry service for about an hour. That slowed everything down, and the immigrants were told some of them would probably have to spend the night on the island."

"So you're saying that the murderer wouldn't have had a chance to make his escape and get off the island?"

"It's possible that a person could have gotten away, taken the boat to the Jersey shore, for example, but most people were held up in the Registry Room because there was no more room on the dock."

"That was convenient, for you," I said. "Otherwise whoever did it could have been long gone and you'd never have known. Unlucky for Rose, though. So other people could have passed that way to the dining rooms?"

Daniel thought about it, then frowned. "Not normally. As you well know, immigrants are not allowed to leave the line that snakes through the Registry Room until they have been fully processed. I'm sure exceptions are allowed for visits to lavatories, usually escorted, I should think, but it seems that the Englishman sneaked out."

"Aha," I said. "Doubly suspicious. First he's an upper-class fellow traveling steerage and then he bypasses the line and just happens to see Rose . . ." I waved a triumphant finger. "I'd say he was the one who murdered the poor man and who seized the chance to pin the crime on someone else."

"Possibly." Daniel nodded. "We haven't ruled him out."

"What does she say about it?" I asked. "I take it you questioned her?"

"Of course. She says that this Englishman, Edwin Cromer, tried to get fresh with her on the boat and she rebuffed him in no uncertain terms. So she reckoned he was trying to get even with her."

"Do you know who the victim was?" I asked.

"That's an interesting point," he said. "No. We don't know who he was. Or at least we didn't when I left for the night. He had no identification in his pockets, which is strange to start with."

"Very strange. In fact impossible. Who wouldn't have identification on Ellis Island?" I agreed. "You have to present your papers to be admitted to the country. Do you think that whoever murdered him also took his wallet? Could it, in fact, have been a robbery gone wrong?"

Daniel frowned, considering this. "That hadn't occurred to me, but yes, I suppose you could be right. If this man had displayed more money than most immigrants have, maybe someone followed him, took a chance to pick his pocket, was caught, and then had to stab him to keep him quiet."

"Stabbed him and then dragged him into the nearest room," I said. "You need to look for someone with traces of blood on their clothing."

He nodded.

"You know what," I went on, warming to the subject, "it could have been an act of utter desperation, Daniel. Perhaps some poor person didn't have the twenty-five dollars, saw someone who had money, and took an awful risk."

"What twenty-five dollars?" he asked.

I looked at him in surprise. "Didn't you know that in order to get into the country you have to show that you have twenty-five dollars on you? If not, you'll be sent back."

"I don't think I knew that," he said.

"You wouldn't. You've never had to do it." The words came out more bitterly than I had intended, remembering that small detail of my whole ordeal. How desperate I had felt at the time. How precariously my life had hung in the balance.

Daniel looked at me, as if reading my thoughts. "This must be bringing it all back for you," he said. "What a lot you went through, my darling." He reached out and squeezed my hand, bringing tears to my eyes.

I gave him a bright smile. "I'd say I landed on my feet in the end, wouldn't you?"

"You could have done worse," he said.

"So getting back to this murdered man." I wasn't about to be distracted by a handsome husband and loving glances. "No identification, so you couldn't work out who he was from the ship's manifest?"

Daniel shook his head. "My men were trying to locate his belongings in the baggage room but with no luck when I left. From his clothing I'd say English or Irish. Tweed suit. Quite good quality, if a little worn. Pipe in his pocket. But the interesting thing is he doesn't match anyone on the manifest from that ship. At least not in steerage on their way to the island."

"A stowaway, then? This gets more interesting by the minute."

Daniel took a last swig and put down his teacup. "More interesting for you, maybe. For me, all I want is my nice warm bed and a few hours' sleep before I'm back on the job. We should know more when my men have dusted for fingerprints."

"Oh, they are doing that more often now, are they?" I asked.

"Oh, yes. It's becoming invaluable, although the evidence hasn't yet been admissible in court. Stupidly shortsighted of the judges.

Fingerprints are the one real piece of evidence we have, now we know that no two are alike." He got up, holding out his hand to me. "Come on. Let's go up."

"So where is that poor girl now?" I asked. "You haven't arrested her and taken her to the Tombs?"

"No, we don't have enough evidence to arrest her yet. She's being held on the island for the night and by tomorrow we might have more idea of what we're looking for." He slipped an arm around my shoulder. "And don't keep calling her that poor girl. She might be a cold-blooded killer, for all you know."

I looked up at him. "I can't help it, Daniel. How can I not see myself in her? Arriving alone, no friends, no one to speak up for her, and being accused on merely circumstantial evidence. I have a feeling that I was meant to be on that island today to save Rose."

Five

The next morning Daniel left while it was still dark. I was only half-conscious of him moving around and muttering as he got dressed in the dark. By the time I was fully awake and had told myself I should get up and make him coffee he had gone. Then I felt a bit guilty. It's a wife's job to take care of her husband, isn't it? Although part of me wished I could be going out to Ellis Island with Daniel and finding out the truth about the murder. I suppose it's the same for many women, finding it hard to accept the lesser role that nature has assigned to us.

Of course the sight of Liam, sitting happily in his crib and playing with his stuffed animals, reminded me that there were real compensations to the role of wife and mother. Especially when he stood up, held out his chubby little arms, and said, "Mama! Up!"

I sat him on the potty, praised him, then carried him downstairs. I got the boiler going, made coffee and then porridge for our breakfast. Daniel's mother appeared as I was spooning out a helping for Liam.

"Daniel came home all right, then, did he? I thought I heard the front door just as I was drifting off to sleep."

"He did," I said, "and left again very early."

"Oh, so it's a big case for him, then? He has men under him to handle the small stuff."

"Strangely enough it's a murder on Ellis Island," I said.

"Oh, the very day that you were there yourself?" The way she looked at me almost hinted that I'd gone to the island with the intent of murdering someone.

"Even stranger than that," I said. "Daniel said that one of the suspects is a woman who looks very like me."

I heard a little gasp from the doorway, turned, and saw Bridie standing there. "The woman who looked like you," she said. "She's accused of a murder now?"

"She's not accused of anything yet," I said. "I'm sure Captain Sullivan will sort it all out today and we'll know more. Now sit down and let me get you some porridge. Will you be going over to the ladies for your schooling today?"

"I don't know," she said. "They might have more warm clothing to hand out."

"I can see this is going to be a disadvantage of having Sid and Gus as your teachers," I said. "They get involved in so many things. They are rarely at home enough to give you a good day's schooling."

"Flitting about like butterflies," Mrs. Sullivan commented. "If it's not doing good, then it's campaigning for votes for women." She shook her head in disgust.

"And what's wrong with that?" I couldn't stop myself from asking. "Don't you think it's about time women got the vote?"

She looked horrified. "I do not. Running the country is a man's job. Ours is the home and the children. Whatever next? Women get the vote and then they'll want to be running for the Senate and driving trains."

"And what's so wrong with that?" I repeated. "I'd quite like to drive a train myself, wouldn't you, Bridie?"

She could tell I was only joking, but Mrs. Sullivan said, "I'd like to see you shoveling the coal into the furnace." She paused. "Anyway, it's up to men to run the country. Speaking of which, it's time Daniel made plans for the future, Molly. He can't go on being a policeman forever. He's already close to the top of the tree and not yet forty. He needs to aim for bigger and better things."

"I think it's up to Daniel to do what makes him happy," I replied, still behaving remarkably calmly for me.

"It's up to a wife to steer her husband in the right direction," she retorted. "Surely you don't want to live in this pokey little place for the rest of your life?"

It did cross my mind to mention that we'd be inheriting a fine residence out in Westchester County when she died, but I was not going to let anyone run down my house. "It's a dear little house and I've loved it from the first minute I saw it."

"So did Daniel buy it for you?" she asked. "I've quite forgotten."

"No, I bought it myself. When I was still running my detective agency," I said.

"Mercy me. Whatever next." She lowered her head and started attacking her bowl of porridge. Bridie and I exchanged grins. When breakfast was finished and washed up, I walked with Bridie, and Liam in my arms because he refused to be left behind, across the street to visit the "ladies," as Bridie always referred to them.

"Here's our little student come for her first lesson," Sid called to Gus. "Come in and have a cup of coffee, Molly, and there are croissants left from the French bakery on Greenwich. I braved the ice and snow to buy them this morning. Gus was absolutely pining for a croissant."

We went through to the kitchen, where the aroma of brewing coffee mingled with the smells of herbs and spices the two always used in their cooking experiments. Gus was sitting at the kitchen table, her long hair falling over her shoulders, rather than in the staid bun she wore outside the house. She was still wearing a robe and furry slippers. She looked up at us and gave a welcoming smile. "Bridie, my love. We spent the evening discussing you and how best to move forward with your education. Sid is absolutely mortified that you've had no Latin so far, neither any French. What were they thinking at that school of yours? The three Rs are all very well and good if you're going to work behind the counter in a shop, but you'll certainly need your Latin if you're to get into Vassar. So we've decided that Sid will give you a crash course to get you up to speed with Latin, as well as geography and history, while I will concentrate on mathematics and sciences—which I'm sure were taught lamentably badly at that dreary institution. We both think we can leave English to you at the moment, as you love to read so much and you can do that in your spare time. We have, however, drawn up a reading list from books we own."

I glanced at Bridie's face. It was alight with joy. "Latin? Sciences? How wonderful," she said. "But are you sure you'll have the time?"

"We'll make the time for the moment while we search around for the best option for your future," Sid said, putting a cup of her noxious black coffee in front of me. It was strong and so thick you could almost stand a spoon up in it. I had never learned to like it, but having drunk it politely when we first met, I didn't have the heart to now say that I didn't enjoy it. I did take the croissant that was offered me. It was still slightly warm, crunchy on the outside and flaky inside. I broke off a piece and gave it to Liam, who ate it with delighted lip smacking.

"Well, I should leave you to your studies, then," I said, feeling suddenly left out and superfluous.

Sid put a hand on my shoulder. "No, sit and enjoy your coffee. We still have to dress and assemble our teaching materials," she said. "In fact it's probably not a good idea to begin today when we have so much on our plate. We have a meeting later with the other members of our committee. We were all so overcome with the level of need out at Ellis Island yesterday that we realized this should be an ongoing thing. There is talk about finding a way to hand out clothes on the Lower East Side on a weekly basis, even of putting women to work as knitters and seamstresses, making the most of discarded yarn and cloth. But for now we are encouraging more donations at all our social gatherings."

"That's wonderful," I said, as a thought crept into my head. "Will you be going back to Ellis Island again, do you think?"

"There is a lot of need in the city itself," Gus said. "Those immigrants from Ellis Island often wind up living on the Lower East Side, don't they? We could serve them just as well there, without the complication of getting out to the island and back—and freezing to death on that dock."

"I suppose so," I admitted grudgingly. What I had been thinking was that I'd welcome an excuse to go back to the island and take a look at things for myself. Not today, of course. I couldn't risk Daniel seeing me there. I'd never hear the last of it. But when suitable time had passed . . . "Although," I continued, "when we hand out clothing on the island, we could also help the immigrants who were taking the train from the station in New Jersey."

"That's true," Sid said, "But we have to be realistic, Molly. We can't help everyone who needs it. We can do our part, but it doesn't make sense to spread ourselves too thin. And Gus and I have to balance our charitable work with our other interests—and foremost of those at the moment is teaching this young person." She ruffled Bridie's hair and Bridie gave a self-conscious grin.

"Guess what?" Bridie said, conscious that all eyes were on her. "You remember I told you about the woman with red hair who looked like Molly? Well, she's been arrested for a murder on Ellis Island."

Both women spun to stare at her.

"Really?" Gus asked.

"Are you making this up?" Sid said. "I rather fear you've become a spinner of tall tales recently."

Bridie shook her head. "No, I'm not making it up. It's true, isn't it, Molly?"

"I'm afraid it is," I said. "Daniel came home very late last night, having been called out to Ellis Island, where a body was found in a disused room. And it seems this woman was spotted coming out of that room."

"How exciting," Gus said, glancing at Sid. "A real murder for you to solve, Molly. Now we have to go back to the island and give you a chance to snoop around."

"Daniel would have a fit if I tried to do that," I said. "He's already told me to stay out of his work."

"But you are good at it," Gus went on. "Look at how you found that missing girl at Christmastime."

"And solved that strange case in Paris," Sid reminded.

"I might have a certain flair for it," I said, feeling my cheeks turning red. "But I also swore that I'd put it aside when I became a mother. I just don't seem to have managed to do that yet. But I'm sure Daniel will handle this one beautifully without me."

"But a red-headed Irishwoman who looks like you, the very same day we went there," Sid said. "It's too delicious to turn down, isn't it?"

"I must admit I'm curious," I confessed.

"Well, then," Sid said, looking quite excited now. "When we have our meeting today, we'll suggest to our Vassar friends that we should return to the island as soon as possible, while the weather remains this frigid. Then we can be on hand to help you with your sleuthing."

Having Sid and Gus as willing, if over-enthusiastic, helpers sent a shiver of alarm through me. They had tried to help me on cases before. But they were my ticket back to Ellis Island. "Good idea," I said, "although I don't know what we'd actually be looking for. The immigrants who came in at the same time as Rose McSweeney will be long gone."

"But we can check out the scene of the crime," Gus said. "We can chat with the guards. One of them might have seen something and not realized it." She gave a little grin. "Sid is an expert at chatting to people."

"I can come too, can't I?" Bridie asked. "Nobody would think twice about a little girl wandering around."

"You almost got yourself in trouble last time, young lady," I said.

"If you're not careful you might find yourself put on a ship back to Ireland."

Gus put an arm around Bridie's shoulder. "I'll take care of her. Of course she must be in on the fun with us."

"It's not fun, Gus," I pointed out. "It's a murder. A man has died. Somebody killed him. It's deadly serious."

"I realize that," Gus said, looking slightly worried at my outburst. I rarely crossed my friends. I was a little surprised at myself. Maybe it was seeing Bridie looking so smug with Gus's arm around her shoulders that upset me. Or maybe it was all the old memories stirred up by Ellis Island. I don't know. I was just in a very unsettled frame of mind at that moment.

Six

The unsettled feeling wouldn't leave me as I carried Liam back from Sid and Gus's and put him down for his morning nap. He was reluctant to leave his favorite people and a place where he often was given small treats and made a big fuss when I tried to put him in his crib, immediately attempting to climb out again. I realized as I watched him that we would need to get him a big bed soon. He had outgrown his baby crib. I stood staring at it, remembering how tiny he had looked when he was first born and how I had pictured having another baby lying in there by now. I shut the door on Liam and walked slowly down the stairs.

I was trying to think what had so upset me. Was it Ellis Island and all the memories it stirred up? Was it the realization that I was not allowed to solve a crime, that I was a wife and mother and not a detective like my husband? Was I actually jealous that Bridie and my friends had become so close and I felt left out? I realized that this had an element of truth in it. They were building a life together that I was not part of. Bridie would be learning Latin and science and discussing books from their library. And I, whose chance for education was cut off abruptly when my mother died when I was fourteen, would somehow be left behind. I suppose I had carried an underlying feeling of inferiority since I met Daniel. I couldn't live up to the standards of his former fiancée Arabella Norton and was amazed that he chose me instead. Daniel's mother had not concealed her disappointment at first, but now her constant pushing us to higher levels of society had rekindled my uneasiness. I had always known that Sid and Gus were better educated and more cultured than me. It had never bothered me before and they had never made me feel less than them. In fact I had delighted in their lively minds, their attempts at foreign cooking, the interesting mixture of guests who frequented their house. So I had to think this sudden stirring had to do with Bridie. I had come to love her like a daughter. She was my one link to my homeland and I cherished her. But now it seemed she was being lured away by what Sid and Gus had to offer that I could not.

I stood at the bottom of the stairs, staring down the hallway to the kitchen. Then I gave myself a stern talking to. "Pull yourself together, Molly Murphy," I said to myself. What was it my mother used to say when I whined that something was unfair? I seem to remember some Gaelic phrase. She had the Gaelic and she used it on us occasionally even though we never quite understood the words, but we got the meaning rightly enough—since it was usually accompanied by a slap or two. I could hear her voice now, but the words were lost to me. But the meaning was clear. No wallowing in self-pity. Life wasn't meant to be fair and I had to get used to it. I realized that I had more than enough to be thankful for. How many girls from my old school in County Mayo could look forward to my sort of life? Most of them were married off before they turned twenty and probably had a brood of children by now as well as long days of backbreaking work in the fields or cutting peat. I had it good. So no more whining. "If you found a silver ring lying on the road, you'd no doubt complain it wasn't a gold one." That was another of my mother's colorful criticisms. I found I was smiling as I walked through to the kitchen.

Daniel's mother was sitting at the table, writing a letter.

"I can put more coal on the fire so that you can use the parlor," I said to her.

She looked up. "There's no need. I'm comfortable where I am," she said. "Where is the young girl? Is she taking her lessons over with your friends?"

"She'll be starting properly tomorrow," I said. "Today they are just getting her set up and deciding who will teach what."

"I don't see this as a long-term solution for her," Daniel's mother said. "I've no doubt that they are highly educated women, but a girl like that needs companions her own age. And I hope she won't be influenced by their . . . attitudes . . ."

She hesitated before that last word, but I got her meaning. She didn't want Bridie getting too many strange ideas about the role of women and especially about Sid and Gus's relationship. She had never admitted that they were more than friends sharing a house, but she certainly knew it. It had become so natural for me that it barely crossed my mind these days. But as for influencing Bridie—well, that was just nonsense. I nodded and said, "I quite agree with you that she needs friends her own age. This is only until we find the right school for her."

"Another thing," she said, wagging a finger at me now. "That girl is growing out of her clothing."

"You're right," I agreed. "She's getting a proper woman's body, isn't she? I can't believe how fast she's growing up."

"She's certainly not a little girl any longer," Mrs. Sullivan said. "You and I should pay a visit to a haberdasher and get some cloth to make her a new dress. How are you with the needle?"

"I did my share of patching, darning, and mending when I had to look after my little brothers," I said. "I've never had the chance to make anything fashionable or dainty."

"And with the sewing machine?"

"Not bad, actually," I said. "I learned to use one when I had to go on an undercover assignment in a garment factory once." The memory of that experience came back to me in horrifying detail, including the disastrous fire. "But I don't own one now."

"We could see about buying you one," she said. "But you've not much room to work on a treadle machine in this little house, have you? Maybe when you move you'll have your own sewing room."

I didn't see how I could say that I didn't intend to move without sounding rude. Before I could say anything, she went on. "I've an idea. Why don't we send a telegram to Martha and have her pack up and send my old sewing machine with a carter? It's the simple turn-the-handle variety but it would suffice for now, and it doesn't take up much room."

"That's very kind of you," I said. "Perhaps you and I can go together to choose fabric for Bridie's dress. When the weather improves we'll go to Wanamaker's Department Store on Broadway. They've a good selection of cloth." I paused, wondering how I could fit sewing a new dress, something I had little skill for, into a day when I wanted to be helping Daniel with the current crime and poor Rose McSweeney. "Of course," I added, "there are also ready-made garments in places like Macy's Department Store these days."

She looked horrified, as if I'd suggested something illegal or immoral like going to a strip club to find clothes. "Better to have it made at home," she said. "We can teach the girl herself to sew. She'll need the skill if her children are not to go in rags."

Was that a veiled slight, that I'd said I didn't sew much? And yet with adoring aunties across the street plus Mother Sullivan's maid Martha I'd never worried about having enough clothes for Liam. "Good idea," I replied.

The day seemed to pass slowly as I waited for Daniel to return with more news of Ellis Island. To keep myself busy I made several loaves of soda bread—one of his favorites. Bridie came home after lunch saying that the ladies had served her matzo ball soup and it was a Jewish dish and it was delicious. She also showed me the stack of books she had brought home to read. I studied her face, excited and animated at the thought of tackling Dickens and Longfellow.

"You don't know how wonderful it is knowing that I never have to face those boys again, Molly," she said. "I can't thank you enough that you had the nerve to face that principal of mine. I always found him terrifying, but you were really brave."

The smile she gave me warmed my heart and made me realize how silly and petty I had just been. Of course she still loved me. I was still her adopted mother. I had prepared a big Irish stew for dinner, just the sort of thing for the bitter weather and one of Daniel's favorites.

"I'm sorry you had soup for lunch and now you'll be getting it again for your supper," I said to Bridie.

"Oh no. I love the way you make stews," she said. "The way the ladies cook is interesting and different, but it's not like the food at home."

And again I felt all warm inside.

Daniel, to my delight, came home on the stroke of six. "It's raining now instead of snowing," he said, brushing drops from his hair as he came through to the kitchen. "I think I prefer the snow. We got soaked through on the boat ride back from the island."

"Go up and change your clothes, then I'll hang these to dry over the fire guard in the parlor," I said as I planted a kiss on that wet, cold cheek.

"Good idea," he said. "Just a minute, son." Liam was holding up his arms to be picked up. "Dadda's all wet and cold at the moment. I'll give you a hug in a minute."

"Dadda all wet," Liam explained to me as Daniel disappeared upstairs.

I had a cup of tea ready for him when he came down again and had to wait patiently while he played with Liam, asked Bridie about her day, and then sat down with a bowl of stew in front of him.

"So what news?" I asked. "Did you find out who the man was?

Have you any more clues to who really killed him?" The words came tumbling out. Daniel shot me a warning look.

"Right now I intend to eat my supper, Molly. This is not the time or place to discuss such things." He glanced over at his mother's inquisitive face. "You know I don't like to bring my work home with me and I've been up since before dawn."

"I'm sorry," I said. "Of course you have. Eat up, then. I made your favorite."

He barely nodded before he attacked his bowl of stew with gusto. Then, of course, it was time to put Liam to bed and it wasn't until after eight that we were finally sitting in the parlor around the fire. I wondered if he was deliberately not wanting to discuss the case with me, but I wasn't about to let him off lightly.

"So can you tell me now?" I asked. "You know I'm dying to hear what you've found out. I'm wanting to hear that by now you've decided poor Rose isn't guilty after all and you've started to pay more attention to that no-good Englishman who tried to incriminate her."

Daniel sighed. "I'm not sure I should be discussing it at all, Molly. It's an ongoing investigation, you know. Not a public forum."

"I'm not the public," I said indignantly. "I'm your wife. And a good detective, too."

"All the same . . ." He glanced at his mother, sitting by the fire knitting away, and Bridie, curled on the sofa with a book.

"He's right, Molly," Mother Sullivan said, not looking up from the clicking of her needles. "Daniel's father made it a point never to discuss a case with me. He always said he left his work at the office."

That was because you were never a detective in your own right, I wanted to say, but with age and experience I had learned to temper my outbursts these days.

"It's just that this case holds special interest for me, Mother," I said. "A young Irishwoman, just like myself, wrongly accused of murder on Ellis Island. I feel I have to get involved and make sure that justice is done for her."

"You can be sure that your husband will do the most thorough and fair investigation possible, just like his father did," she said calmly. "I'd leave it in his capable hands if I were you. When women try to interfere there is always emotion involved. That's why they shouldn't be voting, either."

"I think it's wrong that we women can't vote," Bridie said. "I mean, we are half the population, aren't we? How can a whole country be governed just by half the people in it? That's not fair. We are just as smart as the men are. The ladies across the street are smarter than any man. I was much smarter than any of the boys in my class."

"But we are entrusted with the sacred duty of raising the children, Bridie dear," Mother Sullivan said sweetly. "Isn't that just as important?"

"Not if we don't get to use our brains as well," Bridie said.

"Well said, Bridie." I gave her an encouraging nod. "I can see Sid and Gus are already turning you into a proper little suffragist. And we haven't yet mentioned women's intuition, which has solved many a crime better than the plodding work of policemen."

I got another warning frown from Daniel. "We'll talk about it later when we're alone, Molly. All right? At this moment I'd like a bit of peace and quiet."

"Yes, Daniel." I gave him a meek little smile.

"And you, young lady," Daniel's mother addressed Bridie. "Always with your head in a book. You'll ruin your eyesight by the time you are twenty if you're not careful. Molly and I agree that you're in need of a new dress or two. You're growing like the proverbial weed."

"A new dress?" Bridie looked up, excited now. "For parties or for regular occasions?"

"Let's start with the everyday dress," I said. "We don't exactly go to too many parties."

"But if I'm over doing my studies with the ladies, they might want to take me to plays and things," Bridie said. "All part of my education."

I studied her as she went back to her reading. How could this be the meek and timid little thing who barely spoke up in company? Was it just that she was growing up or was it Sid and Gus's influence on her? I wasn't sure whether that was a good or bad thing. Of course I wanted her to be educated and not feel afraid to express herself, but what if Sid and Gus were offering her a glimpse of a life she couldn't have?

Seven

I was undressed and in bed by the time Daniel came in from the bathroom.

"Now we're alone," I said. "Don't you dare say you're too tired to talk, Daniel Sullivan. I want to know what happened today and I'm going to badger you until you tell me."

Daniel climbed into bed beside me. "I should have married a quiet and gentle little thing," he said. "I could sense you were trouble from the very beginning."

"What if I hadn't found out who committed that murder on Ellis Island by my own wits?" I asked him. "You'd have sent me back to Ireland and I'd have been hanged by now, or at least languishing in jail."

"At least I would have had a peaceful life," he said, but he was joking and he turned to kiss my forehead. "Actually," he whispered, "I wouldn't have changed a thing. You, Liam, they are the best things that have happened to me. And I can't wait for the arrival of little Kathleen and Brendan and Margaret and George . . ."

"Hold on a minute," I said. "Is that your secret plan? To keep me so busy with babies that I'll never have time to get involved with your cases?"

He chuckled.

"I'm hoping for the next one too, Daniel," I said. "It just doesn't seem to be happening. I'm wondering if there is something wrong with me. The doctor said there was no reason, but—"

"These things take time," he said.

"But I keep thinking about your parents. You were an only child, weren't you?"

"Not exactly," he said. "My mother had several miscarriages and one baby that died soon after birth. After that grief she was reluctant to have any more."

"I can understand that," I agreed, having gone through a miscarriage myself last year. I felt a connection of sympathy for Mrs. Sullivan. "You may need your sleep, but I'm not going to let you nod off until you tell me what you found out today."

He slipped an arm around me, giving a sigh. "All right. I suppose I owe that much to you. We are not much further along, but I have to tell you that things don't look too good for your friend Rose. The room and the hallway were dusted for fingerprints and hers showed up not just on the door handle but also on the doorjamb inside the room. She says she opened the door, saw it wasn't a WC, and closed it again. But she's lying. She was in that room."

"And have you found the identity of the man who was killed? Did he know her?"

"That's the strange part," Daniel said. "I told you he wasn't on the manifest of passengers in steerage. At least there was no passenger fitting the description of a single man of his age. Well, we went through all the passengers on the ship that came in from England and Ireland and it appears his name is Henry Darby from Blackfriars in London and he came across in a second-class cabin."

"In a cabin? Not in steerage at all?"

"We verified who he was and we located his belongings in the baggage room. What's more, he only brought one small suitcase with him, with little more than a change of clothes and his shaving kit."

"Meaning that he did not intend to immigrate to America but was just coming on a short visit," I said.

"Exactly. But why go through Ellis Island when he was a second-class passenger? He could just have stepped ashore from the Hudson Piers with little or no formality."

"Perhaps someone was waiting for him on the docks that he wanted to avoid," I suggested. "He took his chance and mingled with the crowd being herded onto the ferry to Ellis Island. But that person he wanted to avoid followed him and finished him off before he could step ashore." I realized that my voice sounded unnaturally loud in the silence of the night and lowered it to a whisper. "Could the person he wanted to avoid have been a fellow passenger on the ship? Someone in first or second class who was waiting for a chance to get at him?"

"We have the manifest, but unfortunately all the first- and second-class passengers had already gone ashore by the time we discovered the murder. We have forwarding addresses for some of them and we'll be interviewing them to see who remembers sitting with him in the dining room or talking to him in the smoking lounge."

"I'll tell you one thing." I turned toward him. "If he was up in a cabin, there was no way he could have met Rose McSweeney during the voyage, was there? I remember we were kept down below for the whole journey. Awful, it was, with people vomiting and unwashed bodies."

"It must have been." Daniel gave me a sympathetic squeeze. "We have sent a cable to Scotland Yard in London asking them to find out who he is."

"If he's from London that proves that Rose McSweeney could have nothing to do with him," I said. "You said she's from near Galway. Didn't she board the boat in Queenstown?"

"She did," he agreed.

"And this Henry Darby?"

"Also boarded in Queenstown."

"So you need to find out what he was doing in Ireland," I said.

"We've sent a cable to the Irish police to find out where he stayed in Ireland and all the details on Rose McSweeney. Anything that provides a connection."

"And what about that Englishman?" I demanded, a little too snappily. "The one who claimed he saw Rose coming out of the room. The one she claimed had tried his luck with her on the voyage. I think he's the suspicious one. Whoever heard of an upper-class young man coming across in steerage? You will be looking into him, I take it?"

"Of course we will. Although I have to say he's been most cooperative so far. Didn't even make a fuss when we told him he would not be free to resume his travels to friends in South Carolina but would have to stay on in the city. He simply said he'd been looking forward to visiting New York and with any luck he'd have enough money to take in a theater or two."

"So where does he intend to stay? The spanking new Plaza Hotel? It just reopened, didn't it? Or does he know the Rockefellers?"

"Why are you saying that?"

"He seems to have expensive tastes, that's all."

"Now who is prejudging?" Daniel asked. "He's taking a room at a boardinghouse near police headquarters for the time being."

"And what of poor Rose? What's going to happen to her? You're not about to lock her up, are you?"

"Hold your horses," Daniel said. "We are not about to lock her up. At least not yet."

"Does she have relatives in the city?"

"She is also being put into a boardinghouse nearby, with a constable assigned to keep an eye on her so she doesn't do a flit."

"Did she come alone?" The thought had just struck me. "I mean, unmarried women are not admitted to the country unless they have someone to vouch for them."

"She has relatives in Chicago. They had supplied her with money for the railway fare."

"I see," I said. "Poor thing. I know how it feels to be so near to safety and yet so far." I was determined to meet this fellow Irishwoman. I sat up in bed. "You know, Daniel, I could go and interview her for you. I suggested that she might open up to a fellow Irishwoman in a way she never would to a policeman."

"Absolutely not, Molly." He sat up too now. "I probably should not have mentioned this case to you in the first place, or shared any details. Well, you have your details, but I forbid you to get involved in any way, shape, or form. This is a police matter. A murder investigation. You could jeopardize the whole thing by interfering."

"I was just trying to help," I said because he was glaring at me now. I could see his eyes flashing in the light of the street lamp outside the window. "I just want to make sure the poor girl gets a fair hearing. I know what it's like, Daniel. To flee from your own country, either from terrible poverty or from some man not leaving you alone, and then to be in a strange place where nobody will believe you and there is no one on your side."

He put his hands on my shoulders. "She'll get a fair hearing, Molly, I promise you. Now lie down and let's go to sleep, for God's sake."

He pulled me down and lifted the eiderdown over us. I snuggled against him, enjoying the warmth of his body. I closed my eyes, then abruptly opened them again. "Did you search her? And her belongings?"

"We did."

"And did you find any blood?"

"We didn't."

"Aha. There you are, then."

"Not so fast, Miss Sherlock Holmes," he said. "The way the man was stabbed, neatly between the ribs, might not have produced blood immediately. Actually he might not even have realized he'd been stabbed initially. I've heard of people walking around not realizing anything is wrong until they collapse and die."

"That would indicate someone with skill, wouldn't it? A trained professional killer, not a girl fresh from Ireland."

"Or someone who was just lucky in their aim," he said. I felt him settling snugly beside me, but there were still a million more questions flitting around inside my head.

"But you didn't find his wallet on her?"

"No, we did not."

"Or the knife?"

"Not that, either."

"Huh," I said. "And was a thorough search made of that part of the building?"

"I think so. No sign of the knife, although whoever killed Henry Darby could have found a way to toss it into the harbor. Now, for the love of God, can we go to sleep?"

"Only if you promise to keep me up to date on what you find," I said. "Otherwise I'll bombard you with questions every single night."

Daniel sighed. "Just as long as you promise to keep your involvement in the case to questions, I'll tell you what I can. Now. Does that satisfy you?"

"I suppose so," I admitted.

"You know what satisfies me," Daniel whispered, nuzzling my ear now. And for a while there was no more talking.

Eight

I have never been much good at doing what I was told. I can't tell you the number of spankings I got for it as a child, or the strap across my hand from the nuns at school. I didn't think Daniel would give me anything more than a tongue-lashing, but I was determined to take the risk. I knew, in spite of what Daniel had said, that I just had to find Rose. She had to know that someone in this big, strange city was on her side and would be fighting for her. I knew it would be a challenge to locate her—New York, after all, is quite a big place—but I didn't think it would be impossible. Daniel had already let slip that they had placed the Englishman (his name was Edwin Cromer, if I remembered correctly) in a boardinghouse not far from police headquarters on Mulberry Street. It would therefore stand to reason that Rose had been placed in a similar boardinghouse, again not too far from police headquarters. And . . . Daniel had let slip that he'd put a constable to guard her.

I had no idea how I would be allowed to see her, though, even if I found her. Would the constable let me in for a few minutes if I said we had been friends on the boat and I was from her part of Ireland? I had baked soda bread and wondered if that would bribe my way in. "I've brought her a loaf of bread from the old country. Surely you don't mind my dropping that off?" It was worth a try—just as long as

Daniel wasn't in the middle of interviewing her when I arrived! But that was a chance I was going to take.

Excited, if a little apprehensive, about my quest, I went through my morning chores at lightning speed, put Liam down for his morning nap, and then told my mother-in-law that I had to run some errands. It was funny, but as I told her that I remembered that back in Ireland we'd called it "the messages." We'd had lots of queer sayings that I'd learned nobody would understand in this new world. Now I sounded pretty much like a New Yorker. I'd learned to adapt and be part of this new life. Hopefully Rose would too.

Daniel's mother looked crestfallen. "Oh, but I thought we'd send the telegram to my Martha today and then go shopping for the fabric, just like we said."

Mercy on us! Mrs. Sullivan was not the swiftest shopper in the world. That would be my whole day gone. I gave her my bright "what a good idea" smile. "You write what we should say on the telegram and I'll take it straight to the post office," I said, "but you know I don't think you should venture out yet. There are still patches of snow and ice out there. Why don't we wait at least until tomorrow and see if things improve?"

She glanced out the window where our tiny back garden was still blanketed in a mantle of snow in the shady spots. "Maybe you're right," she said. "There is no rush until the sewing machine arrives, is there."

"I'll get down to the post office now," I said, as I watched her write the words for the telegram, "and then I've a couple of errands I need to run before lunch. Liam shouldn't wake for a while, but if he does, let him have a little play in that snow before it all vanishes."

Before she could find any objection I went to put my coat on. Then I unpinned my hair, letting it fall over my shoulders as Rose's had done. Instead of my usual hat I tied a scarf over my ears, leaving all that red hair exposed. Then I started off in great haste, first stopping at the post office to send the telegram and then proceeding on my mission. I decided it would be quicker to walk than to wait for a trolley down Broadway. So I cut across Washington Square, past the university, where students were gathering and chatting in spite of the cold. Luckily it was not quite as frigid today and yesterday's rain had washed away much of the snow, leaving patches of slush that clung to the hem of my skirts and slowed me down. I turned onto Wooster and followed it until I came to Prince, then along Prince until it crossed Broadway. Then it was only one block down Mulberry to police headquarters.

This would be where my female intuition should kick in, I thought. There wouldn't be a respectable boardinghouse among those tightly packed tenements of the Lower East Side. So probably not on the Bowery side, which was rather less respectable with its taverns and burlesques. Certainly not down Mulberry toward Mott Street and Chinatown. So my hunch said further south, closer to City Hall and the Tombs, and to the west of Broadway. There might be boardinghouses along Broadway itself, but I suspected they'd housed Rose somewhere off the beaten track where it was easier to keep an eye on her. So I started walking south, going up and down the adjoining streets, one by one. This had become mostly an Italian area these days and I was eyed with suspicion. Youths loitering on a corner called out to me, although whether it was words of appreciation or warning I couldn't tell. No obvious sign of boardinghouses, nor of constables standing guard. This was going to be harder than I thought.

It did occur to me that maybe they had placed her in a boardinghouse closer to where the ferry came in from Ellis Island, but again that wasn't the best of areas. I found I was wandering aimlessly, peering down one street to decide it was not the right sort of place. I stopped short when I came to the Tombs on the corner of Center and Leonard. The impressive Roman-looking building with its columns housed the grimmest cell blocks inside. I knew. I'd been in there myself and I'd visited Daniel when he was wrongly arrested.

I turned away hurriedly and walked back toward Broadway. I heard the bell on a nearby church chiming eleven. I'd better get a move on.

Around Broadway I did spot several boardinghouses, but none of them had a constable standing any nearer than a corner. I did pluck up the courage to go in to a few and ask if they happened to have an Irishwoman staying there. "I'm looking for my sister, newly arrived," I said in my best Irish brogue. But no luck. I started to head north again, up Mercer toward Washington Square and home. Suddenly I heard a shout and a hand was clamped on my shoulder. I spun around, wriggling to escape.

"Let go of me, whoever you are, or I'll call for the police," I shouted.

I heard a chuckle. "That's a good one. You're a lively little thing, aren't you?" I managed to swivel around enough to find I was staring at the brass buttons of a police uniform.

"Jesus, Mary, and Joseph, would you let go of me. I don't know what you think you're doing, but I'm a perfectly respectable—" I was about to say wife of a police captain, but instead he cut in.

"I don't know how you managed to get out and slip past me, but you're going right back where you came from, my girl."

He started marching me down the street, away from Broadway, his hand still clamped onto my shoulder. Suddenly it dawned on me. He thought I was Rose McSweeney! I couldn't believe my luck. I no longer resisted but allowed him to propel me across the street and up the steps into a tall brownstone that had no obvious sign of a boardinghouse. We went into a dark foyer. There was nobody at a reception desk.

"Ah, so that's how you managed to get out, is it?" he said. "I'll be having a word with the manager, you mark my words. They promised us that the building would be safe and you'd be well looked after. Now, up the stairs with you." He propelled me up the stairs at a great rate, opened a door at the top of the landing, and shoved me inside.

"And make sure you stay put this time or it will be the Tombs for you, where the rooms are not so pleasant."

The door closed behind me. I was glad that I didn't hear a key turning in the lock. I didn't have time to catch my breath and look around before a figure jumped up, giving a little scream. She had been sitting on the bed and she stared at me in wonder.

"Saint Michael and All the Angels," she said in a brogue stronger than my own had ever been, "who are you, I'd like to know? What in heaven's name are you doing here? Have they arrested you, too? Are you the one they now think did this terrible crime and there they were, pinning the blame on me, if you please." She came toward me, hand extended. "I'm Rose. Rose McSweeney, and you are?"

"Molly Murphy," I said, reverting swiftly to my maiden name.

"Pleased I am to make your acquaintance, Miss Murphy," she said. Now I had time to observe her I could see she didn't resemble me that closely. She was a real beauty: perfect white skin, enormous blue-green eyes, a delicate little button of a nose, and that gorgeous red hair, cascading over her shoulders in luxuriant curls. She sank back onto the narrow iron bed again. "Jaysus, but it's depressing stuck in here and wondering what's about to happen to me. But it will brighten things up if I've a companion now. Did you come over on the same boat? I'm sure I would have noticed you—us looking so alike."

"No, I've been living in New York for a while," I said, trying to remember how I used to sound before I picked up some New York vowels.

"Then why did they grab onto you if you weren't on Ellis Island? They can't have thought you were involved in a murder there."

"The constable thought I was you," I said, giving her a knowing little smile. "He saw me and thought you'd escaped, which was lucky for me as I was trying to think of a way to get in to see you. With any luck it will take him a while before he finds out his mistake."

"But what are you doing here, then?" Her expression was still a little guarded.

"I heard what happened on Ellis Island and I thought to myself, that poor girl, fresh from Ireland like myself had been. She'll need somebody on her side. And I decided I'd bring you some of the soda bread I'd just baked."

She took it, warily, I thought, then added quickly, "Why, that's so thoughtful of you, Molly."

"Soda bread always reminds me of home," I said. "So I thought you might enjoy some too. Maybe you can ask the landlady to give you a little butter to spread on it. But it's good enough with plenty of currants inside."

"You're a kind woman, Molly Murphy." She took the bread, wrapped in greaseproof paper, and put it on the bedside table. "Won't you sit a while? I'd sure welcome the company."

I took a seat opposite her on a wooden chair in the corner. "I don't know how long they will let me stay," I said, "but they can't deny us a little chat, can they? So cunas a-taw too?" That was how the Gaelic speakers greeted each other in my part of Ireland. I'd never seen it written, but that was how it was pronounced.

"A tall what?" She frowned.

"Do they not greet each other like that where you come from?" I asked. "Around where I lived we had plenty of folk who spoke the Irish language. It's how people said, how are you doing?"

Her face lit up. "Oh, we've switched to Gaelic, have we? What a nice surprise. Do you have the Gaelic yourself, then? I didn't expect to find people over in America speaking my language."

"Sorry." I gave a rueful smile. "My mother spoke it and scolded us in it often enough, but I never did learn it myself. I only know the odd phrase."

"My parents spoke it as well," she said. "I never bothered to learn it, myself. I felt it was old-fashioned, you know."

"I did too." I nodded agreement and we both laughed.

"Anyway, we were close to the city of Galway, where not so many spoke Gaelic. Do you know Galway?"

"I've never been there myself. I'm from further north. Up near Westport," I replied.

"Oh, Galway's a grand place," she said. "Beautiful buildings. I used to love to go into town as a special treat. Looking in all the shop windows, you know. That was before my parents died, of course."

"Your parents died? So did mine," I said. "I had to raise my three young brothers after my mother died."

"You've brothers too? What a coincidence." She gave me a dazzling smile. "I've two older brothers myself. Brendan and Joseph." Then her smile faded. "They both got themselves involved in the struggle for home rule—went off to join the Irish Republican Brotherhood, as they call themselves."

"Mine too!" I exclaimed. "Another coincidence."

"Not really. Any brave and decent young man would want to fight for his country, wouldn't he?"

"I suppose so," I agreed. "So where are your brothers now?"

"God only knows," she said. "They took part in some sort of raid on a police station in Galway. It went wrong, of course. They were betrayed and they had to flee for their lives. And when the police showed up at our cottage, I knew I'd better flee for my life too, or I might find myself in jail."

"So you decided to come to America?"

"I did. Me mother had cousins in Chicago so I wrote to them and they wrote back that I'd be welcome. Even sent me the money for the train fare."

"They must be worrying that you haven't turned up," I said. "If you give me their address I'll be happy to write to them for you."

She shook her head. "No, thanks all the same. I'd rather do the writing myself. It's only right and proper, isn't it? To tell you the truth, Molly, I've been in such a state of shock since this happened that I haven't been able to think straight. I just keep praying to all the saints that they'll find the person who really committed this crime and I'll be free to go on my way to Chicago."

"I hope so too," I said. "Why exactly did they think you had committed the murder?"

"The stupidest of reasons," she said. "Just because I had to obey the call of nature and I had to find the ladies' room in a hurry. I slipped out of the back of that hall and started opening doors to see which one might be a ladies' lav. But they were all dark and empty storerooms and I didn't go into any of them."

"And someone saw you?"

She nodded. "Some English fellow. Creepy sort of type he was. Acted all posh and refined but what was he doing in steerage, that's what I want to know." She leaned closer. "He'd had a go at me during the trip, you know. Started flirting with me and then tried it on in a dark corner. Pinned me against a wall, all hot and heavy breathing and hands where they'd no right to be. I put him straight right away. Told him I wasn't that kind of girl and besides I'd a fellow of my own."

"And have you?" I asked. "Over here in America?"

"What? Oh no. Not really. I just said it to keep that man away. But I reckon he didn't like being rejected and all. So he spotted me in that hallway and told the police he saw me coming out of the room."

"But what was he doing in that hallway, then?" I asked. "Weren't the immigrants supposed to stay in the Registry Room until they were processed?"

"That's what I'm asking myself." She wagged a finger at me. "I wouldn't be surprised if he didn't do the dirty deed himself. I'm hoping they'll find the knife and pin it on him and I can go on my way."

"The man who was killed," I said, cautiously now. "Did you know him?"

She shrugged. "I've no idea who it was. They never let me see the body so it could have been any Tom, Dick, or Harry." She paused, looking at me. "If the word has got out about this crime, are they saying who this man was, by any chance?"

"Not that I've heard," I said. "All they've been saying is a man found murdered on the island. I expect they'll know soon enough."

She reached out and touched my hand. "Molly, you know New York. I've heard bad stories. Do you think the police here will try to pin it on me? Plant false evidence, I mean, just to get the case over and done with?"

"I don't think so," I said. "I'm sure they'll be thorough and fair."

"Not what I've heard."

"I'm sure there are some bad apples, but the detectives in charge are supposed to be good men. And when you think about it, they've nothing to go on, have they? You opened a few doors. They'll find your fingerprints on a doorknob. That doesn't prove you were ever in a room, does it?"

"They say they found my prints on the doorjamb inside that room," she said, "but that's rubbish. All I did was to reach inside and try to find the electric light switch. But I couldn't locate it and I could see it wasn't a ladies' lavatory, so I went on my way."

"Then I don't think they can possibly have enough evidence to arrest you," I said. "Unless the man who died turns out to be somehow connected to you."

"How can he be?" she said. "I came all by myself. I knew nobody on the ship and I met nobody from my part of Ireland." She stared at me, thinking. "You said you weren't on the boat. But you made the soda bread for me. So how did you . . .

"I was on the island that day, helping to hand out warm clothing to the newly arrived immigrants," I said, thinking quickly. "We heard a rumor that a man had been killed and the suspect was an Irishwoman who looked like me."

"But how did you find me?"

This was getting complicated. I stood up. "I should be on my way. I have my shopping to do."

"But how . . ." She continued looking at me strangely. Time to go, I thought.

How could I explain why I had come looking for her without letting her know I was married to a policeman? "I'll come and visit you again if they'll let me. I'll see if I can pick up any more information for you."

"That's kind of you. I appreciate it." She got up and walked over to the window. "Do you have any idea how long they'll keep me here? I mean, I'm awful bored and I have no way of earning money. Are they planning to charge me for the boardinghouse?"

"I don't know," I said. "I shouldn't think—"

"Oh no!" she said. She had been staring out the window. She jumped to her feet, then stepped hastily away from the window, out of sight. "It's that policeman again."

I peered over her shoulder. Daniel was just getting out of an automobile.

Nine

I have to go," I said, already heading for her door. "He can't find me here. I don't want to get you in more trouble."

"What if the constable says that I tried to run away?" she asked, her eyes now wide with alarm.

"Tell him that you just stepped out for a breath of fresh air and you weren't going anywhere." I could see this wasn't the best of answers, but better than saying a woman with similar hair had just visited her. "I must get out of here."

I opened her door. I could hear men's voices downstairs. Obviously I couldn't escape via the front door. Instead I headed down the corridor toward the back of the building. I just prayed there was a second staircase back there. I heard the tread of heavy feet coming up the uncarpeted stairs behind me. I looked around, but no sign of another staircase. I saw the word "Bathroom" on a door and ducked inside. I kept the door open a few inches and waited until Daniel was safely inside Rose's room. Then I opened the door a few inches more—and closed it hastily. The constable was standing guard at the top of the front stairs. I'd be stuck here until Daniel went—and then how would I get past the constable if he was stationed outside the building?

I opened the window and stared out. It was a small square window, not really big enough for me to squeeze through, and I didn't fancy climbing down a drainpipe. Then I saw something that raised my spirits: there was a fire escape outside a window to my left. I held my breath as I opened that bathroom door and slipped into the darkness of the corridor. This was where my red hair would be a disadvantage. My clothing was all dark, but my hair—well, anyone would spot that a mile away. I made straight for the door to the left of the hallway, turned the handle, and stepped inside.

The room was dark. The curtains were drawn and it smelled musty and stale. As I tiptoed forward toward the window I heard a sound. My heart nearly leapt out of my chest. It came from my right. And then it was repeated. A snore. A man was asleep in the narrow bed, his mouth open and snoring loudly. From what I could see in the gloom he was a large man with a shock of black hair and a big black mustache. I held my breath as I tiptoed toward the window. I was halfway across the room when he gave the sort of snort men make when catching their breath from a snore. I froze. He muttered some words—I think they were in Italian. I fled across the worn carpet, praying I wouldn't trip, and tried to slip behind the curtain, but there wasn't much room. At least I wouldn't be quite so obvious if he woke up. I tried to think what I would say to him. That I was escaping from the police? That I was running away from an awful man? My fingers were trembling as I fumbled with the bottom of the window sash and tried to lift it. It was heavy and the wood had warped in the weather. I put all my strength into it. Finally it shifted and I was able to raise it an inch or two. But it made an ugly squeaking sound as I moved it. Again I held my breath. Then I inched it up until I could hoist up my skirts and climb through, out onto the fire escape.

I stood for a few seconds, gulping in fresh, cold air, trying to get my heart to start beating sensibly again. I thought I heard him cough and mutter again. Then I went down that escape as fast as my legs would carry me. The fire escape didn't quite reach the ground. I had to drop the last few feet and nearly careened into a garbage can, but then I was safely standing in a dingy courtyard. There were buildings on all sides—high, faceless brick walls and apparently no way out. I looked around to see if there was maybe a little gate. There were more garbage cans, which had to mean that there was some way for them to be picked up, surely. And if they used the fire escape in a fire, then they'd not find themselves trapped in the courtyard. I saw there was a little door in the wall behind the fire escape, but that would lead me back to the front of the building, where the constable might see me.

Then I smelled a rather appetizing smell. Fish frying. It was coming from the other side of the yard. A door was open. I went across and peered inside. The frying smell was stronger now. A tiled hallway vanished into darkness, but I could hear the clatter of pots and pans. A restaurant, then! Hope surged inside me. I started down that hallway, across the back of a kitchen. White-coated cooks were hard at work, attending to their stoves. I was almost past when one looked up. "Hoi!" he called. "Hey, you. You can't be back here."

"Sorry," I called. "Wrong way." And I fled. Through the restaurant, past astonished waiters, and out to the safety of the street. I had emerged onto Broadway. I gave a little prayer of thanks and hopped on a trolley, heading north.

"Ah, there you are," my mother-in-law greeted me. "Home at last. Did you have a successful morning? All your tasks accomplished?"

"I did. Thank you." I scooped Liam into my arms. "How has the boy been?"

"Good as gold," she said. "We did play a little in the snow, but he complained he was too cold and there wasn't enough snow left for a snowman so we came back inside."

"I'm so pleased you've been a good boy for your granny," I said. "Now we better think about getting you your lunch, then, hadn't we?"

"You're sounding awfully Irish today," Mother Sullivan said with a chuckle. "Are you practicing for St. Patrick's Day? You don't want to sound like an immigrant when you mix with the society ladies. They'll look down their noses at you."

"I suppose it's being with Liam takes me back to my own childhood," I replied. "Now, what are we going to eat? There's plenty of that stew left."

"Mercy me," Mother Sullivan exclaimed. "Have you forgotten it's Friday?"

I had, in fact, completely forgotten.

"Did you not bring home any fish?" she asked. "I thought you were out buying supplies."

"I'm sorry. It must have escaped me," I said. "I've been in such a state this week, what with Bridie's schooling and the visit to Ellis Island and that poor woman accused of murder . . ."

"If you mark my words, young woman, you'll leave police work to the police," she said, wagging a finger at me. "Daniel knows his job. You just put it from your mind. I take it you sent my telegram?"

"I did. First thing."

"Then the machine from Martha should arrive tomorrow and you'll have sewing to occupy you, which is a good thing."

I gave her a half-hearted nod.

After we'd eaten—cheese on toast, which was the only non-meat available—I went out to buy fish. How complicated life becomes when you've a family. I thought of Rose, arriving here all alone, the whole of her life ahead of her to make what she wanted of it, if she could just get through this current nightmare. And I thought of my own life. It hadn't been easy to begin with. I had almost been arrested, almost starved. But I'd come through all right in the end, hadn't I? I should have nothing to complain about with a lovely husband and fine son. Why do we always want what we don't have?

At four o'clock Bridie came home from across the street, absolutely glowing with delight. "I'm learning Latin, Molly. Imagine that. *Puela pupam portat.* Do you know what that means?"

"I've no idea," I said.

"It means 'the girl carries the doll.'"

"And what good is that supposed to do you?" Mrs. Sullivan asked, coming into the kitchen. "How many ancient Romans are you likely to meet?"

Bridie giggled. "Not many. But it's useful for understanding the derivation of words, Miss Goldfarb says. And every educated person knows Latin." She knelt beside Liam. "You are a *puer,*" she said. He looked confused. "That means a 'boy.'"

"He's having a hard enough time with English at the moment," I said. "Don't confuse him."

Bridie picked him up and swung him around. "I've missed you all day," she said. He shrieked in delight.

My family, I thought, and realized how much I adored them. As I prepared the baked cod with a parsley sauce, I was wondering what Daniel might have found out from his interview with Rose today. I hoped he wouldn't be late. Fish doesn't do well if kept in the oven for too long. But he came home soon after six.

I went down the hall to greet him. "There you are," I said, wrapping my arms around his neck while planting a little kiss on his cold cheek. "Right on time and I've your favorite fish with parsley sauce for you."

"Really?" he said. "And did you have a good day? A productive day?" I didn't notice anything unusual in his tone.

"I did. We sent a telegram up to Martha to send down the sewing machine for me to make Bridie a new dress."

"That sounds like a good idea," he said. "And that's all you did?"

"Apart from buying fish for your supper."

He was looking down at me, his eyes bright in the hall light. "So you didn't go to visit Rose McSweeney?"

Holy Mother of God! What could I say? But then, I couldn't lie to my husband. "What makes you think that?"

"Only that she had a loaf of soda bread on the table beside her. An identical loaf to the one I saw, and nearly took a slice of, on the kitchen table this morning. Our kitchen table. And do you know what? When questioned she said a kind lady who had learned of her predicament had brought it in to her." He paused, his eyes now flashing dangerously. "A kind Irish lady named Molly."

"How nice for her," I said.

He gripped my shoulders now. "We are not going to continue this conversation in the hall for everyone to overhear. Into the parlor. Come on." And he propelled me into the parlor, closing the door behind us.

Ten

I have to admit I was more than a little alarmed. It was his steely silence more than anything. I could have handled being yelled at. For a long moment we stood there, both breathing heavily.

"Now," he said. "You disobeyed me, didn't you? Don't deny it. You went to see Rose McSweeney."

"All right, so I did." I stuck out my chin defiantly. "I dropped off a loaf of soda bread. It was a good and Christian thing to do, wasn't it?"

"Since when have you gone around doing good and Christian deeds?" he asked. Did I detect a hint of a grin on his lips? It was hard to tell whether he was angry or not.

"Molly, which of the lads down at headquarters did you get the address from? I've told you not to go down there. Were you in my office?"

"I didn't go near your headquarters," I said, confused.

"Of course you did," he said. "How else did you manage to find Rose McSweeney in the first place? I didn't bring anything home with her address on it. You must have been snooping through my papers."

"I did not snoop!" I retorted hotly. I could tell he thought I was lying.

"So." His voice was laden with sarcasm. "Knowing only that this woman was one of hundreds of Rose McSweeneys in New York and had red hair, you searched the whole city and managed to find her in one day?" He looked at me angrily.

"Yes," I said simply. He stared at me. "If you want to know, I used my detective skills. I decided she'd be put within easy reach of your police headquarters, and not on the East Side, among the tenements. So I worked my way up the west side of Broadway, looking for a boardinghouse with a constable stationed outside it."

He continued to stare. Was this good or bad? "You found her in one day." He paused. "And how did you persuade the constable to let you in?"

I wondered if the aforementioned constable had confessed his mistake to Daniel. I thought not. Or perhaps he never realized he'd apprehended the wrong woman. "Ah," I said. "Well, that was easier than I thought it would be. The constable took one look at me and thought I was Rose, trying to escape. So he bundled me back upstairs again."

"And you didn't set him straight."

"I did not."

"And the constable then proceeded to let you go?"

"Ah, no. I saw you coming, so I climbed down the fire escape and through a restaurant behind the house.

Another long pause. He was staring at me, shaking his head. "What am I going to do with you, Molly? If you weren't a woman, you would be a great detective!"

I stared at him defiantly. "But I am a woman, and a great detective, too. Answer me truthfully. Could one of your men have done what I did today? Being a woman was an advantage."

His voice rose, "But you are not just any woman, you are my wife and Liam's mother! I have to keep you safe! How can I do that if you go haring off? I told you this woman is wanted for murder and you go looking for her. You were alone in a room with a woman who might have stabbed a man, Molly. Did you not pause for a second to consider that?" He was glaring at me now.

"I didn't believe for a minute she would be a danger to me." I went on, "I felt that I'd been sent to Ellis Island on the very day she was there so that I'd be able to defend that poor girl. A message from heaven—that's what I thought, Daniel. All I could see was myself. You can't believe how terrified and trapped I felt that day. I was using another woman's name, wasn't I? Bringing another woman's children to America from their dying mother, and it was that name that implicated me in the first place. And if I told the truth about who I was, the police were looking for me back home in Ireland. I'm sure she's going through the same sort of feelings. Her brothers are with the Irish Republican Brotherhood, you know. They've had to flee for their lives, and she felt that her own life was in danger if she stayed put."

There was a worrying silence while I looked up at him and he stared down at me. "She told you that, did she?"

"Yes, she did. Why can't you admit that I would be an asset on this case?"

"What am I supposed to put on my report, that my wife discovered this information while questioning the suspect? I'm sure the police commissioner would love to hear that."

"And who is going to tell him? Not me. Rose doesn't know I'm your wife. I introduced myself as Molly Murphy, off the boat from Ireland just like her. I thought she might feel free to talk to a fellow Irishwoman."

He was still staring down at me. After a long, icy silence during which I began to feel quite uncomfortable, he asked, "So what else did you learn that we didn't?"

"Did she tell you about her brothers fighting for home rule?"

"It didn't come up," he admitted.

"Aha. That might be important. If she is connected in any way to this murder, then family often plays a big part in Irish crimes. She could be protecting her brothers, or killing the man who betrayed them . . ." I paused.

"Hardly, if the fellow is from London as his luggage says. So go on. What else have you learned?"

I took a deep breath. "I'm not telling you anything else until we get one thing straight. I'm going to work this case with you. I don't want to be your little woman. I want to be your partner. You knew that before you married me."

Daniel paced back and forth. "You could be helpful. I can see that. I can't believe how much you learned in one day, and behind my back." He ran his fingers through his hair. "I don't want to involve you, but every time I tell you to back off you throw yourself in even deeper. How can I stop you, short of locking you in the house?"

"You can't."

"But Molly, it's my job to protect you. You know I've been shot at. Our house has been set on fire. There are dangerous people out there. Why can't you just be content to be a wife and a mother?"

"I don't know," I confessed. "Perhaps you and I are too alike. When I see a wrong, I have to try to right it. Don't you want Liam to have a mother like that?"

He stared into my eyes, and I could see he was afraid and not angry. "I want Liam to have a mother who is alive."

We were silent for a long moment. Then I spoke up. "I propose a compromise."

"I'm listening."

"I want to be part of this case. I'd like to be part of lots of your cases. I'm a good detective."

"Molly—"

"Just listen," I cut him off. "I'm a good detective, but I know I rush into dangerous situations without thinking sometimes. So I propose a compromise," I repeated. "You involve me in your cases and I will follow your orders and not rush into danger."

"What would that even look like?" I was surprised he didn't say no right away.

"Well, for starters you could let me interview Rose again. I already found out more than your detectives."

"If I let you interview her, you would have to be unbiased. What if you find out something that proves her guilt?"

"If she's guilty, then she should pay for killing a man. I won't hide evidence from you. I'll just help you solve this case fairly. You haven't forgotten what it is like to be wrongly accused, have you?"

"I have not." I could see the pain that the memory of that time brought to him.

"You would still be in jail if I hadn't proved your innocence. Let me do the same for Rose."

He shook his head. "I don't see how this is a compromise. What are you giving me?"

"I will tell you where I am going and what I am doing. And I promise not to go into a dangerous situation." I have to admit I added in my head, "unless it is absolutely necessary." What Daniel didn't know wouldn't hurt him.

"Do you promise?" He looked steadily at me. All of a sudden I felt nervous. This was a promise I would have to keep or damage my marriage.

I put my hands in his. "I promise. I won't go off and do anything dangerous or embarrass you in front of your fellow officers, but you will share your cases with me when you can, and let me help."

We had been standing this whole time like two fighters in the arena but now we sat on the sofa. I picked up a pillow and played with the tassels.

"There is one thing more you must promise," he said seriously.

"Yes?" My voice was still soft.

"You'll still have supper ready when I come home."

I threw the pillow at him. He was still grinning when he put it down firmly between us.

"Now, Detective Molly Murphy," he continued, all business. "What else did you learn from the suspect?"

"That's Detective Sullivan, sir. I'm a married woman." I gave a little smile. "She's heard that the New York police are corrupt and terrified you'll want to pin the crime on her just to make it easy for yourselves."

"I hope you set her straight on that, at least?" he said.

"I did. I told her she was in good hands and had the best detectives in the city working on the case. Oh, and I can tell you why you found her fingerprint on the doorjamb inside that room, too. She said she was feeling around inside, trying to find an electric light switch. She's not used to electricity where she comes from. Anyway, she couldn't find it and could see it wasn't a ladies' washroom, so she closed the door again."

"Go on, Sherlock. What else did you find out?" he asked.

"Exactly what she told you about the Englishman. He had not only flirted with her on the voyage over. He had tried to get really fresh with her. Pinned her against a wall and run his hands over her body. Now, that doesn't sound like a decent sort of fellow, does it? You should be looking into him, I'd say."

"You're right. We are looking into him. We've sent off cables to London asking for details of the murdered man and the Englishman, Edwin Cromer. And now we know Rose's brothers were in the Brotherhood we'll see if any links show up there. Although how the Brotherhood ties in with a man from London, I don't know. And an older man at that."

"I'll wager there are no ties. You'll find the poor girl was a victim of being in the wrong place at the wrong time. And here she is, locked away, worrying about when and if she'll be able to travel to her family in Chicago and if she'll be expected to pay for the boardinghouse when she has no money and no way of earning any."

He gave me an understanding look. "I'm afraid it's necessary at the moment, Molly. We've interviewed other passengers from the ship and come up with nothing so far. Most of them have been allowed to go on their way. My men are trying to get in touch with other second-class passengers who might have observed Henry Darby, but as you can imagine most of them have dispersed to the four corners of the country."

"And the guards and government employees who work on the island?" I said. "They haven't always proved to be the most decent of men, have they? Maybe it will turn out to be a simple robbery in the end, as I once suggested. Henry Darby revealed that he had more money in his wallet than could be expected of a steerage passenger. One of the guards lured him to a quiet corner and tried to rob him, but Henry Darby was not the weak and defenseless older man that the guard had taken him for. There was a struggle. The guard stabbed him and dragged him inside the room."

"Except there is no trace of blood in the hallway. No sign of a struggle anywhere. And how would the guard have been carrying such an efficient knife?"

"Maybe he makes a habit of preying on unsuspecting immigrants who dare not report him, thinking they might be sent home. Or . . ." I went on, warming to my subject now, "perhaps he works in the kitchen. Saw the nicely stuffed wallet, went back, and picked up a good knife."

"Possible," Daniel said, staring at me warily, as if I were an unknown species of snake that might strike unexpectedly.

I carried on. "So you did interview guards who were working in that part of the building, did you?"

"We did."

"And did you notice any blood on their clothing?"

"Actually, yes. One man did have blood on him."

"Aha! I knew it!" I shouted, maybe louder than I should.

"Hold on a minute," Daniel said. "This was the young man who found the body. He saw him lying on the floor, turned him over, and found him lying in a pool of blood. He called for help. Another guard ran in. Both sets of fingerprints show up inside the room."

"Aha again," I said. "So what was the first guard doing in what was supposedly a disused storeroom in the first place?"

"Someone told him they saw immigrants in a hallway where no immigrants should be. He was checking rooms."

"Someone told him? Who?"

"He couldn't remember."

"But they said 'immigrants,' not one person. Is it possible this was some sort of planned killing? A group lures Mr. Darby to that hallway, stabs, and robs him?"

"An awful risk," Daniel said. "Why not let him step ashore and deal with him in an alleyway somewhere? It happens all the time."

"That's the good question, isn't it?" I said. "Why was it necessary to kill him on Ellis Island and not wait until he'd gone ashore? So we have the big puzzle: Why did he travel second class but come through Ellis Island? And who wanted him dead before he stepped ashore?"

"I agree," Daniel said. "The big puzzle."

"In which case, the answer should be the simplest one." I paused, staring into the glowing coals on the fire. "One of the guards sees a tasty amount of money on Henry Darby. Lures him away—easy enough to do. 'Please follow me, sir. One of the immigration officers would like a word with you in private.' Stabs him and robs him. Goes back to work as if nothing has happened, convinced that nobody will check that room for days."

Daniel sat for a while in silence. "Although you have to admit the coincidence is remarkable. Guard sees immigrant with money—immigrant who should not have been on Ellis Island in the first place. Guard lures, robs, and stuffs in the very same room, around the same time, as a helpless young lady needs to relieve herself, searches for a lavatory, and opens the very same door, without happening to notice the body lying there. And . . . and is seen coming out of that room, having not noticed the body, by the very man who had tried to get fresh with her."

"If a woman killed every man who tried to get fresh with her, the streets of New York would be piled high with bodies," I said with some heat. Daniel laughed and then paused, staring across the room to where a lump of coal had just spit on the fire. "I don't believe in coincidences, Molly. When I was a young officer in training, they told us always go for the obvious first. Nine times out of ten it will be right."

"When you've learned the truth about this man Edwin Cromer, then you'll probably have your answer," I said. "You'll find a connection between him and Henry Darby. Darby was blackmailing him, or the only one who could identify him at a robbery, so he had to kill him. Or the other way around. Darby was trying to escape from someone connected to Cromer, so he hopped on the ferry to get away, only Cromer followed him."

"We'll just have to wait and see," Daniel said. "Let's see if you can get anything more helpful out of Rose. I'll arrange a time to have you safely escorted over to her boardinghouse to visit her. It can't be an official police visit, though. We'll have to think of a reason for your visit."

"That's easy. Sid and Gus have a room full of clothes right now. I'll take her over a coat against the bitter weather. She had only a small suitcase with her."

"I can't believe I'm letting you do this."

"It will be good for both of us." I put my hands on his face and drew him down for a long kiss. It started sweetly but turned passionate. He put his arms around me and who knows where it might have led, but at that moment there came a thunderous pounding on the door and a small voice yelled, "Mama! Dadda? Where are you?"

Eleven

The next morning there was a tap on the front door, bright and early. Gus stood there, her cheeks rosy from having been outside. She was wearing a cerise coat with a white fur collar and matching fur hat. The whole ensemble looked most charming, as if she were ready for a skating party.

"Gus. You're here early," I said. "Is something wrong?"

"Not at all," she replied. "We realized that we'd been ignoring you lately. We've been so focused on Bridie and her schooling that we've left you out in the cold. So I have fresh croissants here from our favorite bakery and wondered if you'd like to come over for coffee. Just the three of us. Leave the family behind."

"That does sound tempting," I said. "But I'm afraid—"

"Oh, come on. No excuses. It's Saturday. No schooling for Bridie. No meetings for us. No visits to Ellis Island . . ."

That reminded me of my quest to go back there again.

"Well, Daniel has to work," I said. "I doubt he'll take a day off until this case is solved. You know how he is."

"Any further developments on the case?"

"Well, there are a few," I said. "I'm not sure if I should share them with you. Daniel would not approve of my friends becoming involved in a police matter." I remembered that promise all too clearly.

"As if we'd blab about it," Gus said. "Really, Molly. Come and have a cup of coffee and spill the beans—not the coffee beans, of course." And she laughed. I joined in. "The croissants are getting cold," she pointed out.

"Just for a little while, then," I said. "I've promised to take my mother-in-law shopping this morning."

"Not at eight, surely."

"You're right." I went back into the house. Daniel was long gone. Liam, Bridie, and Mother Sullivan were all at the breakfast table eating boiled eggs.

"I just need to pop across the street for a little while. Sid and Gus have something they need to discuss with me. Bridie, keep an eye on Liam for me, please."

"I thought we were all set to go shopping this morning, just you and me." My mother-in-law looked up from her egg. The expression was one of disappointment, not disproval.

"Of course we are," I said. "I'll be ready as soon as you've finished your breakfasts."

"But you've not eaten yourself."

"I'll have coffee and a pastry at their house," I said.

She sniffed, definite disproval this time. "Coffee and a pastry, what kind of breakfast is that? Another of these strange Continental ways of theirs."

"But quite delicious." I gave Bridie a little wink as I went to put a shawl around me to cross the street.

Once in my friends' warm kitchen I felt the tension slip away. It was like walking on eggshells, dealing with my mother-in-law. I wondered when her health might have improved enough for her to return home to Westchester County. Probably not while the weather was so unpredictable. I took a seat at the kitchen table, looked up, and gave them a bright smile.

"What's wrong?" Sid was so good at picking up on everything.

"Wrong? Nothing."

"Of course it is. Is it Daniel? Bossing you around again?"

"Not at all. We're on the best of terms, actually."

"Then it's his mother." Gus pulled up a chair across the table from me. "It's not easy for two women to be living under one roof."

"You two seem to manage it well enough." I gave her a cheeky grin.

"Ah, well. We're different, in case you haven't noticed," Gus said. "What I really meant was two women who are used to being mistress of their own household, and who are competing over one man."

"We are not competing," I retorted.

"Of course you are. She is taking every opportunity to assert superiority over you because she's Daniel's mother. She wants him to like her best and he doesn't. So she takes it out on you."

I frowned at her. "We should never have allowed you to go and study in Vienna with Professor Freud," I said. "All these newfangled ideas when it's probably just plain nasty nature."

They both laughed. "In simple terms she's jealous, Molly," Sid said. "Because she no longer has a hold over him."

"I suppose that's true," I agreed.

"Have a croissant." Gus passed them to me. "They are known to cure everything from gout to grumbles."

I took one, bit into the warm, flaky, buttery interior, and wiped Daniel's mother from my mind. But only for an instant. "I can't stay long. I promised I'd take Daniel's mother shopping. We're going to choose fabric to make Bridie a new dress. As you've noticed she's growing out of her clothes."

"You don't need to do that, Molly," Sid said. "We'd love to buy her some new clothes. They have splendid ready-mades these days. We saw some in Lord and Taylor only the other day, didn't we, dearest?"

"We did," Gus agreed. "It would be such fun to take Bridie there and let her choose."

"I'm sorry, but no," I said, more forcefully than I intended. "I know you meant well and you are incredibly generous, but this is something I have to do. Mrs. Sullivan had a fit when I suggested buying ready-made clothes. She has sent for her sewing machine for me, so I can't back out now. Besides, I want Bridie to see that I can offer her something too. You are taking care of her education. I want her to know that I'm her mother now."

"Of course you are," Gus said gently. She reached across the table and patted my hand. "We're not trying to take your place, Molly. It's just that she's such a delight. We are going to love teaching her and it would be fun to spoil her a little too."

"Not this time," I said. "My mother-in-law already thinks I'm useless at household accomplishments. At least I want to prove to her that I'm handy with a sewing machine."

"Your time in the sweatshop! Of course." Sid glanced at Gus and they smiled.

"But you haven't spilled the beans yet, Molly." Gus turned back to me. "What news of your Irish lass?"

"Well, I found her yesterday," I said. "I tracked her down and had a chat with her. Daniel was actually impressed, but the constable supposed to keep watch on the boardinghouse thought I was her and grabbed me."

"How funny," Sid said. "And a bit of luck."

"I was in the right area, of course," I pointed out. "I deduced she'd be held within easy reach of police headquarters. I must say it felt good to have Daniel looking at me with respect that way. And the fact that I got some information out of her that he hadn't. He's agreed I can go to speak to her again."

"So, do you still think she's not guilty?" Sid asked.

"Absolutely. Everything she told me made sense—how she needed to find a ladies' room in a hurry and started opening doors, looking for one. And a young man who saw her had an axe to grind.

He'd flirted with her on the boat and she'd turned him down. In fact, more than flirted. She said it was more like an attack. And"—I warmed to my subject—"he is quite suspicious himself. He was traveling steerage but he has a very posh accent. He said he had been cast off from his family, but he could just as well be lying. Besides," I went on, "what possible motive could she have? She'd had to leave Ireland because her brothers were involved in the republican movement and were wanted by the police. And the murdered man was from London. An older man, who had traveled second class but ended up on Ellis Island. That's strange to start with."

"How exciting," Sid said. "So what's next?"

"I'm hoping we can all go back to Ellis Island and I can do a little snooping around there," I said. "Maybe question some of the guards. I was thinking the murder might just have been a robbery gone wrong, and perhaps one of the guards was involved."

"We'll do everything we can to help you, won't we, Sid?" Gus said. "We're quite good at flirting with guards."

"That reminds me." A thought occurred to me. "I need an excuse to go back and visit Rose. Do you have any more coats or shawls? She didn't seem to have much luggage with her, poor thing, so it will be a perfect excuse to find out some more about her."

"Do we ever!" She looked at me appraisingly. "I wonder what would be good with your coloring. You said she looks like you?"

"Much prettier, I think, now that I have seen her up close. But her hair is the same shade, so probably nothing red."

"Come and choose some things." Gus led me through to their front parlor, now still unrecognizable under piles of assorted clothing. "This is becoming ridiculous," she said. "Friends of friends have now joined in the clothing drive with such enthusiasm that we'll soon be buried. So we have to get back to Ellis Island before long, and we are going to take some to the settlement house in the Lower East Side. Maybe Ellis Island on Monday? I'll ask about the launch we hired before."

"Perhaps not Monday," I said quickly. "I want to visit Rose again. There were so many things I didn't get a chance to ask her."

"Will Daniel let you do that?" Sid asked. "Or do you plan to sneak there under his nose?"

"He is quite in agreement," I said. "He's come to realize that I can be an asset to him at times."

"Wonders will never cease," Sid exclaimed, shaking her head so that her short bobbed hair bounced.

I selected a lovely dark green woolen cape that I actually coveted for myself but was too proud to say so, as well as a plaid scarf and a blue-and-green woolen shawl. "These will do just fine," I said. "They'll certainly suit Rose and I bet she'll love them. And what's more, they'll make her warm toward me."

"What do you think she might be able to tell you?" Gus asked.

I shrugged. "I have no idea. She's already given me a perfectly good reason why she opened the door to that room. She confirmed what she told Daniel about the young man getting too fresh with her and wanting to pay her back, and said she knew nobody else on the ship. I don't really know what else to ask at this moment. I suspect we'll have to wait until the English police can find out details about the murdered man, and the Irish police can confirm what Rose has told me." I stood there, hugging the clothes to me. "But I have to believe she is innocent, because I can see no reason she'd be guilty. Why would anyone kill an older Englishman on Ellis Island? Think of the risk, for one thing. I suppose she could have robbed him, because his wallet was missing. But I've chatted with her. I can't believe she'd be the sort of person who would rob someone. And if she were that type of person, why not wait until she got to a big city where there are fatter wallets to pick?"

"You'll figure it out, I know you will," Gus said. "We have great confidence in your abilities, Molly, and we are so glad to hear that now Daniel does too."

"I'd better be going." I smiled at them. "Thank you for the croissant. Delicious as always."

"Send Bridie over to model the dress for us when you've finished it," Gus called after me.

Twelve

Mother Sullivan was dressed in her outdoor clothes, ready to go, when I stepped into the front hall.

"Ah, there you are at last," she said. "So how do we get to a haberdasher?"

"The closest is Wanamaker's at Broadway and Ninth," I said. I noticed how frail and gaunt she was looking these days. She had always struck me as robust. "Although I'm not sure if you're up to walking that far yet. There are still pockets of snow and ice around the square."

"We'll not think of walking," Daniel's mother said. "We'll go down to the end of your little street and find ourselves a hansom cab."

I didn't argue with this suggestion. Having grown up really poor and been through some tough times in New York I rarely took any transportation when I could walk and certainly not the luxury of a cab. But I had to admit that it made more sense for an elderly woman, still recovering from pneumonia. I kissed Liam and Bridie, told him to be a good boy, and off we went. Wanamaker's Department Store always felt overwhelming to me—taking up a whole block of Broadway between Ninth and Tenth Streets, it was known as the Iron Palace, having been built with cast-iron columns. Even Mrs. Sullivan was taken aback when we entered the central foyer and stood looking up at all those galleries.

"Mercy me," she said. "You'd need to tie a thread to the front door so that you could find your way out again."

I nodded, smiling. "I believe fabric is on the third level," I said. "We can take the elevator."

"Elevator, too! What next!" she exclaimed.

We rode it up and soon found ourselves among bolts of fabric, as far as the eye could see.

"It will need to be practical if she's to wear it every day," I said. "It shouldn't show the dirt." The selection was overwhelming. I saw fabrics I'd have swooned for as a young girl, but I reminded myself it had to be sturdy and last well. Eventually I fingered a soft navy blue wool with just a little interesting nub to it. "This would go well with her lovely fair hair," I said. "Maybe some bright green trim?"

"Blue and green should never be seen," said my mother-in-law.

"Or red buttons?" I didn't fancy an argument when a sales clerk was hovering behind us. "They'd contrast nicely."

"You'll need to make her a new white pinafore so that she doesn't spoil the new dress," Mother Sullivan said.

"Good idea." I handed the bolt of navy blue to the saleswoman, told her enough for a young girl's dress and that I'd appreciate a paper pattern if they had one. She led me over to a rack and selected one for me. "This style is quite popular this year," she said. "What's more, it can be adapted to a bigger size when she grows in the bust."

While she was cutting I went in search of plain white broadcloth for the pinafore. I had just selected it when I saw a pretty white muslin with little flowers embroidered on it.

"Look at this," I called to my mother-in-law. "I think I'll make her a new party dress to surprise her."

"You've a lot of work ahead of you," she said. "But at least it will stop you from running around and getting involved in Daniel's work."

Oh dear. I wish she hadn't said that, because it was quite true. But I decided there was no rush on the party dress. I'd get in some valuable practice on the everyday frock and then turn my hand to the lighter fabric. I could just picture that dress now—big puffy sleeves, a skirt that twirled out, and perhaps a red sash—the sort of dress I'd dreamed of owning as a young girl. I resolved to keep it secret from Bridie and give it to her as a surprise.

We came home in another cab and I left Mother Sullivan while I went out to the butcher to buy meat for the weekend meals. Maybe we'd treat ourselves to a small roast tomorrow, and today—sausages. They didn't make proper Irish sausages in New York, but what they called bratwurst were quite tasty, especially with cabbage and mashed potatoes.

As I walked back I wondered when the sewing machine would arrive. I was itching to get started on that dress. I opened the door, took off my coat, hat, and scarf, and carried my purchases through to the kitchen.

"Sausages tonight," I said, then I saw my mother-in-law's face.

"What on earth's wrong?" For a second I thought her look of dismay was at the prospect of eating sausages.

She looked up. "I've just had a letter from Martha Norton. You remember Arabella, her daughter. She was once—"

Of course I remembered Arabella. How could I ever forget that she was once engaged to the man I loved? That he didn't love her but could not break the engagement. She had once been my enemy, but by now we were quite civil to each other, since she had married well.

"Something's happened to Arabella?" I cut in.

"Not to Arabella. To her godmother. I don't know if you ever met Miss Van Woekem?"

"Why, yes. I know her well," I replied, realizing that she had not been aware I had once been that lady's companion. I waited for more news with a sense of impending doom.

"She had a bad tumble, down the front steps of her house on an icy day," she said, "and has broken her leg, poor thing. I should like to pay her a visit immediately, maybe take her some fruit. Can one find grapes at this time of year?"

"There is Jefferson Market just across Greenwich Avenue," I said. "I could see what I can find there, if you like."

"Most kind of you. I'll feed the little one his luncheon, then, shall I?"

"Please do," I replied. "There is still some of that stew we can finish up, if you like." (I had learned to call it luncheon the way she and Daniel did, but at home in Ireland it we had always called it dinner. The meal at night was either tea or supper.)

I dashed out to the market and miraculously found someone who imported grapes—at a price—but I was fond of Miss Van Woekem and she was worth it. After the meal I left Bridie in charge, her head in a book as usual, and off my mother-in-law and I went in yet another cab.

Miss Van Woekem lived in an elegant brownstone on Gramercy Park. The private garden with its tall railings looked bleak and bare at this time of year, although in summer it was quite delightful and only available to residents who had a key, as I had once found out when I had been trapped there. We paid the cabby, told him he could return in an hour if he wanted another fare, and went up the steps to the front door. I held my mother-in-law's arm, as there were still traces of snow around and I didn't want a second accident.

The door was opened by a young maid I hadn't met before.

"Yes?" she said in an almost aggressive tone.

This was so different from the reception I'd received in the past with a perfectly starched maid opening the door that I was taken aback for a moment. "Mrs. Sullivan and Mrs. Sullivan to see Miss Van Woekem," I said. "Is she receiving visitors?"

"Wait there and I'll ask," she said, leaving us standing on the doorstep.

"That girl needs some serious training," Mother Sullivan muttered to me. "No wonder the poor woman slipped on the steps. Probably not swept properly."

Almost immediately the maid returned. "You can come in," she said. "She'll see you in the front parlor."

"You should offer to take our coats and hats," my mother-in-law said, and handed the girl her hat and scarf. She took them, under sufferance, and they were all bundled together as she walked off with them, leaving us to make our own way to the front parlor. Mrs. Sullivan looked at me and shook her head. Luckily I had been there often enough to know the way. I tapped on the door and we went through. The old lady was not sitting in her customary high-backed chair by the window. Instead she was in an armchair beside the fire, her leg propped on a stool and covered in a rug. Her face had always reminded me of some kind of bird of prey, with its hooked nose, skin like white marble, and darting little eyes that missed nothing. Today I was alarmed to notice how tired and drawn she looked, as if she were clearly in pain. But when she saw us, a big smile spread across her face and she propped herself up. "Molly and Kathleen! What a lovely surprise. Do come in and sit down. We'll have some tea if that fool of a girl can remember to pass a message to Cook."

"We came as soon as we got the news," my mother-in-law said, taking the armchair opposite Miss Van Woekem.

I was about to go for a straight-backed chair when something brushed against my leg. I jumped a little, luckily not knocking over the table with the Tiffany lamp on it, and looked down to see Miss Van Woekem's large white Persian cat staring up at me. "Mew?" it asked.

"She remembers you fondly," Miss Van Woekem said, smiling like a proud mother.

I didn't have any such fond memories of the cat who was adept at sinking claws into passing ankles. But now she was purring, so apparently all was forgiven. I pulled up the chair and sat beside our hostess.

"We were so sorry to hear of your accident," I said.

"Foolishness on my part, I fear," the old lady said. "I saw some boys trying to climb the railings into the gardens. I ran out to stop them, caught my foot on some ice, and down I tumbled. Lucky it was only my leg, I suppose. It could have been my head." And she chuckled.

"Molly found you some grapes," Mother Sullivan said.

"How very kind. We'll need a bowl to put them in. Where is that girl? Molly, go into the hall and shout for her. Her name is Jewel, if you can believe it. She's certainly not a jewel in my book. More like a lump of coal."

"Where on earth did you get her?" Mother Sullivan asked. "And what happened to your former maid? She was a real gem, I believe."

"She was, and still is. Her mother became very ill so I gave her permission to go home and be with her, and this girl came from a charity home. I'd been meaning to get a girl to train as an under-housemaid. I've had good luck in the past with girls from there but this one is more than hopeless. And of course the timing couldn't have been worse. I have agreed to host a tea party for another of my goddaughters in a week's time. I can't call it off now, but I can't see that girl being able to cope with pouring the tea, can you?"

"I could come and help you," I said. "And I'll bring my ward, Bridie. She's old enough to be useful and she'd love to attend a tea party."

"That is most kind of you, Molly, my dear." She reached out and took my hand. "And I'll accept gladly. It's to meet her new fiancé, you know. Just a few family friends. An intimate little gathering."

I was beginning to feel that I should also volunteer to come and help with the training of the maid, but that would mean that I had no time to help Rose, to go to Ellis Island and to prove to Daniel that I could be really useful to him.

At that moment the girl herself poked her head around the door. "Was youse wanting some tea, then?" she asked.

Miss Van Woekem looked at us and sighed. "Jewel, I have told you before that you come into the room and say, 'Is there anything you wanted, ma'am?'"

"Okay. Is there anything you wanted, ma'am?" She repeated the words, rolling her eyes at the same time.

"Yes, please. Some tea for the ladies. Tell Cook it's tea and cake for three." She paused, then added, "Oh, and ask Cook for a bowl to put these grapes in."

"Okay." She went.

"You really will have to find another girl, Maud," my mother-in-law said.

The old woman nodded. "I have sent a note to the mother superior at the home, but so far nothing has come of it. I'm hoping that Annie will be returning soon. I suppose I could keep on the girl and have Annie train her. Nobody else would want her, poor thing."

"I'm impressed with your charity," my mother-in-law said. "I'd have sent her packing."

I could have pointed out that she had taken on Bridie to train as a maid, but then treated her more like a young relative. We chatted while awaiting the arrival of tea. My mother-in-law told her about her bout of pneumonia, and I brought her up to date on Liam, Daniel, and Bridie.

"You must bring them all to see me when I'm feeling rather more sprightly," she said. "I'm finding it very tedious not being able to go out and meet my friends. I remember quite fondly the time when you were my companion, Molly, my dear. We had some good chats, didn't we?"

I had to smile. "I don't think you were that impressed with me to begin with," I said.

"On the contrary. When you stood your ground on that first day and told me I could not call you by anything but your own name, I decided there and then that you'd be a good match for my wits. I like a woman with spunk."

"Molly certainly has that," my mother-in-law agreed.

At that moment there was the rattle of china outside the door. Fearing the worst, I jumped up and went to retrieve the tray from

Jewel. Miraculously nothing had slopped over. I poured the tea while Jewel handed around the cake. It was a rich sponge cake, delicious as always. That meant Miss Van Woekem still had her good cook. As we ate I looked around the familiar room with pleasure: the Tiffany stained glass lamp on the table, the polished mahogany furniture dotted with silk pillows. The bookcase filled with leather-backed volumes and the somber-looking paintings on the wall, one of which I knew to be a Vermeer given by the painter to Miss Van Woekem's ancestor in Holland. We chatted until I could tell that the old lady looked tired. I gave a nod to my mother-in-law and we stood up to take our leave.

"So Bridie and I will come to help you on the day of your tea party," I said. "But won't you need help before that? Ordering food and setting out china?"

"Oh, I think that Cook can handle that side of things," she said. "It's the pouring and serving I worry about. The women who will be attending have expensive dresses. I'd hate them to end up with tea and cream all over them."

She gave me a wicked little smile, which I returned. "Don't worry. We'll be there. And if you need us before, just send a message."

She took my hand, but looked up at Daniel's mother. "Your son married a sweet girl," she said. "So much more suitable than Arabella."

I was grinning to myself as we went down the steps and back to the waiting cab.

Thirteen

To my annoyance the sewing machine did not arrive until Sunday afternoon. I had hoped to get started on the dress for Bridie, but instead had to play the good wife and mother all day on Sunday, going to church with the family and then, because the weather had turned mild, letting Liam feed the ducks in Central Park. Don't misunderstand me—I enjoyed everything we did as a family. I loved watching my son's eyes light up when he saw riders in the park or a boat on the lake. But also I found it hard to shake off the nagging list of things I had to do: make Bridie's dress. Make the surprise party dress. Help Miss Van Woekem prepare for her tea party—oh, and prove the innocence of that poor girl, shut away in a boardinghouse in a city where she knew nobody!

My mind was churning as I tried to sleep on Sunday night. But when I awoke, everything was different. I don't know why, but I felt a new sense of hope and purpose that Monday morning. The sky was bright blue without a cloud and the air was so crisp and cold that it hurt to breathe as I stepped outside to bring the milk bottles in. I hummed to myself as I made a thick porridge, a song that I remembered my mother singing as she made hers. "Shoo shoo shoo la roo." I had no idea what it meant, but the tune was catchy. I dished out some porridge for Liam, cooling it with a little milk and adding a dollop of cream from the top of the bottle.

"There you are, my babai," I said setting the bowl down in front of him. Being a mother had reminded me of words and phrases my mother used with me that I hadn't thought of in years.

"That smells good." Daniel was already dressed in his police captain's uniform and he gave me a quick peck on the cheek. "You're up early." He patted Liam's head affectionately. Liam, whose whole face was liberally smeared with porridge, gave an endearing grin.

"It's cold today. I wanted you to have something warm before you left for work."

"And . . ." Daniel grinned and it struck me not for the first time that he and Liam had the same smile.

"Look at you pair of ijits grinning at me," I said, smiling in spite of myself. "All right, and I wanted to talk to you before your mother was down for breakfast. I want to go and see Rose today."

"But—" he began.

"Now, Daniel, you promised." I ladled out a big scoop of porridge for myself and sat at the table across from him.

"Let me finish, please," he said. "I was just going to say that it needs to wait till this afternoon. I am busy in the morning and I want to escort you over there myself."

"But—" I began to argue that I was perfectly able to take care of myself.

"Now, Molly, *you* promised. I agree it is important that you meet with her today. We are at a loss on this case. You may find a clue that helps us prove her guilty or"—he held up his hands to stop me from interrupting—"prove her innocent. I think I can trust you to meet me at the station without getting yourself into trouble. If you can meet me there after lunch, I will take you over to the boardinghouse where the suspect is staying. I want to have a word with the constable there and make sure you are safe. Tell my mother you are joining me in the city for lunch. That should keep her happy."

"That sounds perfectly acceptable." I didn't want to show it, but inside I was delighted. Daniel was talking to me as an equal. He might want to escort me to keep me safe, but he was also entrusting me with an important job. Instead of sneaking around to work on this case I was doing it with his blessing and as a partner. "I'm not free this morning anyway. I have to start working on the dress for Bridie while she has lessons with Sid and Gus." I pulled my pocket watch out of its pocket. "I'd better get her up now."

"Sid and Gus won't be up to give her lessons for hours yet." He scraped his bowl clean, stood, and put it in the sink.

"Yes, but I want her to watch Liam while I start sewing."

Daniel looked at me fondly. "What a fine wife you're turning into," he said, smiling. "Handy with the needle and a good cook. Even my mother will have to approve."

"Well, I hope she does today, because I need her to watch Liam while I help you solve a murder case."

After Daniel had left and Bridie was amusing Liam I spread the soft wool fabric out on the front parlor floor to cut out the pieces, using the paper pattern. In the factory we had received the pieces already cut, so it took me most of the morning to position the paper pattern then cut and pin the pieces of a blue day dress together. Bridie went off for her schooling, and my mother-in-law took over with Liam while I kept working. It was horribly cold in the front parlor, but it seemed wasteful to attempt to light a fire just for my use. I kept mistaking my finger for the fabric, one time even drawing blood. It is a good thing it was a dark fabric. I can't repeat here the words I said as I pricked my finger, but I had to say them under my breath because Mrs. Sullivan and Liam were in earshot. I didn't feel much like a perfect wife and mother sitting on the floor surrounded by fabric and cursing, but I did have a sense of satisfaction as I laid the neatly pinned cuts away on top of a chest.

"That's all pinned together," I announced to Mother Sullivan as I came into the kitchen. "And ready to be sewed."

"You'd better check the floor for pins before you let Liam down in there." She looked at my finger that still had a pin prick on it. "Did your mother not teach you to use a thimble?"

I took a deep breath, refusing to let anything bring down my spirits today. "The hard part is done. I'll do the basting now, then sew the pieces together tomorrow and start on her party dress the day after. I want to have it done as a surprise before the tea party next Saturday."

She looked down at my bloodstained finger again. "I'll lend you a thimble."

Because I didn't answer, she went on: "Can you not start sewing the dress this afternoon? The boy will be down for his nap."

"Ah, well," I said. "Actually Daniel has asked me to meet him for lunch for a change. Isn't that nice of him?"

"He always was such a kind, thoughtful boy," she replied, but the look indicated she was a trifle annoyed that she had not been included in the luncheon invitation.

"He wants to discuss some details of a case he's working on with me," I went on.

"Not that Irish woman on Ellis Island?"

"That's the one. The police are no nearer to solving it, so it seems."

She sniffed. "It seems like a hopeless proposition to me. Whoever committed this crime will be long gone by now and nobody the wiser. I think the police have little chance of catching him, or her."

"I'm inclined to agree with you," I said. "It would be so easy in that crush of people to stab someone, get on the next boat and off to freedom, hoping that the murder wouldn't be discovered for hours or maybe even days."

She shook her head. "Ellis Island seems like a very disreputable place. I wouldn't feel safe for a minute there myself. Anyone could get themselves stabbed by one of those new immigrants."

"We are both immigrants as well, Mother Sullivan. I came through Ellis Island. Your parents came in the famine. That's why I want to help this girl. And I want to take an interest in Daniel's work. You understand that, don't you?"

Mrs. Sullivan looked around the parlor at the scraps of blue wool scattered all over the floor. I massaged my back where it was sore from being stooped over all morning, bracing myself for her to say something critical. I knew I didn't measure up to her idea of a good mother and wife. But unexpectedly she smiled and put her hand on my arm. "I do, my dear. He is lucky to have you. Let me help. You had better go and smarten yourself up if you need to be downtown for lunch." She bent and helped to pick up the sewing scraps. Well, wonders would never cease!

I was still grinning as I walked up the steps and into the large brownstone police station on Mulberry Street. First my mother-in-law was approving of me and now I was going to work on a case with Daniel's approval. Of course I had always managed to make my own decisions with or without anyone's approval, but it felt nice to have it.

The officer at the front desk was a young man I had never met before. "May I help you, miss?" he said as I approached.

"I'm Mrs. Sullivan, actually." I smiled at him. "Is Captain Sullivan in his office?"

"No, ma'am. He asked you to wait out on the street for him."

I walked back out the door and down the steps. I looked up and down the pavement, feeling puzzled. Just then an automobile pulled to a stop and honked its horn. Daniel got out with a big smile. "Our newest acquisition. What do you think?" he asked. "Let's see the criminals try to outrun us now. This thing can go over twenty-five miles an hour."

"It looks very impressive," I said, carefully not mentioning that a few days previously I had ridden in an even grander automobile owned by no less than Mrs. Sage. Daniel came around to open the door for me. I gathered my skirts, stepping carefully on the side runner and into the car. Daniel climbed in beside me. "I thought I would take you in style." Daniel was obviously excited to be behind the wheel. We took off a little jerkily, startling the horse that was pulling a hansom cab.

"So you are allowed to use the police automobile to take your wife to lunch now?" I could tell that Daniel was loving it. I had not been in many automobiles, although Daniel had given me a ride in a police auto on occasion. The speed was still new and a little alarming. He wasn't driving as smoothly as the chauffeur had been, and I clutched the door to steady myself.

"When I am on official police business. Which I am now."

"Rose McSweeney can't see me get out of a police car or she will never feel comfortable telling me anything."

"I thought of that. I'll drop you around the corner."

It took only minutes to get to the boardinghouse. I thought with a smile of how long it had taken to find it on my own two feet. The automobile would be a big help to the police indeed! True to his word Daniel pulled up around the corner from the boardinghouse. He insisted on getting out of the car to open my door and help me lift the bag of clothing out of the back of the car.

"Remember, the constable is just downstairs if you need him," he said, giving me a worried look. "Don't take any chances. The woman is a suspect in a murder investigation."

"I'll be careful," I promised. I hoisted the bag and walked up to the boardinghouse.

I was glad to see that Rose was not at the window as I walked up to the building. The constable was standing just outside the door. Presumably he had gotten in some kind of trouble for thinking I was the prisoner the other day and was now showing his superiors what a good job he could do.

"I have some warm clothes for Miss McSweeney," I said loudly in case she was listening. In an undertone I added, "I'm Mrs. Sullivan. Captain Sullivan asked me to speak with the young lady. He is just around the corner if you need to verify that."

"No need, ma'am." The constable looked at me in some awe. "He gave me very specific instructions this morning. I will be listening. If you need anything or the prisoner gets violent, just give a holler."

So I really was there on official police business. Wonders would never cease.

I walked through the dark foyer and up the stairs. I knocked at the door and it was opened just a crack. "Who's there?"

"It's Molly Murphy. I brought you the soda bread? I came back to visit like I said I would."

"Molly Murphy." She opened the door. "'Tis grand of you to come and visit me in my hour of need. You said you would be back, but I didn't really think you would come."

"I thought you might need some warmer clothes." I held up my bag so she could see it. "I noticed last time that you had only a small suitcase with you."

"God bless you. Please come in." She moved aside so I could enter. The room was dark and narrow, with just enough room for a bed and a rickety dresser. "I did have another suitcase, but it was stolen when we were waiting to board on the dock. I didn't realize it was gone until too late."

"Oh, how sad. And worrying for you. Did you lose much?" Rose looked around the room as if wanting to offer me a place to sit. There was nowhere but the bed, so I perched there and opened the bag to take out the cloak.

"Some clothes and my warmest coat," she replied. "And a photograph of my brothers."

"A photograph! You were living it up in Galway. We never heard of such a thing in Ballykillin! A girl I was at school with went into Sligo with her family to a studio and had one taken. My mother wanted to do that too, but she died before we were able. What a tragedy to lose it." I would have loved to have a photograph of my brothers. I only had my memory and I tried to only remember the good times.

"Yes. It was special for us, too. My whole lovely family, back in the good days before the troubles overtook us. We had to go into the city to sit for it. And now they are gone and the photograph is gone. And me not sure if I'll ever see my brothers again." She turned away and wiped a tear from her eye. "I'm afraid I have no idea what to expect in America. To tell the truth I've never been outside my own little village. It's kind of you to visit me and perhaps you might be good enough to tell me a bit about America. They asked me on the island if I was being met by a husband or a male relative. I gave the address of my kinfolk in Chicago and said I was supposed to get straight on the train to go to them. Am I not allowed to travel to Chicago by myself? Would you be telling me that women are not allowed to travel in America unchaperoned? Will my family have to come and get me?"

I laughed. "I wouldn't go anywhere if I had to be chaperoned all the time. Women can go wherever they want. Although I have noticed that women who stand for too long on a city street tend to be taken for ladies of the evening." Rose's face looked so shocked that I didn't elaborate. "There are certain parts of town that a woman shouldn't venture into alone. But you should be fine on a train to Chicago. You certainly won't be arrested for it."

Rose's bottom lip quivered. "I had the money for the trip to Chicago, but the landlady asked for the rent on Monday and I gave her all I had. I don't know what I'm going to do or how I'm going to get there. I can't ask my cousins for more. They have already paid my passage over. I will have to make it myself somehow. But I don't know what I'm qualified to do. Back home women took in washing or worked as a maid or a teacher. I didn't have enough schooling to be a teacher. What do women do here if they don't have a man to support them?"

"Well, the first woman I knew here had a job in the fish market.

Some do work as maids, but I think it is hard without a reference. I'm afraid that even in 1907 you'll find that some shops have 'No Irish Need Apply' in the window. My first real job here was as a lady's companion. That didn't last too long. I'm not good at taking orders. I was too outspoken. That's always been my curse." I laughed, remembering how severe Miss Van Woekem had been. "What is funny is that now I am on good terms with that same lady. She's a friend of my mother-in-law and at the moment I'm helping her since she broke her leg and has no one to take care of her."

"It seems you are a charitable woman, Molly Murphy," Rose said. "An angel of mercy."

I smiled. "I wouldn't quite say that, but I'm happy to help where I can. I just don't like to be bossed around." I paused. "Don't follow my example if you want to get on in New York."

"But you have done so well for yourself! Maybe I should follow it." Rose looked around the tiny room as if despairing of its squalor. "I couldn't hope to start at your level. I'm lucky if the fish market would take me. I've no experience." She turned to the window and wiped away another tear that trickled down her cheek. "What am I going to do?"

My heart went out to her. I had survived but not everyone did. I tried to remember back to that feeling of being in a city where I knew no one. Of course, I had not been completely alone. I had Bridie's family, who had taken me in, not very hospitably, but at least it was a place until I could stand on my own two feet.

"This is for you, then." I took the cloak out of the bag and shook the creases out before I handed it to her. She dabbed her eyes with her sleeves and took the cloak with reverence.

"Oh, how beautiful." She walked over to the window to hold it up to the light. "What a lovely color. You must have chosen this. You know what suits a redhead. But it is too much. I can't accept such a nice piece of clothing."

"I have some friends who have been collecting clothes for those who are . . ." I didn't want to say poor or destitute. "In need of something warm to wear. They have been collecting clothes from some of the society ladies in town. I assure you it won't be depriving me of a coat." I pulled the shawl out. "Here, this is for you as well."

"Heaven bless you for an angel. This is beautiful. And it's freezing in here." She slipped the cloak on and sat on the other end of the bed, which squeaked horribly, took the shawl on her lap, and began running the tassels through her fingers. "I don't know why you would help me. Are you and your friends religious, then?"

"No," I laughed, "I don't think they are particularly religious. And we would be three different religions."

Rose looked confused.

"I grew up Catholic, of course. But I have mostly left it behind except to accompany my mother-in-law to church. I just want to help a fellow Irish girl." I tried to give an encouraging smile, but I could tell she still wasn't sure why I was here. What explanation would make sense without letting her know my husband was a police captain? "I was at Ellis Island with those same friends I mentioned giving out coats on the day you came through. It brought me back to my own stay in the place."

"You said you came through Ellis Island yourself?"

I nodded. "I did and not too long ago."

"And look at you now, quite the successful lady." She looked at me appraisingly. "So are you living in a fine, big house up there by the park?"

"Goodness me, no. We've a dear little house on a back alley called Patchin Place, near the university on Washington Square. That's Greenwich Village. Not at all swanky."

"Sounds perfect to me. I just pray I'll have a home of my own someday, and a good man to take care of me too."

"I'm sure you will. You're so beautiful, I'm sure you'll have no problems."

She gave an embarrassed smile and looked down at the shawl

on her lap. I tried to remember what this city and everyone looked like when I first arrived. I supposed I would have considered myself a toff, although today I had picked a modest outfit, not wanting to stand out in this poorer area.

"Don't worry. Things will get better. You'll be on your feet in no time." I laid a reassuring hand on her arm. "I struggled a lot in the beginning. Sometimes I didn't know where my next meal was coming from. But yes, I am doing well now. I'm happily married with my own home and enough to eat."

"Do you have children?"

"A girl and a boy. Thirteen and two."

"Holy Mother of God." Rose's hands went theatrically up to her face as she said it. "You are never old enough to have a thirteen-year-old-girl."

I laughed. "That is a long story. She is not mine by blood, but she is my ward now and I love her like a daughter."

"And what does Mr. Murphy do?"

I thought quickly. "He works for the city. He is thinking of going into politics."

"Politics no less. You have landed on your feet, Mrs. Murphy. That gives me hope, that does. This city scares me to death. It's so big and there are so many people." Tears shone in her eyes and she looked out the window again. "And before I can even start to get on my feet I have to prove that I didn't commit a murder." She twisted the shawl she was holding in her hands. "It's all a horrible mistake and I'm just praying to all the saints that justice will be served and they'll let me be going on my way."

"Do you have a favorite saint?" I asked. "I've never been one for the saints myself."

She frowned. "I can't say I've a particular favorite. I just like to think of them all working together for me."

"Where I came from it wasn't the saints so much. With the nuns it was all about Knock," I said.

Rose knitted her brows quizzically, "Knock? On what?"

I put my hands together in a pious prayer position. "Our Lady of Knock, Merciful Queen, help us in our hour of need," I chanted, and grimaced at the memory. "The nuns at school didn't teach you about Our Lady of Knock? We had her morning, noon, and night. We were told since we lived so close to her shrine that we'd be specially favored by her. But she didn't stop the English from taking our house. I'd like to believe, mind you, and maybe I even say a prayer when I'm desperate, but why would the Holy Queen of Ireland let the English do just what they please?"

"I didn't have nuns at my school." Rose stared at her fingers, now knotted in the shawl's tassels.

"Are you not Catholic, then? I didn't think any Protestants lived that far south."

"Well, yes. Of course I'm a Catholic," she said quickly. "But I had very little schooling. I had to leave school early to keep house for my brothers. There was just a kind teacher lady in the primary school."

"Lucky you," I said. "I raised my brothers after my parents died as well. Are these the same brothers who went into the Republican Army?"

"Yes, I only have the two."

I realized I had been here for a while and had nothing to tell Daniel. "Were you maybe involved with the cause? Did you help with their resistance work?"

"Oh, heavens no. To tell you the truth I had no idea what they were doing until they were arrested." She looked up, afraid. "Do you think the murder had something to do with the freedom fighters? Was the man killed one of them, I wonder? Or someone for the English cause? Mrs. Murphy, how could I have murdered a man when I don't even know who he is?"

"Call me Molly, please. I did hear something about that man." How could I tell her what I knew without revealing how I knew it?

I decided just to plunge ahead. "I heard that the murdered man was an Englishman, from London."

"From London, you say?" Rose turned those wide green eyes on me. "Fancy that. You don't see many folks from England down in steerage, do you? And I didn't hear anyone talking with that kind of posh accent. Apart from that annoying chap on the boat I told you about."

"I wonder," I mused. "So that man you told me about—the one who attacked you. Did you ever hear him talking politics? Did you see who he spoke to on the passage over?"

"No, I never noticed him at all before he made advances at me, Molly. To tell you the truth, I was quite seasick on the journey. Were you allowed up on deck during your journey?"

"No, we weren't. And it was quite a surprise. I thought we would have a cabin, and instead we were all crammed together in bunk beds like cattle."

"I was surprised too. Horrified, I was. It was quite rough and I felt so sick. And then everyone around me was sick. The smell of it . . ." She grimaced. "I really don't want to think about it. So, that's to say that I really paid no attention to any of the other passengers until that man's attention was forced on me."

"I'm afraid I've had that happen to me too," I said, thinking of the reason I had first fled to America. "How did you get away from him? Were some of the men decent? Did someone come to your aid?"

"There was no one nearby." Her lip curled. "He trapped me in a dark corner where no one was watching. I had to get away myself. I stabbed him with my hatpin."

"I keep one of those handy myself." I grinned at her and pulled one out of my bun to show her. "A woman has to take care of herself. And like you I had to flee in a hurry, from a very similar situation. I was scared all the time that the police were after me. I'll let you into a little secret. I was using another woman's name so that I could bring her children over to America. She was dying, poor thing, and their father had gone ahead to make a new life for them."

"Well, isn't that just the saddest thing you've ever heard?" Rose's voice cracked with emotion. "And how brave you were to be bringing those poor wee things to America. What became of them?"

"One of them is now my ward, Bridie. A lovely young girl. I'm so proud of her."

"You must be. You saved their lives. But then we Irish have to stick together, don't we? Especially against those English."

I nodded. My heart was full. It was as if I'd discovered a kindred spirit for the first time in years.

"Mind you," she went on, "I have to confess I always dreamed of going to London someday, didn't you? London and if not that, then Dublin. Have you ever been to London?"

"Not me. I couldn't even imagine that. I certainly dreamed of Dublin, though," I said. "Big city, bright lights, cultured people. And young men who were not uncouth clodhoppers like the boys at home."

"Oh, those boys where I came from." She shook her head in disgust. "Only wanted one thing, didn't they? And no conversation between them."

"So true," I agreed. "And everyone expecting us girls to get married before we turned twenty and start having babies every year. How did you manage to escape that, or are you not much older than twenty now?"

"I look young for my age," she said with pride. "And I'd set my sights higher than a local farm boy when I was no older than ten. I would have moved away from home sooner, but I didn't like to leave the brothers in the lurch."

"Me too," I said.

"I thought I might get a job in Dublin as a maid to start with. Or even in London. They like Irish maids there, so I've heard. And I had a bit of training, you might say. There was an elderly widow in a big house near us. Lovely old lady, very refined, and I helped out there when I wasn't needed at home. She only had the one servant and the girl couldn't read, so I used to go over and help out. Polish the silver, you know. And then I'd read to her. Chat with her, you know. Cheer her up a bit."

"Did you really?"

She nodded. "To tell the truth I just loved being in her house. Those lovely paintings on the walls and that fine furniture. I used to hope, to dream, that she'd leave me some of it. You can tell I always had big dreams." She broke off, shaking her head. "Of course she didn't. She died and some nephew arrived to take over the lot of it. Not even a thank you or help yourself to one of her books. But that's the way it goes for people like us, isn't it? People walk over us all the time."

"If we let them," I said. "Nobody walks all over me any longer, I can tell you."

"And I don't intend them to walk all over me, either. America, land of the free, isn't that right? Home of equal opportunity. I intend to make the most of it." Rose's lovely face broke into a smile. "And now look at us, here we are. One of the biggest and brightest cities in the world. I'd say we've done all right for ourselves, wouldn't you?"

"I'm doing just fine," I said, cautiously. "But you—we've got to clear your name and get you to your relatives in Chicago."

"They have to come up with the truth soon, don't they?" she asked, her voice faltering now. "I mean, if the gentleman is from London, what could I possibly have to do with him? They searched me. They searched my bags. And what did they find? Nothing at all. And me, never having been to London in my life. Not even left Galway until I had to get out in a hurry."

I took her hands in mine. They were very small and cold. "It seems desperate now, but try to have faith. I'll do everything I can to get you out of here." And at that very moment I had a brilliant idea just how I could do that.

"Well?" Daniel asked as I joined him at the automobile around the corner. "And what great details did you learn? You've cleared her name and solved my case for me, all in one go?"

I chuckled, then shook my head. "Actually I can't say I learned much, except I am sure that she is innocent. She's never left her small village near Galway, until she had to flee when her brothers were arrested. So how would she be likely to meet any Englishman?" I paused, as something nagged at the back of my brain. "And she's a timid, insecure little thing—worried about how she'll make her way to Chicago and how she can earn money. I can't see her stabbing a stranger. What's more—" I went on, warming to my subject now, "she was crying because she'd had to use her train fare to pay for the boardinghouse and now has no money to travel to her relatives. So that rules her out as a thief, trying to steal his wallet."

"It does seem to," Daniel agreed. "You tried. That was the main thing. I'll drive you home."

He cranked the motor and it roared to life, then he hopped in and off we went. I have to confess that I loved that feeling of speed as I had to hold on to my hat, even though the air was still chilly in my face. As we drove I toyed with what I had just said. Something had worried me. I'd said that Rose couldn't have met an Englishman because she came from a remote village, but so did I. And I had to fight off a man who tried to rape me. He lived in the big house, near us in Ireland, but he was the English landowner. An Englishman. Was it possible that this man had a property in Ireland?

And Rose had said that she'd managed to fight off the young Englishman on the boat by jabbing him with her hatpin—something I'd tried myself before now. So she might seem timid, but she could fight when necessary. Having been attacked by a man more than once, I created a possible scenario in my head. If she had gone looking for the ladies' WC on the island and this man had tried to drag her into an unused room to have his way with her, might she have fought for her life? Might she have grabbed a knife and stabbed him? It seemed rather implausible, but if I got to know her better, maybe she'd confess something like that to a good friend like me.

Fourteen

After my chat with Rose I was anxious to get back to Ellis Island and see if I could find anything at all that might lead to the real murderer. So I had gone straight over to Sid and Gus's and asked them if we could possibly arrange for a visit the next day. But things don't always work out as we plan them, do they? The next morning the weather changed yet again. I was awoken by rain hammering against the window. The sky was leaden. I hoped that Sid and Gus would not change their minds and put off the visit to the island. They were not especially good about enduring hardships, having never had to walk to school in the driving rain on many an occasion like me.

"Hurry up with your breakfast, Bridie," my mother-in-law chided as Bridie made herself a second slice of toast with dripping on it. "The ladies will be waiting."

"Bridie isn't getting her lessons today, Mother," I said. "The ladies are going back to Ellis Island with another load of clothing, and we promised we'd go and help them again."

Mrs. Sullivan stared out the window. "They'll surely not be going on a day like this? I'd certainly not be wanting to cross the choppy waters to get to the island. You'll be soaked to the skin if you're not blown away."

"The last boat did have a little cabin," I said. "I expect we'll be fine."

"Can you not put it off for a few days, until the weather clears again?" she asked.

I knew that in theory we could, but who knew when Sid and Gus would tire of this latest philanthropy and find something that excited them elsewhere? Their attention span wasn't always the longest. Also I was driven by the desire to get at the truth. Maybe I could find something on Ellis Island that the police had not managed to unearth. I thought this was unlikely. But then, not all the guards were trustworthy. I had found out this before. They were not above helping themselves to anything that took their fancy in the baggage room. Maybe a fat wallet was too much of a temptation. But how I was going to find out any more on this subject I had no idea. I'd have to rely on a little Irish luck.

"I'll go over and find out if they are brave enough to venture out as soon as I've washed up the breakfast things," I said. "I don't suppose they'll want to leave too soon. They are not the earliest of risers. And by then, who knows, the weather might have cleared."

"It looks like it's set in for days, if you ask me," she replied in gloomy fashion.

"In that case the poor souls arriving here will be sorely in need of warm clothing, won't they? All the more reason to go over there right now."

I gathered the dishes from the table and deposited them in the sink. Then I sent Bridie across the street to see when Sid and Gus might be ready. She returned saying that they thought the weather was simply too unpleasant today and why not put it off until next week?

I was across the street without waiting to put on my scarf.

"I can understand that you'd not want to go today," I said as Gus dragged me in out of the deluge. "But I'm actually helping Daniel with the murder investigation right now. Would you mind much if Bridie and I take some of the clothes and go by ourselves today?"

That, of course, changed their minds. "Molly, if there is something we can do to help with the investigation, then of course we'll come today," Gus said. "You know how we love being Watson to your Holmes."

So an hour later we set off, in two cabs, our laps piled high with more bundles of clothes and, for me, a growing sense of excitement. As I had lain in bed that night I had gone through possible scenarios in my head.

If the murderer was a guard, only attempting a simple robbery that had gone wrong, then it would be harder to find any clues. He'd have had plenty of opportunity to toss the knife into the harbor, obliterate any traces of blood from his clothing, and act as if nothing had happened. But if it was a fellow immigrant—either another opportunist who saw money in a wallet or someone with a compelling motive to make sure that Henry Darby did not step ashore in New York, then things would have been more complicated. The murderer had counted on killing in a secluded spot, then slipping ashore on the next ferry to the railway terminus in New Jersey. It was possible he or she might well have done so and be heaving a sigh of relief at this moment in Chicago or St. Louis or wherever they were headed.

But if he had planned to stay in New York, then the ferry to Manhattan had not turned up, having encountered a minor iceberg. While he was held up on the island the body was discovered and he was instructed not to move. So it was just possible that the murderer had had to hide the knife somewhere—maybe the wallet, too, having extracted the cash. That was another question in my mind: Had the wallet been taken because it contained Henry Darby's identity or was it just a robbery? Was it even possible that the man had no identification on him for some reason? Did he want to be incognito on the island? But then of course he would have needed his travel document when he had to enter the registration room. Those steerage passengers all had labels around their necks stating who they were and which ship they had arrived on. The labels had to match the ship's manifesto. But this man had come over in a second-class cabin. How had he explained that away? And what in God's name had made him take the ferry to the island rather than walk ashore to be lost in the multitudes of New York City? I worried that we would never know.

"So what is our assignment for today?" Sid asked. We were clinging to each other as the little boat bobbed and bucked in the waves, sending sheets of icy spray onto the deck.

"To cover for me while I snoop around and ask questions," I said.

"That's no fun," Sid retorted.

"You can chat with the guards if you like," I added hastily. "Ask them what they know about the murder. Say everyone is talking about it in the New York drawing rooms and they think one of the guards might have done it. See what their reaction is."

"Great idea." Sid looked pleased. "They might well have their suspicions."

I wasn't sure I had been entirely wise with this suggestion. Sid and Gus were more enthusiastic than tactful, and if I were a guard and a well-dressed society lady started quizzing me, I don't think I'd be willing to share any suspicions with them. But on the other hand, it might start them muttering to each other when Sid and Gus were out of earshot. And I might just overhear something useful.

We arrived at the dock and a crew member jumped ashore to tie up the still-rocking boat.

"Welcome, ladies. You're back again, are you?" the same official who had helped us before greeted us. "It's very charitable of you, especially on a day like this. Not the day you'd choose to make a sea crossing, is it?"

"It is a trifle wet," Gus said, accepting his hand as he helped us ashore. By the time we were escorted into the main building we were quite soaked through.

"I think we should help ourselves to some of these clothes, Molly," Bridie said. "I'm horribly wet and cold."

"That's not a bad idea." I smiled at her. "They are certainly better quality than ours, aren't they? I don't suppose Sid and Gus would mind if you found a cape or scarf that suited you if there is something small enough."

Bridie gave a hopeful little smile.

"Now, where should we set you up, ladies?" the official asked as he led us into the building. "Last time you were out by the kissing post, weren't you? I wouldn't advise that today, however. Maybe by the cashiers where the immigrants can change their money after they've passed through the Great Hall?"

"Yes, that should work well, shouldn't it, Molly?" Gus asked. I agreed that it would.

As two tables were set up for us the official asked, "And you'll no doubt be wanting the rest of your stuff?"

"Rest of what stuff?" Sid asked, shooting me a surprised glance.

"Well, the last time you were here some of the ladies didn't finish handing out the bundles they had brought with them." Cordelia Ransom, I thought. She had skipped out early. "We didn't realize there was a pile of clothing waiting to be distributed until the police came and told us not to touch anything." He leaned closer. "You may not have heard, but there was a distressing incident that day you were there."

"Really? What happened? A fight between immigrants?" Sid asked, giving him an eager smile.

He shook his head. "Much worse than that. A poor gentleman was found stabbed in one of the side rooms. It was lucky really that your lady had left the clothes behind, because I told one of our boys to find somewhere to put them until you ladies returned again. He was looking for the right place to store them and opened the door to this particular room and saw the body on the floor. Otherwise he might have lain there for days."

"Good heavens. How amazing," Gus said. I hoped they wouldn't go overboard in their enthusiasm. "Did they find out who killed this poor man?"

"Not that I've heard," he said. "We've had the police here several times, snooping around. Taking fingerprints, if you please. Did you ever hear of such a thing? That's how they identify criminals these days, so it seems. Everyone has a different fingerprint. What will they think of next?" I chuckled. "Well, I shouldn't keep you. We've a ferry coming in from an Italian ship as we speak and I've no doubt they'll be glad of your clothing, poor things. Some of them arrive in next to rags, don't they?" He started to leave, then turned back. "I'll have one of my lads retrieve the clothing that was left."

"Oh, please don't concern yourself," I said swiftly. "My daughter and I can go and find the clothes ourselves. I'm sure you'll be extra busy any minute."

"We will too," he said, "but I can't have delicate, well-born ladies like you lugging big bundles of stuff. I'll find someone to do it."

Darn, I muttered. I had hoped it would give me a chance to snoop in the actual room where the murder took place. Instead I turned to help Sid and Gus, who were already untying bundles and starting to place piles of gloves, scarves, shawls, and overcoats on the tables.

"Children's clothes over here, Molly," Gus said. "I'm afraid we don't have too many of them. I wish we knew more people with children. They were snapped up instantly last time, weren't they?"

"Well, they are beautiful," Bridie said. "Look at the little girl's coat with a fur muff. I would have loved something like that."

"If you want a fur muff, my darling, you shall have one," Sid said. "What kind of fur? White, or died some other color?"

"You shouldn't spoil her, Sid," I said.

"That's not spoiling. Everyone should own a fur muff." Sid gave me a challenging look.

She had hardly finished speaking when the first people came out of the Registry Room and saw us. They hung back, hesitating until Sid said, "You need warm clothes? Please—come and see."

"Clothes? We take? For us?" a woman asked. "Gratis?"

Gus nodded. "Help yourself to something warm."

"Madonna!" The woman turned and called out a stream of Italian. Instantly we were besieged by a throng of women, all fighting to grab what was on the table.

"Ladies. Orderly, please," Sid said in a commanding voice. "Form a line." She demonstrated. "No more clothes until you do."

Some of them must have understood English or at least Sid's pantomime. After much shuffling and pushing, they did so. A young guard arrived, carrying a bin full of clothing.

"This is what was left from before," he said. "Shall I just put it down here?"

"Thank you," I replied. "Bridie, would you like to take out the items and add them to the right piles on the table?" I leaned closer. "If you happen to find something that you could wear, you can keep it back."

Her eyes lit up. "All right," she said, and started digging into the bin. "Ooh, that's a lovely coat," she said.

I glanced quickly. "Too big. You'd drown in it. Here, give it to this lady with the baby."

Bridie handed it over, a little reluctantly, I felt. The woman tried to kiss her and offered up blessings. At least they sounded like blessings from all the saints. Bridie looked a little scared. She turned back to the bin again and started putting out more items. Then she gave an excited little gasp.

"Molly, there's a fur muff. Look—just like I wanted!" She dragged it out. It was white rabbit fur, lined with red satin. "Can I possibly have it, do you think?'

"I think you can," I said. "Your wages for coming to help us."

She gave an excited little smile, hung it around her neck, and slipped her hands into it. The next moment she gave a cry and pulled out her hand.

"What is it?" I asked.

"Something sharp." She was gazing down at her hand in disbelief. "Look. I'm bleeding."

Drops of red blood dripped onto the white fur.

I reached into my pocket. "Here's my handkerchief. It's only a scratch. Let's see what could have done that?"

Cautiously I reached into the muff and felt cold steel. I drew it out. It was a knife with a long, thin blade.

Fifteen

We stood staring at the knife in horrified silence.

"Who would be unkind enough to put a knife into a muff where some girl could cut herself?" Bridie asked in a shaky voice. She was holding my handkerchief to her hand, which mercifully no longer seemed to be bleeding badly.

"I think I know," I said. I looked across to Sid at the table next to me. "Sid, do you happen to have a clean handkerchief in your pockets?"

"I think I do." She reached into pockets on both sides of her coat and brought out a neatly folded linen square. I took it, opened it, and laid the knife on it.

"What on earth's that?" Sid asked.

"I believe it's the knife that stabbed our murder victim," I said. "The killer had to dispose of the knife in a hurry and couldn't get out to the dock to throw it into the water, so he thrust it into the bin of clothing where it wasn't likely to be found for a while. Giving him a chance to be far away when it was found." I examined the knife as it lay on the handkerchief. "I wonder if he thought to wipe the handle for fingerprints. It looks like an ordinary kitchen knife, doesn't it?"

"A paring knife, maybe?" Sid suggested. "Quite a big one. Could well have come from the kitchens here, since the immigrants had to leave their own baggage downstairs."

"I think I might go and ask," I said. "Can you all hold the fort until I get back?"

"And when do we get a turn to charm the guards?" Gus asked.

"When I come back from the kitchens or you run out of clothing." I didn't wait another second but pushed my way through the crowd. Luckily I had been to the island before. I knew the kitchen and dining room were in a building that connected at this end of the Great Hall. I found the hall and hurried along it without being stopped. The clatter of pots and pans and the smell of frying onions told me that I was in the right place. I pushed open a door.

"Can I help you, miss?" A woman stepped out to block my path. She was a thin, scrawny-looking little thing one would have thought too frail to be working in a kitchen.

"We wondered if this might be one of your knives?" I asked, opening the handkerchief to reveal it. She went to take it. "Please don't touch," I said hastily. "This might be a murder weapon."

"Mercy me," she said. I could hear from the way she said it that she too was originally from Ireland.

"You heard that a man was stabbed on the island a few days ago, did you?" I asked.

"We did. We couldn't believe it."

"Do you recognize the knife, then?"

"I'd say it was one of ours, all right," she went on. "Martha got in trouble when it seemed there was a knife missing from the block. Where did you find it?"

"I'm one of the ladies who came to hand out clothing the other day," I said. "One barrel of clothing was left behind and the knife was hidden in it. I suspect the killer thrust the knife in among the clothes, thinking it wouldn't be found for a while."

"Holy Mother of God," the woman muttered.

"I'm afraid I have to hand it over to the police," I said, "but you can tell your supervisor that your friend was not to blame. Someone came into the kitchen and took it." I paused, digesting this. "Did you happen to see any stranger come into the kitchen at any time?"

"They are coming in and out all the time when they are detained on the island and we have to feed them," she said. "That evening, I remember, there was some kind of delay with the boats, wasn't there? A whole lot of immigrants who had been processed but couldn't go any further, so we were instructed to serve them a meal. It was chaos, you know. People coming in and out, grabbing plates and cutlery and bringing back dirty plates."

An ideal opportunity for a murderer, I thought. Nobody would have seen a kitchen knife being taken. This made me realize that it was an opportunistic killing rather than a planned one. The murderer had taken advantage of milling crowds, chaotic conditions. This pushed the crime back later than we had thought. And it also explained why Mr. Edwin Cromer was not willing to wait his turn to eat but had tried to slip out to the dining room via a side corridor and probably back stairs. We might need to rethink a lot of things.

I decided that a fellow Irishwoman might be happy to chat with me. A welcome diversion from peeling potatoes.

"I don't suppose the police will ever find the person who did it," I said. "You haven't heard any gossip about it, have you?"

She gave a tired shrug of the shoulders. "I work in the kitchen, my dear. We don't have time to listen to gossip and besides, nobody talks to us. We're at the bottom of the heap when it comes to island workers. Us and the cleaners and the ward maids in the hospital. All we heard was some poor fellow got himself stabbed. I thought it was probably some kind of fight. Vendetta, you know. Those guys from Sicily are always killing each other."

"It was an Englishman, so I've heard. An older man. Well dressed."

"Really? What was he doing here? We don't often get 'em well dressed, or English."

"I wondered if it might have been a robbery," I said. I leaned closer to her. "I've heard that some of the guards might enjoy helping themselves to the odd item they like in the baggage room?"

"I wouldn't know," she said quickly. "Like I told you, we're stuck here in the kitchen and don't see anything of what goes on." She paused, frowning. "Mind you—funny you should say that. I did see something the other day. I was taking out the rubbish when I saw one of the guards digging into one of the trash bins and he said to his friend, 'Would you look what I just found.' And it was a wallet. A real pigskin wallet."

"Did you see what was in it?"

"I saw him look and say, 'Money in it too.' What was someone thinking, throwing it into the trash?"

"And what did he do with it?" I was trying to stay calm and disinterested.

"His friend said, 'Is there a name in it? We should hand it in and let them find the owner. It must have fallen out of a pocket by mistake. Or maybe a pickpocket took it and then lost his nerve.'"

"And?" I asked.

"And the first fellow says, 'There's no name in at all. So I say finders keepers. If I hand it in they'll only keep the money for themselves, won't they? Here, I'll share with you. Take this.' And the other fellow says, 'What is it?' And the first says, 'Let's take a look,' and he opens this big white-looking piece of paper and he says, 'Well, would you look at that. It says it's an English five-pound note.' And I could see that there were several of them." She looked up at me. "That's a lot of money, isn't it?"

"Quite a bit, I should think."

"What is a new immigrant doing coming in with money like that?"

"Could be his life savings," I suggested.

I saw her brain working, beginning to put two and two together. "Here, miss. You don't think that wallet had anything to do with the murdered man, do you?"

"Quite possibly," I said. "Do you happen to remember which guards they were?"

She grinned. "I do, because one of them is not at all bad looking. Gives himself airs a bit, but he's got a good head of dark hair on him and a fine black mustache. Maybe Italian. But he's tall for an Eyetie. Quite tall." She gave me a hopeful little smile, then added, "The other was a portly chap. Reddish hair like yours, but fairer. Big round face."

"Thank you," I said. "I'll pass along what you told me to the police. You've been very helpful."

"I won't have to talk to them myself, will I? And you won't say I'm the one who told you? I don't want to be seen as one who blabs to the police."

"I understand. I'll make sure everything's smooth sailing for you. I must be getting back to the other ladies now. Thank you again—what was your name?"

"Coleen, miss. Coleen Burke."

"Nice to meet you, Coleen."

As I turned to go I saw her face change yet again as if there was something else she wanted to say. "You're one of the ladies who handed out the clothing?"

"That's right."

"They were giving away some lovely things there, weren't they? I saw some myself. Good warm coats and scarves. Better than we can afford for ourselves. I said to my friend at the time, 'I wouldn't mind being one of those immigrants and being able to help myself to one of those.'"

"Hold on, Coleen." I wagged a finger at her. "Let me go and see what I can find. You've been a big help."

I dashed back to our tables in the foyer. The pile had already shrunk quite a bit, but I rummaged through it and found a lovely wool shawl, black with a pattern of red roses on it. I took it and made my way back to the kitchens.

"For your trouble," I said to Coleen. She gave me a big, delighted smile.

"God bless you, lady," she said. "May all the saints smile down on you."

I wondered if I should try to check out the room where the murder took place myself. But both Rose and Mr. Cromer said they had gone into a side corridor at the back of the Registry Room. Which would mean they hadn't been processed, and therefore were not eligible to get a meal—which was why he tried to slink out unobserved. That alone didn't reflect well on his character, did it? If I wanted to look at that hallway for myself, it would mean going around the outside of the building in that driving rain or through the Great Hall, against the flow of traffic—through that winding maze of benches and iron railings and seething humanity. I'd be stopped. I'd have to explain my reasons. Unlike the rest of the Vassar ladies, I didn't immediately look like a visiting benefactor. No fox fur around my neck. They might not even believe I was not an immigrant trying to avoid the inspection process.

And now that we had located both objects the police wanted there wasn't likely to be anything of interest I could find in that room. They had dusted it for fingerprints, Daniel had said. I glanced down with a look of satisfaction at the object I carried in my hands. What a coup that would be to hand it over to Daniel! And to tell him about the wallet, too. I'd show him his wife was a detective force to be reckoned with.

I was dying to leave the island at that moment, to take the knife in triumph to my husband at police headquarters. But we still had clothing to be handed out and a hopeful line of women waiting for it. Also, as Sid and Gus pointed out, they were supposed to do their share of the sleuthing. They did look like visiting benefactors. I gave them a description of the two guards who had been involved with finding the wallet.

"Now, be tactful, won't you?" I said. "Make it clear that you're not reporting them and you don't want the money but you would like to know what happened to the wallet and if there was any kind of identification on it."

"Got it." Sid gave me an excited nod.

"And if you can find your way to the back of the Great Hall, perhaps you could manage to take a look at the corridor where the murder took place. I'd like to get a feel of the place for myself."

"It's too bad I didn't bring my new Brownie camera," Gus said. "But then the light's not good enough indoors anyway. We'll give you a complete report, Molly. Don't worry. Are you sure you can hold the fort?"

"Bridie and I can do it, can't we, my darling?" I asked.

"But what about my wounded hand?" Bridie asked dramatically as she held out the hand wrapped in its bloodstained handkerchief. "Will I need to go to a hospital or see a doctor?"

"Let me see," Gus said.

Bridie removed the handkerchief and we all looked at her hand. There was luckily only a superficial cut across the palm and it had almost stopped bleeding.

"You'll live," Sid said. "Use the other hand for now." When Bridie saw she wasn't going to get sympathy, she nodded, wrapped her hand in the handkerchief again, and turned back to the waiting line of immigrants.

We kept handing out clothing until it was all gone. The last of the women turned away despondently, making me wish that we could collect more and come back every day from now on. Bridie must have been feeling the same.

"I wish we could have helped them all, don't you?" she whispered. "Did you see that lady's face? The one with the three little girls? Perhaps I should give her my muff?"

"I think the police might want to take a look at your muff, so you'd better keep it," I said, and saw the relieved smile on her face.

"We can't help everyone, my love," I said, putting an arm around her shoulder. "Think of all the starving people in the city, all the children with no home. We can just try to help a few of them."

"When I'm done with my education, I'll want to do something special and important," she said. "Auntie Sid and Auntie Gus do some kind things, but then they go off and try something else. I would want to make a real difference—you know, fight for votes for women or be a doctor and find a cure for cholera."

"Those are grand ambitions, Bridie," I said. "Just keep working hard and believing and I'm sure you'll make them happen."

"I'll be learning a lot from the ladies, but then I'll learn even more when they find a good school for me," she said. I shot a quick glance at her. This was a new, confident Bridie, so different from the scared little girl I had brought across from Ireland. In a way I was proud to see a person emerging, but I didn't want her to be setting her hopes too high—getting above herself, as my mother would have said.

We were ready to leave when Sid and Gus returned, breathing excitedly. "Mission accomplished," Sid said. "We found the big fellow with the light red hair and he seemed very worried that we'd learned about the wallet. He kept insisting that he didn't want to take any of the money but his pal said that the bosses would only keep it all for themselves. He said as far as he could see there was no calling card or any other identification in it, but that Mario had put it in his pocket." She leaned closer. "And listen to this. When I asked where we could find Mario, he told me that Mario had quit at the end of last week. So Gus and I were wondering if there was perhaps quite a bit of money in that wallet?"

"It's possible," I said. "But then we have to ask who would throw away a wallet stuffed with money? It doesn't make sense."

"I agree," Gus said. "And we managed to find out where the murder room was located. It was down a side staircase to one side of the baggage hall. And it was locked. We tried."

I digested this. So the Englishman who saw Rose coming out of the room had gone down a back staircase. That would make sense if he was trying to get to the dining hall. It would be the only way for someone at the back of the line to bypass the hordes waiting their turn to be processed. He could have been spotted slinking out of the hall, but then it was unlikely that anyone else would have seen a person on that corridor down below.

"I think we've learned all we're going to," I said.

"We can't give up now." Sid looked to Gus for confirmation. "We're here, on the island. There must be more we can do. Question other guards? Find out who passed through that afternoon and whether any of them came from near this man in England?"

I tried not to smile. "I think the police have questioned the guards and they have the passenger manifests. And they have cabled Scotland Yard asking for information on the man who was killed. We should know more when we find out who he was and what he was doing in America."

The rain was still coming down as we made our way back to the boat, and we got well and truly soaked as we crossed back to Manhattan. I had intended to deliver the knife straight to Daniel at police headquarters, but then I saw Bridie shivering and Sid and Gus looking quite miserably stoic and decided we all needed to go straight home and change out of our wet clothes. We'd be no use to anybody if we all came down with chills. And if Daniel happened to be out on an assignment, I certainly didn't want to leave the knife on his desk for anybody to find. So we rode home together, squashed into one cab.

"Will you come in and have some hot coffee, Molly?" Sid asked.

"No, thank you. Not this time," I said. "I need to change out of these wet things and so does Bridie, and then I should be taking over my wifely and motherly duties from my mother-in-law."

Sid grinned as I said this. Then she turned to Bridie. "Make sure you come over to us after you've changed your clothes, young lady. We can't have you skipping too many lessons. Today we'll tackle algebra."

"Algebra?"

"A vital skill for any educated woman. And Gus will start you on American history. You can't go to Vassar someday if you don't know how the republic was founded."

"All right." Bridie nodded, trying to muster a bright and confident smile. I'd have felt the same if someone had wanted to teach me algebra, I thought. Although I'd been quite good at arithmetic I had found it a struggle to do pounds and ounces, gills and pints, not to mention rods, poles, and perches.

We went into the house, changed, and warmed ourselves up with the hot potato soup that Daniel's mother had made. Then I sent Bridie off for her lessons while I gave Liam my full attention. He was a bit clingy, which I could understand. I had been out quite a lot lately. I paused to think about this: my life had become confined to my motherly duties. Now I was reclaiming bits of my former self and I was enjoying it. I remembered the excitement of the chase, following clues, homing in for the kill. I had been in danger at times, certainly terrified at times, but I had known I was alive, every single minute.

Sixteen

When Liam was napping I braved the inclement weather and went out to shop for our supper. Since I was eager to show Daniel my brilliant find on the island I decided I'd make it a good meal. One that would put him in the right sort of mood to appreciate his wife and her accomplishments. Should it be steak? I asked myself. Or roast beef? I decided on the latter, had the butcher find me a nice little topside, and put it in to roast with potatoes and parsnips around it, praying that for once Daniel would arrive home on time.

"Is this some kind of special occasion?" Mother Sullivan asked me. "Going to town in the middle of the week? We only ever had roast beef on a Sunday, and then only on special Sundays."

"I just felt I'd been neglecting you all a bit recently," I said. "And the meat was a good price, so why not?"

"Why not indeed," she said. "If you're ever the wife of a congressman or senator you'll be required to entertain a lot. You should start learning to prepare more adventurous dishes."

"To my mind it's hard to beat a good roast beef and two veg," I said. Then I relented. "But you can show me some of your favorites, I'm happy to learn."

"Well now, I'll have to think about that," she said, and I saw that

I'd caught her out. I remembered Daniel telling me that his mother had always served simple Irish food at home and his father had complained once when she had tried something more elaborate like spaghetti. "Don't serve me any more of that foreign muck," he had said.

Once the dinner was cooking I went back into the freezing cold front parlor, where I had set up the sewing machine on a small table, and got to work on Bridie's dress. I needed something to take my mind off that knife, now lying on the sideboard in this room, out of harm's way. I couldn't wait to tell Daniel everything. I could imagine a surprised, impressed look coming over his face. "You accomplished what all my men together couldn't, Molly." That's what he'd say. I grinned to myself as I formed my modest reply.

I found my machine skills came back to me quickly, even though I had never used a machine where I had to turn the handle with one hand while steering the fabric with the other. Even so I breezed through the first of the seams, managed the pleats in the bodice, and was feeling rather pleased with myself until I noticed I had sewn one sleeve inside out. Of course I was just in the middle of unpicking it when Mother Sullivan poked her head around the door.

"I thought you'd be needing a cup of tea," she said, putting one down beside me. "It's freezing in here. Can you not bring your sewing through to the kitchen table? I've cleaned it off."

"You're right, it is freezing," I said, hastily pushing that sleeve under the bodice section. "But I should stop soon anyway. Liam will need to be fed and bathed and Daniel should be home."

"How are you coming along?" She peered over my shoulder.

"Well. I'm about to set the sleeves into the bodice and then it will be the bodice to the skirt, the buttons down the back, and hem everything. I should have it done tomorrow and then I can start on her party dress. I'd love that to be a surprise for her when we go to Miss Van Woekem's tea party on Saturday."

"It was a lucky day when you took charge of that girl," she said. "Who knows where she would have ended up if you hadn't."

"Right now she'd be a household slave for her father and his new wife on their pig farm in Ireland," I said with a wry smile. "I am still impressed with the way she spoke up and defied him. That took real courage."

Mrs. Sullivan gave me a knowing look. "There's more to that one than meets the eye," she said. "She likes to appear as a sweet, meek little thing, but she's already learning how to get her way. Look how she manipulates those two ladies. Has them wrapped around her little finger, doesn't she?"

"Oh, I don't think she manipulates them," I said. "They are thrilled to have a lively young mind to develop."

I went back to my unpicking, and before my hands completely froze I had sewn the sleeve seam the right way round and pinned it to the armhole. As I worked I thought about Bridie. Was she learning to be devious? I had always seen her as sweet, innocent, and compliant. I'd have to watch out for signs that she was learning to get her own way. I put the cover on the sewing machine and went back into the delightful warmth of the kitchen. A little before six the front door opened, sending a blast of cold air down the hallway to us.

"Dada. Dada home!" Liam yelled and ran down the hall to him. I heard Liam give a squeal of delight as Daniel picked him up. "How's my big boy, then?" I heard him say. I waited for him to take off his outer garments and then he came into the kitchen, carrying Liam over his shoulder like a sack of potatoes.

"Look what I found, Mama," Daniel said. "What should I do with this, then? Shall we keep it? Throw it away?" He let Liam fall into his arms. "Or maybe put it in the stew pot for our dinner?" Liam squealed with delight again and I smiled, thinking what a wonderful father Daniel had turned out to be and how much I wanted another baby. Soon, too soon, Liam would be a big boy with a mind of his own and past this stage of delight in his parents.

"Oh, I think we might keep him," I said as Daniel set his son down on his seat at the table.

"What's for dinner? It smells wonderful," Daniel said.

I opened the oven and brought out the roasting pan. "Roast beef and all the trimmings," I said.

"Heavens above. It's not someone's birthday, is it?" he asked. "And I know I didn't miss an anniversary."

"It's just an ordinary night, but I thought we could all do with a treat," I said. "Besides, it's not really that extravagant. I'll be able to get three meals out of this. Now, set the table, Bridie, and we'll eat."

I glanced across and saw her face. It was stoic, and I realized that all the fuss we had been making of Liam had her feeling left out. "After dinner we can try on your new dress," I said. "I might even finish it tomorrow."

"That's good," she said, managing a little smile now.

Daniel carved. We sat down and started to eat. "And what did you do today, Bridie?" he asked, also realizing that we had been ignoring her.

"We went to Ellis Island," she said. "And I cut my hand in the muff and it turned out to be—"

"Later, Bridie," I said. "Let's finish our dinner first."

Daniel was now frowning as he looked at me. "You went back to Ellis Island? Without telling me? Without asking my permission?"

"And why should I be asking permission to go and give warm coats to the poor immigrant women?" I demanded, feeling my cheeks flushing red. "We went with Sid and Gus, just like we did last week. And awfully glad of the clothing they were, the poor things, on such an inclement day."

"I see." Daniel said no more, but his eyes held mine as he picked up his knife and fork and started eating. He knew me well enough to know when I wasn't quite being truthful.

We finished our meal and Daniel said he was going through to the back parlor to have a whiskey while we washed up. I turned to Daniel's mother and Bridie. "Can I leave it to you to start on the washing up? I've something important to discuss with my husband,"

I said. I took Daniel's arm and steered him away from the back parlor. "In here first, please. I've something to show you."

"All right." He gave me a querying look. "Is this something that needs to be done in here? It's like entering an ice house."

"It won't take long," I said, "but I had to make sure everything was safe."

"Safe?"

"Listen, Daniel," I said. "On Ellis Island today we had a bit of luck. There was a bin of clothing left from our earlier visit. Bridie was putting the items out on the tables and she saw a fur muff, just like the one she'd been wanting. She put her hand into it, screamed, and pulled it out all bloody. You'll never guess what was inside that muff." I walked over to the sideboard, picked up the knife, and carried it to Daniel, peeling back the handkerchief that covered it.

"My God." Instinctively he reached out to touch it. I jerked it away. "Don't touch."

"You think this is the knife that killed him?"

"I would guess so, wouldn't you? The murderer was intending to throw the knife into the water but suddenly wasn't allowed to go anywhere. He was trapped in that big hall with hundreds of other immigrants. He couldn't be caught with the knife on him, so he plunged it into a bin of clothing where it wasn't likely to be found until he was safely far away."

I put it down on the table in front of him. "I tried to be as careful as possible so that we didn't wipe any possible fingerprints."

"Why didn't you bring it to me straight away?" he asked.

"I didn't know if you'd be in your office and I didn't want to risk any other officer getting it and maybe claiming the credit for it. What's more, I know where it came from. I interviewed one of the kitchen workers and she said it was theirs and another of the women had gotten in trouble for losing it. And it was a brilliant stroke of luck that I spoke with this particular woman, because she told me that—"

"Molly. Are you trying to tell me that you were doing police work on the island? Interviewing people? Snooping around? Did you really just happen to find the knife or were you actually looking for it?"

"Hold your horses, Daniel Sullivan," I said angrily. "I found your knife for you. Something none of your men had managed to do. And instead of saying thank you you're starting to attack me."

He was still glaring at me. "You went back to that island again without my permission, didn't you? Not just to hand out clothing but to have a good snoop around, so you could prove yourself smarter than the NYPD."

When I am put on the defensive it riles my fighting spirit. "As it happened that wasn't too hard, was it?" I said, staring at him triumphantly.

"Molly, when I agreed to let you interview Rose, I wasn't giving you free rein to take over my investigation. You know damned well—"

"Don't swear, Daniel," I interrupted.

"Sorry. You have me riled up," he said. "You know darned well that I would not have given you permission to go and question people on the island, so you resorted to subterfuge. Do you realize what harm you might have done? If someone who works on the island is involved in any way and you've said the wrong thing, you might have tipped that person off that we're checking on them."

"Speaking of someone on the island being involved," I said, "I can also tell you what happened to the wallet and who you should be looking for."

"What?" His jaw actually dropped. "Molly, now you've really gone too far."

"And what makes you think I'm not as good at asking questions as you are? I'm better, in fact, because a woman working in the kitchen is not going to gossip with you, is she? We were chatting, woman to woman, and she let me know that she overheard two of the guards." And I repeated the whole scene to him. "And now one of those guards has left his job. So if I were you, I'd be looking for a handsome Italian called Mario. He says he found the wallet in a rubbish bin, but who is to say he wasn't the actual robber and murderer? Or in the very least involved in some way?"

Daniel was still shaking his head in disbelief. "I don't know what to do about you."

"You could say 'thank you very much for helping to solve my case for me.'" I came over and wrapped my arms around his neck. "Don't keep scowling like that, Daniel. Contrary to what you are thinking we did find the knife exactly as I've told you. It looked like a big paring knife, and it was when I went to the kitchen to see if it had come from there the woman let slip about the two guards. I wasn't grilling anybody. I wasn't even snooping."

"I'm sorry," he said after a pause. "I suppose I should be grateful to you. If what you were told is correct, then maybe this will turn out to be the simplest of cases—a robbery that went wrong."

"And nothing to do with poor Rose," I replied. "When do you think she can be released from your custody? Her relatives in Chicago are waiting for her and she has no money here."

He was looking down at me in more tender fashion now. "Not quite yet, I'm afraid. She still isn't off the hook, at least not until we have tested that knife for fingerprints."

"I've just come up with a brilliant idea," I exclaimed. "I told you Miss Van Woekem had a fall and at the moment she is stuck with an absolutely terrible new maid who is useless. Rose happened to mention that she'd been a companion to an old lady back home. What if we sent her to help Miss Van Woekem, at least until she finds a better maid?"

Daniel frowned. "I'm not sure that is a good idea, Molly. This is someone who still has not been cleared of a serious crime. We can't put an old lady at risk."

"Oh, come on, Daniel. You can't honestly tell me that you see that poor girl as a murderer? And how, in God's name, could she have any connection at all to a man from London when she had never left her village in Ireland until she traveled down to Queenstown to board the ship? Have you not found out any more details on him yet?"

"As a matter of fact we got a cable today," Daniel replied. He walked over to the window, toyed with the drapes, and then looked back at me. "From Scotland Yard. It seems that Mr. Henry Darby is a private detective. The sort who undertakes discreet inquiries for the upper classes. And they seemed to think he was on the trail of a jewel thief."

"A jewel thief?"

Daniel nodded. "Of course one can't glean much from a cable, but a valuable piece of jewelry was stolen at an exclusive party. Presumably by one of the guests, as the servers have all been thoroughly checked. The piece was a gift to a mistress, hence the man not wanting to involve the police or make it public."

"Goodness!" I exclaimed. "How exciting."

My thoughts were whirling wildly at this new information. "A member of the aristocracy stole a jewel? What kind of jewel?"

"That I can't tell you yet, except that it was valuable and unique."

"And this man was hired to find him and was presumably following him to America. He traveled second class but then got himself on the ferry to Ellis Island. That indicates that the person he was following was in steerage, doesn't it? But why steerage when he could obviously afford a better mode of transportation?"

"I can't tell you that, either," Daniel said.

Then I waved my arms excitedly. "The Englishman who accused Rose. What was his name? Edwin Cromer, right? You said he spoke with a posh accent. Have you searched his belongings? Have you questioned him again? Have any details of him come to light in England?"

"Only that he might have left England in a hurry because of gambling debts."

"So he's the sort of person who would be desperate enough to grab a piece of jewelry if he got the chance, and he flees to America, thinking that nobody is on his tail, but the detective corners him on the island and the Englishman stabs him. And . . . he points the finger at a poor innocent Irish girl who is wandering down corridors in search of a WC."

Daniel stood there for a moment before nodding. "You do make a good case," he said. "Except that his fingerprints are not to be found on the doorknob or in the room."

"Of course not. He's a pro. He was wearing gloves," I said.

"Again that's a possibility," he agreed.

"So you'll keep on questioning him and have Scotland Yard question his relatives—and find out if he was at the party where the jewel vanished?"

"I'm sure we'll do all those things," Daniel said.

I waved my hands excitedly again as I realized the implications. "There you are, then. That takes Rose off the hook, doesn't it? If this man was on the trail of a jewel thief who fled to New York, it's certainly not a girl from a humble cottage in Galway, is it? A girl who has never left Ireland. And if she had stolen an expensive piece of jewelry, she'd hardly be crying as she told me she had no money and didn't know how she'd make it to her relatives in Chicago."

"I suppose you're right," Daniel said at last. "She doesn't seem a likely candidate. All we have to go on is that her fingerprints show up inside that room."

"Only on the doorjamb inside, surely?"

"Yes, but . . ."

"She already explained that to me. She was reaching around to find the light switch because the room was in complete darkness."

"I see."

"And the Englishman chose her because she had fought him off on the ship. She stabbed him with her hatpin. He sounds like an all-around rotter."

There was another long pause. I went over to him and put a hand on his shoulder.

"So would you have any objection to me taking Rose to Miss Van Woekem? That way she'd be helping out a friend, earning some money, and you could put your constable outside the door so that she didn't run away if you were worried."

"I would have to approach Miss Van Woekem myself. Give her all the facts and see how she would feel about having someone like Rose in her house. I still see an element of risk, Molly."

"You can't believe an old lady would be in danger with other servants in the house and a constable outside?" I turned away from him, stalking angrily across the room. "Really, Daniel. You can't tell me that you believe Rose McSweeney is a cold-blooded killer who is so handy with a knife that she kills with one blow?" I warmed to my theme. "And where did she learn those knife skills? Killing chickens in her cottage in the bogs? Oh, and it's so likely that she is a jewel thief from a swank party in London, isn't it?"

"I do find that hard to believe," he said.

"So you'll go to Miss Van Woekem?"

"Very well," Daniel said at last. "I suppose we can give it a try."

I tried not to look too triumphant as we left the room.

Seventeen

I was so excited that night I found it hard to sleep. I pictured Rose's face as I told her the good news and when she saw Miss Van Woekem's lovely home.

"A match made in heaven," I told myself. It felt so good to know that I was doing something to help a fellow Irishwoman, to make up for the way I had been treated when I first arrived and had nothing and nobody. Daniel agreed to visit Miss Van Woekem that morning, after he had taken the knife to the fingerprint experts at police headquarters. If she was agreeable to the suggestion he'd let me know I'd be free to visit Rose.

"I hope you know what you're doing, Molly," he said. "She may turn out to be a complete disaster. Not because of her criminal past, but because she completely lacks housekeeping skills and refinement."

"She certainly can't be worse than the maid," I told Daniel. "She really is hopeless."

"Why does a lady like Miss Van Woekem employ a hopeless maid?" he asked. "She doesn't strike me as the charitable sort."

"Bad timing," I said. "Her real maid, who you remember was an absolute gem, asked to visit her mother, who is gravely ill. So Miss

Van Woekem sent for a temporary replacement from the girl's orphanage. And this uncouth girl was the only one they had available."

He was about to leave when something struck me. "Daniel, Rose doesn't know I'm married to you and I want to keep it that way. Can you find a way to tell Miss Van Woekem to call me Mrs. Murphy?"

Daniel raised his eyebrows at me. "So I'm Mr. Murphy now, am I?"

"No, you are not! I don't want her to know I have any connection to you. Remember, she still might be useful to your case."

So off he went. I waited impatiently for Daniel to send a message. Instead he showed up himself about ten o'clock, saying that he had visited Miss Van Woekem and she accepted the idea with enthusiasm. She said she enjoyed a good challenge and if Molly thought the girl would be suitable, she'd go along with it. Then he suggested he would drive us up to Gramercy Park in the police automobile.

"Then she'll know I am married to a policeman, and I don't want that," I said. "That's why I've called myself Mrs. Murphy. I thought she might open up to me more if I was an ordinary Irishwoman in a strange country, just like her."

"Well, I've warned Miss Van Woekem, but Rose will know the truth as soon as she sees me," Daniel pointed out. "I suppose you can pretend not to know me and I'll just be the policeman driving you."

"That won't work," I said. "I can't seem to be in cahoots with the police." I got up and walked across the room, thinking as I did so. "No, Daniel. Much better that she doesn't connect the two of us before she absolutely has to. If she thinks I'm your wife I'll lose the relationship we've managed to build. She won't open up to me again, will she? She sees you as the enemy, trying to pin a crime on a poor, defenseless immigrant." I shook my head. "I can't have you drive us, Daniel. I'll take her in a cab."

Daniel was frowning. "Molly, she is still, at this moment, a suspect in a murder inquiry. I can't allow the two of you to take off across

New York on your own. What is to stop her from jumping out and making off into the crowds, and we'll never see her again?"

I tried to hide my impatience. "I thought I just told you that she had no money to go to her relatives and that's why she'd be so happy to get this job. But anyway, if you're so worried, let one of your constables accompany us in the cab. We can squeeze in three people."

"I suppose so," he said hesitantly. He took a deep breath. "I trust your judgment, Molly. I know you want to help this woman because she reminds you of your own plight when you arrived in the city, but I hope you are doing the right thing."

"I hope so too," I said. "But now that I've found your knife for you we should definitely know whether Rose was the murderer in a day or two, shouldn't we? And your constable will be right outside the front door, keeping an eye on her, just as much as if she were in the boardinghouse."

"Why didn't I marry a submissive and uninquisitive little wife?" Daniel came over to plant a kiss on my forehead.

"You'd be bored to tears." I gave him a wicked grin. "But on the subject of automobiles, did you come here yourself in the police car? If so I wouldn't say no to a ride to Rose's boardinghouse."

"You see, I do have my uses." He slipped an arm around my shoulder. I was about to put on my coat when I remembered I hadn't asked my mother-in-law to do more babysitting duty. I hurried through to the back parlor, where she was sitting, knitting as usual. Liam was on the floor loading blocks into his toy horse and cart.

"Can I possibly impose on you to watch Liam again for a while this morning?" I said to my mother-in-law. "I know it's been an awful lot lately, but I've managed to find a companion for Miss Van Woekem, just until her real maid returns. I mean, we couldn't leave her to the mercy of that awful creature, could we?"

"Of course not. How clever of you to come up with someone," she said. Then she hesitated. "It's not an acquaintance of the women across the street, is it?"

I knew what she meant—bohemian, different, radical—but I pretended I didn't. "No, it's not," I said. "Their acquaintances mostly move in high society. I can't see any of them wanting to work as a companion. They are more interested in snagging a rich husband or working for the suffrage cause."

Luckily she didn't ask more questions, so I was not forced to admit it was Rose the murder suspect who was to become the companion. So with Bridie at her studies and Liam happily playing I set off with Daniel for Rose's boardinghouse. This time I went up without fanfare, tapped on the door, and went in. She had been bending over a drawer and scrambled to her feet with a look of horror on her face.

"I'm sorry. I didn't mean to startle you," I said. "I've come with good news."

She patted her hair in an embarrassed fashion, although it looked to me perfectly in place. "Good news? I'm free to go on my way?"

"Not that good," I said, "but everything looks hopeful. They have found the knife associated with the crime and if they can match the fingerprints on it, then you're clearly off the hook."

"I have to wait until they have tested the knife?" she said. "How long will that take? And how do they know it's the same knife that killed that poor man?"

"I expect the police will be able to detect traces of blood on it, as well fingerprints," I said. "But until then I've found you a job."

"A job?" She didn't look as thrilled as I thought she might. "What kind of job?'

"You said you were once a companion to an old lady? Well, last time I was here I mentioned an old lady who has had a fall and broken her leg. She desperately needs help right now and I think you'd be perfect."

Rose looked confused. "So did someone tell you I'm free to go now? Why haven't they told me? Because if I'm free I'll be heading for Chicago and my family as soon as I have the money."

I hesitated, not sure how to explain without telling her my husband was a policeman. "You're not exactly free yet, I'm afraid, but my husband pulled some strings to allow you a better situation. Wouldn't you like to get out of here?"

"Why, yes," she said, her face now lighting up. "That would be just lovely. Better than this dump anyway, sitting around all day and not allowed out. Mr. Murphy must be a powerful man?"

I chose not to answer that query and went on. "Well, you'd still have a constable on guard there, too, but at least it's a beautiful house with lots of lovely things in it. And she's not exactly a sweet old lady, she can be quite sharp and critical, but she's good-hearted. And you'll make enough money to send you on your way when you're free to go."

She came over to me now. "You're too good to me, Molly Murphy. I don't deserve it. God bless you for a saint. Truth be told I've been so depressed I've been wondering about just ending it all. And now here you are and I'm finding I have new hope."

"Come on, then," I said. "Let's get your things packed and ready to leave. You said your suitcase was stolen, so it shouldn't take long. Where's the bag? I'll help."

"No, thank you," she said forcefully. Then she gave an embarrassed grin. "I'd not be wanting a fine lady to see the state of my undergarments. Would you mind awfully waiting downstairs?"

"Of course," I said. "I'll let the landlady know that you're leaving. You say you've paid for the whole week. I'll see if I can get some of that back for you."

"Oh no, don't do that," she said. "Now I'm about to earn my keep I really don't mind and I don't want to make a fuss."

"All right." I started for the door. "I'll go and find a cab and then be waiting for you at the front door."

"The police are letting me travel alone? Are they not worried I'll escape?"

I smiled. "The constable is going to accompany us and then there is going to be another policeman stationed at Miss Van Woekem's front door. They are not going to let you give them the slip."

"As if I wanted to, stupid men," she said. "If I've now a chance to stay in a nicer place and earn some money, why on earth would I want to do a bunk?"

I went downstairs and found a cab on Broadway, riding back in it to where the constable was standing. Eventually Rose appeared carrying a battered old cardboard suitcase and now wearing the green cape I had brought for her. To say it suited her was an understatement. She looked stunning in it, the green of the cape bringing out those clear blue-green eyes and contrasting with that luxurious red hair, not wild and uncontrollable like mine but falling in smooth waves to her shoulders. I saw both the constable and the cabby eyeing her with appreciation. Rose was going to set heads turning when she finally settled in Chicago, I thought.

Soon we were heading northward up Broadway and then onto Park Avenue. Rose looked out of the cab with interest, giving almost a running commentary. "Would you look at the size of those buildings? How many floors do you think they have? Must be twenty or more. Holy Mother of God. It's not natural that a building should go up so high. Will they not blow down in a wind?"

"Cathedral steeples seem to manage all right," I reminded her.

"Yes, but they are thin. Oh, but that one is quite thin too, isn't it? Like a slice of cake?"

"It's called the Flatiron Building," I said.

"Amazing." She put her hands to her face. "Do you think there are buildings like this in Chicago? I shall really like living in America. What a change from slow and boring old Galway. And motor cars, too. Did you say your husband has one?"

"Only his employer's that he can use sometimes. We're certainly not rich."

"But you've a house of your own in the city?"

"We do. A small house but quite nice. It's not too far in that direction," I said, pointing as we drove past Waverly Place.

"That seems like riches by my standards," she said. "By Irish standards. It was one room for the likes of us. Well, to tell the truth, one room and the scullery out back and then an attic where we slept on the straw."

"Ours wasn't much better," I said. "Certainly no inside WC and only cold water from the pump."

The constable said nothing, only regarding Rose from time to time with wonder. From Park Avenue we turned onto Twentieth Street and then ahead of us were the railings around the gardens and the lovely tall brownstones on the south side of the square. My eyes quickly scanned the gardens and I noted, with joy, that a few snowdrops were now peeking out around the trees. The first signs that spring was on its way!

"This is the house, ma'am?" the cabby asked, a note of wonder in his voice that the likes of us should be visiting such an address.

"This is the one," I agreed. "Thank you, cabby."

He got down and helped us ladies from the cab seat. I noticed his eyes lingered on Rose and also the quick, flirtatious gaze she shot at him. The constable hovered uncertainly on the sidewalk as I paid the cabby.

"Are you to stay here, Constable?" I asked.

"Captain Sullivan said I should wait until the local man arrives," he said.

"Very good."

"He said you'd take over from here on," he added. Oh dear, I wish he hadn't said that. I hadn't wanted Rose to think I had any connection to Captain Sullivan.

"Yes, I said I'd take over responsibility for Rose until she's settled in this house," I said quickly. "Come on, Rose. Let's go inside."

I shepherded her rapidly up the steps before the constable could call me Mrs. Sullivan and knocked on the door. We had to wait quite a while before it was opened by the same new maid, her cap askew. "Oh, it's you again," she said. "I don't know if she'll want to see you now. She was having a little snooze last time I peeked in."

"This is important," I said. "Please go and wake her gently and tell her that Molly has brought a surprise for her."

"Why don't you go and wake her yourself?" the girl said, eyeing me with what looked like defiance. "She'd take it more easily from you. She can be a proper old grouch if she's woken from a nap."

"All right," I said. "You can take our coats." I slipped mine off and handed it to her. Rose removed her cape and was looking around the front hall in wonder.

"Holy Mother, but it's a big place," she said. "And you're telling me only one lady lives here?"

"And her servants, of which she only has two at the moment," I said.

She shook her head. "Wonders will never cease. If only they could see me at home right now. And Mother McCready saying I'd never amount to anything!"

Didn't that just sound like myself a few years ago? I gave her a knowing smile. "Come on, then. Let's face the dragon." I took her arm and then knocked gently before we entered the sitting room. Miss Van Woekem had fallen asleep with a book on her lap. She looked terribly old and frail and I felt a lurch of compassion and worry. I had become fond of the old lady. I tiptoed over to her and touched her arm gently.

"Miss Van Woekem?"

"What do you want now?" She was instantly awake and glaring at me. "I thought I told you to—" She broke off, staring at me in amazement. "Molly, my dear child. I'm so sorry. I thought it was that fool of a maid again. Jewel, if you please. Did you ever hear of such a heathen name?"

"I've brought someone to cheer you up," I said. "This is the young lady from Ireland that Daniel told you about. Rose McSweeney. Rose, this is Miss Van Woekem."

"Delighted to make your acquaintance, ma'am," Rose stepped forward, giving a charming little curtsey. "I can't thank you enough for giving me this opportunity and for believing in me. God bless you. I hope I'll be able to take good care of you and to let your life run a little more smoothly."

"I hope so too," Miss Van Woekem said, eyeing her with an element of suspicion.

"Saints be praised but it's a lovely room you're having here. And pictures on the wall like a museum or a palace."

"You've been to plenty of museums and palaces?" Miss Van Woekem asked, amused now.

"No, ma'am. I went to the art gallery in Galway once with the school, but I've seen photographs in a book, and I can tell a lovely thing when I see it. I've a great appreciation for beauty, I think."

"I'm glad to hear it, Rose. Then it's a relief to know you'll take good care of my precious objects. I'll hand over the dusting in here to you. I'm terrified every time that girl waves a feather duster over my priceless paintings."

"Oh no, ma'am. You don't need to worry with me. I'll take such good care of everything, I promise you."

The old lady actually smiled. "I've had Jewel make up a bedroom for you. And I want you to understand that you'll be here as a companion, not a servant—apart from the dusting, that is."

"Oh, I don't mind a bit of hard work at all, ma'am. I'm used to it, what with looking after my brothers at home, cutting and stacking the peat, and feeding the chickens and all."

Miss Van Woekem gave a half snort, half laugh. "I can assure you there is no peat and no chickens here. But I will be asking you to make up the fire from time to time. And fetch things from my bedroom, bring my food trays, and read to me. You know how to read, do you?"

"Know how to read?" Rose asked. "There's nothing I love better than a good book. That one you're reading there—*Pilgrim's Progress*—one of my favorites. The way that poor man suffers and comes to glory. It fair moves my heart."

Miss Van Woekem patted her hand. "Then you shall sit and read to me now."

"And I should be getting back, if you don't mind," I said. "I've left my mother-in-law at home with Liam for long enough recently. I'll be back on Saturday to help with the party. Is there anything you need me to get in for you in advance?"

"No, thank you, dear. It will only be a simple tea, with the addition of a little champagne in case a toast is needed. Cook can take care of everything in the food line and now that I've Rose here to keep an eye on the girl we'll make sure the napkins and cups are clean and in order."

"I could come early and help cook set out trays. You may need help setting up the room."

"That would be lovely." Miss Van Woekem smiled gratefully. "I do like things set up in a certain way and I can't do much to help right now."

"I'd be glad to help," I said. "Until Saturday, then."

As I retrieved my own coat from the hall stand I heard Rose's voice, clear and sweet. "'And I saw before me two angels . . .'"

I smiled to myself as I opened the front door. Mission accomplished. I had done a good deed.

Eighteen

All Wednesday afternoon and then on Thursday I waited impatiently for Daniel to bring me the results of his tests on the knife, and to hear whether he had managed to locate the handsome Mario who had found the wallet. In the meantime I made sure I kept busy. Not that it was hard. I had some catching up to do on laundry and house cleaning, as well as finishing Bridie's everyday dress. I decided not to show it to her until both dresses were finished. Having thought the party dress was something I could make at my leisure and show to her at some time in the future, I now had to race to have it finished for the party on Saturday. I realized as I spread out the fabric that I wasn't used to working with something as fine and dainty. I'd better not prick my finger any more or every little drop of blood would show!

I worked until Bridie returned home on Thursday afternoon, then hid my sewing quickly away so that I didn't spoil the surprise. We had heard nothing from Miss Van Woekem, so I had to assume that Rose was settling in well. I waited until Daniel was having a glass of whiskey alone in the parlor after dinner to ask about the knife.

He shook his head. "Plenty of fingerprints on it, and traces of blood, too. So we've got the right weapon."

"But not Rose's prints?"

"No. Apparently not."

"Or the Englishman's?"

"Not his, either."

"Well, you said yourself that the murderer could well have been wearing gloves."

"That appears to be the case. Any prints on the handle were well and truly smudged as if someone was wearing gloves. My men will be taking prints from kitchen workers and guards too, just to rule them out, but it doesn't look as if we're going to find out much more."

"And the Italian man who was the guard?"

"In police custody, arrested for theft."

"They found the wallet on him?"

"Not the wallet, but English bank notes, plus other items he had helped himself to from the baggage room. It seems his superiors had had their eye on him for a while."

"But his fingerprints weren't on the knife?"

"Not as far as we can tell. As I said, they were smudged. And I questioned him myself. He doesn't fit the profile of a killer. Quite the opposite, in fact. An opportunist who would snatch an old lady's purse but would run like mad if confronted."

"So we're none the wiser?"

Daniel sighed. "We are following up on other passengers on that boat. A few possible leads on people who moved in the right circles to be jewel thieves. We've asked Scotland Yard for a list of attendees at the party."

"But that wouldn't explain Ellis Island and why such a person would travel steerage. No more information yet on Edwin Cromer?"

He shook his head. "Scotland Yard doesn't consider New York to be a high priority, I fear. They think we Yanks are a bunch of lawless nobodies and that murders here are ten a penny, I suspect."

"Are you going to let Rose go free yet?"

"Not until we have verification from Dublin of what she's told us."

"At least Rose is in more pleasant surroundings now while she waits," I said. "Miss Van Woekem seems quite taken with her."

"And I," Daniel said, grabbing my hand and swinging me down onto his knee, "am quite taken with you. How long since you and I have had a quiet moment together?"

"It's not easy with your mother and Bridie here," I said.

"Then I think we might have an early night for once," he whispered, nuzzling my ear.

On Friday morning I got right to work. The party dress was already cut and basted and I took the pieces out of the chest and laid them on the table. I had waited until Bridie was safely over with Sid and Gus. I gave myself a little smile of satisfaction as I pictured her face lighting up when she saw the new dress.

"Right," I said to myself. "This should take a couple of hours." To my surprise it went beautifully. I was more used to sewing on a foot treadle, but sewing the blue dress first had given me confidence on the hand-cranked machine. It was only eleven when Mrs. Sullivan walked in and said, "I'll make luncheon, then, shall I, if you are just getting started."

"Actually, I'm finished," I said with satisfaction. I snipped the last thread and pulled the dress out of the machine. "Here it is." I stood and proudly displayed my work.

"Very interesting." Her eyebrows rose quizzically. "Is it a new fashion, then?"

"No, you saw me buy the pattern. Is something wrong?" I looked more closely at the dress. Oh no! I had done it again. The right sleeve that I had carefully fitted and sewn so that the material puffed up perfectly was actually inside out.

"Damn," I muttered.

"Molly!" She looked at me in horror.

"Sorry, Mother Sullivan." I waited until she was out of the room to say a few more choice words then sat to unpick my work and start again.

Three hours later, I knocked at 9 Patchin Place and heard a faint "Come in." Gus was seated in the living room surrounded by an enormous pile of coats and hats. "Oh, Molly, thank God. Can you help me sort these into men's and women's?"

"Holy Mother! More clothes?"

"They keep coming, Molly." She looked a little desperate. "We put out a call for coats and hats and it seems that everyone in New York has cleaned out their closets and sent them to us. I don't know how to get them to stop."

"Will you take them out to Ellis Island again? There certainly is the need for them, but I must confess, now that we have found the murder weapon I don't feel that I can spare another day. I am afraid that Daniel thinks this detecting is taking me away from Liam too much. And his mother certainly agrees with him."

"He should be delighted. You have half solved his case for him and shown you are much smarter than his police force. But, no, we've given up on Ellis Island. There is the Ladies Mission as well as a soup kitchen in the Bowery that will hand them out for us."

I held up a very chic silk hat with pale silk roses on it. "I'm not sure where someone living in the tenements is going to wear this."

Gus looked up, "Yes, well, sometimes the ladies who donate just get rid of everything from last season. They don't think about what is practical."

We piled the women's coats and cloaks on the sofa and the men's on a low table and stuffed ottoman. I looked at some of them with a touch of envy, but once again I was too proud to ask for myself. We bagged up many hats in big canvas sacks, though I rather worried they would all be crushed. When we were finished all of the furniture was covered with garments. I sat on the floor and Gus collapsed onto the sofa in the small space that was not taken up by clothes.

"Do you want some coffee?" she asked. "Only don't ask me to get up just yet. I'm exhausted."

I got to my feet. "No, don't move. I'd better take Bridie home," I said. Now that it was finished I couldn't wait to show her the dress. "How are the lessons coming?

Gus's face lit up. "She's brilliant, Molly, she wants to learn everything we teach her. She was wasted on that public school."

"You two are changing her life." I smiled as I said it, but inside I still felt some misgivings. I wanted Bridie to learn and grow, but would she change too much to be happy as an Irish immigrant girl? Daniel and I could give her a stable home, but she wouldn't have the wealth and connections of Sid or Gus. Would she end up in an in-between world, too educated to be happy as a housewife, but not able to live in their world?

I looked around. "Where are they doing lessons?"

"They are up in your old room. We've been using it as a schoolroom. Go on up."

I climbed the stairs thinking of the days when this house seemed like a palace and Sid and Gus my fairy godmothers. Now that I thought of it, I supposed Bridie saw them that way too. Who wouldn't rather spend time with them, always fun, always cheerful? Sid and Gus could always be sweet and kind to her because they never had to be around her when they weren't in the mood. They didn't have to stay up with her all night through a fever or say no to her schemes because they didn't have the money. They came and went from her life as it pleased them. I had to wonder, would I rather be tucked up in that snug bedroom with Sid and Gus as my fairy godmothers than having responsibility for two children, a husband, and a mother-in-law? I wasn't sure that I wanted to know the answer to that question.

I could hear Bridie's voice as I stepped onto the landing. The door was open and I saw that the room had been transformed. It had been a pretty little spare bedroom when I lived there, now it was a girl's dream schoolroom. A darling white desk sat where the bed had been. The shelves beside it were filled with leather-bound books. A daybed with a lacy white coverlet was against the other wall. The only thing that was the same was the full-length dressing mirror. Bridie was standing in front of that. Sid was sitting on the daybed, her feet curled up under her.

"This is lovely," I exclaimed as I tapped politely on the door before stepping into the room. "When did you do all of this?"

"We wanted our young pupil to have a nice place to work. And it was a good excuse to buy some new furniture. Show Molly what you learned today."

"*Salve.*" Bridie turned and grinned at me cheerfully. "*Ingressus es ad me in domum suam?*"

I'm afraid to say my mouth fell open. "Say that again?" Then I gaped at the sight of Bridie, standing in front of the mirror. She was wearing a much too big purple evening dress. It was topped with a matching purple turban. The centerpiece was a giant diamond.

"It's Latin. It means, 'Hello, have you come to take me home?' At least I think it does." She looked over to the bed a little hesitantly and Sid, who was sitting there, nodded approval.

"It does indeed. Well done!"

"And what on earth have you got on?" I continued.

Bridie went back to looking at herself in the mirror. "I told Aunt Sid that I had a party to go to tomorrow and she said I could pick anything out of her closet. I picked this."

"That's a lovely outfit for dress-up, but get out of it now. It's time to go home."

Bridie looked at me as if I were not very bright. "You don't understand. It's my party outfit. For the tea party tomorrow."

I took a deep breath. Stay calm, Molly. "You are not wearing that outlandish getup to Miss Van Woekem's house tomorrow. It is too big for you, for one thing, it is an evening dress for another thing, it's far too old for you, and for the other thing"—I had run out of things—"it's . . . purple!"

"Aunt Sid says I must not care about the silly conventions of people in society. I should be a free spirit and express myself." She gave a little twirl as she said this and went back to looking at herself in the mirror. I could feel myself turning red and I didn't want to look at Sid. I heard my mother's voice in my head—"That's all very well for the gentry, but not for the likes of you or me." I choked the words back. Sweet Jesus and Mary, was I going to become my mother? Instead I said, "Let's talk about it at home. Get dressed in your regular clothes now." I could already imagine what Mrs. Sullivan would say if she saw Bridie come home in that dress.

Her eyes flashed. "Well, I can at least keep it on for today? Why should I have to change?"

"You are not wearing that. Take it off." Had my younger brothers been there they would have recognized from my tone that my anger was rising. I had raised them after my mother died, and although I had never given them the back of my hand as she did frequently I had given enough tongue lashings that they knew to run when they heard that tone of voice. Bridie, however, did not.

"But—"

"Get that ridiculous outfit off and get over to our house immediately or I will turn you over my knee and paddle you so help me Jesus, Mary, and all the saints!" Bridie had never heard me yell at that volume before. Her eyes opened wide with alarm, then filled with tears. All the fight went out of her.

"Yes, Molly," she said. "Excuse me, Aunt Sid. My clothes are in the closet where I found this." She walked past me out of the room. There was a dead silence.

"I wore that outfit to the opening of Ryan's play last season." Sid looked hurt. The words "ridiculous outfit" hung in the air.

"I'm sorry, Sid. I lost my temper. Lately that girl is making me see red. I keep hearing my mother's voice coming out of my mouth."

Sid put a forgiving hand on my arm. "Come down and have a cup of coffee while you wait for her to change. I have to help Gus sort a mountain of clothes. Did you see them when you came in?"

"I helped her. We're all done."

"Thank God for that. Between you and me, Molly, I am hoping that this phase will wear off. I am all for helping the poor and I feel for them and all that. But it is a lot of hard work. Try to encourage her to go back to her painting. Art gallery openings are much less exhausting, and there is champagne."

I laughed. As we reached the bottom floor I heard Bridie coming down behind us. She was still in the purple dress.

"Don't you look nice?" Gus looked up from the couch as we came down the stairs.

"Yes, she looks very nice," I spoke through gritted teeth, "but, Bridie, I told you to get changed. Now!" You have probably realized by now that I am not a saintly woman. My temper can be hard to control. So the last word came out a little too forcefully.

"I can't undo the hooks at the back." A tear rolled down Bridie's cheek.

"Oh, my darling girl. Don't cry." Gus stood and flung open her arms and Bridie rushed into them and started to sob as if her heart would break. They sank back down onto the sofa, Gus cradling Bridie in her arms.

"Molly shouted at me and she said . . ." The words were lost among her sobs.

"Really! I . . ." I began.

Just then the front door was flung open with a crash.

"I've been knocking for hours and I won't stay on the doorstep another minute! I have returned to you. Come and greet the conquering hero." And our friend the playwright Ryan O'Hare burst into the room, making a dramatic entrance as always. He was wearing a black cape lined with white fur and a French beret over hair that curled down to his collar, and he held a cigarette in a long ebony holder in one hand.

"Oh, hello, Ryan. Were you away?" Gus feigned disinterest as she got up and walked toward him.

"I am cut to the quick! You know very well I went to Europe. I expected you to be counting the days to my return." He accepted Gus's kiss on his cheek.

"How could we count them if you never give us any idea when you will be back?" Gus gave him a playful slap. "Have you never heard of the mail? You could always drop us a postcard from your travels."

"I'm sure all of New York society has to know all about my doings every day. Don't you read the papers? My darlings, I've been the toast of the town in London. Everyone has been talking about me, from royal circles to the Old Kent Road."

"Maybe in the London papers." Sid laughed. "The *New York Times* has not been reporting on your London success, I'm afraid."

"Ignorant philistines," he said. "That's all right. I've brought clippings." Ryan was carrying a very handsome leather satchel. He pulled it open and handed out newspaper clippings to all of us. "Read it and weep!"

"'Sale on women's garments,'" I read deadpan. Gus followed suit. "'Gaiety Girl leaves show abruptly. Cites nervous breakdown.'"

"'Bank shares fall five pounds,'" Sid said with a straight face. Then we all burst out laughing.

"You are all being horribly cruel to the returning hero. I may never speak to you again. Turn them over, you fiends." Ryan retrieved a whole newspaper from the handbag and read, "'O'Hare play a London triumph.' Now read yours properly." We turned our clippings over.

"'Opening Night huge success for *Queen of Diamonds*,'" Sid read.

"'Elsie Hall gives smash performance in O'Hare play,'" Gus added.

"'E.R. was seen with M.E. last night at the private party at Savoy. R.O. attended with the beautiful E.H., fresh from their triumph at the Haymarket theater, and L.L. was present with C.B.' . . . I don't understand this one at all." I looked up, puzzled.

"Oh, it's a gossip column. You have to know all the initials. E.R. is the king, Edward Regis, you know—and M.E., his latest mistress. I am the R.O. mentioned and I escorted my leading actress, Elsie Hall. It is quite a coup to be included in this column. Only the best and the brightest."

"The king attended your opening night and party?" Sid asked. "I thought you were persona non grata in England, especially with the royal family, after that play you wrote satirizing Victoria and Albert."

"Fortunately their son, the current king, has much better taste in art and literature," Ryan said. "Not only did he come to the royal box, but he laughed heartily throughout. And he brought his mistress to my party."

"Well done, Ryan. Won't you sit down?" Gus motioned for Ryan to come in and then realized there was nowhere to sit. He looked around at the piles of clothes covering every surface. "Are you starting a store?" He picked up the silk hat and perched it on his head. "Ladies' fashions?" He walked over to the gilt-framed mirror and examined himself critically. "It suits me, don't you think?"

"Gus has put out a call for warm clothes for the poor. We've been to Ellis Island twice to give them out, but more keep showing up." Sid sounded a little desperate.

"To tell you the truth, it's a little exhausting," Gus confessed. "I would like to get back to some quieter afternoons and my painting."

"Oh, thank God." Sid's relief showed all over her face. "I know, let's have a party to celebrate Ryan's return. We'll have a diamond theme. I can wear my tiara."

"A party! A lovely idea!" Ryan clapped his hands like a small child. "It will have to wait until after opening night, though. I'm going to be working like a dog for the next week."

Suddenly Ryan noticed Bridie perched among the clothes on the sofa. Her face was still streaked with tears.

"Who is this vision of loveliness, this fair damsel in such distress? Molly, have I met this enchanting young woman?"

"This is Bridie, my daughter. I believe you met her once."

Bridie got up and stopped crying instantly. "Mr. O'Hare. It's me, Bridie."

Ryan did a theatrical double take. "That is not possible. Bridie is an elegant young woman and much too old to be your daughter." He swept a stage bow and kissed her hand. She giggled. He looked at me. "Does Daniel know? Do you have a wicked past I don't know about? Does he have a wicked past I don't know about?"

He was just getting started. "You have the mind of a playwright, Ryan," I began.

"And a mind in the gutter," Gus put in.

"I'll tell you the whole story sometime, but the short version is that I brought Bridie over to America when she was tiny girl. She has been in my life for a long time and she's now our ward. But enough about me. We want to hear your news!"

"Yes, let's hear all of it. It's good to have you back, Ryan." Sid gave a genuine smile. "It's been dull without you. How wonderful that your play was a triumph in London."

"It was! Everyone who is anyone came to see it. The king came to see it opening night and we had a party after at an enormous hotel. There was dancing and champagne. All the great men of London were there with their . . ."—he glanced at Bridie—"and very few of their wives. And all the most beautiful Gaiety Girls, and some beautiful leading boys as well." He gave a knowing little wink.

"Who are Gaiety Girls?" Bridie asked. "And what is the king like?"

"Well, Miss Bridie, the Gaiety Girls are the prettiest actresses in London. They are almost as pretty as you and I'm sure you will be one if you ever decide to live there. The king is very fat and very well dressed. I am told his beard is tickly, but he has wonderful taste in plays and champagne."

"Bridie, please go and get changed now," I said, hating to break up this reunion but thinking that if I didn't get to the shops soon we would have nothing for dinner. Bridie looked like she was going to argue, but Sid said, "Come on, I'll help you with the hooks," and they started up the stairs.

"But she's dressed for a night on the town," Ryan exclaimed, "just like one of the Gaiety Girls. Miss Bridie, come out on the town with me tonight."

Bridie turned on the stairs and gave me a triumphant look but kept going hurriedly as I frowned at her.

"Don't encourage her, Ryan," I pleaded. "She's still a little girl."

"Barely," he said. "You'll have to keep your eye on that one."

"So you're bringing your play to New York?" I deliberately changed the subject. The best way to change the subject with Ryan was to ask him a question about himself. He needed no encouraging to do that.

"We are, my darling girl. It opens in a week. Of course, it needed some rewriting. A lot of the jokes were made for the English audience. The Americans have a more pedantic sense of humor. The English are a lot more wicked in general." He winked. "But far be it from me to deprive New York of my genius. So I have returned to bring culture to the masses!"

"What's the play about? Is it as wicked as your others, or are you reforming your ways now you are more established?" Gus asked. "I hope you are not selling out to fame and fortune."

"Moi! Care about fame and fortune? Only inasmuch as it gets me tables at Delmonico with plenty of champagne and I can usually manage to be kept in the style to which I've become accustomed." Ryan typically attracted wealthy young men who were willing to finance his lifestyle. But his true loves were himself and the theater. "You can judge for yourself if it is a sellout. It is a typical love story: Boy meets girl, girl meets more attractive boy. First boy makes a lot of money and wins the girl. Same old story but with a fresh twist, naturally. It's called *Queen of Diamonds*."

"That sounds quite cynical, even for you, Ryan." I smiled. "Some of us married for love, not for money."

"It is wrapped in a pretty bow. I assure you that most of the rich ladies who were purchased by their husbands in a similar manner will have no idea the play is about them. These are what I came to bring." He pulled two tickets out of his leather handbag. "Tickets to opening night. I am counting on you to be there." He handed them to Gus, then looked at me apologetically, "I didn't bring yours with me, Molly, but I'm sure I can get you two tickets as well. Promise me you'll come. I would like to think that three people in the audience understand the play."

"Coffee?" Sid reappeared carrying a tray with tiny cups of strong coffee on it. We all perched on the only chairs that were not hidden under piles of clothing.

"I suppose it is a bit early for anything stronger." Ryan took his cup. It felt so nice to be sitting with Sid and Gus and Ryan sipping horribly strong coffee and laughing as he recounted the many near disasters he had averted by his brilliance and the many people who had told him he was the most brilliant playwright on the English stage.

Bridie came down the stairs, wearing her gingham dress, which I noticed was now too small. She really was growing out of all of her clothes. I sighed. "Duty calls, we had better go."

"I'll make sure they have those two tickets for you at the box office, Molly. Please say you'll come. Next Friday is opening night. And come to the party after. Everyone who is anyone will be there."

"Can I come?" Bridie asked hopefully.

"We'll see. Say goodbye to Mr. O'Hare and the ladies. I have a surprise for you when we get home."

She looked interested. "What kind of surprise?"

"You'll see." I pecked Gus and Sid on the cheek. I held out my hand to Ryan, who brought it to his lips, bowing. "Goodbye, lovely, delicious Molly. Until we meet again."

We hurried across the street.

Nineteen

"I like Mr. O'Hare very much." Bridie said as she took of her coat in the hallway. "He called me a young lady."

"You are a young lady." I looked at her dress that was heading up alarmingly toward her knees. "And getting bigger every day. And speaking of that, your surprise is upstairs on your bed."

"It is?" Bridie tore up the stairs, taking them two at a time. What a strange age, I thought, a lady one second and a little girl the next. I walked into the kitchen and gave Liam a kiss.

"Did you finish the dress?" Mrs. Sullivan looked as if she doubted my ability to have sewn all the pieces in the right places. "It was back in pieces when we left for our walk." She hadn't ever worked at a sweatshop. I had sewn the equivalent of ten dresses a day there. Although I hadn't had to cut the pieces out or tack them together. Apart from my piecing mishap, one dress had not seemed so hard this morning. It seemed my time as a working girl had not been wasted, although I was still not handy with the needle when I had to baste the seams. My fingers were sore from sticking myself.

"I did finish it. Thank you so much for keeping Liam occupied. I just told Bridie she has a present on her bed."

"Oh, so that was the herd of elephants I heard on the stairs."

"Efelants!" Liam agreed. "On de staiws."

"I want to go and see how she likes it. Come on, babai." I scooped Liam up and carefully washed his little hands. I didn't want him to put grimy fingerprints all over Bridie's new dress. "Let's go and see Bridie's new dress."

"Bwidee," he agreed earnestly. "Noo dwess."

"What a talker he is already! Just like his father." Mrs. Sullivan beamed at Liam fondly. She and I might not always get along, but she was a wonderful grandmother.

"Say thank you, Granny," I prompted, giving his chubby little face a kiss.

"Thak yoo, Grandee," he said and laughed, squirming to get down. I put him firmly on my hip and started up the stairs.

The door to Bridie's room was open and I walked in. "Do you like them?" The white party dress was laid out on the bed where I had left it, the navy blue dress beside it and partially under Bridie. She was lying on her stomach across the bed, propped up on her elbow reading a book.

"Oh, yes," she said without taking her eyes from the book. "They're very nice."

"Down," Liam demanded, and I put him down. He grabbed the white dress and I gasped, hoping his just-washed hands wouldn't leave a wet mark. I gently tugged it out of his hands. I smoothed it as I put it back on the bed.

"I made them for you. The blue one is for every day. Mrs. Sullivan and I found the party dress fabric. I thought you could wear it to the party tomorrow."

"When she did her season Aunty Gus had a dressmaker who came all the way from Paris. She said she wore nothing but silks all year."

"Well, she must have been very cold in February."

"Silly, the season isn't in February. It's—"

I cut her off. "Come on, I want to see how they look on you."

"I promised Aunty Gus I'd do this reading before our next lesson. Could I try it on tomorrow?" she said, her eyes returning to the book.

My excitement fell flat. Really, when I thought of all the time I had put into those dresses. I remembered how many times my mother had called me an ungrateful wretch and for the first time it occurred to me that perhaps I had been. I had never looked at things from the mother's point of view.

"You have twenty minutes and then be downstairs and washed up to help me get the dinner," I ordered.

"Okay," she said without looking up.

I bent and picked Liam up. "Down!" he screamed, and squirmed out of my arms. "Liam do it." He carefully turned backward and started scooting down the stairs.

"Let me help you, babai," I cooed.

"Liam do it!" he screamed and flinched away from my hand. He went down each step that way all the way down to the kitchen. I hovered just beside him, ready to catch him if he fell. I tried several times to pick him up, but each time he screamed. Now that I think about it I was already seeing some of my stubborn nature in him. I suppose it was only to be expected. But at that moment I only felt my own frustration building.

"Oh, the poor darling!" Mrs. Sullivan shrieked as she saw him come down the last step. "Why would your mother make you climb down all those stairs? So dangerous."

I gritted my teeth. "I'll be back with some meat for dinner."

"Meat? Are you forgetting that it's Friday again, then?" Mrs. Sullivan exclaimed as she clasped Liam to her as if he had tumbled down the stairs.

"Oh, sorry, right, it's Friday." I forced out the words through gritted teeth. "I'll get some fish!" I clapped on my hat and stalked out the door. Hopefully on the way to the butchers I would find a good murder to solve. I might prefer that to life at home right now.

* * *

Things were rather frosty between Bridie and me that evening. She helped grudgingly with the dinner but rushed back up to bed and her novel as soon as she was allowed. Still, as I awoke the next morning I had high hopes for the party. I'm not sure why. After all, I was going to serve and be a helper rather than an honored guest. But I have never minded hard work, and a party might mean good food and laughter. I decided to enjoy myself.

That resolution was tested immediately as I realized I had forgotten to ask Sid and Gus for the loan of a dress for myself. I knew I was going to be among society ladies, and various disasters—a bomb, a fire—had decimated my own humble wardrobe. I had meant to ask for a tea dress, perhaps with the additional loan of one of the warm, nice coats they had in their living room. But they had gone out before I finished cleaning up breakfast and had not returned when it was time to get ready.

"Oh, well, this is probably better for helping to serve tea anyway," I told myself as I brushed the good wool two-piece. It was not fancy but it would do.

I went in to Bridie's room and she was sitting with just her stockings and petticoat on, still reading her book.

"Let's see how that dress looks, then."

She stood up with a resigned expression on her face. I helped her to put it on. It was a darling dress. The material was finer than I ever would have hoped for as a girl and I had even put some lace around the sleeves and hems. "What do you think?" I asked.

"It's very pretty." Bridie's voice was flat. "Thank you." She looked at herself critically in the mirror. "But why couldn't I wear the one I had on yesterday? Mr. O'Hare said I looked like a Gaiety Girl in it."

"I think he was joking with you. Sit," I ordered. She sat on the bed and I brushed out her hair. My anger was rising to the surface and it made my movements rough.

"Ow," Bridie complained as I brushed through a tangle and pulled her hair.

"Sorry," I said automatically, tying the hair back with a ribbon. Bridie stood and I tied the blue silk ribbon around her waist. "You're beautiful." I kissed her nose. She flinched away.

"When can I wear my hair up like the ladies?"

"When you are a little older." Keep calm, Molly, I told myself. I had spent days making this dress and it deserved more than a lukewarm thank-you. "Don't you like the dress?"

"It is very nice for a little girl's dress."

"You are a little girl." My voice rose along with my temper.

"The ladies say that—"

"Let's leave the ladies out of this for right now." I pressed my lips together tightly and took a deep breath in and out through my nose until I could speak calmly. "Miss Van Woekem will expect you to look and behave like a little girl. And she will expect us to be on time. We'd better go right now. And I want you to be on your best behavior."

"Are you sure you don't want to come, Mother Sullivan?" I said as I walked into the kitchen. "After all, Miss Van Woekem is your friend."

"No, it will be mostly young ladies there and we need someone to watch this little man." As she said this she put an arm out to restrain Liam, who had stood in his chair and was holding his hands out to me. "Careful, my boy," she said as she lifted him into her arms.

"Mama." He reached for me.

She turned her gaze to Bridie, who was standing in the doorway with a look on her face that only disgruntled young girls can give. "Bridie, don't you look pretty, child? I hope you appreciate all the work Molly put into that dress."

"Yes, Mrs. Sullivan," Bridie said flatly. "It's very nice."

"Speaking of which, are you going to wear that, Molly? Don't you think a tea dress would be more appropriate?" Mrs. Sullivan looked critically at my two-piece wool skirt and jacket.

"It would be if I had one," I replied. "You seem to forget that I've lost my wardrobe twice now—in a bombing and in a fire. But I'm mostly going to be helping out so it won't matter too much."

"Mama," Liam's voice raised insistently, and he leaned out of Mrs. Sullivan's arms toward me.

"I had better go," I said hurriedly. "Liam, be good for Granny." I popped off the lid of the blue tin where I always kept the week's spending money. It was quite low. Mrs. Sullivan might have a point about not buying too much meat, but there was enough for a cab to Gramercy Park. I have always preferred to travel on my own two feet, but I was afraid of getting dirty on the way if an auto or a carriage splashed through some of the many puddles of mud on the roads when we were waiting to cross.

We put our coats on and headed down to the end of Patchin Place to hail a hansom cab. The sky looked quite dark for mid-morning. A uniform blanket of gray covered the city and it had begun to drizzle before the cab turned into Gramercy Park and came to a halt outside Miss Van Woekem's brownstone.

I went ahead of Bridie, up the steps, and rang the bell. She hung back, reluctant.

"Come on," I said. "It's going to be fun. Lots of nice ladies like Sid and Gus."

"They'll all think I'm a little girl," she said. "And they'll all be wearing lovely clothes."

"At least you're one better off than me," I replied. "I'm having to wear this because my own nice clothes got burned in that fire. I'm the one who will feel out of place."

I saw her expression soften a little. She went to say something then thought better of it. We stood in silence on the doorstep outside the elegant brick house, shivering slightly in the brisk wind. It seemed a very long while. I was just about to push the bell again when the door was finally opened. Miss Van Woekem's new maid stood in the doorway looking at us and not speaking.

"Can we come in, please?" The girl's face was bright red, and she glared at me. "Miss Van Woekem will want to know we are here."

"I don't know," the girl said without moving. "The lady is changing and I'm not sure if I'm supposed to let people in. She gets real mad if I do the wrong thing."

"Well, we're not staying out here on the doorstep. Come on, Bridie." I pushed past the maid into the hall. "It's all right. You won't get in trouble. We are supposed to be here to help set up for the party."

"I'm not going to tell the old woman." She was still glaring defiantly. "She said not to disturb her until she was dressed and ready."

"Don't worry, you can take our coats, then we'll just go into the kitchen and see what we can help with. Is Rose already arranging things in the drawing room?"

"Rose?" The girl shot me a look of pure venom. "She's helping the lady get dressed."

"Come on, Bridie. Let's see where we're needed." I waited for her to hand her coat to Jewel, then we went through to the back of the house. The kitchen was rather smoky and the cook was busily stirring a batter and turned when she saw us enter.

"Oh no, you get out!" she yelled.

I hesitated, wondering if I should go. "Oh no. Not you, ma'am. You!" I saw the maid had entered behind us. "Not in my kitchen. You've done enough this morning." The maid glared at her, then she turned and fled.

"I'm sorry, Mrs. Sullivan, but that girl has been causing all sorts of trouble. She's made me a bit behind and I'm afraid I won't have everything ready for the party."

"I can help. Just tell me what you want done."

"Oh no, madam. That wouldn't be right."

"I assure you I do all my own cooking at home and I'm happy to help. Bridie can too." I pulled on an apron I saw hanging with others on the wall to show her I was serious.

"That is really kind of you." She smiled. "I have some cream in that bag. Can you top the fruit tarts with it?"

"Easily." I picked up the bag full of cream. It had a darling little metal nozzle and the cream came out in a smooth tube. "Look, Bridie, like a real bakery. Do you want to try?"

I could tell Bridie wanted to but was hesitant she'd make a mistake or look foolish.

"Come on. Have a try and then I can help Cook finish those sandwiches."

"All right." She squeezed the piping bag and a swirl of cream came out.

"Very nice, young lady," Cook said.

Bridie looked up with an expression of delight, and I realized that she was still a little girl at heart, in spite of wanting to be so sophisticated and grown up.

I started cutting the crusts off smoked salmon sandwiches.

"So what was all the commotion this morning?" I asked as I worked.

"It is all that new maid. First she knocked over a bowl of batter that was resting overnight. Then she cleaned the wallpaper right off the wall in the hallway. Then this morning she has hysterics because the new companion has accused her of going in her room to steal her things. She almost got fired right there on the spot, but Miss Van Woekem is too kind a lady. That girl Jewel insisted she just thought she was meant to clean in that room and had no bad intentions. Well, with all the commotion I burned the biscuits and I have to start over and still have the cake to frost."

"At least the tarts are done," I said as Bridie finished the last swirl. "I'll take them through into the parlor and we'll decide where to set up. Do you have a tray?" The cook passed me a big silver tray. We loaded it with tarts and Bridie held the door so I could take it through.

The doorbell sounded as I walked through into the parlor.

"Bridie, bring that little table over here. We'll put it in the center of the room with this platter on it." As we placed the platter the doorbell sounded again.

"Jewel, get the door," the cook's voice called from the kitchen. I waited but the girl did not appear and the doorbell rang again.

"I'll get it," I called back as I walked into the front hall. I opened the door and there stood Cordelia Ransom, looking wet and not pleased at all.

"A new maid already? I knew that other girl wouldn't last." She stepped in, taking off her wet coat then thrusting it into my arms. "Tell your mistress I'm here. I'm her goddaughter."

"Hello, Cordelia." I fought to keep a civil expression on my face. "We've met."

Cordelia looked at me as if a piece of furniture had suddenly started a conversation with her.

"Molly Sullivan. We met giving out clothes at Ellis Island."

She raised her eyebrows. "Good God. I knew Augusta was bohemian but I didn't think she mixed with maids socially."

"I'm not a maid." I gritted my teeth. "I am a friend of Miss Van Woekem."

"Then why are you answering the door?" She looked at me suspiciously.

"I came to help because she is laid up and her new maid is a disaster. I volunteered to help with the party for her goddaughter, whom I now assume is you?"

"Yes." Cordelia now seemed faintly embarrassed and tried to recover poise. "How kind of you, Mrs. Sullivan. Is my godmother in the parlor?"

"She is getting dressed, according to the maid. I think she has been using a downstairs room because of her injury."

"And who is this darling little girl?" Cordelia tried to redeem her rudeness by putting on a sickly sweet smile for Bridie. "How old are you, darling?"

"I'm thirteen." Bridie glared back at her stonily. "And we have met already. I was on the trip to Ellis Island with you as well."

"Oh yes." Cordelia gave a fake laugh. "One doesn't always remember all the help wherever one goes." She raised her voice again as if speaking to a toddler. "I'm sure you were a big help to your mama."

"She's not my mama," Bridie began, but Cordelia had already moved away.

She turned back as we heard someone on the stairs and both looked up. An elegant young lady in a pale blue tea dress and matching hat was gracefully descending.

"How do you do," Cordelia said politely as the young lady reached the hall, holding out a white gloved hand.

The young lady took it equally politely. "You must be Miss Cordelia. Pleased to meet you." I started as I heard her Irish brogue and looked again. The young lady was Rose. She turned to acknowledge me. "Molly, I'm so glad to see you. But I must run this instant. I've been upstairs to get the bracelet Miss Van Woekem wants to wear today and I mustn't keep her waiting." She dashed off down the hall and Cordelia stared at me.

"Who on earth was that? She is dressed like one of the Four Hundred and sounds like someone selling fish. How do you know her?" I wondered where to begin.

"Her name is Rose. She is Miss Van Woekem's new companion. I am as surprised as you to see her dressed like that. When I brought her over here last week, she had only one outfit."

"Well, I can at least explain the dress." Cordelia started to walk into the parlor and I followed her. "My godmother has so many goddaughters, her great-nieces and children of her school friends, and we are always staying the night and leaving something or other here. I expect my godmother didn't want her to look like a beggar woman and had her choose a dress. It could even be one I left here, although I don't remember it. But what do you mean you brought her here?

Is she one of your charities?" She sat on the dainty little sofa, then removed her gloves, setting them on a side table beside her little beaded handbag.

"I came across her through one of my husband's investigations. She is newly arrived from Ireland and needed a job. Your godmother needed a companion. I introduced them." I began to feel uncomfortable as I realized I had overlooked something. Cordelia and Miss Van Woekem knew me as Mrs. Sullivan and the wife of Captain Sullivan. It was bound to come out that my husband was a police captain sometime at the party or soon after. I would have to explain to Rose as soon as possible who I really was or there could be an embarrassing scene.

"She sounds just off the boat. I hope she doesn't steal my godmother blind or murder her in her sleep," Cordelia said with no real trace of concern in her voice. "Do you think you can find somebody to bring us tea? I'm freezing."

"I'm sure the cook has the kettle on. You could check in the kitchen with her." I had not come to serve tea to the likes of Cordelia, whether or not I also sounded like someone just off the boat. Cordelia looked scandalized. Obviously she still intended to treat me like the maid. Just then the door opened and Rose pushed Miss Van Woekem in in her large rattan chair on wheels. It took a minute to get her safely through the door.

"Molly, how nice of you to come. I see you have met my goddaughter," she said as we had her safely transferred to her customary chair by the window. "You're a little early, I think, Cordelia. The servants are still setting up. Please sit. It hurts my neck to look up at you." We sat and Rose took a knitted blanket from a shelf and placed it on Miss Van Woekem's lap.

"Thank you, dear." The old lady beamed up at her.

"Yes, we are already acquainted." Cordelia stressed the word in a way that made it clear that acquaintance was not friendship. "We met handing out clothes at Ellis Island with the Vassar Benevolent Society."

"You were doing charity work? I'm glad to hear that about you, Cordelia," Miss Van Woekem said. "I rather fancied you went in for parties more than good deeds."

"We all have to do our part. Society expects it of us."

"And you were there, Molly? Surely you don't run in Cordelia's society circles."

"I have two friends who went to Vassar. They asked for help with the clothes." Bridie had been standing in the doorway silently for quite some time now, I realized. "It was my ward Bridie's idea that we help those less fortunate than ourselves." I held out my hand to her. Bridie came in shyly and perched on the end of the sofa.

"What a charming little lady. My friend Mrs. Sullivan has so many nice things to say about you, Bridie," Miss Van Woekem began. "I'm so glad you could come."

"Thank you for having me," Bridie muttered, going bright red. I hastily changed the conversation. I couldn't see how to explain that either myself or my mother-in-law were called Mrs. Sullivan to Rose, who thought I was Molly Murphy.

"Cordelia was very helpful with the clothing drive. It was kind of her," was the first thing that came to my mind even though she wasn't and it wasn't. "Are you often involved with charity events, Miss Ransom?" I continued.

"When one is called upon to help the least of these." She looked at me smugly, assuring herself that I belonged with the least of these rather than her circle of society. Then she turned to her godmother. "All the best New York families give back in some way. The day we went out to Ellis Island, Mrs. Sage herself sent her automobile to transport the clothes to the ferry."

"And you thought she might be attending the party today along with her son." Miss Van Woekem gave Cordelia a meaningful look. "I see."

"Godmother." Cordelia blushed. "I'm about to announce my engagement."

"Yes, but you didn't have the viscount on the hook yet. He was not yet arrived from England, as far as you knew." She paused. "Your name was quite connected with young Mr. Sage's name last summer, I seem to remember." The old lady leaned forward and took Cordelia's hand. "Are you sure you want to marry this English viscount, my dear? I've known your mother for a long time and she would do anything to get you a title and a castle in England, but is it what you really want?"

"Of course it is, Godmother. He is completely charming. Now, can we possibly have that cup of tea?" She rose, clearly changing the subject. "The weather is bitterly cold today. Shall I see what has happened to your servant?"

"As long as it is not only his castle that is charming." Miss Van Woekem would not be deterred. "And the maid can get it for you, dear, sit down." But Cordelia marched out of the room. "Oh, dear. Not a good start to the afternoon," Miss Van Woekem said. "Rose, ring the bell for the maid, please. Or go and find her yourself. Really, guests in my house don't have to get their own tea."

We waited but the maid did not come. "I'm afraid she's quite disappeared," I said. "She's probably off sulking. The cook was very upset with her."

I was about to volunteer to find the tea myself when Rose got up. "I'll go and find her. The guests will be arriving soon."

"I can't thank you enough, Molly." Miss Van Woekem looked up with an expression not often seen on her normally stern face. "You have done me such a service." She glanced over to where Rose had just left. "Having that girl around the house is like having a breath of fresh air. I didn't realize how shut in I was becoming until she moved in here." I put my hand on hers in sympathy. She might have a big house, but apart from servants she was all alone. No wonder she would welcome a cheerful presence in the house.

"I think you are making a big difference in her life, too." I said. "I didn't recognize her when she walked in. She looks like quite a lady."

She smiled. "It makes a difference to have my morning coffee brought to me by a pretty face. And she tells me such charming stories about Ireland."

"I know what it is like to arrive in this city without a friend," I said. "And we have to clear her name so she can move on with her life."

"Surely Daniel doesn't still suspect her of anything," she said. "Anyone can see she could have nothing to do with a murder. I'll give him a piece of my mind next time I see him."

"I don't think he does suspect her anymore, or he would never have let her come here. He just has to close his investigation before he can let her move on to her family in Chicago."

Her face fell at the thought that Rose would be here only a short time.

"That reminds me," I said, leaning closer to her. "Please don't forget not to mention Daniel to her, at least not his work. She doesn't know I'm the wife of a policeman and I'd like to keep it that way." There was a sudden crash and we looked up in fright. Rose had come back into the parlor. Around her were the shards of the tea cup she had been holding.

Twenty

"Oh, I'm terrible sorry." Rose stared down at the broken cup. "Look what I've done. Do forgive me, Miss Van Woekem. I'm afraid I caught my shoe in my dress. I'll clean it right up." She disappeared in the direction of the kitchen.

"I'll help." I jumped up and followed her. I almost ran into her as she came out of the kitchen door with a dustpan and broom in her hands and a towel over one arm.

"To tell the truth I've always been a bit clumsy. Saints alive, what would me mother be saying," Rose said with a bright laugh that didn't match the look of fear in her eyes.

"Rose, I know you heard what I said and I want to explain."

"I don't know what you mean." Rose walked over to the broken shards and swept them into her dustpan. She walked quickly by me back into the kitchen, and I followed her.

"Rose, I may have told you a bit of an untruth." She dumped the broken cup pieces into the garbage pail noisily without looking at me. I put my hand on her arm and turned her to look at me. "My name used to be Molly Murphy, but it's Molly Sullivan now. My husband is Captain Sullivan, the policeman you have met."

"You've been pretending to be my friend." Her voice was still low but filled with anger. "You were sent to try and catch me out. You've been trying to prove me guilty and put me in prison."

"Not at all. Absolutely the opposite. Apart from that one fact, everything I told you was the truth. I've been trying to convince my husband that you're innocent."

She blinked back tears. "I thought you were my friend and that I could trust you. I'm all alone with no one to turn to. How do I know you are not trying to put me in prison?"

I took my hand off her arm. "You don't, I suppose. I can only tell you the truth. At first I did have to promise Captain Sullivan that I would help with the investigation, but since we have become friends I have only been trying to help you. Do you really think I would have trusted you with a job at my friend's house if I still suspected you of murder?"

Rose gave a tentative smile. "Oh, Molly, you scared me so much. I want so much to believe you're my friend."

"I am, believe me." I put my arms around her. "I'm sorry I didn't tell you the truth to start with."

"What must Miss Van Woekem think?" Rose looked worried again. "We shouldn't keep the ladies waiting. Molly, I had better get back."

I looked around. "And where's Cordelia? I thought she was looking for the maid to bring her a cup of tea." As we walked back toward the parlor Cordelia emerged from one of the doors in the hall. She stopped dead when she saw us both looking at her.

"Just powdering my nose," she said haughtily, and walked past us into the parlor. We followed. Rose and I spent the next few minutes moving furniture around at her direction.

"Mrs. Sage must have the place of honor beside you, of course, Godmother. Mama and Papa will sit here. Mrs. Sullivan, just move that sofa a little more to the right. I shall sit here with the viscount. My sisters can sit in these chairs here."

We finished arranging the room just as the first guests rang the bell. The maid mysteriously appeared from somewhere in the house to answer the door and admit the guests. I heard a gasp of pain and a cry of "Oh my!" and ran into the hall in time to see Jewel bending a poor middle-aged woman's arms behind her back in an attempt to relieve her of her coat.

"Let me help," I quickly offered. "Jewel, go and announce the guests as they come in." I helped the lady off with her fashionable but very wet coat.

"I dunno her name." Jewel stood there sulkily.

"Mrs. Sage," the lady said quite cheerfully, not put out at all by the ordeal. I decided at once that I liked her. She was a middle-aged woman dressed in a black tea dress, high necked and trimmed with lace. Her hair had the plastered-down forehead curls favored by the rich ladies of her generation. She wore huge dangling pearl earrings and a pearl choker around her neck.

"Mrs. Mage," Jewel announced in a nasal voice in the next room and stalked off. The doorbell buzzed again.

"I'm Molly Sullivan, Mrs. Sage. So nice to meet you." I gave her an encouraging smile as I steered her toward the sitting room. "I'm afraid Miss Van Woekem's current maid is not quite up to snuff. She's just out of the orphanage and not yet trained. I had better help the ladies off with their coats or they'll have her up for assault." She laughed and went into the parlor. So that was the Mrs. Sage I had heard so much about. One of the Four Hundred families that Mrs. Sullivan wanted me to become familiar with if Daniel went into politics. She was not at all what I expected. But then I remembered that she had sent her chauffeur to help give clothes out to the poor immigrants, which I suppose is more than most of the very rich would do.

I greeted the guests as they came in and took their coats as well, blushing a little bit because I was sure that more than one of them took me for the new maid just as Cordelia had done. Jewel finally reappeared just as all the guests had entered the sitting room.

"You had better mop the floor," I said, looking at all the puddles in the front hall, "or one of the guests will slip going out."

"I'm not sure that's my job." She looked at me defiantly, as if she were going to run away again.

I was not going to spend the rest of the party mopping floors. "Who else's job would it be but yours? Now go and get a mop this instant." She slouched off with ill grace and, trying to neaten up my dress a little, I returned to the sitting room.

For all her bravado earlier in the day, I saw that Bridie had shrunk back into the corner as the splendidly dressed ladies and one gentleman entered the sitting room. They gathered around Miss Van Woekem as if she were a queen on her throne and they were attendants. Some perched on the delicate little chairs with high spindly backs and some stood as if they had been posed. Beside Miss Van Woekem on a pink silk cushion was Princess Yasmin, a Persian cat now so large she only just fit on the cushion. I stayed well clear, having been scratched by that cat on more than one occasion.

The young ladies were in pale silk tea dresses that seemed to float off the ground. It was a good thing that Miss Van Woekem's ceilings were high or there would have been no room for the hats that perched on their elegantly swept up hair. Some of the feathers were a foot long! I wished again that I had thought to ask Sid and Gus to lend me a dress before they went out. At least the older women were dressed in all black and thicker fabrics so I didn't stand out too badly.

"And Molly, here is one old friend of yours," Miss Van Woekem called to me across the room. "You remember my goddaughter, Arabella. She was Norton but now Chase." As if I could forget Arabella Norton.

I gave her my sweetest smile. "Nice to see you again, Arabella."

A large number of fashionable heads turned in my direction as I pulled over a chair for myself. Of course Cordelia had neglected to include me in the seating arrangements. "This is Mrs. Molly Sullivan,

Police Captain Sullivan's wife," Miss Van Woekem said, introducing me to the company.

"Mrs. Sullivan is Augusta and Elena's little friend," Cordelia continued as her eyes traveled down me, taking in the unfashionable suit and the small felt hat. "She has been kind enough to help with this little gathering." Cordelia's smile was polite. I bristled at being called little. I was sure I was inches taller than Miss Ransom, unless you counted the hat.

"And how do you know Mrs. Sullivan?" The elegantly dressed woman on the other side of Cordelia sounded surprised.

"We met handing out clothes at Ellis Island, Mother. For our benevolent society, you know. Mrs. Sullivan, this is my mother, Mrs. Ransom, and my sisters, Elizabeth and Victoria." Cordelia's mother looked more like her sister than anyone's concept of a mother. She had a waist even tinier than her daughter's and an impressive bosom, a figure I supposed I might have had too if I wanted to be laced up into a corset. She looked at me sharply, as if wondering if I were good enough to associate with her daughter, even at a charity event. I tried to keep a smile on my face. If going out into polite society was going to mean being judged like this on every occasion, I decided I would just as soon stay a simple policeman's wife.

Elizabeth and Victoria were both younger than Cordelia, Victoria scarcely older than Bridie. They were both dressed like little princesses in pastel silk. I saw them looking at Bridie with the same disdainful look that Mrs. Ransom gave me, and I saw Bridie blush as she noticed this too.

I turned to introduce her. "This is my—"

"You were out at Ellis Island?" Mr. Ransom's forceful voice interrupted me. Cordelia started, rather guiltily I thought. "What on earth were you doing there? I pay the earth to send you to the finest schools in America and Europe and you spend your time with the worst trash in New York? It is positively un-American!"

"Hush, John, charity work is perfectly acceptable for a young lady." Mrs. Ransom looked embarrassed.

My color rose. Trash indeed! My temper, already frayed by that morning's events, almost got the best of me. But I was a guest in Miss Van Woekem's house and I bit back the angry words that threatened to spill out.

"'Give me your tired, your poor, your huddled masses yearning to breathe free,'" a firm voice with an Irish lilt spoke, and I was surprised to see that it was Rose. "That's on your statue in your harbor. What is more American than helping an immigrant coming to the new world?"

"I hope that you will remember, young *lady*"—he put an emphasis on the word "lady" that made it clear he did not think her one—"that the next line in that poem is 'your wretched *refuse*.' Precisely what I said—trash."

"Dear, don't be unpleasant." Mrs. Ransom laid her hand on his arm.

"And I suppose that your family never immigrated from anywhere, then?" Rose looked up at him defiantly.

"She has you there," Mrs. Sage spoke up. "I happen to know that your grandfather came over as a young man. He came to be a forty-niner but never made it farther than New York." The ladies in the room laughed.

Cordelia's father's large unpleasant face now turned a shade of purple as he opened his mouth to defend himself. Cordelia managed to get in there first, turning to Miss Van Woekem with, "Where did your family come from? Your family were one of the original residents of New Amsterdam, weren't they?"

"Indeed they were. We've been here since the sixteen hundreds."

All eyes turned to the hostess as she explained a rather lengthy family tree. I confess I didn't pay much attention. I was thinking about two things that surprised me. One was that I felt a little sorry for Cordelia Ransom and two was that Rose McSweeney had spoken up when I had kept silent. There was a time when I would not let anyone put me down. I was proud of my heritage and who I had become. Had life in New York changed me so much that I wouldn't stand up for my own people? I told myself that I was growing up and learning to control myself. Surely that was a good thing.

I turned to Cordelia, who was still looking quite embarrassed by her father's behavior. "Tell me about your young man," I said. "I understand he is an English aristocrat?" I was gratified to receive the first look from her that was not scornful. She flashed me a grateful smile.

"He should be here any minute, he—" Cordelia began.

"He's English, you know," her mother interrupted, leaning over her and speaking loudly enough that the whole group could hear. "A viscount. Just imagine it, my Cordelia will be a viscountess. Lady Cordelia. I can't wait to go and stay with them at their castle. My dears, I may meet the king. Imagine it!"

"My friend has met the king." I was astonished to see that Bridie was speaking. All eyes turned to look at her, as she was still sitting on the far corner of the sofa.

"Oh, yes, dear?" Mrs. Ransom looked put out. "And you are?"

"I'm Bridie O'Connor. A girl that lives with Molly. And my friend is Mr. O'Hare. He does plays and he did one for the king. There was a big party."

"Bridie is my ward." I shot daggers at her. "A girl that lives with Molly" indeed when I was practically her mother. "Ryan O'Hare the playwright is a friend of ours."

"Did he tell you what this party was like?" Mrs. Ransom turned to Bridie, and she glowed at being the center of attention. I wondered what had happened to the shy girl who hid behind my skirts. Mrs. Ransom looked eager to hear, but I was all too aware that Miss Van Woekem was looking scandalized at a young girl speaking to the whole party. "In my day," I could almost hear her say, "children were to be seen and not heard."

"Yes. The king was there and all the famous actresses that you see in the paper and lords and ladies . . . there was even . . ."

"Just a minute. Excuse me. Eyelash." I felt Rose's finger touch my cheek delicately and looked at her. I was relieved she had stopped Bridie's story. That girl was getting above herself, and who knows what inventions were about to come out of her mouth.

"Oh, I'm sorry, Bridie, I didn't mean to interrupt. It's just that Molly has an eyelash on her cheek and she can make a wish." Rose took my hand and put the eyelash on the back of it. "Now blow and make a wish." I felt foolish blowing on my hand in front of all these people and unable to come up with any wish but to stop being the center of attention as soon as possible, but it was an instant success. Young ladies were checking each other's faces for stray eyelashes, some of them outright pretending to have found them and wishing.

"I know who you are wishing for," Victoria said to Elizabeth. "And his name starts with C." They collapsed into giggles.

"So, Mrs. Sullivan, is that an Irish superstition? Wishing on an eyelash? Like throwing salt over your shoulder or not letting a black cat cross your path." Mrs. Ransom's nose wrinkled slightly as she said this. Silly Irish superstition was written in her body language.

"I'm not sure I ever heard of it before," I confessed. "My family didn't have much time for superstitions, or wishes. Except of course wishing you'd never been born. That was a big one. 'You get those chores done before dinner or you'll wish you'd never been born.' Maybe Rose's family was a little different. Is this a superstition from Galway, Rose?" But Rose wasn't listening to me anymore. She was the center of the wishing girls. Mrs. Sage especially seemed to be enjoying herself quite as much as the younger women.

"Excuse me, miss." The laughter broke off as heads turned toward the door. The maid Jewel had just entered, and a handsome, well-dressed man was standing in the doorway.

Jewel gave an entirely awkward, sweeping, and quite inappropriate curtsy. "The Viscount Brackley, ma'am." Perhaps she thought she was in a castle in a penny dreadful.

"Yes, thank you, Jewel." Miss Van Woekem's tone would have made any other girl leave the room immediately, but Jewel seemed to not even hear it and turned to stare at the man as he entered. He was, indeed, extremely handsome.

"Here he is, the man of the hour." Mr. Ransom was now all smiles as he walked over to the viscount, his hand extended. Cordelia rose gracefully, almost shyly.

He took Cordelia's hand and kissed it. "Cordelia." He smiled charmingly at her. "Mr. Ransom, Mrs. Ransom," he turned to them politely, "please excuse my lateness. I had some business that had to be attended to and I wanted to finish it quickly so I could spend the whole afternoon in your charming company."

"Doesn't he have the cutest accent!" Mrs. Ransom beamed. "Viscount, this is Miss Van Woekem, who is so kindly giving the party. Miss Van Woekem, this is Viscount Brackley.

"Delighted to make your acquaintance, Viscount." Miss Van Woekem held out her hand. I wondered if he was going to kiss it too, but he merely shook it, giving her a little bow. I noticed her looking at the couple appraisingly. Maybe she was wondering if this English viscount was good enough for her young friend. He certainly had charm. His sandy blond hair was impeccably styled and his suit was expensively cut. He was a perfect match for Cordelia, who looked as if she had stepped out of a fashion plate. Not my type, I thought.

That made me think of Daniel, who was definitely my type. It was hard to equate the Daniel I knew now with the confused feelings I had experienced in this very sitting room, knowing that I loved Daniel, but knowing that he could never be mine because he was engaged. I wondered if romance would be ahead in Rose's future like it had been in mine. I looked around to see her. She had retreated to the far side of the room and was staring at the viscount with what looked like awe, nervously patting at the sides of her bun to smooth her hair neatly. So perhaps he was her type. But already engaged to a socialite. Was history repeating itself? I told myself that I had to stop comparing the two of us. We were quite different people. She just reminded me so much of myself, of things I had forgotten about myself until this minute.

"I think the viscount might have an announcement for us!" Mrs. Ransom said excitedly. "Go ahead, Viscount. We're all ears!"

The viscount cleared his throat. "Since I seem to have everyone's attention, and with your permission, sir," he looked at Mr. Ransom, who nodded. "Cordelia and I spent a lot of time getting to know each other when she was in London. And, in short, I have asked her to marry me and she has made me the happiest man on earth." He kissed her hand again. We all applauded politely. Space was made for the couple to sit together.

Mrs. Ransom turned to Mrs. Sage next to her. "Of course he has only seen our apartment in Central Park West since he has just arrived, but we will certainly be inviting him out to our estate on Long Island once all the snow has cleared. It is beastly to be out of the city in this weather. And after the wedding, my dear, we will be traveling to England and staying at his castle. I have always wanted to visit a real English castle. Imagine that. Me, the mother of a viscountess."

An extra-strong gust of wind made the window by Miss Van Woekem rattle. "What a dreary day. I declare I prefer snow to this cold rain," she said to no one in particular.

"Are you cold, Miss Van Woekem?" Rose muttered into her ear. "I'll fetch you a shawl right away."

"That would be lovely, Rose. And get yourself a cup of tea and a biscuit while you are at it. You look quite pale." I was impressed. That was not how she had treated me as a companion! She had made sure she kept me in my place. Here was Rose, just arrived off the boat from Ireland, and she was treating her like a long-lost daughter! I supposed Rose was more considerate than I. Or had learned to be more subservient.

I listened to the conversation in the room without taking it in much. I knew no one there except for Cordelia, and the party was now deep in conversation about colors for the wedding breakfast. Rose did not reappear. Poor Bridie looked quite lost and alone, glancing with envy at Cordelia's beautifully styled young sisters. I motioned for her to come over and sit beside them. Surely she could join in conversation with girls her age, but she shot me a mortified look and shook her head.

"Did I hear your young ward was helping the poor with you out at Ellis Island?" Mrs. Sage began kindly, seeing our exchange. "Were you in my motor car, young lady?" Bridie's face brightened.

"Yes, with all the clothes. We almost couldn't see out the windows." Bridie's animation returned. Mrs. Sage patted the sofa beside her. "Come and tell me all about it." Bridie walked over and began to tell Mrs. Sage all about her trips to Ellis Island. I noticed with some trepidation that she was telling her stories in a rather embroidered fashion again. Mrs. Sage was either very kind or actually entertained. Even Cordelia's sisters began to listen, although they tried to keep the disdainful looks on their faces. Really, I decided, perhaps she was destined to become a novelist, as she described the horror of almost being trapped in the Registry Room and sent back to Ireland, alone and an orphan.

"How did you escape?" Victoria's pretense of not caring dropped entirely, and Bridie turned to her to continue the story with a gratified look on her face.

"I'm afraid the girl has a bit of the blarney, Mrs. Sage," I said softly to her so that Bridie wouldn't hear. "I wouldn't believe everything she says."

"She seems like a gifted storyteller. It takes a lot to get the Ransom girls to take an interest in anything except clothes and young men." Mrs. Sage turned to me.

"Do you know the Ransom family well?"

"It seems as if all the old New York families know each other. I thought, you know, that Cordelia and my son might make a go of it." She spoke comfortably, treating me as if I were someone she had known for years and not a total stranger. "Her mother and I had an understanding from the time they were little. They played together before they could talk. But Odessa has always been fascinated with the English aristocracy. She is so thrilled that her daughter will be a viscountess. My poor Harry didn't stand a chance."

Her manner was so relaxed and easy that I responded the same way. "According to my mother-in-law you are New York aristocracy, Mrs. Sage."

"Who is your mother-in-law? Have we met?"

"I don't think we move in the same circles. She and I are both Mrs. Sullivan. My husband, Daniel, is a police captain." Mother Sullivan would have loved for me to mention politics or Daniel's ambitions at the point, but I couldn't bring myself to do it. I paused to listen to Bridie's story again and realized that she was telling the story of the second visit to Ellis Island as well, in gory detail.

"And then I felt a searing pain and I pulled out my hand and it was dripping with blood!" She matched the action to her words, miming a death wound.

"Oh my." Mrs. Ransom had clearly been listening to the story as well. "Please don't give my girls nightmares. Their delicate dispositions can't take that kind of horror."

On the contrary it seemed that the girls had enjoyed the story immensely and were eager for Bridie to continue. But I was aware of Mrs. Ransom glaring at me. "Let's talk about something else," I said to Bridie. "That's not appropriate party conversation."

"I suppose it is because your husband is a policeman," Cordelia put in. "She must be exposed to more of the criminal element." And for once I couldn't think of a single thing to say.

Miss Van Woekem began a story about a prank that she and Mrs. Ransom had played on their families when they were both still children. I was grateful to have nothing to do but listen. I'm afraid my mind started to wander, seeing that bloody knife again in my imagination. How had it ended up in that muff? We knew that a guard had stolen the money and wallet. Had he been involved in the murder, too? But why would a guard have anything to do with a detective from England?

As the day became quite dark outside, even though it was not yet five in the afternoon, Cordelia's mother started to make her excuses.

"Really, I am not sure we would be able to get home safely through this rain if it gets any darker," Mrs. Ransom said as she peered outside doubtfully. "Maybe we should take our leave now, Maude."

"That might be wise. It looks as if the weather is getting worse," Mr. Ransom agreed.

One by one the guests all rose to go.

"Oh, dear, I've dropped my bracelet." Mrs. Sage got up and started looking under the sofa cushions. "The clasp is weak and it falls off my wrist sometimes. Girls, help me look for it." Cordelia's sisters and Bridie stood up obligingly and began to look behind the cushions and on the floor.

"What does it look like, Mary?" Miss Van Woekem asked, concerned.

"It is a pearl bracelet that matches this choker. I know I shouldn't wear it out, but it matches the necklace and earrings, so I do."

"I'll go and look in the hall," I said, wondering if it might have come off when the maid was jerking the coat off roughly. I searched under the hall chairs but couldn't see any sign of it. The girls had no luck either.

"Don't worry, my dears, perhaps it fell off in the automobile on the way over. I'll have the chauffeur look for it tomorrow." She glanced out the window. "Ah, here he comes now with the umbrella. Please excuse me if I make a hasty exit."

"I'll take my leave too." The viscount kissed Cordelia's hand, and her mother gave a twittering laugh. "Shall we be seeing you tomorrow at the Plaza Hotel at eleven, Viscount?"

"Of course," Cordelia said, giving her mother an annoyed look.

"It will be my pleasure, ma'am. And perhaps I may be allowed to ask Cordelia to dine with me?"

"Oh, how genteel he is," Mrs. Ransom said in a loud whisper to her husband.

"Come on, stop dillydallying," Mr. Ransom said crossly. "Let's go, the chauffeur is getting quite wet. Thank you so much for the party, my dear Maud. Come on, girls."

"Cordelia, you've forgotten your gloves and purse. I'll get them for you." Elizabeth ran to the small table where Cordelia had laid her gloves and purse and snatched them up.

Something flew out of the gloves and landed on the floor with a loud clatter. "Sorry!" Elizabeth gasped, "Whatever is that?" She bent to pick it up. It was Mrs. Sage's bracelet.

Twenty-One

It was raining quite hard when we came out of the house and darkness had already fallen, the street lamps throwing pools of light onto the wet sidewalks. I might have expected the constable on duty to find a cab for us, but he was reluctant to leave his post, guarding Rose. So we had to walk as far as Park Avenue to find a cab and were both rather cold and miserable by the time we climbed aboard. I was still disturbed by what had happened at the party. All these images flashed through my mind: Rose looking so beautiful and almost defiant in that pale blue dress. The viscount was certainly handsome, and I saw that Rose was fascinated with him. Good luck there, I thought. He was about to marry a very rich woman.

But then there was the disturbing incident with the bracelet. Who could have taken it and then put it in Cordelia's glove? What's more, why? To make Cordelia look like a suspect? Who could possibly have wanted to do that? I found my gaze turning to the girl beside me, who sat hunched up and cold as we rattled over the cobbles on the way home. Had she decided to pay Cordelia back for treating me like a servant? It didn't seem likely, as she hadn't seemed that fond of me lately. A more worrying thought crossed my mind: Had she taken it for herself, hiding it until she could retrieve it later?

I decided not to say anything about it.

"Didn't Rose McSweeney look pretty in that dress?" I said, to break the silence more than anything. "She looked quite different."

"I don't like her," Bridie said with conviction.

"Bridie? Why not?"

Bridie shrugged. "I don't know. I just don't. She's just too nice and friendly to you."

"I'm a fellow Irishwoman, so naturally she feels a connection with me. And after all, I have saved her bacon. She's bound to be grateful. Wouldn't you be if you'd been rescued from a horrid boarding-house?"

"I guess," she said. She hunched down into her scarf and wouldn't say any more. We arrived home and changed out of our wet things. Mrs. Sullivan had heated up the last of the cottage pie while I added cauliflower and carrots.

"I don't think we'll be wanting much in the way of supper tonight," I said to my mother-in-law as I swept up Liam into my arms. "There was a marvelous spread of sandwiches and cakes, wasn't there, Bridie?"

She gave a sort of grunt in reply.

I noticed she had changed into her old day dress and not the new blue one I had made for her. "You're allowed to wear your new dress," I said. "It's for every day, to replace that one that you've outgrown. Put the pinny over it if you don't want to get it dirty."

"I'm fine with this now, thank you," she said. "I don't want to go up in the cold room to change again. And I have homework to do."

"Speaking of your studies." Mrs. Sullivan turned to me. "The ladies commented how well you were doing and how eager you were to learn."

"You saw the ladies?" Bridie asked, her face lighting up now.

Mother Sullivan nodded. "They came over a little while ago and asked you to stop by when you came home, Molly. They have something to give you, apparently."

I felt a glimmer of hope that they had found a lovely dress for me among their donations. Or at least one as nice as Rose's. And I desperately wanted to talk to them.

"I'll be back in a minute," I said. "Bridie, can you watch Liam?"

"I should be doing my studies," she said.

"Very well, I'll take him with me. He loves visiting his aunties," I said. I was not going to let her annoy me tonight. I draped my coat over both our heads and we dashed across the narrow street. Gus opened the door. "Molly!" she exclaimed. "We didn't expect to see you this evening. Your mother-in-law said you'd gone out to a fancy party."

"A tea party," I said. "It was over at five."

"And you've brought our favorite man to see us." Gus took an excited Liam from me. "Aunty Sid is cooking in the kitchen, Liam. Go and see if she has any goodies to share."

Liam needed no urging and took off down the hallway.

"We should probably go through to the kitchen too," Gus said. "The parlor is still full of clothes. A complete fire hazard, so I haven't dared to light the fire in there." She walked ahead of me down the hall.

"Mother Sullivan said you had something for me?" I asked.

"Why, yes. Ryan popped in to visit and left two tickets for his opening night for you. He's sorry it couldn't be more, but the play is sold out for weeks. Ryan, as you can imagine, was in his element, glowing so much that one would not need electric light."

I smiled. "It's next Friday, is it? I hope Daniel is free for once."

We came into the warmth of the kitchen, redolent with the scent of herbs. Sid looked up from a pot she was stirring. Liam was sitting on the floor beside her, chewing happily on a carrot. "I'm making a variation on a Moroccan lamb dish," she said. "I'm supposed to have a special pot with a funny lid called a tagine, but we don't have one and I've no idea where I'd be able to buy one."

"It's smells wonderful," I said. "Really I must learn to try some of these exotic dishes one day, if I ever find the time."

"Would Daniel approve?" Sid grinned.

"Probably. I'm not so sure about Mrs. Sullivan," I said. "She never misses a chance to tell me what Daniel's favorite food was before he met me."

"Tell her too bad, he's not her little boy any longer and she's lucky to have you to look after her," Sid said, going back to her stirring.

"I'm trying to keep the peace. It's not always easy," I replied.

"And how is our favorite young lady? Did she have a good time at your tea party?" Gus asked. "Was she able to impress the other guests with her vast amounts of knowledge?"

"Your favorite young lady is becoming rather a handful," I said. "There was that incident with the party dress . . ."

Sid turned to me now. "Yes, I'm truly sorry about that, Molly. All my fault. I didn't really think for a minute that my old ball gown would be suitable for her to wear to your party. I let her have fun and try it on. I'm sorry it caused conflict. But she is growing up, you know. We should encourage that, not try to keep her a little girl forever."

"I just don't want her to have her expectations raised above reality," I said.

"But, Molly, she'll go to Vassar one day if we can bring her education up to the right level," Gus said. "We've already agreed that we'll pay for her. After that the sky is the limit. She can be anything she wants to be, and anyone she wants to be."

I didn't quite know what to say to that. Didn't one need money and position as well as education for the sky to be the limit? And I knew all too well that Sid and Gus were easily distracted, always anxious to try new things. What if Bridie was in the middle of her studies at Vassar when they decided to go off to South America or Australia? I shifted nervously and bent to take a piece of unchewed carrot out of Liam's mouth before he choked on it.

"To be honest, I'm a little worried about Bridie at the moment," I said. "Not that she is defying me. That's to be expected given her age, I suppose."

"Aren't all girls of her age rebellious?" Sid asked. "I know I was."

"Haven't changed much," Gus commented.

Sid chose to ignore this. "And you have to realize she feels secure for the first time in years. She knows she's got a loving home, she has two aunties who adore her. She doesn't have to walk on eggshells any longer, or worry if she could be abandoned. So it's a good sign, really."

"I suppose so," I agreed. "Liam, come back here." I grabbed him as he attempted to run down the hall. "But something happened today that rather disturbed me." And I related the incident with the bracelet.

"You think that Bridie took it?"

"She had the opportunity. She was sitting next to Mrs. Sage and I remember she was deep in conversation and wouldn't have noticed someone unclasping her bracelet. So now I'm wondering did Bridie take it, meaning to steal it, and then lost her nerve, or did she take it and plant it deliberately to make Cordelia Ransom look suspect?"

"You don't want to have a heart-to-heart talk with her? Ask her for the truth?" Gus asked.

"I think that would only make her more suspicious of me. She's not likely to tell me the truth at the moment. Do you think you could broach the subject with her, if the opportunity arises?"

"I suppose so," Gus said hesitantly. "But we have developed such a good relationship with her, Molly. I'd hate to suddenly seem to be mistrusting her. I'd say let it go and maybe she'll tell you herself in good time."

I nodded. Liam squirmed in my arms. "I should take him home," I said. "Daniel will be wanting his dinner."

"Speaking of Daniel, what news on your murder investigation? Have they nailed down the culprit yet?"

"No, but our discoveries on Ellis Island were much appreciated. Remember you found out that Italian guard called Mario had left his post in a hurry? Well, it seemed that he'd been under observation for a while, helping himself to items from the baggage room. When Daniel's men raided his apartment they found the English money from the wallet but other things, too. So he's been arrested as a thief."

"But not a suspect in the murder? They don't think he killed to get the wallet?"

"They may still be looking into that. I don't know. Daniel doesn't tell me everything, and frankly I've been so busy with finishing Bridie's dresses and getting Rose settled and worrying about this party that I haven't had enough time to play the detective. It's hard to be a housewife and mother and try to make time for a life outside the home."

"Which is precisely why we choose the life we have," Sid said.

"Not only for that reason," Gus reminded her. Sid smiled.

"So where would you go from here as the detective?" Gus asked.

"I'm dying to have a chat with that Englishman—the one who claims he saw Rose coming out of the room where the murder took place. He's the only person to have implicated her in the crime so far. He seems very suspicious to me. An upper-class man, traveling in steerage, claiming his family sent him away because of his bad behavior. And Rose said that he made sexual advances to her on the boat. She thinks he told lies about her because she rebuffed him."

"Quite possible," Sid agreed. "Do you know where he is staying?"

I gave a hopeless shrug. "Somewhere in the city. That's all I know. I can't very well ask Daniel for his address. And Daniel is waiting to see if more information on him is coming from Scotland Yard. Apparently they aren't being too helpful or speedy. At least he's not allowed to leave the city for the moment."

"He sounds like a good candidate," Gus said. "Would he have had any connection to the man who was killed? A fellow Englishman, you said."

"Not only that but he was a private detective hired to track down a jewel thief from a party in London, so it seems."

"Ah!" Sid wagged a knowing finger at me. "Hence the desire for justice. One of your fraternity is killed. You seek retribution."

I laughed. "Not at all. I have no feelings for the late Mr. Darby. But I do care about Rose McSweeney. Having been in the same position myself when I arrived and had nobody I could turn to, I want to make sure we get to the truth swiftly, so that she can join her relatives in Chicago. Although . . ."

I hesitated.

"Although what?"

"Having seen her today at Miss Van Woekem's I wonder if she is not considering other options. Maybe a companion's job to a rich elderly lady might be more desirable than what her relatives have to offer her."

"So she has taken to the position well, has she? The old lady is satisfied with her?"

"More than that. She seems right at home, and Miss Van Woekem is clearly enchanted."

"So all's well that ends well, then?" Sid said.

"If it does end well," I replied. I realized that the events of the afternoon had made me uneasy, and not just the loss of the bracelet. Something to do with the arrival of the viscount . . . but when I tried to analyze it I couldn't put my finger on it.

Daniel wanted to know all about the party. He was amused when I told him it was to celebrate Cordelia Ransom's engagement to an English viscount. "So Mama Ransom finally got her way, did she?"

I was surprised. "You know her?"

He looked slightly embarrassed. "She moved in the same circles as Arabella. Lots of mothers on the prowl for good matches for their daughters."

I realized then, with a jolt to the pit of my stomach, that he too had been part of that circle, although I was sure that Mama Ransom would not have looked twice at him as a good match.

"That Cordelia person is horrible," Bridie blurted out. "She looks at Molly and me as if we are servants. She told Molly to take her coat. And then—do you know what—one of the ladies lost her bracelet and guess where it was found? Inside Cordelia's glove on the table beside her."

She said it with such triumph that again I wondered if she was pleased with herself for having managed this coup.

Daniel chuckled. "You're not trying to hint that Cordelia Ransom tried to steal a bracelet? Oh no, my dear. The Ransoms are stinking rich. She could buy herself a bracelet a day if she wanted to. I wasn't there, but the most likely thing is that the bracelet fell off and one of the servants saw it on the floor, picked it up, and put it on the sofa for safekeeping."

That did seem to be a reasonable explanation, except that I couldn't recall a servant in the room. Rose had made herself scarce, and Jewel had only appeared with a new pot of tea under sufferance, making a hasty departure each time. Perhaps it had been put beside the glove but Cordelia had moved it a little, causing the bracelet to be hidden.

"Perhaps she's one of those people who can't help stealing things," Bridie suggested. "I've forgotten the word, but Aunt Gus was telling me about when she worked with Professor Freud and how people have manias."

"A kleptomaniac." Daniel looked at her with interest as if he were seeing her as a person for the first time. "Yes, it's always possible." He took a drink of water. "So, you're studying psychology now, are you?"

"Oh no." Bridie blushed. "It is supposed to be American history, but Aunt Gus tells me things she thinks might interest me. We were talking about the man who shot Abraham Lincoln and then we got on to the man who shot President McKinley."

I knew a little too much about that, having been personally involved, but I didn't think this was the time or the place to tell her. However, Daniel said, "Molly helped to catch that man, you know."

"She did?" She turned to me with wonder.

"It was frightening," I said. "One day I'll tell you about it, but not now."

I noticed that she was looking at me with new respect. As we cleared the table after the meal she came up beside me. "So it's true that you were a real detective, is it? Aunt Gus said you were, but I didn't quite believe her."

"I used to be once," I admitted.

"You should go back to doing it. Aunt Gus said a woman's brain is wasted on domestic matters."

I had to smile at that earnest little face. "Oh, my dear, I'm afraid you're going to find out that the world expects women to take care of domestic matters. We are the ones who have to keep the house and have the babies and there is no escaping that fact."

"That's not fair," Bridie retorted.

"I agree, but it's the way it is." I put an arm around her shoulder. "Nevertheless, a woman can make time for other things if she's a mind to."

"I'm not going to get married, then," Bridie retorted. Oh, mercy me—I hoped Mother Sullivan hadn't heard that or she'd blame Sid and Gus.

"There is a lot to be said for having a loving husband and children of your own," I said, exchanging a glance with my husband. "You'll agree when you find the right man."

"Do you think that viscount was the right man for Miss Cordelia?" Bridie asked.

"I think the idea of a castle in England and being called 'my lady' are more appealing to her than the actual gentleman, although he certainly is handsome."

"I didn't like him either," Bridie said. "He thought too much of himself, didn't he?"

I had to smile. "He certainly seemed to."

I remembered the tickets that Gus had given me. "Daniel, next Friday is the opening night of Ryan O'Hare's new play. It was a huge success in London and now he's brought it here. He's given us two tickets for opening night and then he's having a party afterward at the Knickerbocker Hotel."

Daniel's face was hard to read. "You know I'd love to come, normally," he said, "but I'd hate to have to let you down at the last minute if I was called out to a homicide. And Friday nights are prime moments for that. So why don't you take someone else? Take my mother—"

I didn't say what I was thinking, which was "Jesus, Mary, and Joseph!" Ryan had already hinted that his play was more than a little risqué. Actually Ryan's plays were always risqué. I glanced over to see if Mother Sullivan had heard. She had. Before I could answer she shook her head, "Oh, no, thank you. My days of theaters and late nights are long over. Besides, who is going to put the little one to bed if I'm not here, and keep Bridie company too?"

I tried not to let my sigh of relief show. "That's very kind of you, Mother," I said.

"Your friends across the street will be going," she said. "You can go with them. I've no doubt they feel right at home in a theater crowd."

"They do," I said.

"You could always take me," Bridie spoke up. "I've never been to a proper theater and I'd love to see Mr. O'Hare at his party."

I went over and put an arm around her. "Unfortunately, my darling, I gather this is going to be quite an improper theater. Not a suitable play for young girls."

"I'm grown up." She stuck out her chin. "I know lots of naughty words. You should have heard what my cousins and Aunt Nuala said."

"I can imagine." I had to smile. "But all the same it would not be proper to bring a young girl to such a play and certainly not to the party afterward."

"Certainly not indeed," Mother Sullivan echoed. "Not the sort of people a decent young girl would want to go mixing with."

"But Mr. O'Hare was a lovely man. He told me how elegant I looked," Bridie said.

"He is indeed a lovely man, but some of his friends—well, I wouldn't want you there and that's final. I won't be staying long myself. To be honest, Bridie, I don't feel comfortable in that kind of crowd either. Just as I didn't feel comfortable at the party today."

"You didn't?"

"As a matter of fact I felt most out of place. I wasn't dressed properly and Cordelia Ransom treated me like a servant. If I hadn't promised to help Miss Van Woekem and didn't want to let her down, I would have slipped out early."

"I thought I was the only one who felt that way," Bridie said.

"I thought you were enjoying yourself." I frowned as I looked at her.

"I tried to smile and be polite, but I was sure they were all staring at me. Aunt Gus said once that nobody wears white after Labor Day and I was wondering why I was dressed in the wrong color."

"That rule doesn't apply to young girls," I said. "And it's a silly rule anyway. You should be able to wear whatever color you like. Anyway, I thought you looked just perfect and I'm sure the other ladies did too."

"What will you wear to the theater and the party?" Bridie asked. "You said all your lovely dresses got burned."

I gave a sad little smile. "Well, for one thing I never had lovely dresses. I had a couple of suitable dresses—passed on from Gus, I seem to remember. But we've never had the money to have me fitted for a real evening gown. Not that we go to elegant soirees." I glanced at Daniel and chuckled. I saw he was frowning. Was he picturing a future in which he might be a candidate for office and we would have to be out in society? Was he just now realizing the sort of money that would entail? I hoped it might make him decide he liked our life just as it was.

Twenty-Two

Sunday was cold, wet, and gloomy. We had planned to take Liam out to the park after church, but instead we had to keep him entertained in the house all day, which meant too much pent-up energy and several bouts of tears. Why did I ever think I wanted more children, I wondered as I carried him up the stairs, kicking and screaming. That night the problem of a dress to wear to the theater weighed heavily on my mind. Should I swallow my pride and ask to borrow something from Sid and Gus? Then I thought of that closet at Miss Van Woekem's where Rose had said that the goddaughters left all sorts of dresses behind. Perhaps I could ask to use one of those for the evening. But again my pride wouldn't let me. What if the dress had belonged to Cordelia and she happened to be at the opening night and she saw me and exclaimed loudly, "Why, she's wearing my old dress!" I could just imagine her doing that!

All right. It would have to be Sid and Gus unless I could rescue one of the donated garments and, with my newly acquired sewing machine, make something of my own. I felt more optimistic when I awoke on Monday morning. It was a fine, breezy day so I had to put all else aside, light the big copper for the hot water, and do laundry. With any luck the sheets would dry in the stiff wind. This kept me busy all day, but I had the satisfaction of bringing in a laundry basket full of items waiting to be ironed.

As I worked I found myself toying with the murder case that Daniel had not yet managed to solve. How I would love to come up with a brilliant solution and present it to him. "Do you not realize that the real suspect is so obvious?" How I would love to say that and watch his face. But of course I had no idea who the real suspect might be. The police were looking into that guard who had been pilfering. They might find he had connections to the Cosa Nostra and thus might be a trained killer. That would be a wonderfully simple solution for all concerned. But my money was still on the Englishman. I dearly wanted to have a chance to chat with him.

Daniel arrived home early and beckoned me into the front parlor. "I thought you ought to know," he said as he closed the door behind us, "we've finally had some communication from Ireland. There are twenty-three Rose McSweeneys living in that coastal area outside Galway, but there does indeed seem to be one whose two brothers, Connor and Joseph McSweeney, are known to authorities as active members of the Republican Brotherhood. They were recently arrested and, according to neighbors, Rose herself had left the village in a hurry, intending to go to relatives in America."

I felt a great flood of relief. "There you are, then. She's exactly who she claims to be. She recently left a village in the west of Ireland to come to America. There is no way she could have met a man from London or been involved in any high society robbery, is there?"

Daniel nodded. "There does not seem to be."

"Not seem to be?" My anger bubbled to the surface. "Ever since that poor girl stepped onto American soil you've been trying to find a way to pin the crime on her. It's just not fair. Is it because she's a woman on her own, with no relatives nearby, and she can't fight back? So tell me, did you find her fingerprints on the knife? Did you?"

"Molly!" Daniel put a hand on my shoulder. "Calm down. I'm agreeing with you. I'm saying there does not seem to be any reason why we need to keep Rose McSweeney in New York any longer. Tomorrow you can go to Miss Van Woekem and tell Rose that she is free to leave when she wants to."

"She'll be so happy to hear that," I said. "Although I think she's fallen on her feet in her current position. I doubt her relatives live in such luxury."

"The old lady might well want to hang on to her at the moment if she's proving to be a good companion," Daniel said. "In my experience she's found companions are hard to keep."

I grinned, understanding the reference. "In my case I had a better offer," I said. "I wanted to become a detective."

"I should have stopped you then and there." Daniel chuckled.

"You were the reason I left." My smile turned into a glare. "Your precious Arabella staying at the house. It was more than I could bear."

"I'm sorry." He took my hand. "But it all turned out all right, wouldn't you say?"

"Not too badly at all," I agreed.

The next morning I packed Bridie off to her lessons, waited until Liam was ready for his nap, and then off I went to Miss Van Woekem's. I didn't treat myself to a cab this time but instead took the Sixth Avenue El to Twenty-Third Street and then walked across to Gramercy Park. I had long ago found that walking was faster than taking the jitney across town. The maid Jewel opened the door.

"Oh, it's you again," she said.

"Indeed it is," I replied. "And that is no way to greet a guest, Jewel. When Miss Van Woekem's real maid returns and you're looking for another position, you will need a reference. And I can't see her giving you one at this rate." I was rather surprised at myself. Until now I had firmly been on the side of the underdog, the downtrodden. And here was I sounding exactly like Cordelia Ransom. But I was doing it for the girl's good, I told myself. I continued as I stepped into the front hall, "What you should say is 'Good morning, madam. Please come in. I will ask the mistress if she is receiving callers.'"

I thought I saw Jewel's lips twitch in a smile.

"But you ain't no real lady, not like them, are you?" she asked defiantly. "I saw you working down in the kitchen. Real ladies don't know how to do that."

"Ah, but I'm better than a real lady because I'm a police captain's wife," I replied and was delighted at the look of horror that invoked.

"Oh, I see," she said. "So is it about last night or are you checking up on Rose?" She nodded toward the sitting room.

"Should I be?"

"I don't trust her," Jewel said.

"Why not?"

She shrugged. "I've grown up in the orphanage. When you live with a lot of people, you get a feeling which ones you can trust. And it ain't her."

I didn't know what to say to that. Was she perhaps getting in the jab first because Rose had caught her snooping? I didn't think I quite trusted Jewel, to be honest. I took off my coat, left it on a chair, waiting for her to hang it up, and went into the sitting room. Miss Van Woekem was in her favorite chair by the window and Rose was perched on a stool beside her, reading to her. Whatever was in the book had made the old woman laugh. She looked quite different from the pain-ridden person I had seen two weeks ago. I gave a polite cough. They both looked up.

"Oh, Molly, my dear." The old woman held out her hand to me. "Rose has been keeping me so entertained. She has a natural gift for bringing a book to life when she reads to me. Rose, dear—go and find Jewel and tell her we'll have some coffee."

"Of course, ma'am." Rose got to her feet and hurried out of the room.

"She's an absolute gem, Molly," the old lady said. "Thank you for finding her for me. I don't know how I would have managed alone. Did you have a special reason for the visit today or are you just paying a social call on an old friend?"

"Actually I did have a reason for the visit," I said. "It's good news for Rose."

Rose was just returning to the room and stood poised in the doorway. "Good news? For me?" she asked.

I nodded. "My husband says that they've heard back from Ireland and verified everything you told him about your address and your brothers."

"Oh," Rose said in a flat voice. "That is good news."

"So you're free to go to your relatives whenever you've a mind to."

Rose came across the room and took up her place beside the old lady again. "But I couldn't be leaving dear Miss Van Woekem now," she said. "Not when she's needing me so badly. I have to stay at least until she's up and walking again and her proper maid comes back."

"It's good of you, my dear." Miss Van Woekem smiled at her. "You've such a generous nature. But if your relatives are waiting for you in Chicago, then I can't be selfish. You should go."

"No, no." Rose shook her head. "I'm not about to be leaving you, so don't you be worrying your head with that. I know what's right, and to tell the truth, I know nothing about those relatives. For all I know they may be living in a one-room flat."

"Then you shall stay on here," Miss Van Woekem said. "And we'll both be happy."

A brilliant idea had just occurred to me. "How would you like to come to the theater with me on Friday night, Rose?" I said. "That is, if Miss Van Woekem can spare you."

"The theater?" Rose's expression was wary.

"That's right. My friend Ryan O'Hare has given me opening-night tickets for his new play."

"Ryan O'Hare?"

"That's right. Have you heard of him? He's from your part of Ireland."

"I don't believe so," she said. "It's not like I've ever been to a theater or anything. Is he famous?"

"Very famous, both here and in London. His new play was a great success. Do come. It will be a proper treat for you. You could wear that pretty dress Miss Van Woekem let you wear for the party."

"Oh, I don't think so," Rose said, shaking her head emphatically. "I don't want to leave the mistress alone. Not after last night."

"Last night? What happened?" I remembered now that Jewel had mentioned last night and I'd overlooked it.

"Somebody tried to break in, apparently," Miss Van Woekem said. "Rose heard a noise. She thought it might have been one of the servants coming down from their rooms on the floor above, but then she thought she should check on me."

"I'd been keeping my door locked," Rose said. "Because I caught that girl Jewel snooping in my room once. And I'd swear that someone jiggled my door handle. Anyway, I came out and I found a window open. But apparently nothing had been taken and the mistress was sleeping just fine. I don't understand it myself. I mean, all these lovely things in the house and a burglar doesn't help himself to a Vermeer or a silver vase?"

"It certainly was strange," Miss Van Woekem said.

"Did you call the police?" I asked.

"We had the constable come in and take a look, but when he saw that nothing was taken, he suggested that one of the members of the household opened the window and then forgot doing so. So I suppose we'll never know."

"You're sure nothing was taken?" I asked.

"Anyone intending to rob us could have found my jewelry left on the bedside table, as well as the objects here in this room," Miss Van Woekem said.

"But you still have the constable outside the house," I said. "He didn't see anything?"

"It was a window at the back," Rose said. "Whoever came in must have climbed over the garden wall from the house behind."

"Well, I hope you're wrong and it was no more than Jewel trying to sneak out at night to meet a boy," I said.

"I hope so too." Rose still sounded worried. "I have my doubts about that girl. I'm wondering if she has bad connections. Maybe she opened that window so that an accomplice could climb in, only something startled him and he ran off."

"Make sure all the windows are properly shut and fastened in future, Rose," I said. "Just to be on the safe side."

"And do you think you can ask that husband of yours if we can keep the constable outside a little longer, even though I'm no longer suspected of that murder?" she asked me. "Tell him about the break-in."

"I will," I said. "But please say you'll come to the theater with me. I hate going to things alone. We'll ask the constable to be extra vigilant while we are gone. And I gather it's a wickedly funny play. It will do us both good to laugh."

"Yes, Rose dear. You should go. You deserve a night out after what you've been through. Take a cab, Molly. I'll pay for it."

Rose looked from her employer to me, her expression still hesitant. "Well, I don't suppose it can do much harm to attend a theater, can it?" she said.

At the time I thought it was a strange thing to say.

On the way home, packed into a crowded El carriage, I thought about that break-in. The second strange thing to happen at Miss Van Woekem's within a few days. First a missing bracelet turned up in Cordelia Ransom's glove and now this. Maybe a complete coincidence. Maybe Jewel had intended to sneak out and meet a boy at night but then had lost her nerve when she saw the long drop to the ground, or she had been about to escape when she heard another member of the household stirring. That would seem the most likely.

But I found my thoughts moving to the viscount. Henry Darby had been on the trail of a jewel thief and jewelry stolen from a high-society party in London. The sort of party a viscount would be likely to attend. What if he was an accomplished thief? He had taken the bracelet at Cordelia's tea party only to realize it wasn't worth much. But then why hide it in his fiancée's glove? Unless, of course, he didn't know the gloves belonged to Cordelia. Perhaps he'd had a chance to notice that Miss Van Woekem wore some good jewelry and had come back last night to help himself, only . . . This was where my theory fell down. Why didn't he take it? By the time Rose came down to check on her mistress he was gone. He could easily have pocketed jewels from the bedside table first.

A thought occurred to me: Jasmine! Perhaps the old lady's cat had been on the bed beside her and had woken up and hissed, as she was prone to do to strangers. And the old lady had turned over and . . . But he still could have snatched something. Besides, stealing a valuable piece of jewelry from a London party was very different from being a cat burglar, climbing up drainpipes. Quite beneath a viscount!

So the question was whether he could possibly have killed Henry Darby. But then how could he have been on Ellis Island? He wouldn't have come steerage. But then neither had Mr. Darby. Besides, the viscount said he had only just arrived in New York, by which time Henry Darby had been dead a couple of weeks. I decided this was too farfetched.

The disturbing thought came to me that there was another coincidence here: that danger seemed to be following Rose. First she was accused of murder on Ellis Island and now there was a break-in at the place where she was staying. Two completely different crimes and circumstances. The first had nothing do with robbery or Mario, the Italian guard, would not have wound up with Henry Darby's wallet.

And if the second had nothing to do with robbery either? I'd learned during my years as a detective that there was often something more to coincidence. But Rose's only connection to crime and criminals was her brothers, who had been arrested. Could it be anything to do with Rose's brothers and the Irish Republicans? It seemed unlikely in New York.

I took this a stage further. Could she have been an innocent bystander when a crime was committed? Had she seen something that put her in danger? Something to do with those brothers? Or had she witnessed the murderer leaving the room where Henry Darby lay dead? The murderer was sure she had seen him, but she, occupied desperately with finding a bathroom, had actually not noticed. My money was still on the Englishman. I was determined to find out more about him.

I felt a shiver of apprehension now: If Rose was somebody's target, was I putting Miss Van Woekem in danger by introducing Rose to that lady's house? I just hoped I hadn't been too impetuous again in my desire to make things right for Rose.

Twenty-Three

On Thursday I swallowed my pride, and after Bridie's lessons had finished I went over to Sid and Gus and asked for the loan of a dress for the theater. "I'm sorry to trouble you," I said, "but I have nothing suitable, not since that fire over Christmas."

"Of course, Molly. Delighted to be of assistance," Gus said. "I'm sure most of Sid's clothing would not be to your taste, but I still have dresses that can be worn in polite society."

"I take exception to that," Sid said. Since she was curled up on the sofa, wearing a gentleman's black silk smoking jacket and wide Chinese trousers at the time, Gus and I had to look at each other and laugh. "I can be feminine when I want to," Sid said. "There's that dress Bridie really coveted. I bet you'd look stunning in it, Molly. Come up and try it on."

She went upstairs ahead of me and took the purple dress from her wardrobe. Feeling very self-conscious, I tried it on and Sid fastened the hooks and eyes at the back. It was a tight fit, since my middle had expanded somewhat when I was carrying Liam, but the dress was breathtaking in more ways than one. I looked—well, not like myself.

"You look positively spectacular, Molly," Gus said, coming into the room as I admired myself in the mirror. "You should give it to her, Sid."

"Oh, absolutely," Sid said. "It's yours, Molly, if you want it."

I felt my cheeks flushing bright red. "Oh, I couldn't possibly. I only meant to borrow."

"No, really. Take it," Sid said. "I've been seen in society once in it, so I really shouldn't wear it again. No, you must take it. I insist, Molly."

Embarrassment was still fighting with delight. Looking at myself in the mirror I saw an elegant, almost voluptuous woman. Mercy me. If my mother could see me now!

I felt tears welling in my eyes. "You two have done so much for me and my family," I said. "I won't ever be able to repay you.

Gus put a gentle hand on my shoulder. "You have become our family, Molly. The only family we have these days. And you know it gives us great pleasure to do small things for you."

"If you want to know, Molly," Sid joined in, "I felt horribly guilty when you just said that your wardrobe had been lost in that fire. We should have realized that and replenished it sooner. Why don't we go through our wardrobes now and see what might fit you, and then if you'd like to sort through the clothing downstairs, see if there is anything there?"

"I can't take any more of your clothes," I said, my face still red with embarrassment, "but I don't mind looking through the donations, just in case. Although with my luck I'd choose a dress Cordelia Ransom had discarded and she'd point out with glee that it used to be hers."

"We'll go through our wardrobes and Gus still has trunks full of things in the attic," Sid said, "and we'll make sure that you have enough to see that you are well kitted out. Here, let me help you out of the dress again. You'll be the belle of the theater party tomorrow."

"Will you be riding in the cab with us?" Gus asked.

"No, thank you," I said. "I have to pick up Rose from Miss Van Woekem's."

"You're bringing that Irish girl?"

"I am. I thought it would be a treat for her since she's been through such a tough time."

"Good of you, Molly. I'm interested to meet her," Sid said. "Are you taking her to the party afterward as well?"

"Just for a little while," I said. "She'll probably feel out of place at such a gathering. I know I always do myself."

"But Ryan's parties are always such fun!" Gus said. "Send her home in a cab and you stay on. You can ride home with us."

"We'll play it by ear," I said. "She was reluctant even to go to the theater in first place. She's never been to one in her life."

"I just hope she's not too shocked by the dialogue," Gus said, chuckling. "You know Ryan's plays can be very naughty. She'll probably be crossing herself and invoking the Blessed Virgin all evening."

"I didn't think of that," I said. "I hope I'm not making a mistake."

I went home, having found a good tweed skirt and a couple of jackets among the donated clothing. I'm sure there were more things that would have fitted me, but I didn't want to seem greedy or to deny those who had nothing. I found that I was now feeling anxious about the upcoming theater. Was I doing the right thing by taking Rose with me? Had I actually been thinking of her—wasn't it more this stupid desire to cling to someone like me? Wanting to make her life go smoothy when mine had encountered more than my share of bumps along the road.

It wasn't until the next day when I started to dress for the occasion that I found I was just a teeny bit excited.

"Bridie?" I called. "Can you come and hook me into this dress?"

She came running up the stairs but froze in my doorway. "That's my dress!" she said in a cold, accusing voice. "You're wearing my dress. First you take Rose to the theater instead of me and then you take my dress." She was glaring at me. "You wouldn't let me wear it because you wanted it for yourself!"

"Calm down, Bridie," I said. "That's not true at all. Aunt Sid insisted that I wear this dress for the theater and she only let you play dress-up in it. She wasn't serious about actually giving it to you. It's quite wrong for a little girl."

"I'm not a little girl!" Bridie yelled the words. "I'm almost a woman. In some societies girls get married and have babies at my age. You can't keep me a little girl forever, you know. I'll go and live with the ladies across the street. They don't treat me like a baby. I'll have them adopt me instead."

She ran down the stairs and then I heard the front door slam. Oh, dear. Should I go after her? Then I decided that Sid and Gus would know how to handle her better than I. Besides, I had to finish getting ready and leave to pick up Rose. Sid and Gus would deliver her home again when they too had to leave. I had my mother-in-law hook me into the dress, and she even helped me put up my hair, which always tried to escape from the hairpins. I had to admit the result was pleasing. I would not be ashamed to bump into Cordelia Ransom this evening.

"It's a pity Daniel is not home to see this," Mother Sullivan said. "He'd have regretted not coming with you this evening. He'd worry the other men couldn't take their eyes off you."

I went off with a little smile on my face. Luckily it was a mild spring evening with not a hint of rain or snow in the air. In fact the scent of early blossom wafted toward me as the cab came to a halt at Gramercy Park. Rose was ready and waiting in the front hall, the blue-and-green shawl I had given her wrapped tightly around her.

"I'm not so sure about this, Molly," she said. "I've never been out in public in my life. I couldn't find a dress that was in any way modest either, so I'll be keeping my shawl around me all evening. Me mother would be cursing me from heaven if she saw me exposing my bosoms to the world."

I wondered what she would think of my purple dress that was quite generously exposing my own bosoms.

"You'll enjoy it," I said, now wondering if indeed this was a stupid idea. What if she shrieked or swooned at some of the ribald jokes? Then I decided that Ryan was sophisticated; perhaps most of those lines would go over her head. Well, it was too late to back out now. Rose called out a goodbye to Miss Van Woekem, and I instructed Jewel to keep a close eye on the mistress until we came home.

"I hope she'll be all right," Rose said as the cab took off with us. "That Jewel—I'm not at all happy about her. She's a useless lump of flesh if ever there was one."

"I'm sure it will be fine," I said. "Actually, Rose, it's you I worry about."

"Me?" Her voice was sharp.

"Yes. First you get yourself implicated in a murder—wrongly accused by a young man. And now a break-in? I'm wondering if—" I paused, thinking how to phrase it.

"If what?" She still sounded edgy.

"If maybe you've witnessed something you shouldn't along the way. Maybe you don't even realize it but a person feels you are a threat. You did say someone jiggled your door handle, didn't you?"

"Yes, I did." Her voice was hardly audible above the clop of the hooves. There was a long silence, then she exclaimed, "To come to think of it, Molly, I did see something in Queenstown. The night before we were due to board the ship."

"Go on."

She leaned closer to me. "I had been out for a bite to eat and I was coming back to the boardinghouse where I was going to spend the night, and in this alleyway I saw two men. And one was handing a package to the other and he quickly put it under his cloak. I didn't think anything more about it until now. I suppose I thought that such things go on in cities and around docks."

"But if one of those men had been coming here and had noticed you . . ." I remembered something else. "And you said your suitcase was stolen on the dock?"

"That's right. I'd almost forgotten about it now." She grabbed my arm. "Molly, do you really think I'm in danger? Do you think one of those men is following me?"

"I'm wondering about that Englishman who was the only one who reported seeing you coming out of that room. It's possible he's not who he claims to be but a clever con man and maybe a clever thief."

"Has your husband not looked into his background yet?" she asked.

"He's still waiting for Scotland Yard to verify what he told us. They are being annoyingly slow."

"I wouldn't trust him further than I could throw him," Rose said angrily. "What was he doing in steerage, anyway?"

"A good question," I replied. "We need to find out and sooner rather than later."

I glanced across at her. Her lovely auburn curls were down and over her shoulders tonight, being held back with what looked like an expensive comb—obviously loaned by her employer. She sensed me looking and gave me a shy smile.

"You've been so kind to me, Molly. And I appreciate the way you've put yourself out to take care of me."

"We Irishwomen have to stick together, don't we?" I gave her hand a little squeeze. "And I have to confess that it's nice having someone from the old country to talk to. I'm still a newcomer to New York, you know, and sometimes I feel far from home. I'm sure you will too, but then you'll have relatives who will make you feel that you belong. I had nobody."

"But you married a handsome man," she said, giving me a little nudge. "I'd say you fell on your feet."

"Eventually," I agreed. "And I know his heritage is Irish but he's a

New Yorker, and it's nice to have someone to talk to who remembers the old country. One thing I miss is a good ceilidh, don't you?"

"Oh, to be sure, I'm certainly missing a good ceilidh," Rose said with great enthusiasm. I wondered if she'd be shocked when she realized that a New York social gathering would be very different from our evenings at home.

Twenty-Four

As the cab turned down Forty-Second Street we joined a long line of horse-drawn carriages, cabs, and automobiles dropping their passengers off at the theater. Rose and I watched with fascination all the theatergoers streaming along the sidewalks and up to the theater. In the light of the street lamps I could see a parade of people's torsos and feet passing right by my open window. What a mix of people. Most of those climbing out of autos and carriages were dressed in the latest evening fashions, but some of those walking toward the theater seemed more dressed for a costume party. As I watched I saw two petite figures pass in enormous flowing pantaloons that fastened at the ankle and little velvet slippers. I craned my head out to see more and saw that one had a loose-fitting dress on over the trousers and a veil over her head and the other had a tunic and vest and a small round hat. They turned in my direction, and I saw it was Sid and Gus.

"We'll get out here, thank you," I called up to the driver, jumping out. "Sid, Gus, over here!" Gus spotted me and nudged Sid and the two came over with big smiles on their faces. I paid the cab driver as Rose climbed out more slowly, clearly a little nervous in the crowd of theatergoers. I looped my arm through hers and we followed the crowd through the golden-edged doors and up the wide marble stairs into an enormous foyer that was filled with people.

As soon as we could find a tiny space to ourselves I gave Sid and Gus each a kiss on the cheek and stepped back to take in what they were wearing. "I thought you were going to wear diamonds to go with the play," I said to Sid.

"We pulled these out of the closet from our Turkish phase." Gus grinned. "Much more comfortable than a corset and full skirt to sit at the theater." I saw now that her dress and veil matched Sid's vest. They were a blue silk with gold embroidery and tiny mirrors. Sid's little hat was of blue velvet. They did look like the picture of a Turkish prince and princess.

"They're beautiful," I said truthfully.

"And you look stunning in that dress, Molly," Gus said. "I can't imagine why Daniel isn't here to see it. Why, he might need to keep the other men away."

I laughed. "My mother-in-law said the same thing."

Sid made a face. "Really, Augusta, we are becoming altogether boring and provincial if we say the same thing as mothers-in-law. We ladies shall protect you and keep the men off you." A rather dashing young man in a long well-fitted black coat walked by and she looked after him suggestively. "But only if you want us to. We are not our sister's keeper."

"Sid!" I was shocked and amused at the same time. "You know I'm a happily married woman."

"If you say so." She turned her eyes on Rose. "And this must be your Irish friend. You didn't tell us she was a beauty, Molly. We may need to keep the men off her as well."

"This is Rose McSweeney," I presented her to them. "And these are my friends, Miss Elena and Miss Augusta."

"Pleased to make your acquaintance, I'm sure," Rose said faintly. Just then the lights went briefly off and on again and a musical tone sounded.

"We had better take our seats," Gus said, and we walked into the theater. The Belasco Theater was extremely opulent. Rows of red velvet–covered seats ran down to the stage, and as I looked back I could see the seats also went all the way up to the back with an expansive balcony overhead. At the end of each row was an ornately carved letter *B*. The walls were covered with red velvet and gold designs, and the top of the ceiling was an enormous glass dome.

"It's like a palace," I whispered to Sid as we took our seats in the fifth row. "How on earth did Ryan get his play here? I know he's been doing well, but this is quite a step up."

Sid and Gus gave each other a knowing look. "I heard he is quite chummy with David. They've been seen about town quite a bit together."

"David?" I asked.

Gus nodded toward the carved *B* at the end of the next row. "Belasco. He bought this place a few years ago. He is absolutely rolling in it."

"You know how Ryan likes his rich friends," Sid added. I looked at Rose to see how she was taking all of this. I wondered if it was overwhelming for the poor girl, especially one from an Irish family where surely she had had a strict Catholic upbringing. She was looking around quietly, but I couldn't tell if it was from shock or interest. I tried to remember what it felt like to have never been in a big city before, never been inside a theater or in a crowd of artists, but I found I couldn't do it. It was getting harder to remember the girl I had once been. Of course, I had once had to work on the stage to help an actress solve a mystery during my detective days. So the theater felt like quite a normal place to me.

I still got a thrill of excitement as the lights went down and the curtain came up. The play was brilliant and funnier than even I had expected. The heroine was a poor young girl who worked her way through a number of suitors, trading up each time, and who wound up a duchess with a big wedding at the end. At the curtain call the actors got a standing ovation, and as it was opening night Ryan was called out onstage to thunderous applause.

"Ladies and gentlemen, thank you so much." He bowed and smiled. "I would like to especially thank all the generous patrons of the arts who have helped to make this production possible. And of course, the heart of the Belasco, Mr. David Belasco."

A man in the center front row rose, turned, and bowed to much applause.

Ryan continued, "We will be throwing a champagne reception for you just down the street at the Knickerbocker Hotel so you can meet all of our talented cast. I hope to see you there." He bowed again and some enthusiastic young ladies in the front row threw single roses onto the stage, which he picked up and pressed to his heart theatrically.

We waited for the crowd to thin out before trying to make our way out of the theater.

"Are we truly invited to this party?" I queried. "It sounds a little fancy."

"Don't worry." Gus put her arm through mine as we descended the steps. "We are included. The ladies and gentlemen of fashion love to rub shoulders with bohemian artists at after-parties. We are part of the local color. Come on, I know a shortcut. Follow me."

We walked down the street toward Times Square discussing the play.

"Wasn't Ophelia hilarious?" I said.

"When she said to the duke, 'I am innocent of the ways of the world,' I almost fell out of my seat laughing." Gus gave a booming laugh that made a fashionably dressed couple getting into the back of a sleek black automobile look up, startled.

"You're very quiet, Miss McSweeney," Sid said kindly to Rose. "What did you think?"

"To tell the truth most of it went over my head," Rose said. "I liked that she became a duchess. That was a happy ending."

Gus frowned thoughtfully. "But Miss McSweeney, don't you see that it was about the oppression of women and the institution of marriage? Ophelia was just using the system of oppression that we have all been born into for her own advantage. Funny as it was, the play was pointing out that marriage is a straitjacket for a woman and a cage for men."

"I have been in a straitjacket and a marriage," I said without cracking a smile, "and I assure you that marriage is better." Sid burst out laughing. Gus managed a smile.

"Your marriage might be better," she said earnestly, "but how many women is that true for? Miss McSweeney is an American woman now. And I must insist that an American woman is more than just an ornament to a man."

"Sure, but it would be nice to be a duchess, though," Rose said wistfully, and Gus threw her hands up in exasperation.

"Don't worry, you'll have plenty of time to bring her around to your way of thinking." I smiled at Rose. "I believe you want to stay in the city."

"I think I might do. I enjoy my employment very much. I'm very happy in that house. Speaking of that, should we be getting home? I'm afraid Miss Van Woekem might miss me and that Jewel won't know how to put her to bed properly." She looked around quickly as if looking for a cab.

"Let's just go to this party for a while. I don't want to send you home in a cab by yourself," I said. "I'm sure Miss Van Woekem is already safely in bed and won't miss you a bit." As we crossed Broadway the crowd began to thin out, and I wondered where we were going.

We stopped in front of a long flight of concrete stairs going down under the street.

"Where are we going?" Rose's voice squeaked with fear.

"It's the subway," I told her as I realized. "Is it still running?" It looked completely deserted with no one hurrying up or down the stairs as they would during the day. I had ridden the subway a few times, but the El was much more convenient for all the places I needed to go, so to me it was more of a novelty.

"The what?" Rose was still peering down the steps doubtfully as Sid and Gus started down them. I envied them their velvet slippers. My shoes were much higher and sure to be more slippery on the steps.

"It's a train that goes under the ground. It's a new way of traveling."

"Well, saints preserve us. I never heard of such a thing." She started down the stairs somewhat warily. We came down the stairs and into a tunnel that was dimly lit. The ticket collectors were not in their places. I assumed the station must be closed for the night.

Sid and Gus seemed unperturbed, chatting merrily as if they knew right where they were going. To my left were the tracks and ahead a platform. The roof was circular and made me feel like I was in Aladdin's cave.

Gus looked back and must have seen the apprehension on my face and Rose's because she hurried to reassure us. "It's a shortcut. The hotel is right above the station and there's a door into their basement right up here. We'll skip the reception line and get right to the champagne." She headed for a plain wooden, industrial door I could now see on my right just before the platform ended.

I felt a shake and heard a loud, deep wailing sound coming from behind me. As I turned I saw a light deep in the tunnel. As I watched it grew, and all of a sudden a train burst out of the tunnel. The sound was so loud Rose covered her head with her hands. A huge gust of wind swept across the platform, sending stray newspaper pages whipping up from the floor. Then it was gone.

"Holy Mother of God. That was loud." She put her hand to her heart.

"It was like the devil himself coming out of hell, wasn't it? Mother of God, what a thing."

I put my arm around Rose reassuringly and we headed toward the door. After the noise of the train the station sounded eerily still.

In the silence I heard the sound of footsteps coming down the stairs. They grew louder and echoed in the tunnel. We reached the door just as I heard the footsteps break into a lurching run. A voice called out behind us, but it too echoed so much I couldn't make out the words. A man appeared out of the gloom running toward us. My heart leapt into my throat. I put Rose behind me and stood to block his path.

"Are you following us?" My words also echoed strangely.

"Oh, I say, not at all." The man stopped about six feet away, an apologetic look on his face. "I heard there was a shortcut to the party and I thought you might know the way. I've been behind you since the play." He took in the outfits that Sid and Gus were wearing. "You look like theater folk, what. Always know a back way, in my experience."

"Yes, this is the way." Sid pulled open the door. "Are you a friend of an actor?"

"I'm quite new here." From the way he said "new" I could tell he was English and rather upper class. "At home I'm a bit of a stage-door Johnny. Never miss a show. And of course the parties after are jolly good fun."

There was a light over the door and I got a look at him. He was about my age, well dressed in white tie and tails. His speech was slurring slightly, and I guessed that his "good fun" had already started.

"Let me, ladies." He took the door from Sid and ushered her inside with a theatrical arm wave. "My, what pretty ladies." He was more than a little drunk, I thought. He looked us up and down as if we were actresses on the stage for his amusement. "Very nice."

"Yes, thank you," I said, trying to push Rose through the door after Sid and Gus and get on to the party as soon as possible.

"Wait a minute." The man was staring at Rose. "Wait a minute. I know you! Where do I know you from? Wait, it will come to me. Was it a party in London?" He leered at her as she stepped past him into the corridor beyond.

"Come on, Molly, let's get out of here," Rose said urgently. He stepped toward her and caught onto her arm.

"Yes, a party. Were you at old Artie's party at the Savoy? Why do I know you?"

Rose's eyes blazed and she yanked her arm away. "Get your hands off me. You're a lying drunk. You know me because you accused me of murder."

"What?" the man looked absolutely shocked.

"This is the man, Molly. The lying Englishman from Ellis Island." Her voice was full of contempt mingled with fear. "The one who molested me on the ship that I told you about."

His face registered utter confusion as he tried to put together this beautiful young woman with the poor Irish immigrant he had accused on Ellis Island. "No, I would never."

"You've had the police keeping me under lock and key." She was really angry now. "Well, they know I'm innocent. And to add to that now Molly can testify that you are a drunk. Who will believe you then?" Emotion seemed to overcome her and she pushed past Sid and Gus, who were watching the goings-on with great interest.

"So this is the tale teller that got Miss McSweeney in trouble." Gus spoke as if we were discussing a novel she was particularly fond of. She turned back to him. "What we couldn't figure out is why you were traveling steerage in the first place. I don't suppose you'd just tell us?"

He stared at her, openmouthed. "I don't, that is—I mean, that is, I say!"

"Yes, do tell us," Sid said with great interest.

Gus looked over at me. "I don't want to take over your job, Molly, but we did want to know that answer and we have him here right now. He doesn't appear to be too dangerous. Mr. . . ."

"Cromer, Edwin Cromer." He gave a slight bow, as if remembering his manners.

"Well, Mr. Cromer?" Gus said expectantly.

Mr. Cromer looked around as if for an exit, but the way in was past Sid and Gus. Finally he sighed. "I'm afraid I'm cast out without a bean. I really am a stage-door Johnny, you know, and I fell for a lovely little thing. And the long and the short of it is that I'm cast off to make my fortune in America and she has gone to a cousin in the country for the duration, if you know what I mean."

"I thought it might be something like that," Sid said to me.

"I had my money on opium smuggling." Gus sounded disappointed.

All of this time Mr. Cromer had been standing holding the door between me and the passage. I decided to make a break for it and get past him.

"But how on earth did you know about me?" he asked, bewildered and swaying forward slightly just as I moved so I had to push against him to get through. He's doing it on purpose, I thought. His hand reached out and grabbed my bottom. Really!

"Because my husband is a police captain," I said loudly. The hand disappeared. I turned and glared at him. "And I now have proof for him that one part of Rose's story is true!"

"Wait, please." Mr. Cromer looked very uneasy. "Don't tell him that. Just a bit of fun. I'm afraid I'm a little bit tipsy. I'm normally a nice chap."

I turned to the others. "Come on, let's get to this party." I stalked down the passage.

"Are you sure you don't want to question him some more?" Sid was still looking at him as if he were an interesting specimen. "After all, he's right here."

"Please, let's go," Rose called from down the passage. "I don't want to be around him. Do we go up?"

"Yes, up two flights." Gus started up the stairs and we followed. I must confess that I walked slowly and hung back a bit. Sid was right, I might not have another chance to question Mr. Cromer. There was no chance as we climbed the narrow staircase. I wanted to keep well clear of any wandering that his hands might do. But as we reached the landing and faced a stained glass door through which Rose, Sid, and Gus had already disappeared I turned to him.

"I wonder that you are at the theater, Mr. Cromer, and well dressed too, if you were cast out as you say?"

Perhaps the climb had sobered him up a bit or the knowledge that I was a police captain's wife. He opened the door without answering and then turned back with an enigmatic smile. "Ah, well, one always has friends." He stepped into the room, looking around at the noisy crowd, clearly wanting to get far away from me. "Ah, Brackley, there you are." He walked quickly across the room to shake hands with the man who looked up at his call. It was Cordelia's viscount.

Twenty-Five

I looked around the room, taking it in. The large lobby of the hotel had been turned into an impromptu ballroom. It was very grand with a marble floor, lined with potted palms and small tables, and a beautiful staircase sweeping up into the hotel. From where I stood I could see well-dressed couples coming up the outside steps into the hotel as the actors, still in full costume, formed a reception line to greet them. A champagne fountain was in the center of the room and, as promised, Gus and Sid went straight to help themselves while Rose, who had followed them into the room, was hanging back shyly. In the corner of the room a piano and clarinet were playing "I Just Can't Make My Eyes Behave." Couples were waltzing around a dance floor in front of the piano.

To my annoyance I saw that Cordelia Ransom was standing beside the viscount. Really, I couldn't go anywhere without seeing her these days. Then I laughed to myself at the thought. I was the one who was out of place at fashionable ladies' teas and the theater. Not her. As I walked over to Sid and Gus I felt Cordelia's eyes on me. Perhaps she was also thinking that we saw much too much of each other lately.

"Cheers," Gus said gaily, raising her glass to me as I walked up. She grabbed a second glass and filled it. "I promised this one to Ryan. He is having to meet and greet." She forced her way to the front of the room while Sid handed a glass to me and one to Rose. I sipped it gingerly. I was not a big drinker. Rose took a small sip and a smile spread across her face. She drank the rest down like water. She stopped when she saw me looking at her.

"That's so good. I'm thirsty after the play," she explained.

"You might want to sip that or it will go to your head," I warned.

"But it's so bubbly and light," she said, and giggled. I think it was the first time I had ever seen her actually relax. "It doesn't taste very strong." She took a much smaller sip, however, after my warning. I decided I had better keep an eye on her. I couldn't very well carry her home to Miss Van Woekem's and confess that I had let her drink too much in a group of bohemian actors. We moved away as other guests began serving themselves from the fountain.

"What is the viscount doing here?" I spoke into Sid's ear. It was almost too loud to have a conversation.

"Who?" she asked.

"That man is Cordelia's fiancé." I pointed in his direction. "He is an English viscount. I wondered why he'd be at Ryan's play?"

"Are you detecting or just curious?" Sid looked at me with a smile.

"A bit of both, I suppose. I met him at her engagement party . . ."

"You were at Cordelia Ransom's engagement party?" She nodded to me, indicating I should follow her as she weaved her way through the crowd to some green velvet chairs around the edge of the room. I turned to make sure Rose was following me.

"Tell me all," she said. "I am agog."

I was careful not to stare at the viscount or Cordelia. I didn't want to make it obvious that I was talking about them.

"That was the tea where the bracelet went missing. Mrs. Sage's bracelet I told you about. I can't say that I'm wild about Cordelia. She treated me like the maid!"

"Yes, we're not enamored either." Sid was eyeing them curiously and I was quite glad that a large potted plant made it unlikely they would see us. "We heard her mother took her to England to meet a royal, so I imagine she will be quite happy with a viscount. What does this have to do with your mystery, though?" She gave me an interested look.

"I stayed back a bit to question Mr. Cromer, and he seems to know the viscount."

"Really." She raised an eyebrow. "That does seem strange. If Cromer is mixing in these circles, it seems even more suspicious that he came steerage to America. Why not just borrow some money for the passage?"

"That's what I wonder." I went on, "And I can't imagine what Cordelia and the viscount are doing here tonight. She mentioned that she had not seen the play in London because she had been told it wasn't suitable for an unmarried girl."

Sid chuckled. "Cordelia, the righteous virgin?" She jumped up. "Let's find out. Come on," she said, pulling me up as well. She put a big smile on her face, and before I could stop her she marched right up to Cordelia and the viscount. I had no wish to be looked down upon by Cordelia, but Sid motioned for me to come with her. She looked at Rose, who shook her head firmly and headed for the punch bowl.

"Cordelia, darling," Sid positively gushed, holding out her hands. "Of all people I didn't expect to see you here. And who is this handsome young man you are with?"

"Hello, Elena," Cordelia said stiffly. "May I present my fiancé, Viscount Brackley. Roderick, this is an old college friend, Elena Goldfarb."

"Delighted to make your acquaintance, Miss Goldfarb." The viscount gave a charming bow.

"What on earth are you wearing?" Cordelia's eyebrows couldn't climb any higher as she took in Sid's outfit.

"Oh, we're a Turkish prince and princess. There's my princess now." She waved across the room. "Gus! Over here." Gus was weaving her way across the room, pulling a beaming Ryan in tow.

"Here's the man of the hour. We must toast you," Gus said, thrusting Ryan into the circle. "To a brilliant playwright. Cheers." We all raised our glasses.

"I'll drink to that," the viscount said, taking a long swig of champagne.

"You'll drink to about anything." Ryan laughed. "But I agree, I am brilliant and the play was brilliant. Absolutely everyone says so."

"What on earth does he mean?" Cordelia had turned a very surprised gaze on the viscount. "How do you know Mr. O'Hare? We never met him when I was in London." She turned to Ryan. "Were you in London recently, Mr. O'Hare? How do you know my fiancé?"

The viscount shot a look of pure venom at Ryan and then turned to smile confidently at Cordelia. "He is the playwright, my love."

"Yes. I was back in London after having been banished for many long years," Ryan said. "We put on *Queen of Diamonds* there. It was a sparkling success, as your fiancé knows. He is a big patron of the arts in London," Ryan added with an apologetic glance at the viscount. "Every starving artist needs a viscount." He broke off. "Oh, look, there's David. Must dash." And he waved at someone across the room and disappeared into the crowd.

We were all silent for a moment. Cordelia was looking at the viscount as if considering a completely new idea.

"Well, that's why I wanted to bring you tonight." The viscount sounded completely innocent, but from Cordelia's look she was not taken in. "I met him at the party after his play opened in London. I told you about it—how the king attended. The play was so funny, I knew you would love it." He pushed his hair back from his forehead. "Did you enjoy it, ladies?" He turned to us, clearly changing the subject.

"I liked it very much," I said as my brain raced. "Was your friend Mr. Cromer at that party too?" I glanced across the room to where Edward Cromer was helping himself to a large plate of canapés.

"Cromer?" He sounded puzzled. "Oh, that man over there. You

know, I don't remember. One did see him around the theater quite a bit, but I couldn't say if he was there that night. We are passing acquaintances more than friends."

"It sounds like you spent an awful lot of time at the theater." Cordelia attempted a pretty pout.

"I was just whiling away the time until I could see you again, my dear." Viscount Brackley took Cordelia's hand and pressed it to his lips in a romantic gesture. Sid made a face so disgusted that I almost laughed out loud. "Mrs. Sullivan, it was so good of you to help with the tea the other day. I think I saw someone else here who was at that tea?"

"Oh yes, my Irish friend." I suddenly remembered guiltily that I had left Rose alone in a place where she knew nobody. I looked back at the chairs we had been sitting in, but she was gone. It was strange that the viscount would even remember her, but then he did seem to have an eye for the ladies. Of course he would notice Rose. She had looked lovely and I noticed he had glanced her way with clear interest at the tea. "She is around here somewhere. You know, I assume, that she is a companion to Miss Van Woekem and I thought she should have a nice treat for a night. But I don't see her right now." I hoped that Rose hadn't felt sick after drinking down that champagne so quickly.

"I do remember that. I was quite touched by how attentive she was to your dear godmother, Cordelia." He squeezed Cordelia's hand. "Please tell her particularly that I was asking after her."

"I will," I assured him. "I'd better go and see if I can find her." I worked my way through the crowded room, looking for her. After about fifteen minutes I gave up. It was so crowded that I had no way of knowing if she was walking in the same circles looking for me. I decided to stand by the entrance to the dance floor. Surely I would spot her eventually. I worried that she might have decided to make her own way home, not knowing the city. I had to turn down a number of invitations to dance—which were flattering in their way.

A chair became vacant and I sat to watch some of the actors doing impromptu musical numbers. The reception line was over and they were in their element as the center of attention, telling stories from some of the plays and musicals they had been in. I'm not sure if it was the champagne that kept being refilled every time my glass emptied or just the feeling of laughing and being part of a big happy group, but the tension I had been holding recently just dissolved. I sang along with the musical numbers and toasted the musicians. I was quite startled when I noticed the crowd was beginning to thin and saw that it was after midnight!

I walked over to Sid and Gus, who were waltzing together in a corner of the dance floor, and tapped Gus on the shoulder. "I think I had better find Rose and get home before Daniel sends a search party out. Do you want to share a cab home?"

"What's that?" Gus asked. They stopped dancing and stepped off the dance floor to avoid the couples waltzing past. I repeated my question. "Not yet, Molly dear." Gus shook her head. "There's a party at David's after this, you know. You're welcome to come."

"After this?" I laughed. "I'm asleep on my feet, I'm afraid. I'll have to be up to make Daniel's breakfast tomorrow however much fun I have tonight."

Sid pulled out a velvet drawstring bag that matched her hat. "Do you need cab fare?"

Gus spoke at the same time. "Will you feel safe going home alone?"

"I have cab fare and I feel perfectly safe. I just have to find Rose." I looked around the room as I said it. "You haven't seen her, have you?"

"We've been too occupied enjoying ourselves," Sid said. "Perhaps she went outside for fresh air. It is rather smoky in here."

"All right, then," I said. "I'll see you tomorrow."

"Yes, well, not too early. Perhaps tell our sweet Bridie we will be available in the early afternoon."

"It is Saturday, dearest," Sid reminded her. "No lessons for Bridie."

I nodded to them and moved away. Surely it shouldn't be this difficult to find a girl with bright red hair, I thought. And just as I had the thought I spotted her coming in through the large front doors.

"Where have you been all night?" I said, trying not to sound as if I was scolding as I came up to her. "I was worried about you."

She blushed. "Sorry, Molly, I just needed some air." She gave an almost fearful look around the room, and I tried again to see this evening from her perspective. Perhaps this had all been too much for her.

"Shall we go?" I put my hand on her arm.

She nodded. "Oh yes, please. To tell the truth this is a little much for me. And I'm worried Miss Van Woekem will be missing me."

"I'm sure she is sound asleep with no idea that you are still out," I said as we walked out the hotel doors and down the steps. "But I agree it is time to go." I tried to stifle a huge yawn that overtook me. "I'm dead on my feet. I'll get a cab to drop you off and take me home."

It was quite a shock to step out of the bright, warm, noisy hotel onto a quiet and cold New York street. The music from inside was muffled, and a cold, damp fog made the street look quite eerie. I had told Gus I was not worried going home this late, but that had been easier to say indoors where it was bright and cheery. I wondered briefly if it was too late to get a cab at this hour, but they must have been used to the habits of the theatergoer because one came up the street only minutes after we walked out of the hotel. I was going to hail it, but it pulled up under a street lamp about twenty-five yards from us and I noticed for the first time that there was a small group of people waiting. A man and two women got into the cab, but before it could drive away the man leaned his head back out the window.

"Anyone going our way?" he called. "We have room for one more and we're happy to split the cab fare."

"I'm going downtown, to Church Street." I heard an English voice and I saw Edward Cromer. "New Amsterdam Boardinghouse."

I repeated the name to myself under my breath with a grin. What luck. I had even more questions for him now that I had met him in person. I would be sure to pay Mr. Cromer a visit the next day.

Twenty-Six

I have to confess to waking with a headache. I am certainly not used to champagne. I was grateful I had the sense to come home instead of going to another even wilder party. I could thank my fear that Daniel would worry and also my desire to take care of Rose. She had seemed quite flustered, and I felt a twinge of guilt for bringing her to a situation where she was so clearly out of her depth. The risqué dialogue of the play and then the equally naughty repartee between Ryan and his friends had probably shocked her beyond measure. I know I felt the same way when I first encountered Ryan and his world. Well, at least I delivered her home safely and in good time. I wondered if she too had a headache from champagne this morning. I had no idea how much she had drunk after I lost sight of her.

I wondered how long the party had continued and how long Sid and Gus had stayed at David's. For all I knew they could have just gotten in. I certainly wouldn't dream of disturbing them this morning. I was also still marveling at my perfect timing, because if we had stayed on even five minutes more, I wouldn't have heard Edwin Cromer give his address to the cabby in that clear aristocratic tone. But now I was in a dilemma. I knew I shouldn't visit him, but I just couldn't resist. After last night I had more questions than ever. How did he really come to be traveling steerage if he had friends like Viscount Brackley? And to be frank, I thought that Daniel and his team were not doing enough.

I reasoned it would be easy for me to chat with the fellow. He had seen me at the party last night. I could come up with some excuse for wanting to talk to him again. Of course, it depended on how much he remembered from last night. He had been quite drunk. Would he remember I had told him my husband was a policeman? Or would I be able to pass myself off as an acquaintance? Something along the lines of I realized when I saw him leaving that I knew his family. Didn't they have a place in Ireland? I believe our mothers were great friends.

The very worst that could happen would be that he'd tell me I was making a mistake. But even if I just had a chance to see him, I could gauge his reaction to me. Now he had seen me with Rose I would be able to judge if he had a grudge against her or wanted something from her. If he tried to find out from me where she lived or what her plans were, I would know whether she might still be in danger. The problem was that it was Saturday. Daniel was often home at the weekend. If I wanted to go out he'd probably insist on accompanying me. Which would mean I'd have to wait until Monday.

But luck was with me. Daniel announced he had some papers to take care of at work. He was sorry but he had to desert us for a while. He'd be home in the afternoon and then we could take Liam out for a walk if the weather held. I agreed that sounded marvelous. So off he went. I waited until Liam showed signs of needing his morning nap, then announced I should pop out to run some errands to make sure we had enough food for Sunday's meals. I turned to Bridie, who apparently had come home, sullen and scowling, when Sid and Gus left for the theater the night before. She was still tight-lipped and uncommunicative this morning, and I had deliberately not sought to engage her.

Now I needed to. "Bridie, can I ask you to keep an eye on Liam, please? We don't want your grandmother to have to climb the stairs while I'm away, and he's taken to climbing out of his crib."

She gave me a long, cold stare. "She's not my grandmother," she said.

That was it. My temper, so well kept in check, boiled over. "You're right," I said. "We're actually not your family at all. But you know the good news? You do have a family in Ireland. Your dad and your stepmother and no doubt a whole host of aunties and uncles who'd love to have you live with them. I know your dad and stepmother were keen to have you to babysit and help with the pigs. So you say the word and I'll arrange for a passage on the next boat."

I saw her blink and a look of horror come over her face. "I didn't mean that," she said. "You know that I don't want to go to them in Ireland."

"Well, then, what do you want?" I asked.

Silence.

"If you're thinking that the ladies might adopt you, you can put that thought from your mind," I said. "They wouldn't be legally able to adopt a child, even if they wanted to. Children can only go to married couples. So it looks like you're stuck with us, for better or for worse. Now, Captain Sullivan and I would like to adopt you and make you a legal part of this family. If that's not what you want, you'd better say so now, before it's too late."

She was still staring at me with her mouth open. I could almost see the wheels in her brain working. Then she said, "Of course I do like it here," she said. "It's only . . ."

"If I'm to be your mother, I'm going to behave as any mother would," I said. "The ladies across the street can be your beloved aunties and spoil you. That's just fine. But it's up to me to make sure you grow up to be a fine young woman in every way. And that means learning what it's like to be part of a loving family. I know you've had some bad times, some bad examples, but you're part of us now and we won't always be warm and complimentary and give you your own way. But we will always promise to love you. Is that understood?"

"Yes, Molly, I mean Mom," she said in a tiny voice.

"All right, then. You watch Liam for me and this afternoon we'll go out somewhere that's fun for all of us. Maybe a soda fountain."

She perked up right away, reminding me that for all her bravado she was still only a child.

I put on my coat and left them, hurrying to the Sixth Avenue El and then disembarking at Franklin. Thank heavens I knew where Church Street was. If the boardinghouse had been in one of that maze of streets on the West Side, closer to the docks, I wouldn't have known where to start. Luckily it was a short walk south to the address on Church Street, suitably near City Hall and the Tombs, I thought. Perhaps the intent was to remind the young man where he might be put if he didn't comply. The Tombs were certainly intimidating enough from the outside. And I knew, having visited Daniel when he was a prisoner inside, that they were depressing enough to drive a prisoner to madness.

Anyway, my mission today was more cheerful, and the brownstone building with a sign outside that read "New Amsterdam Boardinghouse" did not look like a bad place to stay. I went up some steps and in through the front door, finding myself in a dark and narrow foyer with a counter and door open behind it. There was no one manning the counter but a bell sat on it, which I rang. A man with impressively large mustaches came out, wiping his mouth with a handkerchief as if he had been caught drinking something.

"What can I do for you, young woman?" he asked, pleasantly enough.

"I believe you have a resident called Edwin Cromer," I said. "I wonder if it would be possible to have a word with him? We were at the theater together last night and my husband asked me to pass along a message to him if I was in the neighborhood."

I said the first plausible thing that had come into my head, having not thought through the first gamut I had to run. But it seemed to work. "I'm not sure if he's up yet," he said. "It must have been some party last night. He didn't come down for his breakfast and he normally enjoys his food right enough. But I don't see any harm in your going to wake him now, seeing that you're a friend of his."

"I appreciate it," I said.

"It's number seven. This floor, at the far end of the hall on the right. Watch your step, it's not too well lit, I'm afraid. We keep meaning to have the electric light put in."

I thanked him and made my way down the hall. It was indeed dark and I had to peer to see the numbers on the doors. I came to number seven and tapped loudly. "Mr. Cromer," I said. "A visitor from the party last night."

I waited but I suspected that Mr. Edwin Cromer was still rather soundly asleep. I rapped again. A door opposite opened. A man's face looked out, glaring at me. "Can't a person have any peace around here?" he demanded.

"I'm sorry. I'm trying to wake this gentleman," I said.

"Nothing but coming and going all morning," he grumbled. "Not a moment's peace."

He slammed the door again. I took a deep breath and tapped again. Surely the man's loud, deep voice would be enough to stir him from his slumber. In annoyance I tried the door handle and to my surprise it turned. I stepped into a dark room. The curtains were drawn and the whole room was bathed in shadow. I could make out the form of a man still in bed. I knew it was quite against propriety for me to go and shake a sleeping man, but I had come all this way and who knew when I would have another chance, so propriety be blowed!

I tiptoed over and touched him, gently. "Mr. Cromer?" I said softly. "Wake up."

He didn't stir. I shook him a little more forcefully. That was when

I made out the red stain on the white sheet. I stepped back in horror. Someone had cut Edwin Cromer's throat.

My heart was thudding so violently that I found it hard to breathe. I managed to stagger across to the window and pull back the blinds, revealing the true extent of the horror. Edwin Cromer had been cut from ear to ear. Someone had taken no chances. What is more, the blood still seemed quite fresh. It had not been long ago that he had been killed.

I looked around the room, wondering if the killer had left any clues. The window was shut and outside was only a small area with garbage cans in it. No clear way of escape there. There might be fingerprints, of course. And the killer could well have gotten blood spattered onto him. Someone in the street nearby would notice a blood-spattered individual running away. But I realized this was not up to me. I took out my handkerchief and carefully closed the door behind me, trying not to disturb any fingerprints. Then I hurried back to the front desk.

"Excuse me," I called, ringing that bell urgently.

"Hold on, little lady," the man said, coming back wiping his mouth. Clearly I had interrupted his meal again. "What's the rush?"

"Please, I need to know. Has anyone else called on Mr. Cromer this morning?"

He shook his head. "You're the only one."

"And who else had gone in and out that you know about?"

He shrugged. "This is a boardinghouse, not a jail. Our gentlemen come and go as they please."

"Any visitors?"

He frowned then nodded. "There was an Italian woman came earlier asking for Mr. Martinelli."

"What did she look like?"

He shrugged. "Like any Italian woman, I suppose. Poorly dressed. Shawl over her head, dark hair, couldn't speak much English. Lots of hand waving the way they do."

"Did she stay long?"

He shrugged. "Not long at all. I was in here, doing the books, when I watched her go past and hurry down the steps."

"Did she say what she wanted with Mr. Martinelli?"

"I told you, her English was poor. From what I could gather he was her uncle or cousin and she had brought something from the family." He paused, sucking through his teeth. "We're quite particular here, you know. We don't let any questionable women visit the men, but this one was about as unappetizing as they come. Clearly not that sort of woman, if you get my meaning." He grinned. "But why all the questions, ma'am?"

"Because Mr. Cromer has been murdered in his bed."

His mouth dropped open. "You don't say. Are you sure? He hasn't just died in his sleep, God rest his soul?"

"Hardly. His throat has been slit."

"Well, I'll be—" He held off saying a swearword in the presence of a lady. "We'd better get the police in right away. There's usually a constable on the corner. Don't you go anywhere, ma'am. You'll be needed to make a statement, I've no doubt."

Oh no. I hadn't thought of that. Of course I'd be required to make a statement—to give my full name and address. And eventually it would get to Daniel. I could slip away now, I thought, but then that would make me suspect number one with half the city on my tail. No, I'd have to wait it out and face the music.

The owner returned almost immediately with a red-faced and panting constable.

"This is the lady who found him," the owner said, pointing to me.

"Which room is he in? Not up on the top floor, I hope."

"No, on this floor. Room seven, on the right at the end of the hall."

I waited while the constable went ahead with the owner following nervously behind. I saw the constable open the door, the owner hanging back, not wanting to see, and yet curious.

I heard the exclamation "Oh my Lord!" coming from the room and the constable backed out hastily again, shutting the door. "I'll need to call for help," he said. "Don't anybody go in there again. Do you have a key to lock the door?"

"I'll fetch it," the proprietor said, and came toward me, looking almost green.

The door opposite was opened and the face peeked out. "What in tarnation is going on here?" he demanded. "Can't a fellow get a minute's peace?"

"We'll be needing a statement from you, sir," the constable said. "The poor man in there has been murdered in his bed."

"Murdered in his bed?" The belligerence deflated like a balloon. "You don't say? What sort of establishment is this if you allow people to be murdered?"

"It's a respectable establishment, that's what it is," the proprietor said. He had returned with the key and I had followed, not wanting to be left out of the action. "I should never have agreed when the police turned up with this man and asked us to keep an eye on him."

"I'm leaving as soon as I can pack my things," the face at the door said. "I'm outta here. I come from Ohio, where people don't go around getting themselves killed all the time."

"You'll need to stay until the detectives can ask you some questions," the constable said. "How are we to know you're not the one who did it?"

"Who did it? I was up late last night and trying to get some sleep," the man said, "but it's been nothing but interruptions all morning."

"Did you happen to see or hear anything that might be relevant to this case?" the constable asked. "Any argument going on across the hall?"

"I heard a woman's voice, once, and doors slamming."

"What did the woman say?"

"I'm not quite sure. Heavy foreign accent. Something about wrong or mistake."

"That would be the Italian woman looking for Mr. Martinelli," the proprietor said. "I told her he was in number five—stupid thing."

"Anyone else?" the constable asked.

"Men on the floor above going off to work early. Each one of them slamming a door and then heavy footsteps that woke me up," the man said. "But no more voices until that woman, just now." He pointed at me. "Knocking on the door like she wanted to wake the dead—" He stopped, openmouthed. "I'm sorry. What an awful thing to say."

The constable had gone off, presumably to send word to his superiors.

"So what are we supposed to do now?" the man behind the door asked. "Wait around until someone comes to question us? I've told him everything I know. And I never even saw the murdered man, let alone spoke to him. I've got work to do, you know. I'm here on business, not vacation. And I can't wait to get back to Ohio if this is what goes on here."

"Just be patient, sir. I'm sure the police will be here in a minute and then we'll all be free to go about our business."

The door slammed shut. The proprietor glanced at me. "Nothing but complaints since he got here," he muttered. "He wants the Plaza Hotel at my prices, that's what he wants."

In spite of everything I had to smile.

Twenty-Seven

It didn't take long. The constable returned, now even more out of breath. "I've sent a message," he said. "And in the meantime I should be taking your particulars. Let's start with you, sir."

He asked questions of the owner, whose name turned out to be, appropriately, Hudson. He'd been running the boardinghouse for fifteen years. "Never had any trouble apart from a brush once with the Five Pointers Gang a few years back. Wanted extortion money. Tried to set us on fire. But they are no more, since the police have tidied up the city nicely." As to visitors that morning, only the Italian lady, but then he was in his private quarters having breakfast and he didn't always notice when the gentlemen came in or out. And yes, someone could have easily slipped past and entered without being seen.

He moved on to Mr. Cromer. "Brought in a couple of weeks ago by the police. Witness to a murder on Ellis Island, I was told. Asked to keep an eye on him until he had been cleared by Scotland Yard in London. He was no trouble at all. Enjoyed his meals. Went out for walks on fine days. As things progressed he started going out a few times in the evenings. Said he was a lover of theater and asked me for recommendations."

"Any visitors?" the constable asked.

"Not that I can recall. He asked me to post some letters for him and I believe a letter came for him. But there's nothing out of the ordinary there." I would have to remember to tell Daniel to look for those letters. They could give a clue as to what he was doing here and who would want him dead. I was rather annoyed at myself for not spotting any letters that could have been brought to Daniel.

The constable turned to me. I gave him my name and address. Then I described how I had knocked on his door, found it unlocked, and went in to waken him.

"Was this man a good friend or family member, ma'am?"

"No. Just someone I met at the theater last night."

The constable looked aghast. "You went into a strange man's room? Without an escort? You could have asked me."

"I know, it was stupid of me," I said. "I only had to deliver a message."

"What kind of message?" He was now looking at me as if I were a gangster's moll, delivering a death threat.

I felt that I was slipping deeper and deeper down a rabbit hole. I attempted a laugh. "Nothing important. Just a question about the play we had seen. I know the playwright, you see. Since I was in the neighborhood I thought I'd pass along an invitation to meet with this playwright. I found out last night that Mr. Cromer was a big fan of the theater."

"I see." He wasn't quite sure that he could believe me.

I was wondering whether I'd have to get Ryan or Sid and Gus involved in this when we heard the tread of heavy feet outside and another constable came up the steps, followed by two men.

"I was able to find the captain, Jones," the constable said. "They were just leaving the Tombs so I brought them—"

I looked up into Daniel's surprised face.

"Molly, what on earth are you doing here?" Daniel asked.

"I came to deliver a message to Mr. Cromer—about meeting

Ryan O'Hare," I said, trying to sound more at ease than I felt. "I found his door unlocked and he was lying there with his throat cut."

"A very brave young woman, I'd say," Mr. Hudson said. "Didn't swoon or have hysterics or anything. Just told me calmly to get the police."

"She is indeed a brave woman," Daniel said, not taking his eyes off me. I got his meaning—brave to have defied him and come here.

"You know her, Captain Sullivan, sir?" the other detective asked.

"I certainly do. She's my wife." He looked at me again. "Go home, Molly. I'll talk to you later."

"Daniel." The look in his eyes was like thunder, but I couldn't let that stop me from giving him important information. "Mr. Cromer sent some letters and got some in reply." I was about to suggest that he look for them, but the look on his face closed my throat up. There was nothing I could say to make things better. Feeling utterly miserable, I caught the El and rode home.

The day seemed to drag on forever. Daniel had promised to come home by lunchtime and take Liam to the park, but of course this was a new murder investigation so I expected he'd be tied up all day. Instead we went to the soda fountain as I had promised Bridie. But I was so quiet and tense that I think she felt she was still in trouble. I had a sick feeling in my stomach whenever I thought about visiting Cromer. Because I knew I was in the wrong, I suppose. I had promised Daniel I wouldn't interfere in his case if he kept me in the loop, and now I had. I wondered how I might bluff my way out of this. Tell him I had chatted with Mr. Cromer at the party and he had acted in a very friendly manner toward me, making me decide that I was in a perfect position to wheedle more information out of him in a way that the police could not.

I decided that might be a good strategy. It wasn't exactly lying, as Mr. Cromer had certainly been overly friendly in a way that would have made Daniel furious if he had known. But then dead men tell no tales. I wondered who had killed him. Were the two murders tied together? Had he seen someone else come out of the room on Ellis Island where Mr. Darby was killed? Could he possibly have been blackmailing someone? That would explain the exchange of letters. On the other hand, if he had been the jewel thief who brought the necklace to New York, planning to sell it to the highest bidder, had he been double-crossed? If he was the usual naïve and not too bright English upper-class lad, had he run afoul of a criminal organization and paid with his life? The Italian woman was a good hint that the Cosa Nostra was involved, and they were known to be brutal. That would also mean the jewel was long gone.

Daniel did not return all afternoon. I made short ribs and baked potatoes for dinner.

"Sit down and rest, Molly," my mother-in-law complained. "You're as jumpy as a bucket of frogs."

It was after seven when Daniel finally came home. I had just put the dinner on the table for the rest of us when he walked in. He showed no sign of anger, kissed Liam, and rubbed his hands at the sight of the meal on the table. "Well, that looks good enough to eat!" he exclaimed as I went to get a plate for him. "I've not eaten a thing all day. That's one of the things that's wrong with this job. No meal breaks!"

We ate, hardly saying a word. Daniel asked Bridie a question or two and got one-word answers. I lifted Liam from his high chair, told him to say goodnight to everyone, and carried him upstairs to bed. I had dressed him in his nightclothes and tucked him into bed when Daniel appeared.

"I came to say goodnight, son," he said, and leaned over to ruffle Liam's hair. Then he took my arm and led me from the room, steering me into the bedroom.

"My, but we're being forceful tonight, aren't we?" I attempted to joke.

His look was grave. "Now, you have some explaining to do. You're lucky I didn't have you hauled down to headquarters for more questioning. How do you think it looks when my wife is the one to find a man murdered in his bed? If it had been any other woman you'd have been the prime suspect."

"I know," I said. "And I'm sorry I put you in an embarrassing situation. I only wanted to help."

"And how did you think you were doing that?"

"I met Edwin Cromer at the party last night." This was the speech I had rehearsed all day. "He was very friendly and we knew some of the same people. He even knew Cordelia Ransom's fiancé. So I thought I might call on him, go out for a cup of coffee or tea with him, and get more out of him than the police ever could."

"And if he had been our number one suspect and we were keeping a careful eye on him? One wrong word from you could have tipped him off and forced him to flee New York, out of our sight."

That, of course, was true. "I'm truly sorry," I said. "It was stupid of me, I realize that now. I just thought it was so coincidental that there I was chatting with the very man we needed to know more about. I'd have continued our conversation last night, but it was so noisy and crowded that we had to shout at each other."

"So how did you get into his room?"

"I banged on the door and nobody answered, so I wondered if he was a sound sleeper. I tried the door and it opened. I went over to give him a shake—"

"You went into a strange man's bedroom? Molly, are there no limits to your impropriety? How would it have looked if you'd just discovered the dead man when someone else looked into the room?"

"Pretty bad," I agreed.

"And did it never cross your mind that this man may well have committed murder on Ellis Island? Stabbed someone neatly through the heart? And yet you breeze into his room, where he could have finished you off with no trouble at all."

It was beginning to dawn on me how stupid I had been. He had every right to be angry. "I'm sorry, Daniel." I sighed. "What a mess. And I wasn't able to be of any help. Did you find any clues in the room? Fingerprints?"

"We might have found telltale fingerprints on the door if my wife hadn't grasped the doorknob," he said. "One of the windows was open a few inches, so someone could have entered and exited that way, although it would be hard to gain access to that courtyard. But from what the owner said it would have been easy just to walk in and out through the front door. His boarders did it all the time. My men went through Cromer's belongings. Nothing suspicious there."

"You didn't find any letters?" I asked. "The man who ran the boardinghouse said that Cromer had sent some letters and received some too."

Daniel shook his head. "There were no letters. None at all."

"That's strange, isn't it?" I asked. "Do you think the person who killed him took them?"

Daniel shrugged. "Or they were of no consequence and so he threw them away."

I thought of Rose and the story she had told me. If she had seen something she shouldn't in that back alley in Queenstown, perhaps Edwin Cromer had as well. Had he been blackmailing someone? But I decided I didn't want to drag Rose back into this now that Daniel had finally decided she was innocent.

"Or they were bills," I said instead. "He had to leave England under a cloud, you know. Perhaps his creditors have caught up with him."

Daniel said nothing. There was still a tension in the room that made me distinctly uneasy. "One strange thing—we couldn't find his wallet. He had a letter of credit in his suitcase but no cash, apart from a few coins in his trouser pocket."

"So the killer took his wallet," I said. "Just like Ellis Island. Which makes you think the two must be connected, doesn't it?"

"Not necessarily," Daniel said. "The wallet may have been an afterthought. A mafia thug is sent to kill him, sees the wallet, and helps himself."

"More to the point, you didn't find the missing jewels," I said. "So if he was the jewel thief himself and he had brought the jewels from that robbery to New York, either he'd already sold them or someone took them when they killed him."

Daniel looked up, animated now. "Exactly. The owner of the place said there had been an Italian woman who asked for Mr. Martinelli. Mr. Martinelli said nobody called on him. When asked to describe her, the proprietor said he couldn't really see her face. She had a lot of black hair, shawl over her head. Quite tall. Low voice—couldn't speak much English."

"Could have been a man in disguise!" I exclaimed.

"Possibly. But if it was mafiosi then we'll never get to the bottom of it. They won't talk."

"So we're no further ahead?" I asked.

"No further at all," he said. "All we can say is that Henry Darby was murdered by one of the several hundred immigrants who were on Ellis Island at the time."

"It makes no sense," I said. "What would any new arrival from Italy or Ireland or God knows where want with an older English gentleman if not to rob him?"

Daniel shrugged. I could tell he hated to be beaten. So did I.

Twenty-Eight

That night I couldn't sleep. A cold wind had come up and seemed to get into every crack of the house. I couldn't get warm, even up against Daniel with all the blankets in the room piled on top of me. I kept seeing that red slash of blood and Edwin Cromer's staring eyes. What had they been staring at? I wondered. Had he seen the man who killed him as he died? The thought made me shiver. The night of the party he had seemed like a typical, somewhat stupid English upper-class young man. Only as he had seen Cordelia's viscount had I seen a flash of something else in his expression. A thought struck me. The viscount had come from England shortly after Rose and Cromer. And he seemed to move in the same circles as Edwin Cromer.

Ryan indicated that he knew the viscount as well. They had been at the same parties in London, parties that Viscount Brackley didn't want his fiancée to know about. And it was at such a party that a valuable necklace had been stolen and the man investigating it had been killed. Had Edwin Cromer observed the theft of the jewel and was now blackmailing the viscount? I could peg the viscount as the thief and murderer except he hadn't arrived in New York when Henry Darby was killed, and he hadn't visited Edwin Cromer the morning his throat had been slit. But it all seemed to fit together somehow. Or was I just making connections that weren't there, wanting to make the different parts of my life and my investigation come together somehow? And where did Rose fit into this other than as an unfortunate observer of something she should not have seen? At the back of my mind something was troubling me. Something I didn't want to address. I drifted into an uncomfortable sleep.

In my dream I was at Ellis Island again. Not as Molly Sullivan coming to help the new immigrants but as I had first come. I was running from someone or something. "I have to hide. I can't be seen," I kept thinking, pulling a shawl over my head and looking for a way out of the building. But I was trapped in the registration room in a line full of people. I was so hemmed in I couldn't move. Mrs. Sullivan was behind me with an enormous wicker basket that kept pushing me forward. "Keep moving," she hissed as I looked for a way to duck out of line. Rose McSweeney was ahead of me, her red hair shining like a beacon. "Look out," I tried to warn her. "They'll see you. Cover the hair." I tried to put my shawl over the both of us, but it shrank in my hands into a white glove and a bracelet fell out. Just then I realized that Bridie was missing. "Wasn't she just here? Where is she?" I looked wildly around the room, seeing only faces I didn't recognize. Then Cordelia Ransom came around the corner, a dagger in her hand that was dripping red blood.

I woke up with my heart pounding. I moved closer to Daniel and he turned over and put his arm around me. I felt the nightmare drifting away. I didn't normally have nightmares, but I suppose that finding a dead body could unnerve anyone. My heartbeat slowed but my brain kept racing.

When Daniel's alarm went off at seven, it was still pitch dark.

"Do you really have to get up so early on a Sunday?" I said sleepily as he climbed out of bed and pulled his robe from the bedpost. "Surely you can have a bit of a lie-in on a Sunday. Church is not until ten."

"I'm afraid I can't, my love." Daniel slipped the robe and his slippers on. "I assure you I don't want to be up. But I have more neighbors to question in the Cromer case and it's never helpful to wait for people's memory to get jumbled."

"Don't you have policemen under you to do that? Come back to bed. It's nice and warm." I patted the covers enticingly.

"I don't like to ask my men to do something I'm not willing to. You know that. But it shouldn't take more than a few hours. I'll be back for Sunday luncheon. You can go back to sleep."

"I don't like you going out into the cold without a breakfast." I got up myself, still shivering, and headed down into the kitchen to get the fire going as Daniel dressed.

"If it will only take a few hours, couldn't you get started a little later?" I said, peering out the window. "The fog is so thick I can't see across the backyard. You'll be wet through in a block."

"Well, if I know my men, they would rather get out there early and get back for their Sunday meals with their families."

"You mean they would rather miss church than dinner," I said with a grin as I put the grounds in the coffee pot and put it on to boil.

"I think that is true," he laughed, "no matter what religion they might be."

"Well, I shall have to tell your mother that you are shockingly irreverent this morning and working for mammon on the Lord's day."

"You shall have to be pious and reverent for me today." He grinned up at me.

"Heaven help you, then." I took the coffee pot off the burner and poured Daniel a big cup of coffee.

"Daniel," I said as I set the mug in front of him, "what is a viscount?"

"Some sort of English lord." He added two big scoops of sugar and I topped it off from the milk jug.

"I suppose I knew that. But what sort of English lord? I have heard of dukes and duchesses, but I'm not too sure what a viscount is."

"Why? Surely my independent Irish lass doesn't want too much to do with English lords and ladies?" He looked at me quizzically.

I raised my eyebrows and tried to look haughty. "I'm moving in highly exalted circles now. The toast of New York City. It's all part of your mother's plan to make you police commissioner or mayor by the age of forty."

"I'm perfectly happy just as I am, thank you. So what is this talk of lords and ladies? I take it that it has something to do with Cordelia Ransom."

"Yes, you're right. I thought of something last night." As I spoke I scooped bacon drippings into the pan and cracked three eggs into a bowl. "At the party Edwin Cromer said that he knew Cordelia's fiancé—the English viscount I told you about. And Ryan seemed to know them both as well. They went to the same theater parties in London. It seemed to surprise Cordelia to hear it." I whipped the eggs and added a little milk from the jug, then poured them into the sizzling pan.

Daniel frowned. "I suppose he wouldn't be the first man to go to parties his fiancée doesn't know about. Surely you can't be connecting the Ransoms and New York high society with a murder at Ellis Island? Or one in a boardinghouse on Church Street."

"But I believe the viscount might have been at the party where the necklace was stolen. What if Cromer was there too, saw it, and was blackmailing the viscount?" I looked up as I scrambled the eggs. "Or Cromer took the necklace and the viscount wanted it? I keep feeling that they are connected somehow. I suppose I could ask Ryan. He moved in those sort of circles in London. He might know how the Englishman and the viscount are connected." I scraped the eggs out of the pan and onto two pieces of buttered toast, putting one on Daniel's plate and one on mine.

Daniel looked at me seriously. "Molly, we had an agreement and you broke it."

My heart dropped. I had expected this. Was I always going to have to choose between following my instincts and keeping Daniel happy? But this time he was right, I had to admit.

"I'm very sorry, Daniel." I looked into his eyes so he knew I was telling the truth. "From now on I won't be doing any investigating without letting you know."

He took my hands in his. "I just want to keep you safe, my love. Anyway. You've done what you set out to do. Rose is free to go." A thud upstairs made him look up. "Our little man is up and needs your time and attention. And I need to get to work." He popped the last bit of toast into his mouth and stood up.

"I'll be interested to hear what the neighbors have to say," I called after him. "I wonder if anyone saw anything. Someone with blood spatters on them, maybe? And I'll see if I can find anything out from Ryan. There may be details about that party that he might not want to tell the police."

Daniel gave me an exasperated look. "Molly, I thought we just agreed."

"No, you agreed. I said I'm sorry for putting myself in danger. But Ryan can't possibly cause me any danger. Don't worry, I'm not even sure where he is staying right now, so if I see him it will be at Sid and Gus's." I started toward the door, not wanting Liam to get into any mischief if he was awake. "You can't forbid me to walk across the street, surely? And I am just as concerned as you that a murderer is on the loose."

"I suppose there can be no harm in walking across the street. But leave the murderers to me from now on." He buttoned his jacket and gave me a swift kiss. "Let's talk about it when I get home."

I hurried upstairs to find a cranky little Liam, who had squirmed himself out of his blankets and fallen out of bed. His skin was ice cold and he was crying. I carried him downstairs in my arms and sat with his little head on my chest, singing softly to him until he gradually stopped shivering and fell back asleep. The foggy morning seemed to mute the sounds of the city. I suppose it was the fact that I had not slept well and the warmth of the stove, but as I listened to the rhythmic breathing of my little man I fell back to sleep as well.

"Are we sleeping in on the Lord's day, then?" Mrs. Sullivan's voice sounded quite peevish. I woke with a start.

"What time is it?" I said, not wanting to leave the warmth of the blanket I had wrapped around the two of us.

"It's nine o'clock. We'll be late to church if we don't get a move on. I'll put the tea on." She stalked over to the sink with the teakettle. I must confess that before Daniel's mother came to live with us I was more likely to go for a walk in the park or over to Sid and Gus's for coffee than to put my Sunday best on and head out to church. But I didn't want to be accused of raising Daniel's son to be a heathen so, sighing, I dragged myself out of the chair.

Why am I doing this? I wondered to myself as I rushed around the house dressing myself and Liam, getting a sleepy Bridie up and down to a quick breakfast. Why am I doing this? I wondered again as I saw Mrs. Sullivan looking disapprovingly at the pan and dishes in the sink.

"Daniel had to go into work early," I explained. "I got up to make his breakfast."

It sounded strange to hear myself trying to explain my actions to Daniel's mother. I had never been like this with my own mother. I was always one to fire off a cheeky reply and regret it later.

"I'm a bit worried about him," I confessed, peering out the back window. "It is thick as pea soup out there. Perhaps we should stay in today ourselves. It may be dangerous to be on the street if we can't see our hand in front of our face."

Bridie looked up at me with a hopeful face, then looked down gloomily as Mrs. Sullivan spoke again.

"Our Lord suffered and died for us and the least we can do is come to worship him once a week. You may choose to do as you wish, of course, but I will not be committing a mortal sin this morning." She walked out of the kitchen into the front hall and began to put her coat on. Of course then I had to go. How could I tell Daniel that I let his mother go out in this fog all alone? But he and I would be having a serious talk very soon. If he didn't speak up for me with his mother, I was going to do some speaking up for myself, and quite loudly.

It was eerie as we stepped out into the fog. I trundled Liam's buggy onto the street and put him in it with a big blanket tucked around him. He was almost too big for it, I reflected. Bridie pulled her hood up over her head and started down toward Eighth Street. In about five steps she had completely disappeared.

"Bridie, come back," I called. "Put one hand on the buggy so we don't lose you." My voice was a little shaky. Seeing her disappear into the fog had reminded me of my dream. And my mind went to the hours I had spent during the night thinking of Edwin Cromer with his staring eyes. Pull yourself together, Molly, I muttered, and set out with a determined stride. I tried to keep up a cheerful conversation as we walked, but my voice sounded strangely echoing yet muffled in the fog. As we crossed Eighth Street an automobile came roaring out of nowhere and passed us with an echoing rumble that bounced off the tall buildings before disappearing into the gloom.

The church looked brighter and more inviting when we entered and made our way to the front. I preferred to sit at the back if I went at all, still feeling certain that a priest might point at me during the service and tell me I was a sinner. However, Mrs. Sullivan liked to sit in the front pews and sing loudly during the hymns, so we made our way down the center aisle. The Latin and the rhythm of standing and sitting made me think of my church back home. The statues as well; there was even one that looked like Our Lady of Knock that I had recently remembered from my childhood. Talking to Rose had brought back so many things I hadn't thought about in years. Strange that Rose hadn't known about that apparition of Our Lady. Even if she went to a secular school, there was church every Sunday, surely? I shifted uneasily in my seat as thoughts I had stifled crept into my brain.

I stood with the rest of the congregation and muttered the prayers. How those nuns drilled all the prayers into us. Our Lady of Knock, pray for us . . . I always associated her with the nuns and the cane. Today, though, I looked at the statue of a kind woman and the child in her arms and realized that she was a mother.

I looked down at little Liam, for once sitting quietly beside me and not trying to climb over all the pews, and thought, How could a mother always scowl at her children? I ventured a little prayer, "Mother of Mercy, keep Daniel safe in this fog. Help me keep my temper." I looked down the pew to Bridie, who had a look of wistful contemplation on her face. I wondered if she was thinking of her own mother. "And help to make us a family." Nothing happened, which I suppose is a good thing. At least there was no lightning bolt or thunderclap telling me I was in no state to be praying for anything.

As we left the church we walked out into a newly sparkling world. The winter sun had burned off the fog and a breeze had sprung up, blowing the haze of coal fires out to the Hudson. It crossed my mind superstitiously that it was an answer to my prayer. I laughed at myself for that, but my fears of the night had been blown away with the fog and I looked forward to the rest of the day with a cheerful optimism.

I put our small leg of lamb in the oven as soon as we got home and by the time I had changed out of my work clothes into a comfortable housedress, the smell of roasting lamb filled the house. I had noticed that morning that the parlor rug was looking quite dingy, and I took advantage of the sunny weather to take it out to the clothesline and beat it with Bridie's help. In New York in February you never know when you will get another sunny day. The weather seemed to have lightened Bridie's mood as well, and we joked as we beat out the rug, choosing some people we would like to be beating instead.

"Your principal!" I joked.

"Those snowball-throwing boys!" she added.

"Cordelia Ransom." I gave the rug a particularly hard whack.

"Rose McSweeney!" Bridie whacked the other side so hard that the dust made me cough.

"Bridie, what's wrong with Rose?" I asked, surprised. "She's only been sweet and kind to you. And we have to help those who are newly arrived just like we were helped by others."

"I don't dislike her because she is Irish, Molly," Bridie said. "She treats me like a little girl. She's a fake, too. There's something not right. She's too precious and sweet."

Oh dear. I wish she hadn't echoed my own uncertainties. "But look at how kind she is to Miss Van Woekem. She's a nicer person than I am. I'm sure Miss Van Woekem is thankful for her."

"I suppose." We beat in silence for a few minutes until no more dust would come out. Bridie poked her head around the rug and made a face. She was covered in dust and I realized I was too. We both started laughing.

Mrs. Sullivan came out the back door and looked at us like we were crazy. "Well, St. Michael and all his angels preserve us. I'm living in a madhouse." That of course made us laugh harder. "And a heathen one too," she went on, her voice rising now, obviously angry that we were laughing. "When I was a girl we were taught that working on the Sabbath was a sin. I would not have dreamed of making light of the Sabbath in this way."

"And who do you think will do all this work if I don't?" My temper flared as well. "If you want to live in a clean house and eat nice food, then I have to clean and cook it. I don't see our Lord and his angels coming down to do it no matter how holy I am on the Sabbath day."

"Blasphemy!" Mrs. Sullivan glared at me, reminding me of the nuns at school who had frequently accused me of the same sin. I was glad she didn't have a ruler to hand. "And, as I have been telling you, Molly, you should have a girl in to do this work so you can be a proper wife to Daniel."

"You may have noticed, Mother Sullivan," I said, the words spilling out now before I had a chance to edit them, "that all of our bedrooms are occupied. We are quite full up. To have a girl come and live in, someone would have to leave." I spat out the last word and stood glaring, my hands on my hips and my head thrown back defiantly.

"Such rudeness."

"What's going on out here?" I heard, and looked up. Daniel was standing just inside the back door looking out at all of us.

Twenty-Nine

Instantly I regretted my words. Hadn't I just said a prayer to keep my temper and my family together? But, on the other hand, I was right. I was tired of being put down constantly in my own home.

"I think Molly is a very proper wife," Daniel said, and I wondered how long he had been observing us. "It is certainly nice to come home to such a nice smell in the house. What are you cooking, my darling girl?" He came down the back steps into the garden, put his arms around me, and twirled me around, finishing his gesture with a little kiss.

"Daniel, I'm filthy, you'll get dust all over your suit," I cried, trying to wriggle away from him.

"Don't care," he said, holding me even tighter. Mrs. Sullivan looked at us and gave an audible "Hmmmph" before walking back into the house and closing the back door loudly enough I suspected she was just barely refraining from slamming it. "What was that about?" Daniel gazed down at me.

I sighed. "Oh, your mother doesn't think I should be cleaning on the Sabbath."

"And she made us go to church in the fog," Bridie's voice piped up from the other side of the rug.

"Who's there?" Daniel looked around in pretend astonishment. "Is our backyard haunted now?"

Bridie giggled and came out from behind the rug.

"It is a very dusty ghost." He smiled at her. "So you wanted to give mass a miss this morning?"

"Yes, the ladies said it is 'très gauche' to get up before ten on a Sunday. I need my beauty sleep."

Daniel and I both exchanged a look and stifled a laugh.

"It's your life to live, Molly." Daniel turned back to me, a serious look on his face. "You have a hard enough one as a policeman's wife anyway, with me coming and going at all hours. You shouldn't have to live by anyone else's rules, even if that someone is my mother. Don't worry, I'll have a talk with her and, as soon as the weather warms a bit, you'll have your house back to yourself."

I put my arms around him, no longer caring that the dust was getting on his suit. "That would be lovely."

The rest of the afternoon was wonderful. The lamb was just perfect with deliciously crispy skin. After lunch we walked down to Washington Square, just the four of us, as Mrs. Sullivan said she had a headache and would take a nap. The breeze was brisk enough that Daniel was able to fly a kite with Liam, and Bridie and I walked all the way around the park to keep warm. As we walked back along Sixth Avenue we were laughing and joking. I realized that I hadn't even asked Daniel how his investigation had gone. Even more strangely, for that moment I didn't care. I was glad just to be Molly with a son and a daughter and a husband by my side going home to a warm house. "Thank you," I sent up in gratitude to whoever heard the prayers of people like me.

My peaceful mood lasted until Daniel and I were lying in bed that night. Then my curiosity, never far from the surface, bubbled back up. "So, what did you learn this morning? Did anyone see anything strange? Have you found the wallet?"

"No, nothing from the people on his street," Daniel said. "But I did learn some news, and it is a damn headache."

"Daniel." I pretended to be shocked.

"My dear, if you can handle the details of a bloody stabbing you can take a little bad language." I couldn't see him in the dark, but I could hear the chuckle in his voice. "It turns out that Edwin Cromer is the youngest son of an English earl. His father may have thrown him out, but now we have Scotland Yard breathing down our police department's neck about his murder. And they think it is connected to the theft of the necklace that our first victim was investigating."

"I think so too," I said. "It would be too much of a coincidence if it wasn't."

"And to make matters worse," he went on, "a newspaperman has got a hold of it. If we don't solve this case soon, it will be splashed all over the *Times* with some sort of headline like, 'Inept Police Leave Murderer on the Loose.' The commissioner wants to see me tomorrow first thing. And I'm sure it's not to give me a medal."

We were silent awhile, then Daniel said, "Molly, I want you to do me a favor. You said you might pay a visit to Mr. O'Hare?" For a minute I thought I had fallen asleep and was having a strange dream.

"To Ryan?" I asked, thinking that I must have misheard.

"Yes. I want you to ask him some questions. It seems from what you've said that he might have been at the same parties as this Edwin Cromer. He might know who would have had the means or the motive to steal that necklace. Scotland Yard can't question most of the people involved because they are all important society people. But you have a friend who was on the spot."

"I was planning to see him tomorrow for coffee with Sid and Gus," I said. "I'd be happy to ask him whatever you want. Do you want to come along and ask him some questions yourself?" I could feel him shake his head.

"No, I'm not sure he'd speak freely in front of me. And frankly I'm not sure what to ask. But I do know that a necklace went missing at a party that Mr. O'Hare attended, then a man investigating that theft was killed at Ellis Island, and now another man who was at that same party or at least knew people who were has been murdered. It has to tie together somehow."

"Do you think Edwin Cromer stole the necklace and killed Mr. Darby?" I tried to talk the problem out. "But if so, where is the necklace? Could he have fenced it already?'

"We've thought of that," Daniel said. "We have officers circulating his description in the diamond district and at pawn shops. I doubt he would try to sell such a valuable necklace at a pawn shop, though. More likely he would have broken it up and sold off some of the smaller stones for cash."

"But then you would have found part of the necklace."

"Unless the person who murdered him took it and whatever cash he had on hand." He yawned. "It's a puzzle. But I'm too tired to think more about it."

I slept well that night, safe and warm beside Daniel.

The next morning as I made coffee I had to laugh to myself. I had already been determined to pump Ryan for information about the case. Now I was doing it with Daniel's blessing as an official investigator.

"Well, I'm off," Daniel said, poking his head into the kitchen.

"Daniel, you haven't even had your coffee," I chided him, taking the steaming kettle off the burner.

"No time, I'll have a cup later at headquarters. I've asked my mother to take Liam out this morning and have Bridie as a helper."

"You've cleared the way so I can have a tryst with another man?" I teased.

"Properly chaperoned by your two friends." He smiled.

"I'm not sure I would consider Sid or Gus proper chaperones, but I assure you Ryan is quite safe. I was only teasing."

"Well, I can't keep the commissioner waiting." Daniel gave me a peck on the cheek and was gone.

As I prepared breakfast I realized that Monday was a school day for Bridie and yet her teachers had already planned a coffee morning with a friend. How was this going to work? I wondered. I mentioned it to Bridie when she came downstairs. She didn't seem too perturbed.

"That's all right. They have given me plenty of work to do. I could start on an essay they have given me on the Greek myths."

I had quite a bit of time to do some household chores and get Liam warmly dressed for his outing. Sid and Gus were not early risers, and it would be impolite to go over before ten even for coffee and croissants. Mrs. Sullivan was a little reserved but polite. I wondered if Daniel had already spoken to her or if my angry remark about our full house had made her think.

As Sid opened the door to my knock I could hear that Ryan had already arrived. Loud laughter came from the kitchen as I walked in.

"Molly, darling! You look ravishing!" Ryan embraced me in a bear hug as I walked in, the cup of coffee in his hand dangerously close to spilling on my back. "I can't wait to hear your news. What did you think of my new play?"

I laughed. Typical Ryan. His only interest in my news would be juicy gossip or what I thought of him. "I loved it, as I told you that night." This morning Ryan's self-obsession was just what I needed. I could ask him anything I wanted and as long as it had to do with him he would never question why I asked. "Ryan, tell me about London," I started. "You said the play was a big success there, too."

"It was, my darling. I was the toast of the town!" Ryan beamed fondly at me. "And miraculously dear David was across the pond and fell in love with my play and invited me to do it at his lovely Belasco."

"He wasn't just taken with the play, by what I've heard." Gus arched an eyebrow at Ryan.

"Yes, well, you know how I like to be taken care of. And David is so sweet."

"And has a theater." Gus smiled.

"Don't be catty. It doesn't become you," Ryan admonished.

"Come, Molly dear," Sid said, putting a cup of hot coffee into my hands. "Let's go and sit down. Warm croissants on the table." As we walked through into the sitting room I noticed it was now coat free. The sofa had been pushed back and large purple cushions surrounded a low table in the center.

"No more donations?" I asked as Gus sat gracefully on a cushion and tore a piece off a croissant.

"No, thank God," Gus said. "One of the other members is storing them. We felt so hemmed in and claustrophobic that we decided to go minimalist. You know in Japan it is quite normal to sit on the floor. We may even knock down that wall between this room and the kitchen and put in a sliding rice paper panel."

I looked back at the pretty blue wall with white crown molding and hoped that they were out of this phase before they started tearing down their house. I knew that Sid and Gus were perfectly capable of demolishing the whole ground floor if the mood took them without stopping to think which walls were holding up the house. We sat and ate in silence for a minute, and then I ventured into my "interrogation."

"So, Ryan, you and David were at lots of parties in London? Was that Englishman there? Edwin Cromer."

"Who?" Ryan spooned a large amount of strawberry preserves onto his croissant.

"The young Englishman I pointed out to you at the party. Edwin Cromer was his name. He called himself a 'stage-door Johnny.'"

"Oh, his name does ring a bell. Cromer, you say? I do think I saw him at some of the parties with an actress. Why are you so interested, young Molly? He doesn't seem your type." He dipped his croissant into his coffee and took an enormous bite.

I decided truth was the best option. "He's been murdered."

Ryan choked and waved his arms dramatically, then took a large swig of coffee.

"When? How? Where?" he said as soon as he got his breath back.

"The night after your play. His throat was cut in his own bedroom."

"And I am involved how? Does your brute of a husband consider me a suspect? Am I to be dragged down to the station and wrongly accused yet again?" He lifted his hand to his brow in a theatrical gesture.

"No, my brute of a husband actually wants your help." I smiled at his surprise. "We think that the murder is somehow tied to a necklace that was stolen at a party after your opening night in London. Daniel was wondering if you could remember who was there and if you noticed anything suspicious. He thought you might know the gossip."

"Oh, the gossip. Well, I can help you there. Let's see. I told you that the king was there. That's not mentioned to the press because he was with his mistress, but that was true of a lot of men." He paused dramatically. "In fact, I have heard that the necklace that was stolen from the neck of Lord Harpenden's mistress actually belonged to his wife, who is currently suing for divorce."

"That would explain why he hired a private detective. He probably hoped to get it back without a scandal. Could Edwin Cromer be the thief? Was he at that party?"

"I really don't remember him. I do think there was some gossip connected with him, though. I think one of the actresses had to disappear to the country rather rapidly because she had found herself—you know—in the family way."

"Yes, he told us that much himself." Gus was sitting forward eagerly, clearly enjoying being part of the investigation again.

"Oh, speaking of disappearing actresses, you asked for scandal. It seems that Lily Love has disappeared from the London stage."

"Who is Lily Love again?" I asked.

"One of the darlings of the music hall," he said. "She was supposed to open in a review last week, and no one has seen her. Of course, she was going around with some lord or other as well, so the rumor is she might be in the family way herself."

"You do live an interesting life." Sid took her last bite of croissant and dipped it into her coffee, eating it with relish.

"What's a review?" I had heard the term but had never been sure exactly what it was before.

"It is a hodgepodge of different songs and scenes. A lot of comedy and some sweet young girls. Lily will be sorely missed. I wouldn't be surprised if it closed early without her. She brought the house down in the last one I saw. Oh, I wish you could have seen her." He chuckled to himself just thinking about it. "She started with putting on a flaming red wig, almost like your gorgeous hair, Molly, dear. Then she put on the thickest Irish brogue you have ever heard from the deepest bog. Then she acted like a virtuous young maiden telling the audience how she had kept her chastity as all these wicked men approached her. Everything she said could be taken in an entirely wicked way, but the censors can never call her on it because all the words are completely innocent. You know, talking about a man's shillelagh—one of those big sticks that Irish brutes use, when she meant something quite different. And as she gets more and more wicked she starts every exclamation with "To tell the truth." Ryan started to laugh helplessly. "She was absolutely brilliant! So convincing."

I felt myself go cold all over.

"And she was at the party? Where the diamond was stolen?" I could hardly force out the words. But Ryan was doubled over laughing.

"To tell the truth, sir, that's your shillelagh." He laughed so hard that he fell over sideways and Gus quickly moved his coffee out of the way.

I stood up. "I have to go home right now."

Sid looked up, concerned.

"What is it, Molly? What's wrong?" Just then there was a loud knock at the front door, and before Sid could go to open it, we heard someone come in.

"Molly!" It was Daniel's voice, strained with tension. He came into the room clutching a telegram in his hand. "Hello," he seemed to remember his manners as he saw the frozen tableau that we had become. "Good morning. I'm sorry for barging in."

"Any time, Daniel dear," Gus said, rising, unflappable as usual. "Can I get you a coffee?"

"No, thank you." Daniel didn't even look at her. He was staring at me. "Molly, we have to go home now."

"What is it? What's happened? Tell me now before I die of fright." My heart pounded, but somehow I think I knew what he was going to say.

"My office has been receiving telegrams from Dublin and England all morning about the Cromer case."

"Yes." I looked steadily at him, my heart in my throat.

"This one just came from Dublin, part of our investigation of every suspect in the case."

"Yes," I said again. For God's sake, could he just tell me?

"Rose McSweeney is dead. She fell under a tram three weeks ago in Queenstown."

Thirty

"Are you sure?" My head spun as I tried to make sense of the words. "Perhaps that was a different Rose."

"I don't know, Molly. It's a little hard to believe that one Rose McSweeney was killed in Queenstown. And then another Rose McSweeney takes a boat from Queenstown to New York that same day?" He looked at me with compassion. "I'm sorry. This is obviously distressing when you believed in this woman and did everything you could for her."

I shook my head. "I'm afraid there's more, Daniel." Quickly I related what Ryan had said about the actress Lily Love.

"Rose is dead?" Gus's question reminded me of where we were. "That bright young Irish woman? The one at the party?"

"I don't know what to think." I felt like my head was spinning. "I think Daniel is saying she may not be Rose McSweeney at all, but an actress from London instead."

"Doesn't she live with your elderly friend?" Gus looked up, concerned, and suddenly my head cleared.

"That's right. Daniel, we have to warn Miss Van Woekem right away. I hope I am jumping to a wrong conclusion, and may God forgive me. But if that girl is not Rose McSweeney, she may be the real murderer. Do you have the police automobile here?"

"Yes, I drove over as soon as I got the telegram. But, Molly, you are not going anywhere. I have my men on the way to Miss Van Woekem's house."

"But Daniel," I said, "if she is a killer we can't risk sending police over. Let me come with you. I can invite Rose out of the house in a normal way. And if she is innocent," I added, "perhaps she has a perfectly reasonable explanation. After all, I came into New York using another woman's name and I was not guilty of murder." I turned to Sid, Gus, and Ryan. "Thank you for the coffee."

"I had thought of both those things, Molly." Daniel sounded impatient. "The police will wait outside until I get there."

Sid stood. "We'll come with you, Molly. I've always wanted to be in on an arrest. It's so exciting."

"No, stay." Ryan waved her down again. "It is much too early to chase criminals. You promised me croissants and coffee. Molly and her intrepid Daniel will brave the danger."

Daniel was already halfway to the door, and I was not about to be left behind.

"Thank you for the offer, but this is my mess to fix. I'll tell you all about it, I promise," I said as I briefly turned back to them, then dashed out the door and across the street. Daniel was already closing the driver's side door on the police automobile that was stationed in front of our house. I ran to the passenger side, opened the door, and jumped in.

He looked at me with a pained expression on his face. "Molly, this might be dangerous. Please stay home."

"Don't be ridiculous. You're wasting time. Let's go."

He could tell there was no point in arguing with me at that moment, so he put the auto into reverse gear and steered cautiously down Patchin Place. Then he swung into the busy traffic of Greenwich Avenue, and turned north onto Sixth Avenue. "I don't want any nonsense, Molly. I'll leave you at the corner and go in and get Rose."

"But it would be safer with two of us, especially as she won't sense danger if I'm there. If you go alone she may decide to fight."

"I think I can handle a young girl." I couldn't tell now if he was angry or just concentrating on navigating his way through the traffic of horses and automobiles on the road.

"I'm sure that is what Henry Darby thought too." I put my hand on his arm and then grimaced as he missed his gear and the auto lurched with a loud grinding sound. "So maybe I should go in alone and lure her out to you. I am in no danger from Rose. I will invite her out for a walk around the square. She will come outside with me and you can safely arrest her with no risk to Miss Van Woekem."

"Molly, don't be stupid—" he began, but I cut him off.

"Why should I be in danger? We have been together as friends for weeks." As I said this I realized how much I wanted this whole chase to be for nothing. Surely there would be a logical explanation. I had been so sure that I had made a friend who truly understood me. But then I thought of Ryan's theater story and I felt sick inside. Wasn't "to tell the truth" a phrase that I had heard Rose use over and over? And wasn't her accent hard to place—could it be the thick stage brogue Ryan had mentioned? And hadn't she seemed puzzled about some Irish expressions I'd used and taken for granted? I realized how she had played me—picking up my clues and making them her own: she had brothers because I had brothers. She had worked for an old lady because I had told her about my own experience. I had to face the fact that she was as Ryan had described her—a brilliant actress who had me completely fooled. Suddenly I felt sick and scared, but I wasn't going to let Daniel see that.

"You can come and wait on the front steps if you like. Or even inside the front hall." I saw he was about to argue again. "It's the safest way, Daniel. She might be sitting with Miss Van Woekem. We wouldn't want her to be harmed, would we? And you'll be within reach."

Daniel screeched to a halt as he turned onto Gramercy Park,

still a ways from the house, getting astonished and indignant looks from well-dressed pedestrians. Luckily a uniformed policeman was standing guard near the front steps, and Daniel spoke with him briefly as he handed over the keys to the automobile and gave him instructions. I climbed out and waited impatiently. Daniel came over and took my arm. "Are you still determined to do this, Molly? Are you sure you won't wait here?"

I just nodded tightly. "I'm sure." Daniel took one look at my face and saw he wouldn't change my mind. He knew me well enough to realize that if he left me behind at this point I was liable to sneak in the back way. "Smile," I said, and took his arm as we walked around the corner. "If anyone sees us coming I don't want to look distressed."

We rang the bell and the door was answered by Jewel, looking just as sloppy and belligerent as ever.

"Oh, it's you again." She looked Daniel up and down. "And who's this, then?"

"Please tell Miss Van Woekem that Mrs. Sullivan is here." I was happy to hear that there was no quaver in my voice. The sight of Jewel and her rude reception actually steadied my nerves and made what I had come to do seem ridiculous.

She disappeared into the parlor and I heard her say, "Do you want visitors?"

"You can come in," she said as she returned, giving Daniel and me a defiant stare.

"Why don't you wait for us on the front steps, Daniel?" I said, giving him a sweet smile. "We'll be right out."

Miss Van Woekem and Rose were sitting side by side. Rose was holding a large ball of wool as Miss Van Woekem was knitting. They looked up with smiles as we walked in.

"Molly, what a nice surprise." Miss Van Woekem looked less severe than I had ever seen her. Her normal pinched face was serene and her smile was genuine. "Can I get you some coffee or tea?"

"No, thank you. I hope you don't mind, but I actually came by to see Rose. Rose, dear, I am meeting my husband before he has to go back to work and I thought I would like to introduce him to you and see if you would care to join us. Would you, Rose?" I turned to Rose and smiled. "I thought we might stop for a coffee or hot chocolate. Mrs. Sullivan is watching Liam and I always jump at the chance to enjoy a few minutes of escape with a friend." I felt a pang as I said it. Whatever Rose was after this she would not be my friend. Even if she was innocent, she would no longer consider me warmly after I turned her in to the police.

"That would be lovely," Rose said with a smile. "If you can spare me, dear Miss Van Woekem?"

For a second I thought she would ask if Miss Van Woekem could come as well, and my heart beat so loudly I was sure that she could hear it.

"No, you go ahead. Enjoy this brief sunny spell." Miss Van Woekem smiled up at her. "I'm quite content."

"I'll just go up to get my hat and coat. I'll be right down, then." Rose left the room and I could hear her run lightly up the stairs. I followed her into the hall. The front door was still slightly ajar. I motioned to Daniel, who sprang into action, slipping into the sitting room and putting his finger to his lips as he came over to Miss Van Woekem.

"Please trust me," he said to Miss Van Woekem.

"What on earth?" she began, but he shushed her hurriedly.

"You're in danger. Molly, stay here with her. Explain what is going on." Daniel turned to go back to the hall, but at that moment Jewel burst in.

"God almighty that's a lot of police. What are they all doing outside the house?" She ran over to peer out the front window.

"Jewel. Keep your voice down," I said in an urgent whisper. I moved forward to take her arm.

"Why, what's all this about?" Jewel didn't lower her voice. She moved away from me, a mingled look of suspicion and excitement on her face.

Daniel looked at me helplessly. If Rose came downstairs right now, she would be instantly suspicious. I decided to improvise.

"They're here to arrest you for being the worst maid in the history of New York."

She gaped at me. "You're joking, aren't you?"

I shook my head and watched an incredulous look spread across her face. At least I had stopped her talking for a moment. She took a breath and before she said another word I continued, "But if you go up to your room right now and stay there, I think I can talk them into leaving you alone. Only if you are gone in thirty seconds, though."

"But," Jewel started to argue, "my—"

"Go on. Go now. They are coming in that door to get you in fifteen seconds." I examined the dainty watch that was pinned to the front of my dress. "Ten, nine, eight, seven—"

Jewel stared at me while I counted down, glanced out the window at the policemen, and then fled. I heard her footsteps clattering up the stairs and then a door slam at the top of the house.

"Molly, it scares me how good a liar you are." Daniel was looking at me strangely.

"Well, at least she's gone." I looked toward the door and steeled myself. "We just have a few more lies to tell and Rose will be safely outside."

"No, now that everyone is out of the way the time for lying is over." Daniel's voice had a note of steel in it. I looked over at him and saw that he had his revolver out. "Rose, or whoever she is, is coming to the station with me. You stay here with Miss Van Woekem." This time I didn't argue. As he headed for the door we heard footsteps coming toward us. Daniel and I waited in tense silence as the door knob turned. The door was flung open and Daniel raised the revolver.

"What on earth?" The cook's jaw dropped open in terror and she threw her hands up. "Don't shoot."

Daniel lowered his revolver.

"I'm sorry, Cook. We thought you were Rose. She needs to come to the police station with my husband," I said, going to put a comforting hand on her shoulder.

"That's what I was coming in to tell you. I thought it was the strangest thing, but I guess I understand it now. Rose just ran out through my kitchen, out the back door like a bat out of hell, and climbed over the back wall."

Daniel pushed past her and disappeared in the direction of the back door.

"Will somebody please tell me what's going on?" Miss Van Woekem looked both scared and annoyed.

"I am afraid Rose has run away. Cook saw her go out the back garden." I was suddenly filled with remorse. Who had I brought into Miss Van Woekem's life? Had I put her life in danger? "I'm sorry. I think perhaps I made a mistake bringing her here in the first place."

"Mistake? What sort of mistake?"

"It appears Rose might be a wanted fugitive," I said.

But the stern old lady looked defiant. "I won't believe it until she tells me herself. She's a sweet young thing. Why, she may be only hiding in the back garden because you scared her. She didn't have the easiest life in Ireland, you know. Let's go and look." And she limped determinedly through the kitchen toward the back door. Daniel still had the revolver in his hand, and when she saw him she gave a little cry of fear.

"Put that away! Don't hurt her. I'm sure this is a misunderstanding."

Daniel looked back at us and holstered his revolver. He stooped, picked up something from the ground at his feet, and brought it over to us.

"I'm sorry," he said, holding up the object. It was a wig of long, curly red hair. "Rose is gone."

Thirty-One

"Stay with Miss Van Woekem and explain." Daniel walked quickly through the house. "I must send out the alert to look for her right away."

I felt so guilty that I didn't argue. I looked at Miss Van Woekem standing stock still, absolutely bewildered. God help me I had no idea how to explain what had just happened. I was still confused and hurt myself. I wondered which would make her angrier, that I had brought Rose to her or that she was gone. I knew that the young woman had brought a real joy and companionship into the old lady's life. I resolved to make up for it somehow. I led her inside and explained what I knew. It wasn't much of a success. I don't think I made myself very clear, and she was not in a state to take in very much that I was saying. An impatience was building inside me to be home. I wanted to be safe with my family and also to be close to the telephone in case Daniel called with any news.

"I'll come back tomorrow to see if you need anything," I promised. "Will you be able to manage on your own?"

"Yes, I can hobble well enough to get to my room and back. And I suppose that awful maid will manage to bring me my meals even if they are cold and late." She rang the bell. I started to retrieve Jewel from her room. But to my surprise Jewel poked her head around the door.

"Are those police gone now?" she asked. Then she saw me and her face contorted into a look halfway between fear and a defiant scowl. "Oh, you're still here."

"Everything is fine now," I hurried to reassure her. She might be the worst maid in existence, but Miss Van Woekem couldn't manage at the moment with no one to take care of her. "The police are gone. And they won't be back as long as you do a good job taking care of your employer." I could tell by the puzzled look on her face that she was not sure whether to believe me or not. But I couldn't wait to get home, so I stood up and said goodbye, promising Miss Van Woekem that I would come by the next day to give her the news and to make sure she was all right. I hurried out the door, thanking the Lord that I had had the presence of mind to bring my purse with me so I could catch a cab home.

I hate to admit it, but on the way home in the cab where no one could see me I let myself have a little cry. I couldn't tell if they were tears of anger at having been tricked and lied to or sadness at losing a person I thought was my friend. I felt so foolish, too. I had never doubted that Rose's story was my story, that I had to defend her as I had defended myself all my life. But now I realized that most of the things I thought connected us she had told me about after I shared them with her. I had heard that a confidence trickster could take in gullible people; in fact some years ago I had watched two confidence tricksters take in the rich and powerful. But I had never thought I could be taken in myself. The cab pulled up at the start of the cobblestone street and I jumped out, eager to be home. As I approached my front door I looked with fondness at my little house.

"I'm home," I called as I walked into the front hall and took off my coat. "Has Daniel telephoned?"

Mrs. Sullivan appeared from the kitchen, Liam in her arms, and he reached out for me.

"Come here, little man," I said, taking him and kissing his little cheeks. "No news from Daniel, then?" I asked Mrs. Sullivan.

"He has not been home. Do you expect him early today?" She was looking at me curiously. I realized that she knew nothing of what had happened and I felt too tired to explain it all.

"I doubt he will be early. I'm late thinking about our supper, though. I think I'll get Bridie to push Liam in the buggy and we can walk to the shops to get some meat. Would you like to come?"

My mother-in-law was frowning. "But Bridie's already waiting for you at the soda fountain. I thought you'd be there with her ages ago."

"What do you mean?" I asked, confused. Had I promised to take Bridie to the soda fountain as a treat? I did sometimes, but surely she would have waited for me to walk over with her. I didn't like her walking about the city on her own.

"Your friend came for her, that lovely Irish girl. She said she was treating you both to a coffee and pastry to thank you before she left town."

My blood froze. "My friend? You mean Rose?"

"Yes, that's what she called herself. Ever so pleasant, although she wouldn't step inside. She just said you had sent her to get Bridie to come out for a treat and would Bridie help her to choose a goodbye present for you on the way to the soda fountain." She saw my shocked face.

"Don't worry, I had Bridie bundle up in her warmest coat. I could tell it must be freezing out by how that woman kept her cloak around her, never even took down her hood."

"Was it the green cloak?" I thought of the cloak I had brought her. That would be easy to see in a crowd. "Which way did they walk?" I handed Liam over to my mother-in-law. My mind was whirring and my heart pounding so strongly I couldn't catch my breath.

"Yes, a pretty green cloak. They walked down that way." Mrs. Sullivan waved down toward Washington Square. I didn't even wait for her to finish the sentence and I took off at a run.

"Watch Liam for me!" I shouted over my shoulder.

"What is it? What's wrong?" I could hear her startled cry of alarm behind me, but I could not stop even for a second to explain. I ran down and crossed the street, looking up and down at the cabs coming and going and the people milling in and out of Jefferson Market. Think, Molly, think. Where would they have gone? There was always a policeman on the corner outside the police station. I ran up to him asking if he had seen a woman in a green cloak with a little girl.

"I suppose I have seen a few hundred women in green cloaks," he said, looking meaningfully around at the crowded market. "I don't remember a particular one."

I was in an agony of indecision. I knew that Daniel could have every police officer in the city looking for her. I could tell this policeman that Captain Sullivan's ward had been kidnapped. He would telephone headquarters and let Daniel know. But what would happen next? He would keep me here filling out police reports and answering questions and every second Bridie would be getting further away from me.

I couldn't stand that, I decided. I had to find her myself. Who would have noticed a woman in this crowd? My eyes lit on a little street sweeper in raggedy clothes with the universal soft gray cap. I suppose what drew my attention with Bridie filling my whole mind was his resemblance to little Seamus. Her brother Seamus had looked just like that when I had cared for them both after first arriving in New York. And he and his cousins had often gone out to act as street sweepers, trying to earn a coin or two from passersby. I myself had made use of them in my detective business to get news.

I ran up to the boy. "Have you seen a lady in a green cloak and a girl a little older than you?"

"I might have." He rubbed his fingers together in the universal sign for money. "I might not. My memory might need some help."

I fished in my bag for a quarter and held it out, then snatched it back as he tried to take it. "Information first," I said, and produced another quarter. "And two if your information is helpful."

A smile split his face and he spoke rapidly, "I did see a lady in a green cloak. She and the girl were getting into a cab. There was a big gust of wind and the dame's hood came off and her hair got in her eyes. Then the girl screamed and the lady grabbed her."

"Did you hear them tell the cabby where to go?" I was already flagging down a cab, desperately impatient to be going as quickly as I could.

"I mighta." He held out his hand for the money. I put one quarter into it and showed him the second. "The truth, please. My husband is a police captain, and if you lie to me I'll send the police to arrest you."

"You wouldn't know where to find me," he sneered with an uneasy bravado. "But I know where she went and it ain't no lie. The girl yelled it out of the cab. 'Grand Central.' She yelled out to no one. It's almost like she knew you would come asking."

She did, I thought, putting the second quarter into his hand. "Thank you. I'm sorry I threatened you. If you go and tell the Jefferson Market policeman that same story and tell him that Mrs. Daniel Sullivan said her daughter has been kidnapped and is being taken to Grand Central station, I will make sure you get a reward."

I didn't have any time to waste to see if he carried out my instructions. I jumped into the cab and told the driver to go to Grand Central station as quickly as possible. We plodded through the traffic up Sixth Avenue so slowly that I felt I could have run faster. My only consolation was that their cab must have had the same traffic. I might not be too far behind them. I should have asked Mrs. Sullivan how long ago they left. The traffic eased as we crossed Fourteenth Street, but clogged up again as we turned up Park Avenue. It crawled to a halt as the gold domes of the station came into view and we ran into construction. Then I did decide I could run faster. I paid the surprised cabby and jumped out. I ran the last two blocks, only to find that the Park Avenue entrance was also under construction. I ran around the side of the building and into the big airy terminal. I stopped just inside, trying to catch my breath. Rose would be fleeing as far away as possible, wouldn't she? Somewhere where the police wouldn't catch up with her. I looked up at the big board. Was there a long-distance train leaving in the near future?

Then my heart did a little flip. The 20th Century Limited was in the Grand Central Terminal and was due to leave for Chicago in ten minutes. That had to be the train she'd take! I took off running again, not stopping until I had found the right platform and was in sight of the gleaming metal train. I pushed my way onto the crowded platform, past porters with carts of luggage and through families saying their goodbyes. A smartly uniformed attendant was standing at the door to each car, checking tickets. While he was occupied with an older couple I slipped behind him, into the first car. I resisted the urge to yell out Bridie's name, thinking it might get me thrown off the train.

I thought I saw a flash of green disappearing though the glass door at the end of the carriage I was in. In the carriage men and women were lifting heavy bags along the center aisle. I squeezed past them, hearing some murmurs of disapproval behind me as I trod on some toes and pushed people out of my way. I opened the door into the waiting area between the two cars. I heard the conductor's "All aboard," as I pulled open the door to the next car.

It was clearly a lounge car, filled with elegantly dressed men ordering drinks already from a highly polished bar and equally well-dressed women sitting in the velvet-backed chairs. A woman was removing a green cloak and laying it over the back of her chair. I couldn't see her face through the crowd of people, but I pushed through, determined to get to her. Just as I reached the table the train gave an enormous lurch and I fell forward, clutching her back to keep from falling. She gasped and spun around.

"What on earth?" She was a stout, middle-aged woman. "Young lady, watch where you are going."

Thirty-Two

I grabbed onto the back of a chair again as the train gave another jerk, there was a hissing of steam, the clanging of a bell, and we started to move. "I'm so sorry," I said, my eyes scanning the lounge car for any sign of Bridie or Rose. So now I was heading to Chicago whether I liked it or not.

"Where is the first stop?" I asked a man who was looking at me with interest.

"It stops once more just outside the city, in Harmon," he said. "Then Albany."

I nodded, thinking that I had enough money on me to pay for a ticket as far as that if I were stopped by a ticket collector. I began to move up the car, then into the next that was being set up for dining, then a saloon car with a bar, where white-clad waiters looked at me questioningly.

"We're not open yet, ma'am,' one of them said.

"I'm just passing through," I said, in what I hoped was a haughty voice. I pushed open the door, stepped through the swaying connection, and came to the first of the sleeping cars. It had a central gangway with booths on either side, an upper and lower, each concealed by a curtain. I stood, listening for Bridie's voice, or Rose's. Tentatively I pulled one curtain aside.

"Hey!" a man exclaimed.

"I'm sorry. Wrong compartment," I said, hastily letting the curtain fall again. I hesitated before daring to lift the next curtain, but the thought of Bridie with that woman drove me on. They didn't appear to be in the next car or the next. Then I came to the grander private cabins. Surely Rose didn't have the sort of money one of them would require? But then if she really was Lily Love, a famous entertainer, she might actually be quite wealthy. And quite dangerous, if she had already killed two men, I reminded myself.

There was a smartly attired attendant standing at the far end of the carriage.

"Do you have a woman with a young girl in one of these compartments?" I asked.

"I'm not allowed to tell you who sleeps where," he said, with a broad grin. "More than my job is worth."

"Don't you have a list?"

"Name?" he asked.

"Lily Love?" I suggested. "Rose McSweeney?"

He shook his head. Of course she'd be using a false name, wouldn't she? Or perhaps she hadn't even bought her ticket yet. I moved on to the next car and the next, feeling fear and frustration rising in equal amounts. Could I tell one of the attendants that this woman had kidnapped a girl? Would they believe me? The blinds to the corridor were down in most of the compartments. I listened but heard only a low murmur of voices. At last I could stand the tension no longer.

"Bridie?" I yelled. "Bridie, are you here?"

And from down the car came her voice: "Molly! I'm here. Come and—" The words were broken off abruptly, but there had been enough for me to identify where they came from. I sprinted down the car and flung open the door. Rose, or rather Lily Love, had an arm around Bridie's throat and the girl was staring at me in terror. I saw that Rose's other hand contained a knife.

"Get inside and shut the door," Rose said, "or I'll slit her throat just as I did that fool Edwin Cromer's."

I did as she said. Bridie was staring at me with big, terrified eyes. I confess I wasn't feeling much less afraid myself.

"I should never have trusted you in the first place," Rose said. "Pretending you were working hard to prove my innocence when all the time you were just assisting your policeman husband."

"I was working to prove you innocent," I said. "I believed in you. How can you do this? What has an innocent child ever done to you?"

"I needed security," Rose said. "A human shield in case things got messy. You should have not been so bloody smart, Molly Murphy. I'd have let her go once we reached Chicago and I was on my way to the West Coast. Now I'll have to kill one of you. I can't risk two hostages. Probably you."

"And you don't think they'd find a body on the train?"

"I'd throw you out when we're well clear of the city," she said. "Now, sit over there and don't try to move." She shoved Bridie down at one end of the bunk and I sat at the other.

"The attendant will come in to make up the bed," I said.

"Not until after dinner." She smiled then. She really was a beautiful woman, and it struck me how stupid she was to have given up a glittering career to be essentially on the run for the rest of her life.

"Why would you do this?" I asked. "You were the toast of London, according to Ryan O'Hare. You didn't need a jewel."

"I needed to be free," she said.

"Free?"

"Of a certain man and his hold over me." She gave me a scornful look. "You wouldn't understand. Happily married with children. Never been in my position when success depends on whose bed you are willing to share."

"So you stole a necklace to make you free of a man?"

"I stole a necklace because a man forced me to do it," she said, and I now heard the bitterness in her voice. "But once I'd got it in my hands I realized it was my chance to run, to hide, to escape. So I grabbed the red wig and fled to Ireland. And then I met this girl—Rose McSweeney was her name—in a café. She told me she was leaving for America in the morning. We came out onto the street together. A tram was coming. All I had to do was give her a little shove. Then I gathered up her purse and blended into the crowd. I thought with any luck they'd not be able to identify her and I could travel in her place."

She paused, looking out the train window as we rattled over a railway bridge over some water. "It all worked well until I realized that man was following me. The detective from London. On the same boat."

I nodded.

"And then that idiotic Cromer person. When he saw me in a theatrical setting, I knew he'd put two and two together. And now they are all gone and I only have—"

The carriage door slid open. Rose took a step back and gasped. The viscount stood there, a gun pointing at her.

"Well, well. I didn't expect a party," he said, stepping in and shutting the door hastily behind him. "How delightful to see you, Lily, my darling."

"Don't call me your darling," she snapped, but I heard the fear in her voice. "You have a new darling, don't you? That society woman—with all the money. What's she going to say when she finds out that you're not really a viscount with a castle?"

He smiled. He had the most charming smile, and I could tell why women were attracted to him. "I rather fear that an accident might happen to her when we visit my ancestral home in Scotland. Those rugged mountains, you know. So easy to lose one's footing. After I have transferred the right amount of money, naturally." The gun was still pointed at Rose, and he motioned that she should sit. She sat next to me.

"I always intended to come back to you, Lily. Until you ran off so stupidly with the necklace. Where is it?"

"Safely hidden away," she said.

"I have all the time in the world to find it."

"The attendant will be in soon."

He smiled. "A generous tip, a wink, and the knowledge that we were not to be disturbed. No, I think you'll find that nobody will enter all the way to Chicago. But these two—" He turned to us. "What were you thinking?'

"I grabbed the girl as a hostage, just in case," she said. "But this woman followed us."

His gaze focused on me. He had the coldest eyes and he was giving me an appraising stare. "I've met you before. At the old woman's and the party after the play. I remember the hair. But what are you to do with this matter?"

"She's a policeman's wife. She found out who I really am," Rose said before I could answer.

"How annoying," he said. "Did your husband send you in pursuit?"

"No. I came when I found that Bridie was missing. She's my daughter. I had to try and rescue her."

I saw his smile broaden. How stupid of me. I should have told him that the entire New York police force knew we were on the train.

"So we wait until the line runs beside the Hudson and then we throw her out," he said, addressing Rose as if I weren't there. "We'll keep the girl. As you said, my darling, a hostage is a good idea. Just in case." He lowered the gun and sat opposite her, next to Bridie. "Don't worry, little girl," he said. "You'll be quite safe as long as you do what we tell you."

"What about Molly?" Bridie said, her voice quivering even though she stared at him defiantly. "You're not going to hurt her. She came to save me. That's all. She doesn't want your stupid necklace."

"A policeman's wife is too much of a risk, my dear," he said. "But you, Lily my sweet. What a dance you've led me. Running away from the man who adores you?"

"Adores me? And about to marry that Ransom woman?"

"I did it for us, Lily darling. We make a good pair, don't we? Such a successful team. Just give me time to get things sorted with my new bride, then I'll join you wherever you decide to go. Where are you heading, exactly?"

"San Francisco, I hope," she said. "And if that gets too hot maybe Mexico."

"Ah, Mexico. That sounds nice and lawless," he said. "But you'll need to sell the necklace first, won't you? And you don't have my connections. I will make us both rich. So you'll give me the necklace. I'll sell it to the right person and I'll join you."

I saw her face. She was desperately thinking of the right thing to say. He said it for her. "Of course, if you don't agree and hand over the jewel, I can just as easily throw you out of the carriage after the policeman's wife. As you've told me enough times I have no conscience."

There was a long pause.

"So what do you say?"

"All right, Charlie," she said at last. "You win."

I could see that we had left the city behind. The train slowed and pulled into a small station. Harmon, read the sign on a wooden board. I looked longingly out the window, hoping to attract the attention of a stationmaster or porter. The viscount stood again with his back to the door and the gun in his hand.

"Not a sound from anyone," he said.

I was desperately trying to think what I could do against a knife and a gun. Nobody passed us on the platform. There was a whistle, the shouted "All aboard," and we jerked forward again, gathering speed rapidly. Now the river was right beside the tracks. The carriage shook and lurched as we crossed over points to another track, causing the viscount to lose his balance for a second. As he stumbled forward Rose sprang up and plunged her knife into his chest. He gave a gasp. "What have you done? You stupid woman—" he started to say. Blood spurted out, staining his yellow silk waistcoat. He clutched at his front. She grabbed the gun from him as he pitched forward.

Rose looked up at me triumphantly. "That's that, then," she said. "I'm finally free of him. He used me for years, you know. Making use of my invitations into high society and then training me to do his dirty work for him. He knew I was trapped. But not anymore. We'll throw him out and nobody will be the wiser."

"What makes you think we'll help you?" I said.

"I have the gun now, in case you haven't noticed." She gave a sweet smile.

"You kill one of us, then you'll have two people to dispose of," I said. "I don't know how you'll handle that. And a shot would be heard."

I saw uncertainty in her expression. "You'll do it," she said, "because otherwise I'll slit the child's throat." She yanked Bridie to her feet, still holding the gun, then reached to grab the knife in her other hand. Bridie gave a little gasp.

"Go on. Open the window. All the way down."

I obeyed. Cold sooty air, mixed with smoke from the engine, blew in, stinging my eyes.

"Right now, you and the girl pick him up. Go on." Bridie and I exchanged eye contact. I could tell she was waiting for me to give her a direction, but I couldn't think of one.

"He's too heavy," Bridie whimpered. "I can't lift him. I'm not strong enough."

"Oh, for heaven's sake," Rose said.

"She's a delicate little thing," I said. "Since she had the typhoid."

"That's right." Bridie spoke in a weak little voice. "There's not much I can do anymore."

She looked at Rose appealingly, then she added, "Except this."

And she flew at Rose, knocking the gun from her hand. It fell to the floor. I reached to snatch it up as Rose lunged at Bridie with the knife. The carriage rocked as we changed tracks again and she had to step back to keep her balance. I took my chance and yanked on the emergency communication cord. There was the screech of brakes and we lurched to a stop. Rose looked from me to the open window, deciding what to do. But I held the gun.

"Sit down," I said to her. "And put the knife down on the seat there."

At that moment the carriage door was flung open. A railway policeman and the attendant stood there.

Rose stood up. "Oh, thank God you've come," she exclaimed, sobbing. "These people have killed my darling fiancé and were trying to rob me. She has a gun and a knife."

The railway policeman stepped into the compartment, his own gun drawn. "Hand over the gun, ma'am," he said to me. "Don't make it worse on yourself."

"I'll put it into your handkerchief," I said. "That way the fingerprints won't be smudged too badly."

"What?" He looked confused now.

"Fingerprints on the gun. And on the knife over there. They will tell you who the real criminals are."

"Fingerprints?" Rose asked.

"They use them these days to identify a suspect," I said. "Everyone is different, apparently. They'll find yours are the only ones on the knife that killed him."

"Don't believe her. She's talking nonsense," Rose said. "This man was my beloved fiancé, Viscount Brackley, and I'm Lady Hortense Wainright. We have the highest of connections and this woman wanted to rob us."

"That's not true! She kidnapped me," Bridie said, pointing at Rose. "And my mother, Molly Sullivan, came to rescue me. And my father is Captain Sullivan of the New York police."

"Sullivan?" The railway policeman looked at me with new eyes. "Captain Sullivan? Of the New York police?"

"My husband," I said.

"My apologies, ma'am," he said, his eyes darting nervously from me to Lily Love. "And who is this woman, then?"

"We know her as Rose McSweeney," I said. "She committed a murder on Ellis Island, but her actual name is—"

I didn't finish the sentence. Rose fought her way to the window and with remarkable agility squeezed herself through. I reached to grab her cloak. The clasp broke and the cloak came off in my hands.

"Hey, you. Come back here," the policeman said.

We rushed to the window. She had landed in a heap, as it was a long drop to the cinders beneath, but she staggered to her feet and then went to cross the tracks to freedom. At that moment there was a whistle, a blast of air, a flash of color, and an express passed us on the next track. I pulled Bridie away from the window. "Don't look, my darling," I said. "It's going to be all right now."

And for the first time she burst into tears in my arms.

Thirty-Three

The next moments passed in a blur. I sat with the cape in my hands, still too shocked at what I had seen. As my fingers moved over the soft wool I felt a hard lump. I examined the lining and slipped my hand into a little pouch. My fingers closed around something cold and smooth. I drew it out and saw the sparkle of gemstones. Hurriedly I shoved it into my purse before anyone saw.

I gave statements to the railway police, then again when the local police arrived from the nearest town, and the decision was made that the train should return to New York. Naturally this did not sit well with the passengers, but when they were told there had been a brutal murder on board they saw the importance of having the whole train checked. Bridie and I were taken to the saloon car and both given a sip of brandy for shock. I don't much like the taste of brandy, but I have to admit its warming effect was just what I needed.

Bridie coughed. "It burns," she said. "It's horrible. What is it?"

"Brandy," I said. "You're only allowed to drink it when you have been kidnapped."

Bridie sat beside me, leaning close against me. I put an arm around her and she sank her head to my shoulder. For a while we sat in silence, then she said, "I still can't believe that you found me. I thought I was lost forever or she'd kill me. You really are a clever detective."

"You were the smart one, my darling, shouting out that you were going to Grand Central Terminal," I replied. "Otherwise I'd have had no idea where to look."

"It was only when she told the cabby where to go that I realized she had tricked us. And I saw her dark hair. She was so nice and friendly until that—telling me that we were meeting you for a treat at the soda fountain."

"She was a very clever woman," I said. "She tricked me, too. She had me believing that she was a kindred spirit—the sort of connection to home I'd been longing for. She played me beautifully. And you never liked her."

I glanced down at Bridie and she met my gaze. "I was jealous that you liked her better than me," she said. "But I don't think that was everything. There was something about her I didn't trust. She just didn't sound or act like the Irish people I know."

"You're right," I said. "Now I think about it there were several occasions when her response surprised me but I didn't let myself be too suspicious as I wanted her to be that new friend."

"In the carriage she told me I was trouble," Bridie said.

"Trouble? She hardly knew you."

Bridie squirmed uncomfortably against me. "Do you remember that bracelet that was stolen at the tea party? She thought I'd noticed her taking it. Actually I was sitting right there and I thought she was being rude because she leaned across to take my teacup before I'd finished. But she was really picking up the bracelet, I guess."

"So she meant to steal it," I said. "But she thought you'd noticed her, so she stuffed it into the nearest glove. She certainly liked to live dangerously, didn't she?"

"She's definitely dead, is she?" Bridie asked.

"I'm afraid so. She stepped right into the path of that express train." I stared out across the car as we rattled over a bridge. "Probably the best thing, really. She'd have been hanged." I gave a small sigh. "But it's all behind us now. We can go back to our ordinary lives."

There was a long silence, then Bridie said, in a small voice, "I'm sorry I was so awful, Mom. Here you were being so kind to me and taking me in and looking after me, and I wasn't grateful."

I looked down at her and smiled. "You were trying out your independence," I said. "I've been a young girl too, you know. And it must have been a wonderful feeling to have two ladies making a fuss of you. I like it when they spoil me, too. But they are your adoring aunties, you know, and we are your family. We won't always let you do what we don't think is good for you. But it's because we care about you, you know."

"I know." She gave a little sigh of content.

Daniel was waiting to board the train as we pulled into a freight platform outside Grand Central.

"You're all right. Thank God," he said, sweeping both me and Bridie into his arms. "Do I understand that Rose McSweeney is dead?"

I nodded. "And Viscount Brackley. He was her accomplice in the jewelry robbery."

"Ah, yes. We've already had a reply to our cable about him. A confidence trickster. Not really a viscount at all. He's dead too?"

"Rose stabbed him. Then she jumped from the window in front of a train."

Daniel shook his head. "Well, they've made it tidy for us, but you two should never have had to go through such an ordeal." He turned to frown at me. "Now do you see why I want to keep you from any more detecting, Molly? I can't have you putting yourself into danger like this. My own work is dangerous enough. I can't have to worry about you as well. You do understand that, don't you?"

"Yes, Daniel," I said meekly.

Bridie caught my eye and she grinned.

"Now I hope we can recover those gems," Daniel said. "I presume they were somewhere in her luggage, if not on her person."

"Or right here," I said, producing the necklace like a rabbit from a hat. With satisfaction I saw the incredulous stare on Daniel's face.

"Molly—how did you . . ."

"Call it female intuition," I said, handing the necklace over with great reluctance. I knew I'd never touch anything as beautiful again.

"Sometimes you amaze me," he said. "I don't know what to say."

"You could say, thank you, my dearest wife."

"I do thank you, even if I'm still furious that you took off on your own—I know, it was for a good reason, but—"

"No more, now, Daniel. Bridie and I are still a bit shocked."

He nodded with sympathy. "I'll have one of my men take you home. You can make an official statement later." He had us escorted to a waiting automobile, and soon we turned into Patchin Place.

"There you are at last," Daniel's mother greeted us. "Where in heaven's name have you been?"

On the way home I had wondered what I should say to her about this. I started to tell her we'd had to stop Rose from escaping, but Bridie exclaimed, in an excited voice, "I got kidnapped by a woman with a knife and then a man with a gun came in and she stabbed him and then she jumped out of a window and was killed by a train . . ."

"Mercy me." Daniel's mother fanned herself with an imaginary fan. "That child's imagination gets more outlandish every day. If I were you, Molly, I'd keep her at home with us and not let those women across the street put any more wild ideas into her head."

Acknowledgments

As always, our heartfelt gratitude to the world's best agents, Meg Ruley and Christina Hogrebe, to Kelley Ragland and all the team at Minotaur, and to John and Tim for their input and encouragement.

Read on for a sneak peek at
Rhys Bowen and Clare Broyles's new novel

All That Is Hidden

Available Early 2023

Prologue

New York, Summer 1907

I would never have paid attention to the small news article in the *Times* if Daniel hadn't pointed it out to me. "I wonder if my letter to my mother has been lost?" he asked without much concern. "Listen to this." And he read the item out loud.

The paper didn't seem to know exactly how it had happened. The passenger train heading out of New York City and into Westchester County brought the mail just like every other day of the year. Just like every day the postman, having sorted the letters in the mail car, bundled them up into the heavy postal bag and lobbed it out onto the platform at Mount Vernon to be collected.

But something must have been different that Friday night. Perhaps the train was running slightly late, or the postman had not quite finished sorting as they pulled into the station and rushed to get the postal bag off the train. However it came about, one strap of the bag caught below the wheel of the train. As it pulled out in a cloud of steam it dragged the bag about a mile down the track until it broke and letters exploded out. The rain of correspondence floating down over the tracks contained the everyday doings of mothers and daughters, fathers and sons; deals to be made or broken; everyday joys and disappointments.

When the broken bag was discovered the next day, a hunt was on to find the missing letters and restore them to their owners. Some were lost forever or rendered illegible by the mud and mist of the night they spent outside, most were found and sent on, battered and dirty as they might have been. And one found its way into the hands of the wrong person.

I couldn't have guessed all of this as Daniel read the story in the *Times,* but it did catch my fancy. I amused myself by thinking of the letters floating about in gusts of wind. Since I didn't know a soul in Mount Vernon, I thought it could have nothing to do with me. But I was wrong. Dead wrong.

One

New York, Sunday, October 6, 1907

"So, what is this big surprise?" I asked as I pinned my hat onto my head, checking that it was straight in the entryway mirror.

"Ask me no questions, I'll tell you no lies." Daniel wrapped his arms around me from behind and gave the back of my neck a little kiss.

"Well, it can't be a romantic surprise or we wouldn't be bringing Liam," I mused. "And we are walking so it can't be too far away. Unless we are walking to a train station?" I shook my head. "But we haven't any baggage."

"Molly Sullivan, this is not a case and you are not detecting." Daniel gave me a mock reproving look. "You will find out soon enough." He pushed the pram out of the front door while I lifted Liam, carried him out, and set him in the pram.

"You are getting too heavy to be carried, little man," I said, rubbing the small of my back as I straightened up.

It was a gorgeous day, one of those clear October afternoons with bright sunshine and a cool, clean breeze. We had made it to church that morning, an occurrence that had become rare since

Daniel's mother had left, and I felt clean and bright inside as well. Our ward, Bridie, was with our neighbors, getting help with her algebra homework. I had told her we wouldn't be gone long.

Daniel pushed the pram and I followed in silence as we turned south onto Sixth Avenue. All he had told me was to put on my coat and hat and bring Liam. He had a surprise for me. I tried to judge from the set of his shoulders as he strode ahead whether it was a nice surprise or a nasty one. To tell the truth he did look a bit tense. We crossed the street and walked into the shade of the big trees in Washington Square. The fall colors glowed brightly on the trees, contrasting with a deep blue sky above. The perfect day for a family stroll, I thought. I found myself enjoying the quiet rhythm of our footsteps crunching on the gravel until Daniel slowed to walk beside me. He put a hand on my arm and cleared his throat.

Saints preserve us, he is nervous, I thought. My stomach felt a jolt of fear. Daniel was normally quite direct and forthright. It wasn't like him to make a song and dance about something.

"Where are we going, then?" I asked, keeping my voice light and cheerful.

"We're not going anywhere just yet. I thought it might be best to walk and have a little talk first." His hand squeezed mine reassuringly. "Molly, I want you to trust me." He was not looking at me but straight ahead as we walked. "There are some things I need to do to take care of this family and I hope you will trust I know what I am doing."

"If this is about a helper to look after Liam I'm sure I can sort that out. Your mother has sent me some recommendations of agencies I can try." Daniel's mother had lived with us during the last winter while she recovered from a bout of influenza but was now safely back at her house in Westchester County. I was sure she had been writing to Daniel telling him how unsuitable it was for a police captain's wife to be doing all of her own cooking, cleaning, and child minding. I didn't mind the work, though. I preferred to keep busy and active and spend time with my son.

But Mother Sullivan had plans for Daniel to advance. He had been the youngest-ever police captain in the New York Police Department and his mother was hoping for a career in politics for him. I was fine with him and with our life just as it was. We lived in a sweet little house on Patchin Place that I had purchased myself when I ran my own detective agency. Although I had given up being a detective when I married Daniel, I had found myself doing the odd spot of sleuthing since, and between ourselves I did sometimes help him with his cases. That was why I was not opposed to Mrs. Sullivan's plan to have a girl live in and help with Liam. It had been useful, I reflected, to have Mother Sullivan around to watch Liam if I wanted to go out and investigate.

"No, that's not it exactly, although it will change our domestic situation." He cleared his throat while I looked at him expectantly. "It's actually very good news. I've been asked to run for sheriff and I'm going to do it."

"Sheriff? Of what? Of where?" My mind immediately went to the Wild West. Men galloping on horses and firing guns.

"The County of New York. It includes the five boroughs," he said. "It's an important position."

"Asked, by whom?" Questions swirled in my head. A ball came whizzing over our heads followed by a group of laughing college students from the university on the other side of the square.

"Ball. I want da ball." Liam stood up quickly in the pram. I rushed to grab him before he managed to climb out and lifted him down beside me.

"Take Mama's hand, darling." I walked with him in silence for a moment and then turned to Daniel. "It's an elected position? And someone has asked you to run?"

"Actually, I'm on the Tammany ticket. They will be announcing it tomorrow at Tammany Hall."

"Tomorrow?" I stopped and looked at him in astonishment. Liam tugged at my hand.

"Mama. Ball! Liam wants to play." I held on firmly while I tried to compose my racing thoughts.

"But you hate Tammany and all those bribes and kickbacks. Why on earth would you run on their ticket? And who is the sheriff of New York when he's at home anyway?"

Daniel gave the pram a big push and replied without looking at me, "There are a few things I can't explain, Molly. That's why I need you to trust me. The sheriff is a bit like the police commissioner, only his mandate is broader. He runs the prison system and the courts, not the police department. You know how much that needs reforming. The Tammany man who was supposed to run has gotten himself involved in a scandal and has left the city for a while until it blows over. I'm sure you will read about it in that Hearst rag in the next few days. They asked me to step in as a last-minute replacement."

"But why would you want to? Surely you love being a police captain, especially since you've been in charge of homicide. It's a prestigious job, Daniel."

Daniel continued pushing the pram, still staring straight ahead. "It's my chance to do some good, Molly. If I get in as sheriff I can do away with some of the corruption. You remember what it was like when I was in prison myself. I nearly died in that hellhole. I can really do some good."

"But with Tammany Hall? Daniel, they will never let you go your own way. You know that. You'll owe them for your position and they will make you pay them back."

"I'm sorry, Molly. It's settled." Daniel's voice was now firm. "I have said yes and I expect you to support me. There are some things you don't understand."

"Because I'm a woman?" My temper flared. I should mention that red hair and a quick temper are my two leading characteristics.

"Because there are things you don't know and I can't tell you." He turned back toward the arch. "There's more to this surprise. Follow me."

"Jesus, Mary, and Joseph! My heart can't take any more." Daniel put a protesting Liam back in his pram and lengthened his stride so much I had to hurry to keep up. We swept through the Marble Arch at the entrance to the park and then up Fifth Avenue. I wondered where we were heading. To Tammany Hall? "Daniel, slow down, where are we going?"

"You'll see." He looked back at me, gave me an encouraging smile, then strode ahead. A good surprise this time, then. On the other side of Ninth Street Daniel stopped at an impressive flight of marble steps with a wrought-iron railing leading up to a white door framed with a decorated arch.

"Let's pay a call, shall we?" Daniel lifted Liam out of the pram and into my arms then climbed the steps and rang the bell.

"Wait, Daniel," I called after him. "Who are we visiting? You should have warned me. I'm not suitably dressed. A stroll, you said."

Daniel looked back and smiled. "You look fine," he said. "Don't worry."

I came up the steps beside him and stood rather nervously on the stoop. Really, I like a surprise, but this was going too far. Was sheriff that high a position that Daniel would now know people who lived in Fifth Avenue houses like this? Had we been invited to tea and here was I in my usual two-piece costume and not a tea dress? It had probably never occurred to Daniel that women like to know in advance what to wear for every occasion. Honestly, men can be infuriating. But it was too late to turn back now.

The door was answered by a maid who didn't show any surprise at seeing us. "You must be Captain and Mrs. Sullivan," she said, giving us a shy smile as she dropped a curtsey. "You are expected, please come in. I'm Mary." We walked into the front hall and Daniel took off his hat and hung it on the hat stand, then helped me off with my cloak and hung it up as well. The marble floor echoed as I set Liam down and he stomped his foot experimentally then headed toward the staircase in front of us.

"Shh. Liam, come here." I grabbed him hurriedly and lifted him up again. The maid waited and then indicated we should follow her through a curtained doorway. "The parlor is through here, sir."

I walked in with a bright smile on my face expecting to be introduced to the man or lady of the house, but the parlor was empty. A fire burned in the marble fireplace. A table in the center of the room under the electric chandelier held a priceless-looking vase, and ornate shelves across from me were full of decorative plates, cups, and figurines. I instinctively clutched Liam a little tighter, making sure his hands were safely out of the way, and decided that putting him down here was not a good idea.

"The family drawing room is back here, sir." She led us through another doorway and into a comfortable-looking drawing room. The room was crowded with delicate embroidered sofas and chairs and carved mahogany tables in many sizes. There was a beautiful Persian rug on the floor and a large tapestry on the far wall. But still no people. My mind spun. Had Daniel brought me to a murder scene? Hardly an outing to which you bring your son. Were the owners of the house very shy?

"The dining room is at the back of the house and bedrooms are upstairs, sir, if you will follow me." Mary continued after a pause as we looked around the empty drawing room. The bedrooms?

"Daniel." I turned to him in exasperation. "Why are we seeing the bedrooms? Is the owner an invalid?"

"No," he replied, already heading toward the stairs.

"Daniel!" I called after him. "What is going on? Whose house is this?"

He turned to me with a big smile. "Yours." He put his arms around both Liam and me. "Ours. Welcome to your new home, Mrs. Sullivan!"

TWO

Sunday, October 6

For perhaps the first time in my life I was speechless. So many things came into my mind at once that I couldn't utter a single word. Was this a joke? Would Daniel really move us across town without my opinion? What about my house in Patchin Place? How on earth could we afford a house like this, let alone a maid who seemed to have expected us? That last thought made me remember that the maid was hovering a few steps up the staircase, waiting for an answer, and I broke away from Daniel's hug. "Let's talk about this later, Daniel," I said, smiling through gritted teeth.

"Thank you, Mary. We would appreciate seeing the bedrooms," Daniel said hurriedly. He knew my temper and that I was inclined to speak my mind in any situation. The girl led the way up the stairs. Liam insisted on being put down and climbing each stair himself, holding on to Daniel's hand. Mary waited patiently at the top of the stairs. If my head had not been spinning I might have enjoyed the fact that I was going to see the upstairs of a Fifth Avenue house. I had often wondered about their layout with the front door not in the center but at the right-hand edge of the house. Now I could see that the stairs went up two stories along the right side. At the top of the first set of stairs was a landing.

"There is a main bedroom here." Mary indicated the room on her left. A young girl in a maid's uniform was standing in front of the door clearly waiting to greet us. "This is Aileen," Mary introduced her. Aileen bobbed a curtsey. She looked to be no more than sixteen. Her unruly light brown hair was spilling out of her maid's cap. She had blue eyes and red cheeks full of freckles. Her eyes lit up when she saw Liam.

"Who's this little man, then?" She crouched down to his eye level. "I'll bet that you want to see the nursery. There is a horse and everything." She had a soft country lilt that took me instantly back to my childhood in County Mayo.

I expected Liam to shrink back against me, but instead he perked up. "Horsey?"

"Is it all right if I take him, miss?" She looked uncertain. "I mean Mrs.?" She made it a question.

"Mrs. Sullivan," I offered.

"See the horsey?" Liam piped up.

"Yes, all right, my boy, go and see the horsey." Daniel patted him on the back and he put his little hand in Aileen's outstretched one. They started up the stairs to the third floor.

Mary looked after Aileen, rather disapprovingly I thought. She showed us around the bedroom, decorated in the frilly Victorian style. There was a lace doily on every surface and the bed was covered with embroidered cushions. There were two dressing rooms, one very masculine-looking with dark wood surfaces and the other just as frilly as the bedroom with a rather sweet embroidered daybed and an enormous mirror. Bridie will love this, I thought, then immediately reproved myself. As soon as we left this house I would have plenty to say about whether we would be moving here or not! Until then, I decided I would play along with the pretense that we were moving here. The rest of the level had two more bedrooms, a spacious bathroom with a large claw-footed tub, and a lavatory. A thought struck me.

"Daniel, those bedrooms have no fireplaces. Aren't they bitterly cold in winter?"

Mary answered before he could. "The whole house is on steam heat, Mrs. Sullivan. Did you see the radiators? The rooms are so warm the family has to open the windows sometimes. Even the lavatory!" She looked at Daniel and looked away with a blush as if embarrassed she had mentioned the lavatory in front of him.

The second staircase led up to the maids' rooms and the nursery. We could hear thumping as we walked down the hall to the nursery and as we opened the door we saw Liam in full gallop on the most enormous rocking horse. It had soft velveteen hair, a braided mane, button eyes, and a bright blue leather saddle and bridle. I could imagine that any child would fall instantly in love with it.

"Giddyup!" Liam was shouting as Aileen stood beside him, arms outstretched in case he fell. The rest of the nursery was like a picture in a book. It had a sweet little child's bed with a lace coverlet, low shelves full of books, wooden blocks and toys, and a tiny desk and chair.

"That's enough now, Mr. Liam," Aileen said, and helped Liam off the horse. To my surprise he put up no fuss at all but just stood by her side holding her hand.

"Mrs. Sullivan, I would be happy to watch little Liam whenever you might need it," Aileen spoke up. "I can still do my work," she said quickly as if we had raised an objection. "Lord knows I've watched my own brothers and sisters and kept house for my da at the same time. Not a house as grand as this," she hastened to add, as if I would be offended by the comparison. "But I do miss the little ones."

I wasn't sure what to say. I could hardly say, "I will not be coming to live here after Captain Sullivan and I have had a talk and I have no idea why we are here or who is going to pay your salary." So I said, "That sounds lovely, let me talk to Captain Sullivan about it and I will let you know."

Mary led us back downstairs. "When will you be moving in, Captain Sullivan? So I can let Cook know," she asked as we came down into the front hall.

"This Thursday. We will be sending our things over on Wednesday evening," Daniel said without looking at me. "Luncheon will be our first meal. Is the cook here?"

"No, sir." Mary shook her head. "A new cook has been hired. I'll write and let her know when you are coming."

"Where is the kitchen?" I realized I had not seen a kitchen in our tour.

"Downstairs, ma'am," Mary replied. "There is a staircase in the butler's pantry just off the dining room, and one from the tradesman's entrance at the front of the house." I realized that I had seen a staircase going down to the left of the impressive front stairs and those must have been the windows of the kitchen that were below street level.

And why on earth would we need a cook, I wanted to demand of Daniel, when you seem perfectly happy with my cooking? But I decided to hold all of my questions until we were alone.

Long ago I had been educated at a rather grand mansion, the local girl who was allowed to learn alongside the young ladies of the family because the mistress took a fancy to me. So I was not unused to seeing maids, butlers, and footmen in a big house. But I never expected to be the mistress of one, even one that was quite modest compared to an Irish manor house. I never expected to have two maids handing Daniel his hat, helping me on with my cloak, and bundling Liam up in his coat before putting him into Daniel's arms. They both stood and watched as we went down the steps.

Outside the front door Daniel turned back. "Until Thursday, then, Mary."

"Very good, sir," she replied. "You'll find everything in order, and if you care to send over your trunks of clothing before then, we'll have them all pressed and properly hung for you."

The front door closed. Daniel retrieved the pram from inside the railings and deposited the now complaining Liam into it. "More horsey!" he yelled, kicking out as Daniel strapped him in.

"You'll be getting plenty of horsey soon enough, my boy," Daniel said.

We walked up Fifth Avenue in silence until we were out of sight of the house. Then I exploded. "Daniel Sullivan, by all the saints and the Blessed Mother, have you lost your mind?" Several well-dressed ladies turned to look in our direction and I lowered my voice.

A hurt expression crossed his face. "You don't like your surprise?"

"You knew perfectly well how I would react to you choosing to move us to a new house without consulting me." I had so many objections I wasn't sure where to start. "Patchin Place!" I began. "Do you expect me to give up my own dear little house?"

"Do I expect *us* to give up *our* pokey little house to move into a brownstone on Fifth Avenue? Is that seriously a question you are asking me?" Daniel put the emphasis on *us* and *our*. His eyebrows rose. He had a point. I loved my house and the fact that I could run across the street to my neighbors and best friends Sid and Gus at any time, but perhaps any reasonable wife would think that moving to Fifth Avenue was a dream come true.

"Besides," he continued. "We don't have to give up Patchin Place. We are just going to live in the brownstone for a while. Perhaps the next six months, perhaps longer."

I tried a different tack. "But, Daniel, how on earth can we afford it? Unless you're going to start taking bribes left, right, and center like half the New York police do."

People were definitely staring now. Daniel looked around embarrassed. "Molly, for heaven's sake lower your voice," he said. His tone said that he believed I was the one being unreasonable. This infuriated me.

"I will not! Not until you explain to me how we can possibly afford a house on Fifth Avenue on a police captain's salary."

"I'll explain it all, just please lower your voice." He grabbed the handles of the pram roughly and turned quickly as we crossed at Tenth Street. Liam started to cry.

"Now look what you've done," I began angrily, feeling like crying myself. An automobile passed behind us and I hurried up onto the curb behind them. Daniel stopped, lifted Liam out of the pram, and let him cry on his shoulder. The sight of the two of them couldn't help but soften my anger a bit. Daniel is a good man, I told myself. At least give him a chance to explain. "Let's get Liam home. He's tired of sitting still," I said in as calm a voice as I could muster. We walked in silence for a few minutes, but I felt too impatient to continue another step without hearing more. "Now, can you please explain what is going on?"

"Molly, I have never pretended that I didn't want something better for our family." Daniel appeared to be choosing his words carefully. "I have an opportunity here. And it has come through the police commissioner so I can have my job back if it doesn't work out." I started to interrupt, but he stopped me with a look and went on. "Okay, you need some political background. You know that Hearst's Independence Party has been taking votes away from Tammany and they are fighting to keep control over the police and the docks." I nodded. I had been reading about that in the papers.

"Big Bill, he's the man who pulls the strings at Tammany Hall right now, needs a Tammany candidate to run for county sheriff. If the Hearst man gets in he will be able to make things very difficult for Tammany. But the chosen candidate, as I told you, got himself involved in a scandal and has had to leave town to ride it out. Big Bill—well, that's what everyone calls him, his real name is William McCormick—wants someone who can bring the police on board, so he asked the police commissioner to suggest someone and he came to me." He paused, inviting me to ask a question.

"How could the salary be enough for us to afford a house like that? Even if the salary is enormous, how could we pay for it before you are elected?" I matched Daniel's calm tone.

"The house belongs to Big Bill. He lends it to any candidates he wants to promote. I gather that he even pays the staff. He has offered it to us for six months and said that if I win we can talk about prices then."

"I don't understand how it helps Mr. McCormick if you are the sheriff. How does he benefit?"

"He has been an alderman and he plans to run for mayor. The Independence and Republican Parties are threatening to join forces against him. If they get the sheriff's office they will find all sorts of ways to keep Tammany voters away from the ballot box."

"But, Daniel." My voice began to rise again. "This is how Tammany works, you know that. Someone does you a favor and then you owe them a favor. Someone with a salary of a thousand dollars a year ends up with twenty thousand dollars in the bank. What if they ask you to stuff ballot boxes or keep opposition voters away? You've always fought against that type of corruption. We don't need to get ahead that way. We're doing just fine."

"I do understand how it works and I do not intend to take any kickbacks. This house belongs to Mr. McCormick and he pays the staff. I've checked into it and it is all legal." He looked uncomfortable. "As I've mentioned, there are a few things I can't tell you, but trust me, I am on the right side here."

"Well, don't forget how quickly the police department turned against you once before when they thought you had taken bribes," I said angrily. "I was the only one who stood by you then." We stopped walking and stood looking at each other, both remembering that horrible time when Daniel was in jail and we had no idea how to prove him innocent. The Sixth Avenue el thundered by.

"I will never forget, Molly." Daniel lowered his voice. It seemed suddenly very quiet after the passage of the el. We waited to cross

Sixth Avenue. "I will always take care of you. I want to weed out corruption at Tammany Hall. This is my way of doing it. Will you trust me?"

Did I trust Daniel? I suppose it all came down to that. After all, he wasn't asking me to live in a tenement or go out to the Wild West. He was asking me to live in a fancy house on Fifth Avenue and have all the help I needed. My gut was telling me that he was being naïve; that he was playing with fire and going to be burned. But he had stood by me through my many harebrained schemes. I would have to stand by him in this one, even if it all went wrong.

"So, shall I put on my red, white, and blue sash and come to your political meeting tomorrow?" My smile told Daniel that the fight was over, for now. "I will trust you. But if you find you are in over your head, remember that I don't need to be some highfalutin sheriff's wife to be happy."

"That's good, because I haven't got the job yet." Daniel settled a now calm Liam back into the pram. "And no, a political meeting is not a place for a woman. But thank you for offering."

The sidewalk became crowded as we neared the Jefferson Market. We walked in companionable silence, but my mind was racing. I was determined to pump Sid and Gus for information just as soon as we got home. Daniel might trust this Bill McCormick, but I was going to check him out for myself.

By the time we turned into Patchin Place Liam had fallen asleep in his pram, his thumb in his mouth, his little tearstained face now looking quite angelic. I stood still for a moment, taking in the scene before me. I had never seen my quiet little backwater looking more inviting or attractive. It is really not much more than an alleyway—a small cobbled street of ten houses on either side—simple brick homes fronting the cobbles. But today the red-brown of the brick glowed in the late afternoon sunlight. A pot of yellow chrysanthemums stood beside a front door. It looked peaceful and safe and quite perfect. I felt a lump rise in my throat.

We said no more about it that night. Every time I thought of another question to ask, I decided not to spoil the quiet calm of a Sunday evening. My last Sunday evening in my little house, I thought with a pang. I didn't even tell Bridie as we sat together at the supper table. She had had enough upheaval in her life and I decided to wait until my head stopped spinning to tell her.

Duke Morse Photography

RHYS BOWEN is the *New York Times* bestselling author of the Anthony Award– and Agatha Award–winning Molly Murphy mysteries, the Edgar Award–nominated Evan Evans series, the Royal Spyness series, and several stand-alone novels, including *In Farleigh Field*. Born in England, she lives in San Rafael, California.

Timothy Broyles

CLARE BROYLES, who is Rhys Bowen's daughter, is a teacher and a musician. She has worked as a composer and arranger in the theater for both Arizona Theatre Company and Childsplay, and was nominated for an Arizona "Zoni" Theatre Award. Clare is married to a teacher and they have three children.